Attica Locke's widely acclaimed debut novel, *Black Water Rising*, was nominated for a *Los Angeles Times* Book Prize, an Edgar Award, and an NAACP Image Award, and was shortlisted for the Orange Prize. As a screenwriter, Locke wrote scripts for Paramount, Warner Bros., Disney, Twentieth Century Fox, Jerry Bruckheimer Films, and HBO. She was a fellow at the Sundance Institute's Feature Filmmakers Lab and has served on the board of the Library Foundation of Los Angeles. A native of Houston, Texas, she lives in Los Angeles with her husband and daughter.

Praise for *Black Water Rising*

"Started reading *Black Water Rising* with my morning coffee and barely set it aside until I'd finished it that evening – that's the kind of grip it has. Attica Locke serves up a rich stew of venal politicians and legal chicanery in which staying alive is hard enough and hanging on to your integrity harder still. Longshoremen, Civil Rights and Big Oil – John Grisham meets *Chinatown* in 1980s Texas" John Harvey

"*Black Water Rising* is a terrifying reminder of how recently America was a very bad place to be young, gifted and black. This is an authentic, atmospheric debut that burns with an entirely reasonable anger" Val McDermid

"What a ride! *Black Water Rising* is a superlative debut; a wonderful treatise on the Texas of the 1980s – the best bad town novel in some time. Attica Locke is a stand-out in every imperative young-writer way" James Ellroy

"*Black Water Rising* is a stylish, involving literary thriller with a strong emphasis on human politics and character. An auspicious debut from Attica Locke" George Pelecanos

"The most impressive crime debut I've read this year" Marcel Berlins, *The Times*

"[An] atmospheric, richly convoluted debut novel . . . she is able to write about Jay's urgent need to behave manfully and become a decent father with a serious, stirring moral urgency akin to that of George Pelecanos or Dennis Lehane . . . subtle and compelling" Janet Maslin, *New York Times*

"Attica Locke's real achievement here is a virtually seamless marriage of social comment and slick crime action . . . It's a debut that propels this young African-American writer into the upper stratum of crime fiction" Christopher Fowler, *Financial Times*

"A powerful and skilfully constructed conspiracy thriller – *Chinatown* without the air of despairing fatalism . . . Locke has an extraordinary gift for reinvigorating tired thriller conventions" John O'Connell, *Guardian*

"Superbly written and hugely compelling debut crime novel . . . *Black Water Rising*'s depths and concerns are much wider than the simple thrills it also provides. Locke is excellent at bringing the city to life . . . An impressive, well-plotted and intelligent crime drama" *Independent*

"Smart, gripping tale set among the fallout of America's Civil Rights movement . . . Rich with details drawn from the lives of

Locke's parents, for the most part this serves as a thoughtful, albeit often depressing look at the way in which the idealism of the 1960s ground to a halt, ripped from both within and without" *Metro*

"An even better book than its author had in mind . . . This book cleverly replaces the kind of cold-war paranoia that used to animate thrillers with racial paranoia instead" Charles McGrath, *New York Times*

"Attica Locke's debut as a crime writer has been hailed on both sides of the Atlantic: in her native US, the acknowledged greats such as James Ellroy and George Pelecanos have saluted her, and here our own enthusiasts have been equally excited. So what's it all about? Partly it's about the ideal combination of plot and author, something which, when it works, is guaranteed to whet the public's appetite . . . A complicated, sinister narrative follows, with many twists and turns of perception and many well-plotted surprises" Antonia Fraser, *The Lady*

"A stunning debut . . . Attica Locke has conjoined crime noir and the Afro-American fight for justice and created a powerful literary pot boiler" *Bookseller*

"Locke's debut crime novel unapologetically raises the thorny issues of racism and social injustice. Expect plenty more great reads from this talented author" *Image*

ATTICA LOCKE

The Cutting Season

A complete catalogue record for this book can be obtained from the British Library on request

First published in the USA in 2012 by HarperCollins Publishers, New York

First published in the UK in 2012 by Serpent's Tail,
an imprint of Profile Books Ltd
3A Exmouth House
Pine Street
London EC1R 0JH
website: www.serpentstail.com

HB ISBN 978 1 84668 912 3
PB ISBN 978 1 84668 803 4
eISBN 978 1 84765 850 0

Designed and typeset by Crow Books

Printed by Clays, Bungay, Suffolk

10 9 8 7 6 5 4 3 2 1

For Odell & Odelia

We navigate by stories, but sometimes we only escape
by abandoning them.

—Rebecca Solnit

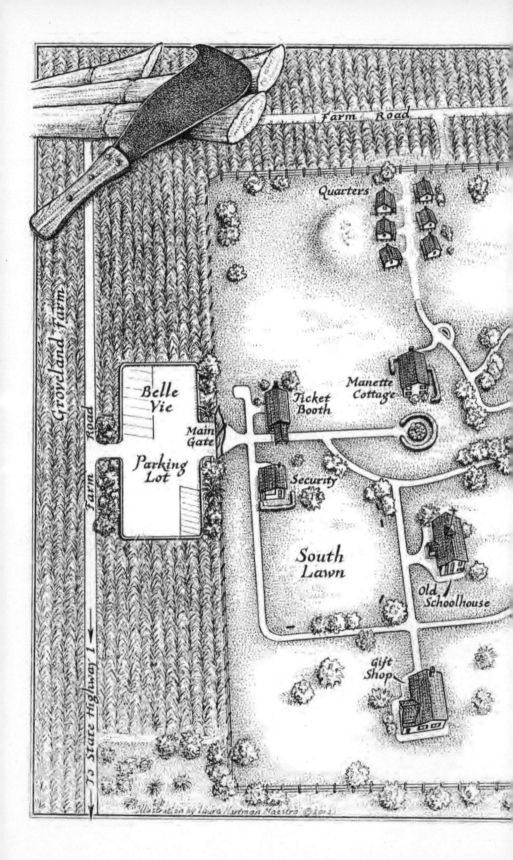

Farm Road

Groveland Farm

Farm Road

To State Highway 1

Quarters

Belle Vie

Main Gate

Parking Lot

Ticket Booth

Manette Cottage

Security

South Lawn

Old Schoolhouse

Gift Shop

Illustration by Laura Hartman Maestro ©2012

Groveland

Farm

Welcome to Belle Vie

Mississippi River

LE VEE

W

S ✦ N

E

Le Roy
Cottage

River Road

North
Lawn

Groundskeeper's
Shed

Kitchen

Vegetable
Garden

Front
Gate

Big House

Garden

BELLE VIE

Willow
Grove

Library

A
Haunting
Discovery

1

It was during the Thompson-Delacroix wedding, Caren's first week on the job, that a cottonmouth, measuring the length of a Cadillac, fell some twenty feet from a live oak on the front lawn, landing like a coil of rope in the lap of the bride's future mother-in-law. It only briefly stopped the ceremony, this being Louisiana after all. Within minutes, an off-duty sheriff's deputy on the groom's side found a 12-gauge in the groundskeeper's shed and shot the thing dead, and after, one of the cater-waiters was kind enough to hose down the grass. The bride and groom moved on to their vows, staying on schedule for a planned kiss at sunset, the mighty Mississippi blowing a breeze through the line of stately, hundred-year-old trees. The uninvited guest certainly made for lively dinner conversation at the reception in the main hall. By the time the servers made their fourth round with bottles of imported champagne, several men, including prim little Father Haliwell, were lining up to have their pictures taken with the viper, before somebody from parish services finally came to haul the carcass away.

Still, she took it as a sign.

A reminder, really, that Belle Vie, its beauty, was not to be trusted.

That beneath its loamy topsoil, the manicured grounds and

gardens, two centuries of breathtaking wealth and spectacle, lay a land both black and bitter, soft to the touch, but pressing in its power. She should have known that one day it would spit out what it no longer had use for, the secrets it would no longer keep.

The plantation proper sat on eighteen acres, bordered to the north by the river, and to the east by the raw, unincorporated landscape of Ascension Parish. To walk it—from the library in the northwest corner to the gift shop and then over to the main house, past the stone kitchen and the rose garden, the cottages Manette and Le Roy, the old schoolhouse and the quarters—took nearly an hour. Caren had learned to start her days early, while it was quiet, heading out before sunlight—having arranged for Letty to arrive by six a.m. at least three days a week, while Caren's daughter was still sleeping. Six mornings out of seven, she made a full sweep of the property, combing every square inch, noting any scuffed floors or dry flower beds or drapes that needed to be steamed—even one time changing the motor in one of the gallery's ceiling fans herself.

She didn't mind the work.

Belle Vie was her job, and she was nothing if not professional.

Though she could in no way have prepared herself for the grisly sight before her now.

To the south and west, across a nearly five-foot-high fence, where Caren was standing, the back five hundred acres of the Clancy family's 157-year-old property had been leased for cane farming since before she was born. Over the fence line, puffs of gray smoke shot up out of the fields. The machines were out in the cane this morning, already on the clock. The mechanical cutters were big and wide as tractor trucks, fat, gassy beasts whose engines often disturbed the natural habitat, chasing rats and snakes and rabbits from their nests in the cane fields—and come harvest time each year, the animals invariably sought out a safe and peaceful living on the grounds of Belle Vie. Luis had run them out of the garden, cleared their fecal waste from his tool shed, and, on more than one occasion, trapped and bagged a specimen to take home for God knows what purpose. And now some critter had dug up the dirt and grass along the plantation's fence line and come up with this.

The body was face down.

In a makeshift grave so shallow that its walls hugged the corpse as snugly as a shell, as if the dead woman at Caren's feet were on the verge of hatching, of emerging from her confinement to start this life over again. She was coated with mud, top to bottom, her arms and legs tucked beneath her body, the spine in a curved position. The word *fetal* came to mind. Caren thought, for a brief, dizzying second, that she might faint. "Don't touch her," she said. "Don't touch a thing."

She'd been up since dawn, that cold Thursday morning.

It was a day that had already gotten off to a wrong start, before she'd even stepped foot out of the house . . . though for an entirely different reason. She'd woken up that morning to a message on her cell phone, one that had set off a minor staff crisis. Donovan Isaacs had had the nerve to call in sick for the third time in two weeks, this time leaving a nearly incoherent voice-mail message on her phone at four o'clock in the morning, and keeping Caren in her pajamas for over an hour as she sent e-mails and placed phone calls, searching for a replacement. She didn't know if it was because she was a woman or black—a *sister*, as he would say—but she'd never had an employee make so little effort to impress her. He was chronically late and impossible to get on the phone, responding sporadically to text messages or nagging calls to his grandmother, with whom he lived while taking classes at the River Valley Community College and working here

5

part-time. His salary, like those of the other Belle Vie Players, was paid by a yearly stipend from the state's Department of Culture, Recreation, and Tourism, which made firing him a bureaucratic headache, but one she was no less committed to pursuing. But that was later, of course. Right now she needed a stand-in for the part of FIELD SLAVE #1. She was about a heartbeat away from making a call to the theater department at Donaldsonville High School, willing to settle for a warm body, at least, when finally, at a quarter to seven, Ennis Mabry returned one of her messages, saying he had a nephew who could take over Ennis's role as Monsieur Duquesne's trusty DRIVER, and Ennis could step in to play Donovan's part, which, he assured her, he knew by heart.

"Don't worry, Miss C," he said. "The kids'll have they show."

Letty was on the kitchen phone when Caren came downstairs a few minutes later. She was standing over the stove, talking to her eldest daughter, a girl Caren had met only once, on a day when Letty's '92 Ford Aerostar wouldn't start and Gabriela had to drive all the way from Vacherie to come pick her up. She was a good kid, Letty reported at least once a week. She was on the honor roll, had held a job since she was fifteen, and didn't mess around with boys. And three days a week, Gabby made a hot breakfast for her younger brother and sister, packed their lunches, and drove them to school, all so her mother could come to work before dawn and do the very same for Caren's child. At the stove, Letty was hunched over a pot of Malt-O-Meal, talking about Gabby's little brother and speaking Spanish in a coarse whisper, only a few words of which Caren could make out at a distance: *thermometer* and *aspirin* and some bit about *hot tea*.

Caren had two school tours scheduled before lunch and a cocktail reception in the main house that evening, the menu for which had yet to be finalized. She couldn't do this day without Letty or her rusty van or the Herrera kids up and well enough for school. They were all tied together that way. Caren's life, her job, depended on Letty being able to do hers. She gave Letty's shoulder a warm squeeze before walking out, mouthing the words *thank you* and mentally making a list of all the creative ways she might make it up to her, knowing, in her heart, that any such token is worthless when your kid is sick. It was not something she was proud of, skipping out like that. But very little in Caren's life, at that point, was. Pride, as a method of categorizing one's personal life and history, was something she'd long given up on. There was her daughter, and there was this job.

The air outside was cold for October, and wet, still drunk from a late-night rain that had soaked Belle Vie, and again she thought it was wise to warn the evening's host against outdoor seating. Still, she would need Luis to pull at least one of the heat lamps from the supply closet in the main house. A number of Belle Vie's paying guests liked to take an after-dinner brandy on the gallery, to say nothing of the smokers who routinely gathered there. The plantation had finally gone smoke-free the year before—in the main house, at least, and the guest cottages. Caren's living quarters, a two-bedroom apartment on the second floor of the former *garçonnière* and overseer's residence—which also housed the plantation's historical records—still carried a heavy scent of burnt pipe tobacco, a faintly sweet aroma she had come to think of as home.

She had, for better or for worse, made a life here.

She had finally accepted that Belle Vie was where she belonged.

Her work boots, a weathered pair of brown ropers, were waiting where they always were, just outside the library's front door. She slipped them over her wool socks, zipping a down jacket and pulling a frayed tulane school of law cap from the pocket. She slid the hat over her uncombed curls, feeling their thick weight against the back of her neck. On her right hip, she carried a black walkie-talkie. On her left, a ring of brass keys rode on her belt loop, bumping and jangling against the flesh of her thigh as she started for the main gate. She'd cover more ground in less time if she borrowed the golf cart from security. The plan was to drive along the perimeter first, then double back, park by the guest cottages, and walk the quarters on foot. She was always careful not to leave tire tracks in the slave village. She was responsible for even this detail.

It's not that Belle Vie wasn't well staffed.

There was a cleaning crew that came several times a week, more if there were guests in the cottages or events scheduled back-to-back on weekends. And Luis, who had been on the payroll since 1966—when the Clancy family fully restored the plantation that had been in their family for generations—could probably run the place himself if he had to. Still, she was surprised by the little things that got overlooked. She once found a used condom on the dirt floor of one of the slave cottages. Drunken wedding guests, she had learned, were by far the horniest, most unscrupulous people on the planet: neither a sense of the macabre nor common decency would stop them once they got their minds set on something, or someone. And Caren didn't think any third-grader's first school field trip ought to include a messy, impromptu lesson about the mating habits of loose bridesmaids.

From high overhead, sunlight studded the green grass with bits of coral and gold, as she rode along beneath a canopy of aged magnolias that shaded the main, brick-laid road through the plantation; their branches were deep black and slick with lingering rainwater. Mornings like this, she didn't try to fight the romance of the place. It was no use anyway. The land was simply breathtaking, lush and pure. She drove past the gift shop, then north toward Belle Vie's award-winning rose garden, which sat embedded within a circular drive just a few feet from the main house. The nearly two-hundred-year-old manse was held up by white columns, and adorned with black shutters and a wrought-iron balcony that overlooked the river to the north and the garden to the south. Luis and his one-man maintenance crew had done a grand job with *le jardin*, coaxing rows of plum-colored tea roses and hydrangeas into an unlikely fall showing. Mrs. Leland James Clancy, had she lived, would have been most proud.

All along the drive, Caren made mental notes.

The hedges in front of the guest cottages could stand a trim. And whatever the latest fertilizer formula or concoction Luis had sprinkled on the hill behind the quarters, it wasn't working. There was still a narrow patch of earth out that way—grown over the foundation of some building long forgotten and not appearing on any plantation map—that remained as stubbornly dull and dry as it had even when Caren was a kid, no matter what Luis tried. Food scraps and horse shit, or cold, salted water.

Down by the quarters, grass simply refused to grow.

Caren was, at that moment, a mere thirty yards or so from a crime scene, but, of course, she didn't know it yet. She saw only the break in the land, where the earth had been disturbed. But from afar, it looked like a rabbit or a mole or some such creature had been digging up the ground along the fence line that separated the plantation from the cane fields—another problem, she thought, since the Groveland Corporation took over the lease on the "back five." Ed Renfrew, when his family farmed the land, always made a point to monitor his side of the fence. If a critter tore up the dirt or left any such blot on the landscape, he'd always tend to it right away. But Hunt Abrams, the project manager for the Groveland farm, had never uttered more than ten words to Caren, had never gone out of his way to acknowledge her existence. She lifted the walkie-talkie from the waistband of her jeans, using it to alert Luis to the problem, telling him to get somebody out there to clean up the mess. "Sure thing, ma'am," he said.

Later, two cops would ask, more than once, how it was she didn't see her.

She could have offered up any number of theories: the dirt and mud on the woman's back, the distance of twenty or thirty yards between the fence and Caren's perch behind the driver's seat, even her own layman's assessment that the brain can't possibly process what it has no precedent for. But none of the words came. *I don't know*, she said.

She watched one of the cops write this down.

But it was the quarters, wasn't it?

The reason she had missed that girl, the dirt and the blood.

The slave village had always been a dark distraction, its craggy, crooked shadows blackening many a morning at Belle Vie. It was the part of the job she liked the least. For Caren, the dread usually started before she even set foot on the dirt road, and today hadn't been any different. It was still dark out when she'd started to the south. Not black, but cold and dim, a heavy, leaden gray. And from the time she set out this morning, she'd fretted over the task of inspecting the quarters, putting it off until the last possible second, until, finally, she parked the golf cart near the guest cottages, walking the rest of the way on foot. She folded her arms tight, putting the bulk of her down jacket between her body and the wind. The air in the quarters was always a few degrees cooler.

Even in the dead of summer, more than few people had reported feeling a chill on this very path. A sign of spirits in their midst, Caren had been told her first day on the job. Among the staff— the ones who didn't know the first thing about her background, the plain facts of where she was born and raised—it was a perverse kind of hazing, a way to test her resolve, perhaps, to lay bets on how long she would last. That she refused to walk the quarters the first few weeks she worked here was a fact greatly whispered about. Anytime she came within even a few feet of the slave village, her chest would tighten to a point no wider than a pinprick, and she felt she couldn't breathe. She would get as far as the dirt road and stop.

They all gave her a week, tops.

But they didn't know the whole story.

Truth is, avoiding the slave village was an old, old habit of hers, and one that long predated the job. Caren had grown up in Ascension Parish, in the shadows of Belle Vie; she had grown up with the ghost stories, childhood rants, and the rest of it. They were almost as old as the plantation itself. She had no proof, of course, that the quarters were haunted, but it is absolutely true that one morning during her first year back, she stood at the mouth of the village, staring down the length of dirt road. And in the morning fog, the graying clapboard cottages lined up on each side, she said a short, fervent prayer, and the spell was effectively and immediately broken. The space opened itself up to her only after she privately acknowledged its power. It was the only way forward.

She repeated the prayer this morning, mumbling the words softly.

The wind lifted and changed direction, pushing at her back, nudging her on.

She passed the bronze marker first, the heels of her boots sinking into the soft, damp earth. Raised some three feet off the ground and set just inside the gate to the first cabin, it dated the village to 1852, the year Monsieur and Madame Duquesne bought the land from the Mississippi all the way to the back swamp, christening it *La Belle Vie*. The six cabins were all that remained of what was once a thriving village of plantation workers. She wiped the words with her jacket sleeve, clearing the dew. Inside the first cabin, she paused long enough for her eyes to adjust to the darkness of the one-room shack. The air was thick, even the halest breeze unable or unwilling to cross the threshold. Caren gave the cabin a quick survey: straw pallet on the dirt floor; antique field tools hanging from rusty nails on the walls; a pine table with a tin cup and a kettle resting atop; a broom of twigs and brush; and a crudely made bench with a threadbare quilt lying on one end. It was neat and clean and ready for showing. Caren backed out, ducking her head beneath a low beam.

The others were all the same: four leaning walls beneath sagging, shingled roofs, each with an open doorway but no actual door, and out front a tiny, square patch of dirt and weeds where vegetables and wildflowers once grew—a historical fact which Raymond Clancy had pointedly refused to re-create, even in a nod to verisimilitude, for fear of being accused of painting too pretty a picture of slave life, of being called an apologist or worse. Raymond hated the slave cabins, hated every damn thing they stood for, he'd said, and had more than once made a fervent pitch to tear them down completely, fairly begging, knowing that this was one curatorial decision he'd have to run by his father, Leland, a man beloved in the parish for preserving an important piece of history, for Louisianans and black folks, in particular. Raymond had tried to rope Caren in once, asking her to author a memo on company letterhead stating all the ways it would boost the plantation's bottom line if the unsightly cabins were done away with. They could build a second reception hall, he'd said, or expand parking. It was the only instance, in all the time Caren had worked for Raymond, maybe even in all the years she'd known him, that she ever told him *no*.

Raymond, she remembered, the one they used to call chicken.

Caren and his baby brother, Bobby, used to spend long, rain-soaked afternoons daring him to walk alone through the slave village, daring Ray to spend even ten minutes inside the last cabin on the left, the one Caren was standing in front of now.

Jason's Cabin, they called it, because that was her mother's name for it.

She could still hear her hot, honeyed soprano.

She could still hear her mother whispering that name.

He was some kin to her, so the story went, some distant branch on the Gray family tree, thin and reedy as it was, pruned by time and circumstance; Caren was an only child, as was her mother before her, great-aunts and -uncles long gone. Jason, her great-great-great-grandfather on her mother's side, she'd been told, had been a slave, born across the river on a neighboring plantation, brought to Belle Vie when he was just a boy. Her mother had always said he was a man to be proud of, slave or no slave. The stories her mother told, bits and pieces of history passed on from one generation to the next, painted a man who had lived with his head up and his back straight, a man who had lived a life of peace and fidelity . . . until he went mysteriously missing sometime after the Civil War. No one really knew what happened to him, but plantation lore was ripe with speculation. Some said he had tired of cutting cane and walked out of the fields after the war, leaving a wife and child. Some said he had problems with drink and women and that's why he ran. And still others, like Caren's mother, thought he had likely met trouble here on the plantation; that he'd died at Belle Vie, and his soul never left the grounds. Bobby's tales

were the most gruesome, often involving knife fights and fisti-
cuffs and blood in the cane fields, anything his twelve-year-old
mind could conjure to color his ghost stories, his proof of a
real plantation haunting, a man without a final resting place.
He would whisper in Caren's ear, tap-tap her shoulders to the
beat of spectral feet wandering the slave village, messing with
her until she either screamed or fell into a fit of laughter, chest
burning as she ran and ran, always looking back, hoping Bobby
Clancy would catch her. Tall and lean, it never took him more
than a few strides. He would throw himself down, rolling on
the grass at her feet, strands of his black hair pasted against
his damp, pink forehead. "Honest," he would say, panting to
catch his breath, staring up through a tangle of trees. Jason's
Cabin was haunted.

Caren rested her hand on the cabin's low-lying gate.

It was washed over with rain, and the door was standing wide
open.

She paused over that, thinking it odd, that one detail.

But it wasn't until she crossed the dirt yard and stepped inside
the cabin that she felt something was really wrong. Someone
had been in here, she thought, inside this very cabin. It was the
stillness that spooked her. Not the kind of emptiness that comes
with actual vacancy, but rather a kind of strained quiet that was
trying too hard, the tightness that comes when someone somewhere is trying very hard to be still, to restrain every twitch and
wayward breath.

She felt, for a moment, that she wasn't alone.

She couldn't see two feet in front of her, the daylight stingy
and withholding and stopping stubbornly at the door. She was
standing in utter darkness, the air thick and dusty. She felt her
chest close, her head go light. She'd had moments like this before, in this very cabin, when she'd felt overcome with dread, a

heavy weight pressing in on her sternum. But today the feeling was worse. And Caren did something she'd never done, not in all the years she'd worked at Belle Vie. She didn't wait for her eyes to adjust, didn't wait until she could actually see . . . the tools on the wall and the rusting sugar kettle made over for laundering, a bar of lye soap and a hand wringer inside; the straw bed and pine table and the shallow pit in the floor that was dug out for cooking. She simply turned and walked out, cutting her inspection short. This cabin, the one set closest to the fields, was exactly the same as the others. At least that's what she told the cops.

Her last stop was the staff kitchen, located in a squat, stone-and-brick building a few yards from the main house. In the old days, a chance kitchen fire could mow down a Southern mansion in a matter of minutes, and the distance between the two buildings was meant to provide a measure of protection, and keep the big house cool in the worst summer months. The kitchen was an eight-hundred-square-foot box, one room that was bigger than any of the places Caren had lived in with her mom when she was a kid: guesthouses and garage apartments and one unbearably damp and hot summer spent in a two-room trailer parked on the back of somebody's land. They were cheap rentals that provided shelter, but little else, places Helen Gray cared little for. The plantation's eighteen acres were the whole of Caren's only real idea of home, the only constant in her life. Belle Vie *is* home, her mother would say. *It's in our blood, 'Cakes.* Caren had spent part of her childhood in this very kitchen, thumbing through her schoolwork or watching television. She'd learned to write her cursive letters in a single afternoon, sitting at one of the small tables by the stove, waiting for her mother to get off work.

The kitchen's door was propped open. Inside, Lorraine, the current cook, had her feet up on a card table covered with vegetable scraps and newspapers and discarded oyster shells.

"Morning, baby," she said, seeing Caren at the back door. Lorraine called everyone *baby*, and Caren had long learned not to take it personally.

In the hot, steamy kitchen, she unzipped her down jacket.

"You have a menu for me, Lorraine?"

"Now, what you think, baby?"

Lorraine had a bottle of hot sauce sticking out of the pocket of her stained apron and was sucking down raw oysters for breakfast and watching *Fox & Friends* on a small black-and-white television set. Caren could have stood there all day before she moved an inch. "Lorraine," she sighed, because they went through this every time.

"Yes, baby?" she said, in a way that suggested she had already carried this conversation farther than she intended to. Lorraine was openly suspicious of Caren and her sudden return to Belle Vie four years ago. It was possible that she even held an irrational belief that Caren had come for her job, to claim her rightful place in line. That Raymond Clancy had made her general manager, Lorraine's boss essentially, certainly didn't help things. Lorraine delighted in small acts of insubordination, putting through purchase orders without Caren's permission, serving pickled chow-chow out of crusty jars from her home kitchen, and often changing menus at the last minute. She considered herself an artist, and not one to be tied down by fixed pricing. To Lorraine, Caren was a nuisance, with her little clipboard and her endless list of questions. Worse, she saw Caren as a woman who was rootless and unsure of where she belonged—and therefore not someone who, by Lorraine's standards, ought to be consulted about the intricacies of local cuisine. Lorraine was tall and black and unabashedly fat, carrying most of her excess weight around her middle, wearing it as a walking billboard for her talents, and she likewise regarded Caren's relatively lean frame as further evidence that she shouldn't be trusted in a kitchen. She was nothing like her mother, Lorraine was fond of saying.

"Lorraine, we have eighty-five guests due here at five o'clock."

"Plenty of time."

"The host is expecting a five-course meal," Caren said, repeating a fact of which she knew Lorraine was well aware. "I'd like to be able to tell them just what all that might entail."

Lorraine pondered the request before deciding, impulsively, to grant it.

"What'd we say, Pearl?"

She glanced over her shoulder at her line cook, a child-sized black woman in her sixties who had to stand on an orange crate to man the stove, which she was hovering over now. She didn't bother to look up from the pot that was fogging her glasses.

"'Gator," Pearl said.

Lorraine turned, reporting this news to Caren. "'Gator."

"And?"

Lorraine sighed then, making a grand show of being ordered onto her feet. She crossed the kitchen to a large, stainless-steel fridge. There, she planted one hand on the curve of her right hip and stood in front of the open refrigerator door, searching the stored contents with her eyes. After a few moments of silence, she ticked off the night's menu: "Grits, rolled with smoked Gouda, spinach, and bacon; chard out of the garden, with garlic and lemon; and potatoes creamed with butter and drippings." She bent down a little, checking a lower shelf. "And I guess I could do a mushroom soup to start." Then, nodding to her assistant, she added, "Pearl did a cobbler last night."

"Peach," Pearl said.

Lorraine turned to Caren. "Peach."

Caren nodded. "Sounds great."

Of course it did, she thought. She and Lorraine both knew those were Caren's mother's recipes. Lorraine held her gaze for a moment, narrowing eyes the color of burnt butter, and daring Caren to say something about it. "Oh, yes, ma'am, baby."

Caren's office was on the second floor of the main house, above the formal parlor. It was long and narrow and always warm, as the room's single window faced south. She could see a swatch of the parking lot from here, and the cane fields beyond.

She was never allowed in the main house as a kid.

She and Bobby had the run of the grounds and would sometimes sneak over the levee to hide from Raymond. But she never once stepped foot inside Bobby's bedroom or sat to dinner with the family. And her mother never made it past the foyer. She would cook, but Helen would not *serve*, leaving trays of hot food on a pedestal table by the back door or sending Lorraine in her stead. The Grays, for generations, had stayed clear of the main house, either by fate or by choice. And now, six days out of the week, Caren sat comfortably at her desk, looking out over fields where her ancestors had cut sugarcane by hand, both before and after the Civil War. Days she felt tempted to sit and ruminate about mistakes she'd made, choices that had led like a series of stale bread crumbs back to the gates of Belle, there was always this one thought. She had gone farther and risen higher than anyone in her family might have dreamed. It was not nearly the life she thought she'd have, not at thirty-seven. But it was something.

The machines were in the fields today.

October to January, they were out from sunup to sundown,

mowing row after row, plucking ripe stalks from the ground and stacking the bounty in advance of its long ride to the sugar mill in Thibodaux. Every year, during the cutting season, she watched them from her desk for hours on end, their whole repetitive existence providing the background hum of Caren's life on the plantation during the fall.

That Thursday was the first dry morning in a week.

Though the air was still damp and thick as wet cotton, fogging up her office window with tiny beads of dew, there was no rain today, and that meant there were laborers in the fields. She watched them work in teams of two. They dropped whole stalks of cane into shallow furrows dug into fields that had been left empty and fallow; they were planting for next year's crop, work that ordinarily would have been completed by early September, well before the harvest, if this season hadn't been so unusually wet. They'd had nearly fifteen inches of rain in August alone, the stuff of records. And every wet day was a day a farm couldn't plant, putting Groveland and everybody else behind for the season—and creating a small band of underemployed field-workers hanging around outside the Ace Hardware or the T&H Superette in Donaldsonville, looking for extra work. Ed Renfrew always hired locally, mostly blacks and poor whites, as had the Clancys when they still ran the farm, but for the past three years, the Groveland Corporation had been pulling in laborers from out of state, as far west as Beaumont, Texas, and even some coming all the way from Georgia and Alabama; they were Mexicans mostly, and some Guatemalans, plucked out of rice fields and fruit groves for a few months of working Louisiana sugarcane, before moving on to somewhere else. If the weather had held, the cops would later say, Inés Avalo would have already been gone. She would have likely still been alive.

The plantation was about fifty miles south of the capital.

Out here, they got only a few radio stations, mostly out of Baton Rouge, an endless stream of adult contemporary and country, Lionel Richie and Randy Travis. The music played softly as Caren got to work on the morning's first task: a memo to her supervisor, Raymond Clancy, outlining the particulars of the Donovan Isaacs problem.

It had started over the summer.

Mr. Isaacs, an "actor" with the Belle Vie Players who'd had a lead part in *The Olden Days of Belle Vie* for over a year, had taken a basic, first-year U.S. history course at his community college and come out a new man, he said. He'd had a personal awakening of sorts and suddenly taken grave issue with the staged play, refusing to utter, on principle, the scripted words that were being "put into his mouth."

The play was, admittedly, bad, a fact that Caren didn't drive home in her memo.

It was written by a state senator's wife, following Belle Vie's formal recognition as a historical treasure (worthy of state funding), and not a period or comma had changed in the twenty-five years hence. It was as soapy as *Gone With the Wind*, full of belles and balls and star-crossed lovers, noble Confederates and happy darkies and more dirty Yankees than you could count. And the tourists *loved* it. Senior groups and war buffs and New Englanders in shorts and flip-flops. And middle school teachers, of course, many of whom ordered items in bulk from the gift shop as takeaways for their students.

Caren had a certain appreciation for Donovan's newfound rage and even let him vent in her office for a solid twenty minutes, as he enumerated the many ways "this cracker-ass bullshit" fell well short of the *real* history of plantation life across Louisiana. Donovan wanted the whole play axed, which Caren was in no position to authorize. She did admit to encouraging

20

him, though. It was actually her idea that he create some kind of alternative document, "like a history report," that would tell a more accurate version of antebellum life, using Belle Vie's own library, if he wanted, and that he present it to the Clancy family and the state's Department of Culture, Recreation, and Tourism, which paid his small salary. She was thinking of a one-sheet, something they could photocopy and include as a hand-out along with the play's programs. But Donovan had taken it a step further. He showed up in her office one hot July morning, clutching a stack of wrinkled yellow legal papers, smudged with pencil marks and ink. He had rewritten the play, top to bottom. Even the title was new: *Truth and Consequences: The Straight Story of the South.* The handwriting was illegible and difficult to follow, and at first she thought he was joking. "I'm as serious as a heart attack," he said, leaving the pages on Caren's desk.

She never even got past the third page, on which, as far as she could tell, a slave revolt took out half the French Creoles in Ascension Parish. There were three beheadings in a single paragraph. The whole thing read like bad comic-book fan fic-tion: slaves firing weapons without any gunpowder in sight, Yankee soldiers making telephone calls in the middle of the Civil War, and there was at least one musical interlude. It was an absolute mess, a boyish fantasy, an overcorrection that fa-vored Donovan's own misguided ideas about power and score-settling over any real semblance of the truth. And besides, it wasn't exactly the kind of feel-good fare that pulls tourists in off the highway. Raymond Clancy said as much when she'd pitched the idea over the phone. His instructions could not have been more explicit: the play, and Belle Vie itself, his family homestead, would stay the way they had always been. When she reported this news to Donovan, he nodded stoically, as if he'd been expecting this. Then he threatened a walkout of the whole cast in protest—inducting Shauna Hayes and Cornelius McCrary on the spot, before finally convincing Dell Blanchett, Nikki Hubbard, and Ennis Mabry to join the fight if push came to shove—leaving Caren with the task of figuring a way to run Belle Vie without any slaves. He'd left her office that day with a parting admonition that the truth would come out, one way or another.

In some ways, Caren understood Donovan.

She understood his pining for a history he could take some pride in. She was the daughter of a plantation cook, after all, the great-great-great-granddaughter of slaves, facts that had caused her no small amount of shame when she was Donovan's age.

She just didn't like him much.

She didn't want to be his *sister*.

He was a twenty-two-year-old kid, undereducated and over-entitled, of a generation long out of the shadow of the hard work that had made a life like his possible. He had nice clothes and a decent car, paid for by his grandmother, no less, the same grandmother who scrounged up bail money from emptied-out coffee cans whenever her boy got in trouble, which he did on an almost quarterly basis. It was little stuff mostly—petty theft or disorderly conduct, drunken fights outside of nightclubs and house parties. They were the impulsive acts of a knucklehead, not a hardened criminal, which in Caren's mind somehow made them worse. She'd been in court with kids who didn't have even half the resources Donovan did, kids who would spend their lives in jail, most of them, kids who had no chance. She thought Donovan should have known better, shown some self-restraint, made his grandmother's heart ache less. Betty Collier was in her eighties now, had raised him since he was in grade school. She would some days keep Caren on the phone at all hours, wanting her to know how hard she worked to keep her grandson out of trouble, often ending these calls by asking if there was more Caren could hire Donovan to do on the place to keep him busy. And Caren would have to explain that the only open work was for maintenance jobs, and that Donovan had made it plain he wasn't putting his hands in any dirt.

"What the fuck I'm in college for?" he'd said.

These unexplained absences were his latest stunt. Caren was listing them in chronological order, starting back from August, when the news finally reached her. There was a faint crackle at her hip, then Luis's lilting voice on her walkie-talkie.

"Ma'am . . ." he said.

She lifted the clunky device from the waist of her jeans. "Luis, could you or Miguel make sure to pull one of the heat lamps from the storage closet for this evening?"

"Uh . . . Mrs. Gray?"

She sighed.

She must have told him at least a dozen times she wasn't married, repeating just as frequently that she, thirty years his junior, was the one who ought to be calling him *sir*.

"Yes," she said, still typing. "What is it, Luis?"

"There's something out here, ma'am, something you need to see."

2

Her first call was to the Sheriff's Department.

They sent a kid in uniform, hardly older than the high school students who came through on the big yellow buses for field trips. He was, bless his heart, trying to secure the scene, where already a small crowd had gathered: Luis and Miguel, who kept crossing himself every five minutes and kissing his rosary; Lorraine and Pearl, who was craning to see, as was Gerald from security; and a few members of the cast. Nikki Hubbard was standing behind Bo Johnston, peering wide-eyed over the rise of Bo's broad shoulders. There were two snow-white iPod buds in her ears. Her red-and-black letterman's jacket was zipped all the way to her chin. Caren could see her breath.

She wanted everyone out of there at once.

She repeated her earlier instruction that no one was to touch anything.

To the Players—Nikki and Bo, Shauna and Dell, Cornelius McCrary and Ennis, who was already wearing Donovan's ill-fitting costume—she told them to wait in the old schoolhouse for further instruction. Lorraine started for the kitchen on her own, if only to rob Caren of the satisfaction of ordering her to do anything. Pearl followed her leader in silence. Caren asked Luis and Miguel to pull the heat lamps from the storage closet. Both men nodded in silence, as did Gerald, who moved away from the scene without being asked. In less than a minute Caren had accomplished what the young sheriff's deputy had been unable to do, and he seemed to take her ease with the task as an affront, spitting in her general direction a reminder that no one was to leave the premises and ordering her to wait by the gate for homicide detectives.

As the group began to disperse, Danny Olmsted could be seen coming over the short hill behind the quarters. Having heard the news by now, he was walking fast, almost jogging, toward them. His trench coat was open and flapping behind him, and both of his shoes were untied. Caren wondered if he'd slept in the library again last night instead of driving back to his office or apartment or wherever it was he went when he wasn't here. He was an adjunct professor in the history department at LSU, working on what must surely be the world's most long-anticipated dissertation. Years ago he'd cooked up some arrangement with Leland Clancy giving him use of the plantation's library, eventually acquiring his own key—a show of scholarship Caren had long suspected was bullshit. She had come upon him catnapping in the library's Hall of Records one too many times not to know better. The plantation kept him off campus for long stretches of unsupervised time, and it provided a rather effective romantic backdrop for the seduction of unsuspecting coeds. He'd let more than a few of them paw through Belle Vie's historical documents on file.

He arrived breathless at the mouth of the grave, ignoring the young deputy, who was telling him to stand back. Danny, who was tall and thin, and sloe-eyed behind his smudged glasses, put his hands on his hips and bent at the waist, peering down at the muddy corpse. "Jesus," he whispered, his mouth hanging slack in a way that made him look drunk or stupid, as if he couldn't make sense of what it was he was seeing.

"Y'all need to get on away from here," the deputy said, hiking his pants up, the weight of his parish-issued sidearm pulling at his britches. Danny took a step backward, turning clumsily on his heels, coming, for a brief moment, to stand face-to-face with Caren. His was flushed, and a faint sheen of perspiration across his upper lip caught sunlight against his pale skin. He mumbled unintelligibly, then stumbled back the way he came, cutting through the quarters, which she'd asked him many times not to do.

The young deputy, still tugging at his waistband, turned to Caren next.

"You, too, ma'am," he said. "I need to keep this area clear."

The bus from St. Ignatius Middle School was already in the parking lot. They were the only ones Caren couldn't get on the phone.

Ernest N. Morial Elementary had, luckily, gotten her message before its fifth-graders left school grounds in Orleans Parish. The school's vice principal thanked her for the update and promptly agreed that today might not be the best day for a tour of the plantation, what with police detectives en route, as well as the coroner.

A Ms. Patricia Quinlan—administrative assistant to Giles Schuyler, CEO of Merryvale Properties, Inc., the host of this evening's dinner reception—said she would have to get back to Caren once she knew more about how Mr. Schuyler wanted to proceed. The woman sounded nervous, but also faintly an-noyed, as if the discovery of a dead body on the property was something Caren should have been able to anticipate.

But no one in the main office at St. Ignatius could get the stu-dents' chaperones or the bus driver on their cell phones, which left Caren standing in the parking lot, trying to explain a set of most unusual circumstances to two sixth-grade history teachers, one of whom was wearing a black sweatshirt with the state of

Louisiana painted in gold glitter. Behind them, the kids were all out of their bus seats, jumping across the aisle, their high-pitched squeals enough to melt metal. Neither teacher looked as yet prepared to endure another ninety-minute drive back to Metairie.

Caren felt herself starting to sweat.

She offered them coffee and a sincere apology and promised a truncated tour of the property, one that would skirt, in a wide arc, anything unseemly. She personally escorted them to the old schoolhouse, where performances were held three days a week and all day on Saturdays. As the students shuffled into rows of plastic folding chairs, Caren ducked into the back room—a spacious closet behind the stage that acted as a greenroom for the cast. She told Ennis Mabry to feel free to draw out some of Donovan's monologues, ad-libbing if need be, to fill time. Ennis stood, twisting a handkerchief in his arthritic hands. "Sorry, Miss C," he said, before relaying the news that his nephew, the stand-in for the part of the plantation's driver, had backed out of playing the part. "He don't want nothing to do with no cops," Ennis said.

"Just do the best you can," she said to the cast.

The Belle Vie Players were unusually quiet this morning.

They looked spooked.

Cornelius McCrary, who was wearing a faded red-and-blue OBAMA '08 T-shirt over the tattered muslin pants that were his official FIELD SLAVE #2 costume, was staring at the floor. Nikki Hubbard, the plantation's SEAMSTRESS, was playing with the zipper of her letterman's jacket. Dell and Shauna, MAMMY and YOUNG HOUSE SLAVE, respectively, were tying each other's aprons in place. Bo Johnston, who had the very important task of filling the boots of TYNAN, the former overseer and distant forefather of the Clancy clan who took over the plantation after the war, was putting on his costume. He and Dell kept looking over at Eddie Knoxville.

Caren couldn't help the feeling that something was going unsaid.

She tried to put them at ease.

"Okay," she said, because she had some basic sense of how this would go. She'd been around the mechanics of a criminal investigation before. It wasn't so long ago that she didn't remember. "Here's what will happen next. There'll be homicide detectives here. They're going to want to ask you some questions, each of you individually probably. It's not something at all to be afraid of." Here she tried to smile, and felt how incredibly tense she was, and afraid, all the while she was telling them to relax. "Just answer their questions simply and honestly," she said. It's what she used to tell her clients.

The room was dead quiet.

Val Marchand, or MADAME DUQUESNE, according to the playbill, was drinking a Pepsi, sitting next to Kimberly Reece and Terry "Shep" Shepard, who played the Duquesnes' two grown children, MANETTE and LE ROY. Shep, a former high school football star, seemed anxious and fidgety, his left knee pumping up and down. Val rubbed a fleck of pink lipstick off her teeth. She wasn't saying anything either. Eddie, who had played the part of MONSIEUR DUQUESNE ever since he retired from a water treatment plant in St. Charles Parish, was either elected or self-appointed as the one to speak. He took a wide step in Caren's direction, standing close enough that she could smell the morning's amaretto on his breath. His voice was flat and dry, just above a whisper. "Where *is* Donovan?" he said. The others were all looking at her, too.

The question about Donovan's whereabouts did not seem casual, and she actually paused before answering. At her hip,

Gerald's voice cut through a wave of static. From his roaming post, he announced, "Policemen are here, ma'am."

She lifted the walkie-talkie from her waist, answering Gerald. "Okay."

To the cast, she said, "Just let me know when the show is done."

Not until she stepped outside did she realize her hands were shaking.

She closed her eyes and saw the blood and the dirt again, the open grave and the curl of that woman's back. She leaned her weight against the trunk of the nearest tree, pressing a hand against her navel, holding it in, willing herself not to throw up, just as she had in those first months of pregnancy, when she had refused to be brought to her knees.

Letty's van was already gone from the parking lot. She and Morgan were probably halfway to school by now, a good thirty miles away in the tiny hamlet of Laurel Springs. Caren thought it was possible her daughter had made it off the property without the faintest idea of what had happened. She could hope, at least.

The bus driver from St. Ignatius was still behind the wheel, talking on her cell phone and eating a honey bun out of a saran wrapper. Her voice spilled out of the bus's open windows, softened to a low hum in the humid midmorning air. The sun was higher now, baking the wet earth and encircling the southern end of Belle Vie with the damp fragrance of jasmine and dogwood. In another hour, it would be warm enough for short sleeves. Across the asphalt parking lot was a single-lane farm road, which, at a distance of several hundred yards to the east, curved around to meet State Highway 1, the road from which the detectives would have traveled, coming from the sheriff's main office across the river in Gonzales. She didn't see their car in the parking lot, only a dark red truck, rusted along its sides, chugging along on the farm road, eventually doubling back and passing in front of the parking lot a second time.

She thought the driver might be lost.

She started for the fence line, thinking the detectives must have already found their way to the grave. By the time she made it back by the cane fields, she saw that a crime-scene team was already in position. There were three of them, each decked head to toe in a crinkly, white synthetic fabric, with plastic booties over their shoes. They looked like moonwalkers, out of place in this verdant landscape. They hovered over the dead woman's body, one technician photographing the scene while another measured the distance from the body to the nearly five-foot-high fence made of whitewashed steel. There was cane swaying on the sugar side of the fence. Through the bars, Hunt Abrams was watching the entire scene, two fists jammed into the pockets of his Wranglers. He was wearing a black GROVELAND FARMS windbreaker. Caren had met the man only once before, one particularly productive harvest when his machines were going eighteen hours a day, seven days a week. She'd sought him out one desperate Saturday morning, wading through rows of shoulder-high cane until she found the double-wide that housed his office in the fields. She had a sixty-thousand-dollar wedding starting at three o'clock that afternoon and fairly begged the man to halt his work, for a few hours at least. His answer was a polite, "No, ma'am." Then he offered her a ride back to the plantation. She sat in the front seat of his black pickup truck, beside a loaded shotgun he kept propped within arm's reach. "For the snakes," he said.

Two police detectives stood a few feet from Caren.

They were already interviewing Miguel, Luis acting as a very nervous interpreter. One of the cops was taking notes on a small steno pad. He was tall and thick-necked, with a deep, ruddy complexion that gave the impression he was exerting himself even though he was standing perfectly still. The other detective was smaller and more compact. His hair was flecked with gray and cut in a stylish manner, his stance one of cool repose. He was making quiet calculations, his eyes scanning the pieces before him: the body, the black soil at his feet, the tall fence, Luis and poor Miguel, who was sweating openly, rubbing his forehead with the back of his hand.

It was the larger cop who noticed Caren first.

He nodded to his partner. "Nes," he said.

Then he went right back to questioning Miguel, who was whispering something to Luis. The cop shook his head. "Tell him I don't give a shit about Immigration." Then, speaking more loudly, he said to Miguel, "No *migra*—get it? Just answer the questions." Miguel was only nineteen and half the cop's size. He looked scared out of his mind. He lived in a one-bedroom apartment across the river in Galvez with his girlfriend, her parents, and his two-year-old son. He was good-natured and quick to laugh and always on time. And now, of all days, Caren realized she would have to let him go. This was the first she'd heard that the Social Security card he showed when he was hired might not be worth the paper it was printed on. The plantation received state funding. Caren wasn't allowed to take any chances. She was management now.

She felt her stomach turn.

She hated this part of the job.

She wanted to lie down somewhere and start this day all over again—Donovan on time, and no body in the ground, and none of this news about Miguel's status.

The slim detective was walking toward her. "Caren Gray?" he said.

31

"Yes."

"Sergeant said you're the one who made the call?"

"Yes."

"I'm Detective Nestor Lang, ma'am." He held out his right hand.

"You can call me Caren."

"Yes, ma'am."

He turned and surveyed the scene with a small sigh.

"Well," he said. "Tell me what you know."

"Miguel," she said, nodding to where he was standing with the other cop. "He alerted Luis, who alerted me, and then I called the station. I don't really know any more than that." Detective Lang nodded, reaching for his cell phone at his waist. He checked a text message, then nodded to the kid in uniform. "Go on and escort Dr. Allard back this way," he said, "and let him know the crew from CID is already here."

"Yes, sir," the deputy said. He jogged across the grass toward the parking lot, keeping a taming hand on the loose waistband of his pants as he ran. Lang slid his cell phone back inside the leather case on his belt. From his jacket pocket he pulled out a small pad, identical to the one his partner was using to take notes. He clicked the top of an ink pen and said, "So who all has access to the property, ma'am?"

"The staff, during the day."

"Can I get a list?"

"Yes."

"And the property's locked at night?"

"Unless we have an event, yes."

"That's right, that's right," he said. "Y'all put on parties out here."

She didn't believe that *y'all* for a second. It was a folksy air, put on in an effort to disarm her, she thought, to make her feel at home with him. He was watching her closely, studying her face, the way she had both hands shoved down deep in the pockets of her jeans, making clear by his expression that he hadn't yet decided on which side of his internal ledger she belonged, openly compliant . . . or trouble. He threw a glance over his shoulder, nodding toward the main house and the quarters. "Strange place to throw a party," he said, testing her reaction, trying to get a feel for what kind of an employee she was, perhaps one who might go off-script outside her boss's earshot.

"Well . . . we host weddings, too."

This made him smile.

He thought she was being clever.

"The event fees help cover the cost of maintaining the property," she said matter-of-factly. "The Clancys feel it's the best way they can preserve the space for history."

"Was there something going on here last night?"

"No," she said, shaking her head. "The last was a luncheon yesterday."

The Baton Rouge Ladies' Lunch Bunch, she said.

"And who all has keys to the property?"

She ran through the list aloud. "Gerald, our security guard, is on nights when we have an event. He has keys for the main gate and most of the buildings. Lorraine, the cook, she comes in early sometimes. She has a key. And Danny has one, too."

"Danny?"

"He's a graduate student, a professor, I guess. He has a key to the main gate and access to the library. He kind of comes and goes as he pleases. He doesn't work for me," she said, making that distinction clear. Lang was writing all this down.

"Is he here now?"

"He was earlier, yes."

"Good," he said, writing this, too.

"And of course the Clancys have keys," she said.

"The owners."

Caren nodded. "Leland and his two sons, Raymond and Bobby. Leland is nearly bedridden these days, and Bobby rarely comes around. Raymond is the one who runs the plantation's LLC. But he hardly ever comes out here either," she said.

Lang pointed toward the main house.

"We came in that way," he said. "That's not the main entrance?"

"No, the main gate is actually around back, by the parking lot."

It was a common mistake, she explained. The front of the big house—which faced the water and was visible from the "river road," a paved street that shadowed the Mississippi like a plain and faithful twin—hadn't been used as the plantation's main entrance for more than a hundred years, back when the river was the primary mode of travel into or out of Belle Vie. These days, nearly everyone entered through the back gate.

"And that's the only way in or out? I mean, besides the house?"

"Yes."

"And they would have both been locked last night, the gate and the house?" he said, glancing at his notes. "The last event was midday, a luncheon, you said."

"That's right," she said. "Everything was locked last night."

Lang nodded, jotting this down. "I didn't see any cameras out here." He nodded in the direction of the main house, the cottages, and the manicured grounds.

"There are actually two security cameras," she told him. "They're both fixed to the main house. But they were both inoperative when I took the job, and Raymond Clancy has repeatedly declined to repair them." Lang glanced again at the grounds, the multimillion-dollar view, making a humming sound at the back of his throat. "I've seen people put floodlights and spy cams on a mobile home," he said.

She shrugged. "We haven't had any problems out here."

"Sure, I understand."

A few feet away, his partner was still talking to Luis and Miguel. Miguel was staring at the ground, and Luis had his ball cap pressed to his chest, shaking his head.

Caren felt bad for both of them.

"And who all was on the grounds last night, ma'am?"

"I was the only one here," she said. "I live on the property."

"Alone?"

"It's me and my daughter."

The detective nodded, writing.

The deputy in uniform was just now returning with a white-haired man whom Caren took for the coroner, Dr. Frank Allard. She voted for him in last year's election, even though she'd never seen the man in person. He'd actually run uncontested, but it was 2008, and she'd felt weird about leaving any of the spaces blank. She didn't want to lose her say on a technicality. She'd gone over that ballot three or four times, standing alone in the booth, tracing a finger under the first line, the word *President*. She wondered what her mother would have made of that, if she'd lived to see it.

Dr. Allard was wearing tan ropers and slacks, and he carried a leather satchel in his right hand. He nodded to the moonwalkers in white before bending deeply at the waist, peering down at the body, its nose down in the dirt.

"How long have you lived here?" Lang asked.

She'd already decided she would answer only the literal questions put to her; it's what she would have told her clients. No need then to bring up her childhood, Belle Vie as her playground, or her mother's three decades of service to the Clancys.

35

She would not say her name out loud.

She hadn't in years.

"Since 2005," she said.

Four years, she thought, and I'm still here.

She turned away from Lang, glancing again at the coroner. He was lifting mud from the back side of the corpse, using a tool like a small paintbrush, working in tight, tiny circles. "And all of your staff is accounted for?" she heard the detective ask.

There was, of course, one person who was missing.

She actually hesitated before mentioning his name.

"Donovan Isaacs, one of our actors," she said. "He didn't come to work today."

"You have a phone number for him?"

She nodded. "In my office."

"We'll need that, too."

"Fine," she said, glancing at her watch. They were probably just entering the Civil War at the schoolhouse, a few minutes away from the sudden death of Monsieur Duquesne and the eve of Reconstruction and Belle Vie's near demise. Which meant the show was almost done, and she would have to improvise some other time-filler. Maybe giveaways at the gift shop. Or Pearl could scoop out ice cream for the kids.

"What about the cane fields, ma'am?" Lang said. "That's the Groveland Corporation out there?" He nodded toward the machines and the rows of sugarcane.

"Yes, they've held the lease for the past year."

"Your staff have any dealings with their people, or vice versa?"

"Their workers aren't allowed on the grounds of Belle Vie," she said. "Raymond Clancy has always been very clear about that."

"Sure, I understand, ma'am," Lang said, closing his notepad for the first time. "But I guess I'm just wondering in any case if there's ever been any contact between your people and the workers over there, any *conflicts* that you know of?"

"Most of the workers out there don't speak English, Detective."

"I know it," Lang said, nodding. "And that might be precisely a source of conflict," he said, adding, "for *some*." He paused, waiting on her reaction; the gesture was presented as an act of courtesy, an invitation to unload in safe company any pent-up feelings about the parish's immigrant population, which swelled every planting season, like the Mississippi after a storm, seeping into a historically tight-knit community. Every year, the feelings of resentment, among locals—blacks in particular, many four and five generations deep—only strengthened, often souring into vocal posturing about "these new people coming here, making themselves at home."

Most black folks with roots in Louisiana could trace their people back before the war, when slaves had built the state's sugar industry with their bare hands. And they all had a good yarn about a great-great-uncle or a distant cousin or somebody who fought with the Union, or a great-great-great-grandfather who served as one of the first blacks in Congress during Reconstruction. There were bits and pieces left behind, letters and faded newspaper accounts, but for the most part this was a history that existed on the wind, in stories passed down through the years. Caren had these stories in her family, too, tales her mother had heard growing up, from elders who were told the very same stories when they were kids. Caren's mother was born and raised in Ascension Parish, and she was always clear that the Grays were sugar people, that she and Caren came from a line of men who lived and died by what they could produce with their hands. Her granddaddy cut cane, and his daddy before him, all in the fields behind Belle Vie. Her mother loved the whole of this land, and she wanted Caren to love it, too, to know where she came from. She had a piece of history for every corner of the parish, pulling bedtime stories out of the dirt Caren played in, the details changing a little with each telling. She peopled their lives with the hazy stories of men and women Caren would never know, in place of where a father might have been, a sibling or two.

Caren stopped listening after a while.

These days you could often hear whispers in town, rumblings about things not being the way they used to be, talk about the lack of good-paying jobs for black folks. One AM radio host even went so far as to publicly blame the Groveland Corporation for high unemployment among the locals, for knowingly hiring illegals and flooding the parish with cheap labor. "Hell, you can't even get a job bagging groceries at the Piggly Wiggly anymore without knowing how to speak Spanish," he'd scoffed.

"Your staff have any problems with the field-workers over there?" Lang asked, more directly this time. Caren didn't get it initially, what this question had to do with the matter at hand. She looked from the woman in the grave over to Hunt Abrams, who was watching them from his side of the fence. She got it then, what Lang was thinking. Or rather *who*. The body in the dirt, discovered just a few feet from the cane fields, had been its own first clue. The inquiries about the farm and the field-workers, Lang's gentle but persistent pushing about the tensions over the fence, all of it added up to an early deduction as to the woman's identity. She was a cane worker, Caren realized.

"The only man I personally know who ever had a problem with Groveland, or the farm, was Ed Renfrew," she said.

"I know Ed."

"His family farmed on the place for years."

"And the company drove them out?"

"They beat him out for the bid. Raymond said it all came

down to dollars and cents, said his hands were tied. Ed huffed quite a bit about it. I don't think he ever had much respect for corporate farming, the kind of business they're running over there."

"Ed hired his people locally," Lang said, more statement than question.

"That's right."

"Black people," he said.

Caren frowned at the implication, where she thought he might be heading with this line of thought. "Some," she said tersely. Whatever note the detective made of this he kept to himself, his notepad now tucked away in the front pocket of his jacket.

"Anybody else express any political views that caught your attention?"

She wasn't sure Donovan's slave rant in her office counted as true political discourse, and, besides him, she'd never spoken with the staff about any subject deeper than work schedules or parking passes—though she did remember Val Marchand saying once that she admired Sarah Palin and would vote for her again if she could. But Caren had never heard anyone at Belle Vie mention a word about the farmworkers.

"No," she said.

"Okay, then."

Behind him, the moonwalkers had formed a tight semicircle around the grave.

Dr. Allard was standing now, nodding his head. "Let's turn her."

Detective Lang shot a look to his partner. "Jimmy," he said.

The two men inched nearer to the grave site, just as the crime-scene techs set gloved hands under the dirt-covered corpse. On a three-count, they lifted the body.

A swarm of blowflies shot two feet into the air.

Caren actually staggered back.

In the rapidly warming air, the scent of death had blossomed. It was worse than spoiled milk or rotting meat or piles of dead fish lying out in the sun . . . though some inventive combination of the three may have come close to matching the putrid smell.

The crime-scene techs turned the body, laying it gingerly on flat grass.

There, on her back, she stared up at them.

Her skin and hair were dappled with dirt, and there was dried blood staining the front of her rose-pink T-shirt. Her arms were pressed against her chest, and her mouth was open, as if a final scream were lodged in her throat, trapped somewhere in the butterflied flesh around her bloody neck, where the woman had been nearly cut in two.

Caren's knees gave out.

She turned from the sight, stumbling slightly, trying to get away.

"You okay, ma'am?" Lang said.

The voice seemed very far away, like a whisper at the bottom of an oil drum, hollow and useless. She bent over, put her hands on her thighs to steady herself, to catch her breath. When she finally raised her head again, the first thing her eyes landed on was the quarters and Jason's Cabin, the last one on the left. She felt a stone-sized pain in her chest. It was the same heaviness, the same dread, she'd felt this morning when she'd no sooner stepped into that very cabin than she'd had to stop and walk out.

"Ms. Gray?"

"Just give me a minute."

"Ma'am, we're going to get the investigative team in and out of here and get this whole thing cleaned up as soon as possible, I promise. Now, if you wouldn't mind gathering the staff, we can start those interviews right away." She nodded and said, "Sure," and then she started for the old schoolhouse, anything to get far away from here.

"And we'll need to speak to your daughter, of course."

Caren stopped cold. "She's only nine years old."

Ten actually, come December.

It was a number frequently on Caren's mind these days.

"We need to talk to her, too, ma'am," Lang said.

"I'll think about it." That was all she would give him.

"You're welcome to be present during the interview."

"I'm aware of that," she said. "I'm also aware of my right to refuse."

Lang shot her a funny look, as if the clouds in the sky had made a sudden unexpected shift, showing her up in some new light that did not in any way flatter. "You're not a lawyer, by any chance?" He gave her a wry smile, enjoying the sheer improbability of it, the idea of Caren, in her ropers and faded jeans, a doctor of law.

"No," she said plainly. "I'm not a lawyer."

He glanced at the TULANE SCHOOL OF LAW ball cap still on her head, but offered no further comment.

Behind them, one of the moonwalkers unzipped a rubber body bag. Overhead, a lone black buzzard circled the whole scene.

"I understand your concern here, ma'am," Lang said. "But we need to talk to everyone." She nodded, but didn't feel any better about it. She hadn't yet given thought to how she might explain to her daughter what had happened here today, the fact of a woman murdered, found dead in the dirt, right where they live. She had up until this point felt one of the gifts of coming home, coming back to Belle Vie, was the sense of safety she felt here, deep in the countryside, fifteen miles from the nearest town. Instead of Caren worrying, as she might have if they'd stayed in New Orleans, about her daughter getting lost on city streets or hunted by predators or shot, for that matter, Morgan, most afternoons, rode her bike down the plantation's main lane, as she herself had once done; and even on nights when Letty wasn't working, Caren only ever required that her daughter be home by sundown. Inside these gates, Morgan had always been free.

3

She ended up giving Letty the day off anyway, eventually arranging with the two police detectives for Letty to be interviewed as soon as she was back on plantation grounds, so she could be done with it and get home to her kids. After her own second, more extensive, interview with the two cops, Caren left Belle Vie at two o'clock, starting the thirty-minute drive north toward the capital to pick up Morgan.

There was a red car behind her on the highway.

It was a pickup truck with a dented grill and ten years of gathering rust.

She didn't make much of it at the time.

She was busy thinking of just what she was going to tell her little girl.

Morgan's school was brand-new, in the planned, gated community of Laurel Springs, just south of Baton Rouge. Raymond Clancy, whose practice was in the state's capital, had pulled a few strings to get Morgan placed at the school, one of the few conditions Caren had pressed upon him before taking the job. Clancy's own kids were at the Laurel Springs Middle School across the street. The town's three schools shared the same campus, and their pooled resources included an aquatic center, a state-of-the-art computer science center, and a library run by graduate students from the Library and Information Sciences Department at LSU. It was a school that would have cost her

43

at least ten thousand dollars a year if they were still living in New Orleans. Instead, she'd managed to sock away nearly twice that for each year she'd been living rent-free at Belle Vie. She had no mortgage, no possessions that couldn't be packed up in a single afternoon, and her car was eleven years old and paid off. Morgan, when the time came, could pay for any college she wanted to go to, preferably one far away from here.

Caren took two calls on the drive.

The first was from Raymond himself, the day's news having finally made it to him through his secretary. "My God, Gray," he said, calling her by her last name, an affectation he'd picked up years ago, when he'd first gone off to school (returning that first semester with all kinds of ideas about how a Clancy man ought to conduct himself). He was a lifelong member of Sigma Chi and seemed to think this manner of speaking was a winning way to show affection and intimacy, even where neither existed. Raymond and Caren were not particularly close, never had been. It was Bobby to whom she'd always been drawn, Bobby who let her tag along places, who never made her feel any different for being born a girl . . . and black. Raymond had mostly ignored her. Nearly fifty now, he was tall and good-looking, and pointedly sheepish about the good fortune he'd been born into, which some women mistook for charm. He was well-liked and well-regarded in his city, a successful civil litigator who represented everyone in the region from Shell Oil to CenturyTel. And every four years, like clockwork, he was courted heavily by the local business community about making a run for office, for his last name as much as anything. He'd turned out to be a decent-enough boss, hands-off and loyal—though she'd heard that heated words had been exchanged between Raymond and the last general manager, who'd been accused of pirating knick-knacks off the property. Clancy had fired him on the spot. Just her luck, it was a week before Caren had called him up, out of the blue, asking about a place to stay, and a job, if he had it.

"So what are the cops saying?"

"Only that it was a woman who was killed," she said. "She was dumped along the fence line, down by the cane fields."

"She one of Hunt's?"

"It looks that way, yes."

"They know who did it?"

"Right now they're just asking a lot of questions."

"My God," Raymond mumbled. "You talk to Schuyler yet?" Giles Schuyler was the host of tonight's prepaid event and CEO of Merryvale Properties, the real estate development firm that designed the town of Laurel Springs. "Maybe we ought to think about canceling his deal tonight."

"The detectives seemed to suggest that we would be able to conduct business as usual," she said, knowing on some level, even then, that nothing about Belle Vie would ever be the same. "They'd already finished the staff interviews before I left."

"Well, that's good to hear," he said, though he sounded vaguely displeased.

"Let's keep a lid on this as best we can, Gray," he went on. "No reporters, hear?"

"Sure."

"This is just awful. I mean, the timing couldn't be any worse."

There was a coolness in his voice that caught both of them by surprise. It was callous and unkind, and Clancy immediately fell silent. There was nothing but the sound of the highway humming along beneath her car. In the rearview mirror, she saw the red truck again, only this time the sight of it bothered her. She'd seen that truck before, hadn't she? It had been passing by, riding slowly, back and forth, on the farm road, the one right outside the gates of Belle Vie—or it was certainly one that looked just like it. It was odd, noteworthy to say the least, to see the red truck now, trailing behind her on the highway, never more than a single car-length away. She couldn't make out details about the driver, only that it was a man, a sun visor shielding the better part of his face.

Raymond cleared his throat then, searching out a more sober tone. "Listen, Gray," he said. "I'd just as soon not have Daddy know a thing about this, okay?"

"Okay," she said, though she thought that went without saying.

She hadn't spoken to Leland Clancy in years, not since she was first hired for the job in 2005. Already well into retirement by then, he used to drive down from his house in Baker for lunch a few times a week. Lorraine would make him a hot plate—chicken and gravy or crawfish with red beans and rice or sometimes just pea soup and biscuits. And after, Leland would sit with a book under one of the old oak trees, his long legs stretched out toward the river. Or some days he would take a nap in the library. He was newly widowed then and alone a lot during the day, and he seemed to appreciate the company he found at Belle Vie, where someone was "always home," as he put it. He took a particular liking to Morgan, plying her with peanut butter candies, which seemed to stream in an endless supply from the pockets of his patched cardigan sweaters, which he wore year-round, and sometimes he read storybooks to her in the rose garden. He asked after Helen from time to time, forgetting she was gone.

Caren liked Leland, always had.

It often pained her to ask him to please move from his post on the front lawn so they could set up chairs for an outdoor wedding reception or request that he not park in the spots reserved for school buses and chartered vans. He always did as he was told, thanking her for the job she was doing. But his demeanor struck her as lonely and displaced; he could spend whole afternoons wandering the grounds of his property, as if he were searching for something he'd lost. He'd inherited Belle Vie from his father, who'd inherited it from his father, a long line of ownership that went back to Clancy's ancestor William P. Tynan, who acquired the land after the Civil War. Leland raised his own family there for a while, until his growing law practice in Baton Rouge required them to move. The family eventually settled into a four-bedroom split-level ranch just north of the capital, and Belle Vie became his wife's pet project, in time lovingly restored to its original antebellum glory and eventually becoming a state showpiece—a long way from the overgrown land, weather-beaten and forgotten, that had been Leland's boyhood home. Though the Clancys were beloved in Ascension Parish for what they had done, making the land available to the public and preserving the history for posterity (not to mention the scholarships they had endowed, the money they poured into local, and mostly black, schools), he once confessed to Caren that he wished he'd never bothered with any of it, turning Belle Vie into an events venue and tourist stop. He was eighty now and in failing health, and once a month Lorraine carried a plate up to his house in Baker, as Caren's mother had done, in the years when Lorraine was her number two.

Caren had made the trip with her mom only once before, when she was barely a teenager. Twelve years old, she'd ridden in the front seat of her mother's white Pontiac, finally working up the nerve to ask her mother something painfully delicate. She knew Helen didn't like her spending so much time with Bobby Clancy, didn't like the way he sometimes looked at her, lingering sideways glances that hadn't escaped Raymond's attention either, even though she and Bobby were both just kids, more brother and sister than anything. And once that last thought took hold, Caren locked on to it and wouldn't let it go. It was an answer, maybe, an explanation for the life that kept them both pinned in place, tethered to a plantation. Caren told herself she could accept it, her mother's job, her devotion to Belle Vie, if she could just make sense of it. And that day, on the car ride, she asked her mother, point-blank, if Leland James Clancy was her father. Helen laughed out loud, the muscles in her neck rolling like waves, up and down. "Oh, 'Cakes," she said. And then just as suddenly she fell into a cold, stony silence. She barely spoke to Caren for three days after that, pulling into herself. Caren had felt shamed by the incident, but also confused.

She hadn't seen Leland in a long time.

Raymond was the one who signed her checks.

"Daddy ought not have any unnecessary stress, and that's straight from the doctor's mouth," he said. "This kind of thing would just mess with his head."

"Sure, Raymond."

"Bobby neither, hear?" Clancy said, and Caren found it amusing that Raymond, all these years later, still imagined she and Bobby had some special connection, when the two of them had seen each other only once in four years, a brief encounter in town that had been awkward and somewhat strained. "Let's keep him out of this, too. There's a whole lot in this world my brother doesn't hardly understand, and he's liable to take something like this personal, somebody leaving that gal out there like that. He still calls the plantation home." Caren nodded, though she suspected Raymond was working himself up for nothing. Until very recently, Bobby had stayed out of Ascension Parish, even skipping out on a seventy-sixth birthday party Lorraine had arranged for his father. "You let me break the news to him," Raymond said.

"Sure."

She glanced again at her rearview mirror.

The red pickup truck was gone.

A few minutes later, she got a second call on her cell phone, just as she was exiting State Highway 1 for the decorative gates of the town of Laurel Springs. It was Mr. Schuyler's assistant, Patricia Quinlan, informing Caren that she would be arriving at least one hour before the guests, to make sure there were no more surprises.

"Have they removed—"

"The coroner took the body late this morning, yes," Caren said.

On the other end of the phone, Ms. Quinlan sighed heavily. "Well, Mr. Schuyler would greatly prefer if the news of this morning's incident did not reach our guests."

"Understood."

"Good, then," Ms. Quinlan said. "I'll see you at four."

The kids were already pouring out of the elementary school when Caren pulled into the circle drive in front, into the crush of SUVs and minivans. The three schools, for grades pre-K through twelve, were a mile past the Unitarian church. The campus spanned both sides of Main Street, with a raised walkway bridging the elementary school to the other buildings, all of which were done up in a vaguely neocolonial style, with lots of red brick and black shutters and eaves trimmed in white. The girls wore smock dresses of navy and green plaid. The boys were instructed to wear khaki pants. Otherwise, their tops were to be all white, polos or cotton button-downs only.

Morgan was one of twenty black students in the lower school, which made her easy enough to spot in the crowd. She was sitting cross-legged on top of her backpack, set a few feet back from the curb, and she was reading a library book. She looked up once, scanning the line of cars in the circle drive, only to go right back to reading her book. She was, Caren knew, expecting Letty's van. Caren honked her horn, even though that was generally frowned upon by the school's staff. Morgan looked up again. She saw Caren this time, and smiled widely. She started to gather her things. By the time Caren reached the end of the curved driveway, Morgan was already waiting at the curb, her navy backpack over her shoulder. "Where's Letty?" she asked.

"Artie's sick."

Morgan's eyes narrowed ever so slightly, an almost comic expression of skepticism on a nine-year-old. "She didn't say anything to me about it." She was standing at the open passenger window. She still hadn't made a move to get into the car. Behind them, the line of waiting cars had grown even longer. "Just get in, Morgan, and we'll talk about it, okay?" Caren said. This only served to confirm her daughter's suspicion that something else was behind her unscheduled appearance at the school. Up ahead, the traffic guard was looking in their direction, waving the Volvo forward.

"Get in, Morgan."

"Did you get my ticket?" Morgan said, changing the subject.

Caren didn't want to have this conversation right now.

"Get in the car," she said.

Morgan pouted openly. She climbed into the backseat, tossing her backpack across the floor, and didn't speak again until they were ten miles outside of Laurel Springs. She kept her eyes glued to the passing landscape, lined with bookstores and gun shops and roadside stands selling oysters on ice, which eventually gave way to naked Louisiana swampland, as they rode shotgun alongside the river. Morgan put a finger on the cool glass of her window, lifting it every few seconds to see the patch of heat and sweat left behind, then pressing down again.

"You promised," is all she said.

Caren glanced at her daughter's face in the rearview mirror.

Morgan was still carrying some of her baby fat, which softened what would otherwise be duplicates of Caren's own sharp features, the L-shaped jawline and cheeks like two wide conch shells beneath the skin, the heart-shaped hairline passed down from *her* mother. It used to embarrass Caren, how much they looked alike, as if she'd huddled alone in a dark room and sculpted the child from her own flesh. It seemed greedy, like she was taking more than her fair share. These days, Caren wore her hair long, tightly pulled and pomaded into a cottony ponytail or a single chignon-like braid on event nights. Morgan, on the other hand, had demanded to wear her hair short for as long as Caren could remember, even attempting to cut it herself when she was only four years old. Even then she seemed to sense that where a line couldn't be drawn between them, only heartache and trouble would follow. In that way, she was a lot smarter than her mother, Caren thought. Now, at nearly ten, Morgan wore her curls in a short, floppy 'fro, pushed back by a headband—but she'd also been trying a myriad of different styles, pin curls one week, a flatiron the next, long afternoons spent in front of the bathroom mirror. Caren loved her desperately. To date, theirs was the most enduring relationship of her life, and one she was determined not to fuck up. This job, this life way the hell out in the country, it was all for Morgan, she told herself daily.

Morgan saw it differently.

She was presently in the early stages of a growing resentment about their living arrangements, especially the distance from her father. She would sometimes go days without talking, often alarming her teachers and the few school friends she'd made. The school's staff sent home notes, worried over her shy and withdrawn nature. But Caren knew better. Morgan could be quite charming when she wanted to be, winsome even, when she wanted someone's attention. At Belle Vie, that usually meant Lorraine, but especially Donovan. She had probably seen *The Olden Days of Belle Vie* at least fifty times, and Donovan's part she could recite by heart, from start to weepy finish. Caren had long suspected that Morgan was developing something of a schoolgirl crush on Donovan—harmless but for the fact that it further signaled the limits of her maternal influence. She had dreams in those days of following her daughter through an endless series of rooms, round and round short corridors, walking in a tight, coiling circle.

"'Cakes," she said.

They were almost to Modeste, and she was running out of time.

"I need to talk to you about something, okay? Something important."

Morgan was busy tracing her finger along the rear window's glass. She didn't even look at her mother. "There's been an incident at Belle Vie," Caren said, because she couldn't immediately think of another way to put it. "Someone's been hurt badly."

In the rearview mirror, she caught her daughter's eye.

"What happened?"

"Somebody died."

In the backseat, Morgan was silent a moment. "Oh," she said finally.

"There'll be police officers there when we get home," Caren said, making an effort to keep her tone even and flat. She didn't want to scare her, but she needed her daughter to understand how serious this was. "They're going to want to talk to you."

In the mirror, their eyes met again.

"I want you to know you didn't do anything wrong."

"I know."

"I mean, no one thinks you did anything wrong. They're talking to everyone at Belle Vie, and because you live there, they want to talk to you, too. It's going to help them understand what happened. And I'll be with you the whole time."

"Who died?"

"It's no one you know. Everyone at Belle Vie is fine."

Morgan didn't say anything. She twirled her index finger on the smudged glass, moss-covered cedars along the highway casting shape-shifting shadows across her face, like dark clouds passing over, then breaking wide again. "I have to prep for an event tonight," Caren said. "But after that we can talk about your plane ticket, okay?"

"My dad said he would pay for it."

"I know. We'll talk about it tonight."

A car shot around them on the two-lane road, passing at eighty miles an hour, at least. It raced ahead of them, growing smaller in the distance. Caren couldn't read the license plate number, determine the make or model. But it was a red pickup truck, she was sure.

4

In the time it took her to drive to Laurel Springs and back, the detectives had turned the old schoolhouse into a base of operations. They were each on their cell phones when she and Morgan entered, Morgan with her backpack in her hands, pressed against her chest. Some of the chairs had been rearranged, and Lorraine had sent over coffee on a room-service tray meant for the guest cottages. Caren put an arm around her daughter and waited for one of the detectives to notice them. The bigger cop, Detective Jimmy Bertrand, was off the phone first. He told them to have a seat. Caren reached for Morgan's hand, holding tightly as Morgan pressed herself into Caren's side. They chose two seats near the raised platform where the play was performed. By then, Detective Lang was off his phone as well. He joined them near the stage. He smiled at Morgan and asked if she'd like something to drink, water or juice, though Caren wasn't sure just where he thought that was going to come from. There were no vending machines at Belle Vie, and it was a ten-minute walk to Lorraine's kitchen. Morgan shook her head; Caren could feel a damp heat radiating from her small, round body. Lang opened a clean page in his notebook, then looked again at Morgan. "So," he said, starting with the barest of facts. "Morgan Gray?"

"It's Ellis," she said, correcting him. "Morgan Ellis."

Lang looked briefly at Caren, but she offered no clarification on this point.

This interview was merely an act of courtesy, a show of good faith.

Lang looked at Morgan again and smiled. "I'm Detective Nestor Lang, Morgan, and this is my partner, Detective Bertrand." Morgan looked back and forth between the two men. Bertrand was on his feet, a hand on his waist. Caren could see a patch of sweat growing in the pits of his dress shirt while he sucked down a cup of black coffee. Detective Lang had meanwhile pulled a chair in front of Morgan. "We just want to ask you a few questions," he said to her. "This shouldn't take too long at all."

"Okay."

"What grade are you in, Morgan?"

"Fifth."

"So that makes you, what, about ten?"

"Nine."

"That's right, your mom said that."

He wrote this down, too.

"And you live here with your mother?"

Morgan nodded.

"Well, I assume she's told you . . . there's been an 'incident' here."

"Someone died."

"That's right," Lang said. "Someone did something very bad, Morgan, and my partner and I are here to find out what happened."

"And put someone in jail."

Lang looked over in Caren's direction. "She's sharp, this one."

Caren glanced at her watch. She would need them to move this along if she was going to be ready for a walk-through with Schuyler's assistant at four. The waitstaff, hired out from a catering company in Baton Rouge, was due to arrive any minute now.

Detective Bertrand stepped away to take a phone call.

"Okay, Morgan," Lang said, continuing. "Can you tell me if, in the last couple of days, you've seen any strangers around the plantation?"

"There are strangers here every day," she said. "It's basically a museum."

Lang smiled, more tightly this time, his expression pinched by the reminder, from a preteen girl, no less, of the challenges inherent in this case. "Maybe a better way to put it is to ask whether or not you've seen or heard anything out of the ordinary in the past few days." He was, without even realizing it, clicking the top of his ink pen up and down, up and down. The rhythm was catching. It set Caren's nerves on edge.

"Like, out of the ordinary . . . how?"

"Well, you tell me. What comes to mind?"

At first, Morgan hesitated, stealing a look at her mother. Then, she tested the room, starting with something small. "Well," she said, "Pearl found a stray cat in the parking lot, and she's been feeding it leftovers from the kitchen, and when Lorraine found out she got really mad 'cause she said it was just throwing good food away."

"Okay, Morgan," Lang said patiently. "What else?"

"Nikki and Bo Johnston were kissing in the Manette house."

Caren turned to her daughter. "Who told you that?"

Morgan seemed to relish this telling of plantation gossip. "Oh, and Donovan quit school," she said.

A few feet away, Bertrand nodded to get his partner's attention.

"Nes," he said, waving his cell phone in the air for emphasis. "We've got a preliminary from Dr. Allard, and that gal from the state lab is on her way down."

"Hold on a sec," Lang said.

To Morgan, he asked, "Where did you hear that? About Donovan?"

This was news to Caren as well. "Morgan?"

Morgan looked from her mother to the two police detectives.

They were all staring at her, waiting. It was clear that some-thing, though Morgan seemed uncertain as to what, hinged on her answer. For the first time, she looked nervous about the po-lice interview, the big men in suits, and the questions.

"Is he in trouble?"

"No," Caren said before Lang had a chance to. She wanted her daughter to tell the truth.

Lang nodded. "It's okay, Morgan," he said. "Where did you hear that?"

"Danny told Eddie Knoxville."

"When?" Caren asked.

"Yesterday. They were smoking cigarettes behind the kitchen."

"Okay," Lang said, making a note on the nearly empty top sheet of his pad, listing one of the few details he'd gathered from this interview. "Now, your mom tells us your bedroom is above the library. I need to know if you heard anything last night, some sound or something out of the ordinary that might have woken you up."

"You mean like the wind shaking, spooky stuff like that?"

"She's heard ghost stories," Caren volunteered.

"Something particular to last night, Morgan," Lang said. "Did you hear anything last night?"

"Just the rain."

"*Before* the rainstorm, Morgan," Lang said, wanting to clarify. "Sometime between midnight and two in the morning . . ." It was their best guess as to a timeline, Caren knew, of when the woman was killed. They'd asked her the same question during her second interview late this morning. They'd gone over this point several times, Lang circling around it, like a seagull hunt-ing for something in the sand. Morgan was in bed by nine, she'd said. Caren had checked her e-mail and was asleep herself by ten-thirty.

"Did you hear anything about that time last night?"

Morgan shrugged. "Like what?"

"Strange voices, arguing, something like that?"

"Huh-uh."

"What about screams?"

Morgan shook her head.

Lang closed his notepad. "Okay, then."

From the seat of a nearby folding chair, which was serving as a makeshift desk, he lifted a thin sheet of sketch paper. On one side was a pencil drawing, the smudged lines of which suggested an image made in haste. The mouth was closed, and the eyes had been brightened by the artist's rendering . . . but it was her all right, the woman from the grave. Her eyes were small, set close to the bridge of a thin, pointed nose, and there were soft, feathered lines around her eyes. There was single star-shaped earring in her left earlobe. She was young, much younger than Caren, in her twenties maybe.

"You seen this woman before?"

"Huh-uh."

Lang looked at Caren next. She shook her head. "No."

"Okay, then." He stood, still holding the picture.

Detective Bertrand was waiting just inside the doorway to the schoolhouse, texting on his cell phone. Lang held out his right hand to Morgan, who seemed unsure of what to make of the gesture from a grown man, a cop no less. She gingerly shook his hand, barely making contact. "You be sure to let your mom know if you think of anything else." Then he nodded to Caren, motioning her into a private conference, out of her daughter's earshot. She patted Morgan's leg before standing to follow him, wanting her daughter to know that she did well. Caren was glad this part of it was over. She crossed the old schoolhouse, the heels of her boots sinking on the loose boards of the plank floor. The building had originally been used as a chapel a house of worship for the master's family and a temporary sanctum for any traveling preachers wandering through the parish. It earned its current name sometime after the Civil War when the Freedmen's Bureau ran a school for ex-slaves, during the years when the federal government held brief ownership of the land. Colored schoolteachers, earnest, mostly unmarried women devoted to uplift and a life of learning, came south in droves. There was a pretty schoolteacher at Belle Vie in those days, a Miss Nadine something or other, as Caren's mother had often told the tale. Next to the kitchen, Helen Gray loved the old schoolhouse best of all. Men had learned to read in this room. Men like Jason. Using their laps for a desktop, they practiced their letters, struggling with a whole new set of tools. Nadine taught them to make the marks that make the letters that make the words. It was a system, like the making of sugar from cane.

Lang stopped near the table that held the play's programs. He put his hands on both hips and sighed heavily. "We need to get a hold of that young man."

"Donovan?"

"Yes, ma'am," he said. "Unfortunately, we've had no luck so far with the numbers you gave us." There was a faint hint of accusation in his voice, as if he thought it was altogether possible that Caren was shielding the boy.

"Those are the only numbers I have, his cell phone and his grandmother."

"Well, I imagine there are ways of getting him on the telephone," Lang said, lowering his voice some. "Say, if you left a message for Mr. Isaacs about some trouble with his paycheck, I imagine he wouldn't waste any time calling you back."

"The state pays his checks, not us."

It was a plain statement of fact, but Lang took it as an inclination toward noncooperation. "Well," he said, "it was an idea." He stared at her for a long while, trying to read something about her that wasn't immediately clear to him. Caren could smell his musky cologne, mixed with the scent of stale coffee and hair grease. He was nearing sixty, she guessed, his skin a tawny Cajun hue that was hard to date.

"Let me ask you something, ma'am," he said. "Did you happen to know of Mr. Isaacs's legal troubles before you hired him?" He pinched his lips together, waiting on her answer. He appeared to be rolling something over in his pocket, coins maybe.

So that's what this is, Caren thought.

Donovan's criminal record.

She couldn't help feeling that something had shifted in the cops' investigation since she'd gone and returned to the plantation, that they were now circling around a specific, but as yet unstated theory. And Caren didn't like it. No matter her personal feelings about Donovan, she didn't think it was fair. Donovan was a lot of things, and law-abiding was not necessarily one of them. But murder was murder, a theft of a soul, requiring a depravity touched by something not of this world. Caren didn't think Donovan had it in him. He was a simple kid, both feet planted in the material world.

"I knew about it, yes," she said. "It was on his application." Not that it would have disqualified him, she might have added, not at this end of the employment pool.

"Oh, he's got a record all right," Lang said, rolling and rolling those coins in his pants pocket, so that she thought she might go dizzy trying to follow the sound. "Some property crimes and misdemeanors," he added. "But he also spent time in the parish jail down to Donaldsonville on battery charges last year."

She knew all of this.

Lang lifted and replaced his slim necktie, smoothing it down along the center of his shirt. "Look, I'll be honest here and say we're up against it with this one. We've got a pretty good read on the time of death. It's the *where* of this crime that's causing us trouble. That rain came down hard last night, and as far as we can tell, washed out any trace of a workable crime scene. There's no blood, no sign of a struggle, nowhere to start. That's why the more information we can get from you folks about what you know or what you may have seen, the easier it'll be for us to put this one down." He smiled here, really selling it, his implied offer of something like a partnership, he and Caren playing for the same team. "If you could help us get a hold of Donovan—"

"Don't push it, Nes," his partner said.

Lang looked at Detective Bertrand, but said nothing.

Then he looked again at Caren.

"You're Helen's girl, right?"

He smiled, not waiting for an answer. "It took me a minute to put it together."

Congratulations, she thought.

She did not want to talk about her mother, not like this, and not with him.

She glanced back at Morgan, who was folding the hem of her plaid skirt across the palm of her hand and kicking one of her sneakers against the edge of the stage. Caren felt tired all of a sudden, aware in every bone that her day had started at dawn. She saw that woman's face again, those narrow, black eyes, that one, tiny star-shaped earring, the other lost along the way. She wanted to take her girl and go home.

"She was a good woman, your mother," Lang said. "Loyal."

Caren nodded vaguely.

"Thirty-two years at Belle Vie," he said, whistling at the

breadth of it. "And Leland Clancy never had any trouble with her," he said, glancing at Detective Bertrand, who was following this bit of the conversation with a kind of detached appreciation for his partner's style and approach. "How long ago did she die again?" Lang said.

"I'm sorry, but what does this have to do with your invest igation?"

"She must have missed you something awful when you went off," the detective said. "Dillard, then two years at the law school at Tulane. You spent time out there working in a legal clinic, isn't that right?" So Donovan's wasn't the only background they'd looked into, she thought. "Kind of strange, you not mentioning that fact."

"You asked me if I was a lawyer, and I answered the question correctly."

"Didn't mention your mother working here neither."

"Didn't think it was relevant."

"'Relevant,'" Lang said, playing the word back to her. He glanced down at the tips of his black dress shoes, which were marred now with damp grass and dirt. He was still fiddling with the coins in his pocket. "Well, Tulane," he said. "I sure hope you weren't gone so long as to forget where you came from, what this land means for the Clancys, who've been very good to people like your mother, Ms. Gray, people like you. We're hoping we can count on you to do the right thing here. Point of fact is, somebody killed that girl out here. Now, my gut on this deal is that we're talking about somebody local, someone who knows the landscape out here, and who might well come back. We need all the cooperation we can get, and that includes getting a hold of Donovan."

"Dumped her here, you mean," Caren said, correcting him.

Detective Bertrand shook his head. "We considered that, ma'am."

"But thing is," Lang said, "you already told us the gates were locked last night."

"That's right."

"Every entrance, everything was locked, you said."

"Yes."

"Which means, ma'am," Lang went on, laying out the facts as gently as possible, sensing he had not been as forthcoming as he should have been, like a doctor speaking of surgeries and pills and next steps, without ever mentioning the word *cancer*. The danger they were potentially in was a lot closer than she thought. "It means I don't think we're talking about someone getting inside these gates with a body, but someone who was trying to get *out* with it. That fence out there is, what, five feet?"

"It's four feet, ten inches," she said flatly. She'd once had it measured for a bride who wanted a line of Douglas firs to greet her guests for a Christmas wedding.

"And that gal out there was well over five feet tall and weighed about a hundred and forty pounds. Even a particularly strong man would have had a hard time lifting that amount of dead weight over a vertical fence, without leverage of any kind. My guess is somebody killed that girl here, on the property, and then tried to move her out. And we believe," he said, glancing at Bertrand, "it was the fence that stopped them."

"Mom," Morgan said, "can I walk over to the kitchen now?"

"No, you stay right there."

Morgan slumped in her seat, rolling her eyes.

Caren turned back to Detective Lang, feeling a flush of heat all of a sudden.

"It's more likely than not, ma'am, that we're talking about a murder that happened here last night, on the grounds of Belle Vie, while you and your daughter were sleeping . . . so I would think you'd want to help us solve this in any way you can."

"I'll try," she said.

The words were a mere exhale, taking with them the last of Caren's strength. She felt fear, of course. But also a choking dread, creeping up like floodwater, rising from her navel to her neck before she had a chance to take a second breath.

She knew the trouble that was coming, for all of them.

She would try to find Donovan, she said.

"'Preciate that, ma'am," Detective Bertrand said.

"And we'll keep Deputy Harris on duty, at least through the night."

"The kid in uniform?"

Lang buttoned his suit jacket, even though the air in the schoolhouse had grown thick and hot, and Caren was by now sweating openly. "You couldn't be in better hands," he said. "And anyway, we'll be back first thing in the morning with the search warrant." He let those last words float in the air, hanging like smoke between them.

5

She told her daughter none of this, of course, as they started for home, veering together off the main path and walking through grass shaded by a grove of willow oaks. The branches were lifted, once and then again, by a stiff late-afternoon breeze. It woke the leaves, stirring them to conversation, the wind like a whisper over their heads.

It would be dark soon.

She'd ask Gerald to stay, put him on post right outside their front door.

Detective Lang had made it plain. There was a killer on the loose.

Morgan was a few feet ahead of Caren. She was humming a song her mother didn't recognize, her overstuffed backpack hanging by a strap in her right hand, swinging and knocking against the backs of her bare knees. "I'm hungry," she said when they were past the rose garden and the library was in sight. Their apartment was on the second floor of the building, which was made of painted brick and stone. It was without columns or a balcony, but in every other way resembled the main house, only in miniature. The black shutters on the top corner window opened to Caren's bedroom.

The house had been Tynan's once, the plantation's overseer.

The man was seen as a hero around here, cited in all the literature of Belle Vie and in the coffee-table books sold in the gift shop, and featured heavily in the staged play *The Olden Days of Belle Vie*. The original owners had fled during the war, and Tynan was eventually hired by the United States government to manage the cane farm. Grant's administration had seized Confederate land all across the South, Belle Vie included, for the purpose of establishing schools and a cash-based labor system for ex-slaves—but also keeping some of the sugar profits for itself. Tynan did well by the feds, and it was therefore a surprise to no one when the government deeded him the title to the land. In this parish, Tynan was regarded as an industrious planter who, by the good Southern values of hard work and discipline, had wrested back the land from a greedy federal government and made it something good again. He lived in this very building until the day he died, turning over the main house to his youngest daughter as a wedding gift on the eve of her marriage to a man by the name of James Clancy. The newly married Clancys had been the first occupants in the big house in nearly a decade.

"I'll bring you a plate from the kitchen," Caren said, as they approached the front door, which was always unlocked during business hours. There was no separate entrance for the upstairs living quarters, but up until now safety hadn't been much of an issue. Tourists never made it back this far, only Danny and his laptop. She had a sudden vexing thought about his gate key, his freedom to come and go as he pleased.

"You have homework?" she asked her daughter.

"I already did it." Caren glanced at her daughter's backpack, aware that it was likely filled with library books and magazines instead of textbooks, plus the cookies she saved from her lunch tray at school. Morgan was a straight-A student and therefore allowed a lot of leeway on the subject of academics. Still, Caren always swore she would never raise a child who lies.

"All of it?" she said.

"Yep."

Morgan pushed in the front door with her elbow.

Caren slid out of her muddy ropers before crossing the threshold.

Inside, the front parlor was dark, waning sunlight casting dusty gray shadows about the room. She turned on a floor lamp, then crossed to each of the room's front windows, closing the velvet drapes. "I want you to stay inside tonight, Morgan."

She was rifling through the drawers of an antique writing table.

She seemed to remember there being a spare key inside. "Letty's not here, and there's an event in the main house, and I want to know exactly where you are."

The key, she realized, wasn't there.

"Can I watch TV?" Morgan said.

There were two doors off the main parlor, on opposite sides of the room. To the right was the doorway that led to Belle Vie's Hall of Records, a room the size of a walk-in closet, lined with storage cabinets and bookshelves. To the left was a closed door leading to the first floor of their apartment. There was a small kitchenette when you first walked in, next to a narrow, poorly carpeted stairway that led to four rooms upstairs: a bathroom, two bedrooms, and a small living area. It was not wired for cable and the "TV" was really a desktop computer on which Morgan downloaded programs she heard girls talking about at school. She was not allowed a Facebook page, and there was a parent-protection lock on the computer, a program that had taken Caren all of one afternoon and into the next to install on her own. She was a single mother out here, leaning on Letty and any other help she could get to raise her girl as best she could. "'Cakes," she said. "I want you to tell me if you hear about things going on around here. Bo and Nikki Hubbard, they're not supposed to be going into the cottages, no matter what they were in there doing." She stopped there rather than get into any specifics about what all she thought they were doing. "If you hear of somebody breaking the rules, I want you to tell your mother about it, okay?"

"Uh-huh," Morgan said, in a way that suggested she had no intention of ever doing any such thing. She had no playmates out here, no kids her own age; all the students from her grade school lived miles away, in Laurel Springs. Instead of friends, Morgan had the staff: a cook, two gardeners, and a cast of slaves. And she spent nearly every moment out of her mother's sight in their company, preferred it most days.

Caren walked into the kitchen.

She didn't find the spare key in any of the drawers in there either.

But by then her mind was made up. "I'm going to lock that door, Morgan."

In the parlor, Morgan was leaning her rump against one of the leather armchairs, fingering a line of brass tacks on the chair's left arm and following her mother's movements with her eyes. "I'll have my cell phone with me," Caren said, picking up her daughter's backpack from the floor and setting it on the chair. "You can call me if you need anything, and I'll have Gerald stay with you until I come back."

She unhooked her key ring from the belt loop on her jeans.

The library's key was sandwiched between the one for her aging Volvo and the small, round-tipped brass key that used to open the front door of their place in Lakeview, one half of a Victorian duplex, a building that didn't even exist anymore. Four years had passed, and she still couldn't bring herself to throw it out. There were twenty or so work keys on her ring: the short brass one for the main house; the color-coded keys to the cottages, Manette and Le Roy; plus the dull silver one that opened the groundskeeper's shed. She paused over this one . . . the key to Luis's shed. Inside, she knew, there was a cabinet that housed a 12-gauge shotgun and a .32-caliber six-shooter, a weapon small enough to fit comfortably in the palm of her hand. They'd only ever been used for killing snakes or wood rats in Lorraine's vegetable garden—shotgun or pistol, depending on Luis's mood, or the size of the creature in his sights. Caren was the only one with a key to the cabinet—the shortest on her key ring, the one with the tiny diamond-shaped head. This was the first time, in all the years she'd worked here, that she'd thought to go into that cabinet on her own, without a word to anyone else. It was the first time at Belle Vie she'd felt the need to have a gun on hand.

She turned toward her daughter. "Why don't you come with me tonight?" she said, already running the calculations in her head, how she could do her job and watch her daughter at the same time. Surely, the night's hosts wouldn't mind a nine-year-old girl tucked in some quiet corner of the ballroom, a book in her lap. Morgan lifted her legs off the ground, letting her soft, pudgy body fall into the center of the armchair. She sank down into the cracked leather, pulling her scuffed knees under her chin. She looked distracted, worried about something. "Why isn't Donovan here?" she said.

"I don't know, 'Cakes."

Then she repeated her earlier idea. "Why don't you stay with me in the main house tonight? Or you could sit and watch Lorraine in the kitchen," she said.

But Morgan was surprisingly uninterested.

She shook her head. "I'm tired, Mom."

Caren kissed the top of her daughter's hair, which smelled of wet grass and thick, late-day clouds, the salted sweat of recess.

She couldn't believe that come December Morgan would be ten years old. She could still remember whole afternoons when Morgan wouldn't leave her mother's lap. She kissed her again, inhaling everything. It was Morgan who pulled away first. She yawned, sinking further into the leather chair, laying her head across the armrest. "I'll have Gerald stay tonight," Caren said. "And I'll be back to take a shower and bring you some dinner." Morgan nodded. It was a quarter to four when Caren closed the door, her only child on the other side.

The Belle Vie Players had left for the day, all but Shauna and Dell, who would each earn an hourly wage for staying on as "greeters" for the night and part of the set dressing—which, at $10.75 an hour for standing around in tattered calico and a head scarf, was not a bad way to make some extra cash. Dell Blanchett, in her late forties, had a second job at an outlet mall off I-10 and a mountain of debt from a second marriage. Shauna was in her twenties and, as far as Caren could tell, spent most of her money on a leased Lexus LS, black with tinted windows. She was a cute girl, young and stylish, managing, even, to pull off the antebellum look, the apron and floor-length rags that made up her slave costume. Both women were in the kitchen by the main house when Caren came in, just minutes before the final walk-through. They were crowded at Lorraine's card table, eating an early dinner along with three of the cater-waiters who were on duty tonight, one of whom was talking on his cell phone. The air in the kitchen was clouded with the smoke of fried bacon and the sizzle of sautéing greens. Caren's eyes watered, and her stomach turned over with hunger. Pearl was standing on her crate at the stove, hovering over a big, dented drum of a pot, stirring creamed potatoes. Lorraine was leaning against the open back doorway, sharing a smoke with Danny Olmsted.

"How are we doing in here, Lorraine?" Caren asked, feeling encouraged by the bustle of culinary activity in the kitchen. "The client's going to be here soon. I assume we're pretty close?" Lorraine didn't address her directly. Instead, she blew out a long, coiling stream of cigarette smoke and glanced at her assistant. "Pearl?"

Pearl squinted through the steam. "Yeah, all right," she muttered.

"Great," Caren said, her manner full of forced cheer for the troops.

In truth, the sheer effort required to remain upright at the end of this long day was making her sweat. She felt a cold line of it running down the center of her back.

At the rear door, Lorraine blew cigarette smoke through her lips, waving the air in front of her face. She offered a drag to Danny, but he turned it down, biting at the white meat of his thumb. He was still in his trench coat, even though the air in the kitchen was warm and sticky. He'd had his eyes on Caren since she walked in.

"So what'd the cops say?" he asked.

"They'll be back tomorrow," she said, not wanting to get into any of it right now, not with the hired waitstaff present.

"And there's been no word from Donovan?"

"No."

The room was exquisitely, almost achingly, quiet, with only the sound of the gas range, the hum and hiss of heat coming from the stove. The staff was tight-lipped, just as they'd been this morning in the schoolhouse. Caren looked back and forth between Danny and Lorraine, Dell and Shauna and Pearl, all of them quiet as church mice.

"Look, if you guys know where he is, you should tell me now," she said. "Trust me, the longer he waits to talk to the cops, the more trouble he's making for himself."

Danny cleared his throat.

"He's not returning any of our calls," he said.

Shauna nodded in agreement, brushing her long, black hair off her shoulders. She, like the others, seemed concerned, but none of them as much as Danny. He looked downright disturbed, his pallor that of skim milk, and he wouldn't, or couldn't, stop gnawing at the flesh around his fingernails, tearing at himself like a dog working a bone.

"The detectives just want to talk to him," Caren said, trying to sound reassuring.

Lorraine tossed her smoke through the back doorway. "Talk to him about what?" she said. "Donovan ain't have nothing to do with them Mexicans back there."

"Oh, hush, Lorraine," Dell said, fanning herself with a paper plate. She lifted and pushed the folds of her prairie skirt up above her knees, courting a breeze down there. One of the waiters, a white kid in his twenties wearing suspenders and black dress pants, his shirt still undone, looked back and forth between Dell and Lorraine.

"Hey, what are you guys talking about?"

"Nothing," Shauna mumbled. She and Dell seemed to regard this as a family matter and not a subject for open discussion, and Caren felt an unexpected surge of affection for both of them. Shauna stood and dumped her leftovers in a gray trash bin. Caren reminded her and Dell that she would need them in position by five. She told both women to keep an eye on each other tonight, no wandering around the grounds. "Not tonight," she said firmly. After dark, she wanted everyone to stay in pairs.

She started for the door and then stopped.

She turned back to Danny and asked about his key.

"The police detectives have informed me that all but essential personnel need to turn over their keys." It was a lie, of course, and she didn't know why she said it.

Danny stared at her for a moment, then looked at Lorraine, who raised an eyebrow but said nothing. He patted the front of his trench coat, felt inside its pockets and the pockets of his trousers, coming up with nothing. "Sorry," he said. "I must not have it on me." And that's how they left it. She turned and walked out of the kitchen.

The walk-through went off without incident. Lorraine was on her best behavior in the kitchen, "yes, ma'am"ing Ms. Quinlan to death, but also letting her have a taste of her mushroom soup and plying her with an early glass of homemade rum, made from molasses and caramel. Caren knew the drink's power, its buttered sweetness, the way it made your tongue go numb. It was her mother's signature drink, a cocktail and tonic all in one. Caren was allowed exactly one swallow on cold mornings, mornings her mother would sit with the heat on in the car while she finished getting dressed for school, so Caren's toes wouldn't go cold. Helen would smoke cigarette after cigarette, waiting, blowing smoke through windows cracked open a fraction of an inch, and sometimes she would grow sleepy and let Caren drive, all the way into town, even though she was only fifteen. "Oh, 'Cakes," her mother would say. "You got my life in your little hands either way, behind that wheel or not." Something Caren never fully understood until she'd given birth, until her mother was already gone, and she had a girl of her own.

She tried to make it once, her mother's homemade rum.

It was during those months when they had stopped talking, when Caren was living in New Orleans—a disastrous event that ended in tears, Eric cleaning up the sticky mess while she sat on the kitchen floor. They were still in that ground-floor apartment in Carrollton back then, Eric and Caren, him out on the front porch most nights, studying and drinking cold beer while she made dinner. He was still in law school at Tulane, while she was bringing home pilfered produce and day-old bread from her shifts at the hotel, where she'd worked since dropping out of law school the year before. This was back when they were still thinking they'd get married someday.

At the start of the official inspection, Caren escorted Ms. Quinlan to the main house, making sure to walk her around to the entrance by the rose garden instead of using an unadorned side door. Patricia Quinlan was a middle-aged woman with a secretary's hips. Her hair was limp and her shoes were cheap, the fake leather peeling at the heel of her pumps. Caren pictured her at a desk all day, under fluorescent lights, vacation photos from Gulfport or Biloxi taped to the walls of her cubicle. She was, like so many others, charmed by the breadth and the beauty of Belle Vie, which photographed handsomely but showed its best face in person. Caren walked her across the circle drive, fine gravel crunching underfoot, where an antique carriage—all polished wood and maple-colored leather—was parked theatrically a few yards from the big house.

Then . . . she swung open the doors to the house, stepping back to reveal a vista that extended from the parquet floors of the foyer to the curved staircase and all the way into the dining hall, where round-top tables draped in cream linens were set with silver and centerpieces of roses and freesia. Nights like this, in early fall or temperate spring, they often left the "back" door open, broadening the view to include the aged live oaks on the north lawn. Their thick, purposeful arms reached out, meeting over the length of a natural alley, carpeted by green grass and framing, at this hour, a sunset horizon over the Mississippi.

Ms. Quinlan gasped, a small, sharp sound of astonishment. She touched her fingers to her plump, flushed cheeks. She was bowled over, and maybe just the teeniest bit drunk. "Well," she said. "Mr. Schuyler will be very, very pleased."

Upstairs, Miguel was waiting in Caren's office.

She'd actually forgotten she'd called him to a meeting and had no idea how long he'd been sitting here. He was still in his work clothes, belted khakis and a T-shirt, both of which were stained with potting soil and grass and rings of sweat. He looked up when she entered the room, and, at first, his expression was hopeful. She had a fleeting thought to tell him, *Never mind.* Go home, and she'd see him tomorrow. But for all she knew the cops had already passed news of his immigration status to Raymond Clancy, and she'd lose her job for not taking action. She knew she didn't have a choice.

This is what her life had become.

She was management now.

Miguel was perched on the edge of his chair, clutching a worn ball cap, resting the sole of one work boot against the instep of the other, his hooded, hazel-colored eyes tracing her movements across the room. By the time Caren took a seat at her desk, leaning forward just so, he seemed to understand where this was headed.

"*Lo siento,*" she said.

Miguel lowered his head, shaking it slowly in disbelief. He was rolling the bill of his cap between his rough and callused hands. "I like you, Miguel, I do," she said. "And you've done very well here. *Pero si estás aquí* illegally . . . *no hay nada que puedo hacer.*"

He held up a single finger, nicked and cut by garden tools. "*Una semana más,*" he said. Then, in near-perfect English, he pleaded with her, "One more week, miss."

"I can't."

He was still holding his finger aloft. On his left ring finger she spotted a slim band of gold. It shone brilliantly against the dust and dirt of his fingers. Either she had never noticed it before or it was brand-new. Caren felt her throat close. She stared down at her desktop, the purchase orders and accounts receivable, the letters and numbers blurring as she felt her eyes mist over. He stared at her for what seemed an eternity, waiting for his fate to change. "I can't," she said. Finally, Miguel lowered his head, replacing the cap over his black, greasy hair. He stood and walked out of the room. She followed the sound of his boots all the way down the stairs until the sound was gone and she was alone. The radio was still playing from this morning, those empty moments before the frantic summons from Luis, when she was still working at her desk—and her biggest problem was Donovan Isaacs. She reached into her jeans pocket for her cell phone, logging into her voice mail to replay his last message.

The digital operator put the call at 4:07 this morning.

She still couldn't make out half of what he was saying, only that he sounded drunk or high, or else half asleep. The words "Can't make it back out there, man" were nearly rolled into one. The rest of the message was unintelligible, even after playing it twice. She turned off the voice mail, staring at her cell phone.

Can't make it back out there, man.

Can't make it *back* out there.

They were his own words, spoken as if he'd just pulled a double shift. Only Donovan hadn't been on the schedule yesterday, and hadn't shown up the day before. His last day of work had actually been Saturday, when the cast had done three performances back-to-back. So why would he be calling her at four o'clock this morning, sounding completely disoriented, saying he couldn't make it *back* to Belle Vie?

Caren hesitated, then she dialed over to his grandmother's house, using her desk phone. She waited through six rings before finally leaving a message on the machine about a scheduling issue that might affect Donovan's hours and pay. She ended by asking him to call her back right away, before setting the phone back in its cradle. She swiveled in her desk chair and stared out the office window at the Groveland fields in the distance and the nearly five-foot-high fence that separated her people from theirs.

It was four-thirty by now.

She still had to shower and get dressed.

But she was slow to move from her desk. She was bone tired, for sure, but it was more than that. She couldn't stop thinking of the slim band of gold on Miguel's left hand and the young woman she imagined waiting for him at home, with a warm pot of food cooking on the stove. At her desk, Caren set her head in her hands and cried.

The sun was down by the time she stepped out of the shower.

Wrapped in a towel, she moved in darkness through the second floor of her apartment, careful not to wake Morgan. She'd been asleep in her bedroom when Caren came home, tangled in the sheets on her twin bed, still in her school uniform. Caren hadn't been able to wake her and so let her be, leaving her dinner on the kitchen stove and instructing Gerald to make a quick sweep of the property and return in fifteen minutes.

In her bedroom Caren braided her hair by lamplight into a single, thick strand, pinning it at the nape of her neck. She slipped into a bra and panties, but couldn't find the black crepe wool dress she'd planned on wearing, which she'd laid out carefully on the rocking chair beside her bed early this morning. She thought Letty might have moved it, thinking it had already been worn or that it belonged in a different place. Her first day on the job, Letty had rearranged all of Caren's kitchen cabinets without asking, and she regularly reorganized the books on her shelves. It had been Letty's idea to move the home computer out of Caren's bedroom. She had three bright, healthy kids and a husband who adored her and was therefore immune to any suggestions from Caren about how a household should be run. Caren was in no position to complain.

She checked Morgan's room first, picking through her dresser drawers, finding, among other things, a pearl necklace and a pair of her gold earrings, both taken from Caren's jewelry box without permission. She made a point to leave them on top of the dresser, so Morgan would know she'd been in here, so she would know that Caren knew what she had done. She picked through a few more drawers but didn't find the black dress. In her slip, she started for the laundry closet downstairs in the kitchen.

The dress was not in the pile of clothes on top of the washer and dryer. She made a careful double-check, plucking the articles one by one, like pulling petals from a wilting flower, and dropping them on the floor. They were Morgan's school things mostly: plaid dresses and white oxford shirts and navy gym short with red piping. There were inside-out socks; a shell-pink camisole; and a worn gray T-shirt from Kingston Mines that her dad had sent her when he still lived in Chicago, just after he and Caren split. The elastic on the neck band was sagging and there was a dime-sized tear under the left arm. Morgan had slept in the shirt for years, treasuring it above all other gifts her dad had sent her over the years: books and toys and, one particularly generous Christmas, a brand-new guitar (the lessons, twice a week after school for six months, Caren paid for herself).

The black dress, however, was still missing.

It was only when Caren bent down to scoop the dirty clothes from the floor that she noticed the stain on one of Morgan's school shirts. It was on the right wrist and quite large, stretching from the very edge of the sleeve to a spot above the cuff line, spread over several inches. The pattern of the stain was immediately familiar to her, a reminder of a time when Morgan was much younger, when she used to come home with the tips of her sleeves dipped in paint and ketchup or crusted with dried mud—a crude report of her day, the things she'd gotten her hands into. Standing alone in her kitchen, Caren stared at the cuff of Morgan's white shirt. The cottony material was stained a dark copper-brown and stiff to the touch, and it looked frighteningly like dried blood.

6

Upstairs, she settled on a gray pencil skirt and a cashmere sweater.

She dressed in silence and then walked across the hall to her daughter's bedroom. Morgan had rolled onto her stomach, her breath a soprano whistle. Caren turned on the lamp by the bed. She pulled the quilted comforter off her daughter's legs and waited for her to stir. "Morgan," she said, repeating the name twice when she didn't move. Caren knelt beside the bed, placing a hand on the girl's forehead. The skin was warm and plump, but not feverish, and Caren couldn't understand why Morgan was sleeping so soundly, almost five hours before her bedtime. "Morgan," she said, shaking her. When she finally opened her eyes, Caren was standing over her, holding the stained shirt. "Sit up," she said. Morgan pushed herself onto her elbows, her body still sluggish with sleep. "I'm hungry," she mumbled, rubbing her puffy eyes.

"What is this, Morgan?"

"What is what?"

"*This.*" Caren held the large stain beneath the lamp's light. "Why is there blood on your shirt?" Morgan stared at the shirt for a long time, her expression as flat as pond water. She wrinkled her nose but didn't say anything. Her hair was mashed on one side from where she'd been sleeping, and her school uniform was a mess of wrinkles. There was dried spit in the corners of her mouth. Caren sat down on the edge of the bed. Across the hall, she heard the crackle of her walkie-talkie, followed by Gerald, who was still out making his rounds. "First guests arriving, ma'am," he said.

"What time is it?" Morgan said, in a voice that sounded small and sleepy. She scratched at a bug bite on her leg, then tugged on her cotton socks, each of which had slid past her heels. When she swung her legs off the bed, the soles of her feet didn't even reach the worn, pea-colored carpet. Caren set the shirt on top of the rumpled sheets. Morgan glanced at the brown, half-moon-shaped stain, as if she were looking at a stone on the ground, a common enough sight and certainly no cause for concern.

Caren felt her veins pulse, a throbbing behind her ears.

"How did you get blood on your shirt, Morgan?"

"What are you talking about?"

"*This* . . . this stain on your shirt."

Morgan shrugged. "I don't know what that is."

Caren reached for her arms and pulled at them, yanking at the skin, searching for a scratch or a scar or anything that might explain the amount of blood on her clothes.

"Did you hurt yourself?"

"No."

"Did someone else hurt you?"

"*You're* hurting me!"

She snatched her arms free, scooting as far away from her mother as she could, pressing her back against the bed's painted headboard and knocking it gently against the rose wallpaper. Caren asked her again, "How did you get blood on your shirt?"

"Why are you yelling at me?"

"I am not yelling," Caren said, even though she was. Her voice had taken on that thin, high-pitched quality it did when she got really scared. And there, in her daughter's bedroom, the

81

bloodstained shirt between them, Caren was quite possibly the most afraid she had ever been in her life. "Did someone hurt you, Morgan?"

"No."

Which left open another possibility, the thing that frightened Caren the most.

She reminded herself to breathe.

"This afternoon," she said, speaking carefully and deliberately, drawing a line of emphasis under each word, "when the police asked if you saw or heard anything last night, you were telling the truth, weren't you, 'Cakes?"

Morgan mumbled something.

"Morgan?"

"I said *yes*." She rolled her eyes, this new thing she'd picked up at school that Caren couldn't stand. She wanted to swat her little legs to get her attention, the way she might have when Morgan was just a tot and danger meant something as real and present as a lick of fire burning on the stove. But her daughter wasn't a preschooler anymore. She couldn't put her in a corner or physically wrest the truth out of her. At this stage, the two of them, mother and daughter, were left with the crudeness of language, the imprecision of words. "What is going on, Morgan?" she said. "Why do you have blood on your shirt?" Her voice was shrill. She was yelling again.

Across the hall, she heard Lorraine's voice on the walkie-talkie. "Miss White Lady is looking for you, baby," she said, speaking of Ms. Quinlan. "I do believe they are waiting for someone to call an official start to this thing." The two-way sputtered in static, and then Lorraine was gone. It was after five, for sure. Caren was late and due in the main house. But she didn't care. The world outside this room could wait.

She started again, slowly. "Morgan . . ."

And then suddenly her daughter had something to say, something by way of an explanation. "Maybe it's not even my shirt," she said, her tone hopeful, courteous even, as if she really was trying to help, to solve a mystery as benign as where her mother may have misplaced her car keys. But the more Morgan talked, and the harder she tried to sell it, the more Caren realized how much trouble they were in. "Sometimes our uniforms get mixed up in PE," Morgan offered. "They're all the same. And you said you would sew my name in the back but you never did, and so it probably just got all mixed up. I bet I just picked up the wrong shirt after gym class."

"'Cakes," Caren said, swallowing hard, "I need you to tell me the truth."

"I am."

Caren could hardly look at her. She lowered her eyes, her gaze falling on the stain, lying face up between them. She saw its twin in her mind. She saw the open grave and the dead woman and the shock of blood that soaked the front of her clothes.

"Did you leave the house last night, Morgan?"

"No."

"Tell the truth, 'Cakes."

Not that Caren would have any way of knowing.

For the cops, she'd already tried to recall anything odd about last night, and now tried again to divine her daughter's movements after dark. Morgan, even at nine, still had bathroom issues at night, a partial explanation for why she refused even the few sleepover invitations she received. She used to come to Caren at night, cradling her wet sheets. But since the start of this school year, she often changed the bedding herself in the middle of the night, shamed even to tell her mother. And, anyway, Caren had had wine with dinner, a lot actually. She'd slept soundly and heard nothing at all.

Morgan had her back pressed against the headboard.

Again, she was mumbling something Caren could hardly hear.

"What is it, 'Cakes?"

What came out was barely a whisper. "You said I didn't do anything wrong."

"Oh, Morgan," Caren whispered.

She felt a brick-sized lump forming in her throat.

"I'm only going to ask you this one more time. How did you get blood on your shirt?" But when her daughter gave a small shrug and said, "I don't know, Mom," Caren simply accepted it. She knew it was all she was going to get. "Okay," she said calmly. She pushed against the side of the twin bed, rising slowly to her feet. She picked up the soiled shirt. And because she had no better idea, she tucked it into the top drawer of Morgan's wooden dresser. "Gerald will be here in a few minutes. You are not to leave this building under any circumstances, do you understand?"

"Yes, ma'am."

"Okay, then."

She didn't intend to stay long, just until the guests were seated and she'd shaken hands with Giles Schuyler, the chief executive of Merryvale Properties. He was not at all what she'd pictured. He resembled something of an aging football player, with broad shoulders that no suit could contain with any grace and jowls thick and going soft with age. On his right hand, he wore a small mountain of gold, in the form of an LSU class ring, the center stone cheap and dull. If you'd told her he'd just gotten off his shift at Sears selling Amana washer-dryers, she would have believed it. His appearance was that of a simple man, a local boy, not one you'd necessarily expect to be running a company that traded on the New York Stock Exchange. He was affable and warm, patting her on the back and offering to fetch her a flute of champagne, as if they were standing in his living room. He was completely at home, an aperitif in hand and his suit coat undone. Whatever, if anything, Ms. Quinlan had told him about the body out by the fence, he didn't seem fazed in the least. Ms. Quinlan, on the other hand, hadn't let a glass of butter-colored rum too far from her lips. She was glued to Schuyler's side, taking one small sip after another and eyeing closely the goings-on in the room, tracking the invited guests.

"I understand your little girl is at Laurel Springs Elementary."

"Yes," Caren said, glancing down at her watch, trying to think what time it was in D.C., how soon she could get to a phone. "We've been very happy there."

"Well, that's what we're all about," Schuyler said. "Building communities where families can thrive." It was a line right out of his brochure. He took a sip of his drink, gesturing toward the gathered crowd. The guests in the dining room were in their midthirties and older, part of a generation late to home owner- ship, men and women whose first home might very well be their last. Each of them had been brought here, beneath the crystal chandeliers, as an invitation to take part in a once-in-a-lifetime opportunity: to become founding investors in Louisiana's next great upscale living community, Douxville Estates, for which residential plots were currently being sold. The houses in the brochure were an echo of the historical elegance of a place like Belle Vie, only with new plumbing, of course, and custom- made granite countertops. It was an offer to retire inside of a Margaret Mitchell novel, to a time of opulence and refinement where you could end each workday as your forefathers had, sit- ting out on the front porch with a drink, imagining land that stretched for acres and acres instead of stopping crudely at the end of a concrete driveway. Mr. Schuyler opened the evening by asking the guests to stand and toast their new neighbors, before reminding them, with a salesman's flair, that time was running out. There were only a handful of plots left. "Act now," he said.

"Who is *that?*"

Patricia Quinlan had slid beside Caren. She was nodding her head at someone across the room. Schuyler was just then getting into the meat of his presentation, the PowerPoint displays of floor plans and computer models and testimonials from residents of Merryvale's other success stories: Oakwood Village in Dallas; Sweetwater Estates in coastal Virginia; and, of course, the town of Laurel Springs, right here in Louisiana. Caren wasn't listening closely. She was still trying to find a way to steal upstairs to her office when Ms. Quinlan pointed to a man standing near the hors d'oeuvres table, picking at the displays of food without a napkin or a plate—and, what was likely worse in Ms. Quinlan's eyes, he wasn't wearing a name tag. "I don't believe he's one of our guests," she said, glancing down at a tiny clipboard, small enough to fit inside her purse. "We don't want to be letting just *anybody* in here," she added.

"He's not just anybody," Caren said, feeling a flush.

Across the crowded dining hall, Bobby Clancy was stuffing his face.

He dabbed at the corners of his mouth with his fingertips and took a sip of whatever it was some waiter had put in his hand—in this case a '96 Burgundy he guzzled unceremoniously—before setting down the empty glass and reaching for another from a passing tray. He was wearing black jeans, faded in places, and an olive-green T-shirt that hung loose on his frame. He was underweight, and his hair had thinned over the years. Drink and time had laid a road map to middle age in the lines of his pale face, but he was a Clancy and therefore slyly handsome still, with black hair and broad shoulders and eyes of a color both blue and gold. He seemed to be enjoying himself royally, dipping into the bounty at the buffet table, and his presence was thoroughly irksome to Ms. Quinlan, no matter his last name. "Why is he *here*?"

Caren offered to refill Ms. Quinlan's glass. She would take care of this, she said.

She crossed the dining hall to greet Bobby, thinking how strangely out of place he looked in the chandeliered hall. In his faded street clothes, he looked for all the world like a man who didn't belong here, a man who could hardly afford even the most basic of Schuyler's starter homes, instead of a Clancy, a man whose family had owned Belle Vie for generations. Bobby, she remembered, used to play in this very room.

He was swallowing a buttered roll when she approached.

She set down Ms. Quinlan's empty glass and handed him a clean saucer.

"Bobby Clancy," she said. "What's this? Two times in, what, less than a week?" They had seen each other in town just a few days earlier.

"I'm spoiling you, I know."

He signaled a waiter for more wine.

Then, turning to Caren, he smiled.

He eyed the getup, the dress and the French braid in her hair.

"I'd better be careful," he said. "You may start to get the wrong idea here, me coming around again."

She smiled, despite herself. He still had a sense of humor.

"What are you doing here, Bobby?"

"Checking up on the family business, that's all," he said. "Seeing what my brother's up to." He looked around the ballroom, the chandeliers and the starched tablecloths, staring at the dozens of strangers standing in what used to be his living room.

"What's this, a five-, ten-thousand-dollar deal?" he said.

"Something like that."

Across the room, Ms. Quinlan was staring at them, her lips pursed.

Caren sent a waiter to see about a fresh drink for her.

"I liked it better the way it was, the way it used to be," Bobby said. "Just family, you know. Daddy and Ray, me and Mother. And all the old-time folks on the place, your mama and her kin, the cutters in the field." He popped another bun in his mouth, a roll baked around a hash of zucchini and potato, smoked sausage and chives, something Lorraine had thrown together at the last minute. Bobby swallowed it whole, wiping his mouth with the back of his hand. "I liked your mama's cooking better, too." He craned his neck, looking around, still hunting for that second or third glass of wine.

Caren wondered if he knew about the murder.

This was the most she'd seen Bobby since she'd returned four years ago, and she suspected something had to be behind his sudden appearance on plantation grounds. Raymond had sworn her to secrecy, made her promise he would be the one to break the news to Bobby. Twenty, thirty years ago, that wouldn't have counted for much. But these days Raymond was her boss, and the truth was, she and Bobby weren't friends anymore, not really, not for a long, long time. He had followed in the family's footsteps to Ole Miss, picking up, along the way, Raymond's ideas about how Clancy men ought to behave, including not spending so much time with the help; Raymond had teased him mercilessly about his particular fondness for Caren. She was only thirteen years old when Bobby went off to college. He stopped hanging out with her after that. No more dropping by the kitchen for teacakes and milk, tugging on the curls in her hair; no more racing her up the trunks of trees, or through the grove of willow oaks; and no more ghost stories in the quarters. Caren kidded herself as long as she could that it was the age difference between them that had suddenly come to significance. And when she couldn't kid herself any longer, she simply accepted the truth as she knew it. She was the daughter of a plantation cook, the descendant of slaves. Bobby had been born in the big house. He played his role, and she played hers, biding her time until she could get out of there, away from Belle Vie. Still, it had stayed with her a long time, the lines that were drawn, reminding her of where she came from.

Older now, she didn't hold it against him.

People grow apart, move on.

Of the brothers, she probably still liked Bobby best. But his nostalgia for the old days was of a color she could not match. "Raymond know you're here?" she said.

Bobby skipped over the question.

"There's a cop out there, you know, sniffing around."

"Deputy Harris."

Caren had forgotten about the young cop and his planned night watch, and now had a panicked thought that Lang had put him on duty as a ruse, a way to keep a watch on the plantation, but also a watch on *her*. It was an irrational worry, a fear that Lang somehow already knew what she knew, that he could see what she had seen: the blood on her daughter's shirt.

Bobby leaned in, hovering over her. "I heard you were the one who found her."

"Raymond told you."

Again, Bobby didn't react to his brother's name.

"A fucking shame," is all he said, reaching for the nearest cocktail tray, settling for a pale glass of champagne and downing most of it in one gulp. "I could have told him that company out there wasn't going to bring nothing but trouble."

Caren wasn't sure what Groveland had to do with it.

"The cops seem to be looking closer to home," she said.

"Hmph," Bobby muttered.

She didn't know if it was the liquor or the bewitching hour, the faded sunlight through the leaded-glass windows, but she couldn't miss the grayish crescents beneath his eyes, the washed-out color in his cheeks, and the bleakness of his expression. There was deep sadness there, but also anger. "It's the money, is what it is," he said. "Every goddamn thing with Raymond is money. You watch yourself with him, Caren." He reached for her arm, all six feet, two inches of him blocking nearly all the available light, throwing her into shadow, standing so close she could count the hairs on his chin.

"Be careful, is all I'm saying," he said.

Caren felt light-headed, overheated, and overwhelmed.

She wanted to get upstairs to her office, alone.

She grabbed a drink from a passing tray and said, "It was good to see you, Bobby. But I left some work on my desk. You can stay if you want to, but I know they'd rather you didn't," she said, motioning toward Ms. Quinlan across the room.

Let her deal with him, Caren thought.

She turned and walked out before the first course was served.

Upstairs, she closed the office door behind her. Hot and slightly rattled, she cracked open her office window, propping a parish phone directory under the painted wood frame to hold it open. She sucked down the warm red wine, and then stood over her desk, watching her trembling fingers as they dialed Eric's home phone number.

Lela answered.

Caren knew that decorum called for her to pause here, to ask Lela how she was doing, to ask after her family or inquire about her work, and ordinarily her own ego wouldn't allow for any less. She had never met the woman and had always known Eric to show good judgment; it would be tacky, frankly, to be anything less than cordial. But she also thought she had earned the right, in an emergency, to skip all social graces.

"Is Eric home?" she said.

There was a pause on the other end. She could hear the hum of Mr. Schuyler's amplified voice from the PA system downstairs, coming up through the floorboards.

On the phone, she heard her name.

"Caren?"

"Yes."

There was another pause, and then Lela's voice, cooler than before. "He's here."

Caren heard a dull thump, and then silence, Lela setting down the phone.

When Eric picked up the line, almost a minute later, he seemed in a good humor, almost cheerful and happy to hear from her. "Hey," he said. Then, picking up on some ongoing conversation, the last e-mail or a voice message she didn't remember, he said, "You know, I think it's best, Caren, if you just let us go ahead and buy the plane ticket. American has a direct from New Orleans to D.C. right now for less than four hundred."

She hadn't seen Eric in almost a year.

His last visit, sometime in the spring, he and Lela had picked up Morgan while Caren was in Baton Rouge meeting with a vendor. Morgan had stayed in a hotel with them in New Orleans through the weekend and was dropped off in Laurel Springs that Monday morning in time for school. Lela had never been to New Orleans, and Morgan came home with three disposable cameras' worth of pictures. It had made Caren sad to think of her daughter as a tourist in the city in which she was born. And though she promised more than once to sit down with Morgan and look through the photos, she never got around to it. Eric's fiancée, therefore, remained a mystery to her. She had, embarrassing as it was to admit, initially pictured her as something of a rival: tall, with bigger breasts maybe, and a law degree. For weeks, she even wondered if Lela was white. It was Morgan who put that idea to rest, reporting, unsolicited, that Lela was brown, of average height, with a "very pretty smile." "She kind of looks like you, Mom," she said. Eric, on the other hand, was always the same in Caren's mind: tall and lean, with close-cropped, tightly coiled hair and round, rimless glasses. They talked on the phone at least once a month, e-mailed more often, mostly about Morgan's schooling, but she had not stood with him, face-to-face, in quite a long time. "I think Morgan is starting to worry you're changing your mind about her coming up here," he said.

"I'm not calling about the trip, Eric."

"Oh," he said, briefly clearing his throat. She wondered if Lela was listening.

"We have a problem, Eric."

"What's going on?"

"There's been an 'incident' here," she said, regretting the weak choice of words almost as soon as they were said. She didn't want to soft-pedal, or be in any way misleading. She wanted him to have all the facts. "The police were here this morning."

"Are you okay?" he asked, his voice sharp and alert. He sounded genuinely concerned, and for a brief moment she felt a warm lump in the back of her throat.

"Yes."

"Is Morgan?"

She hesitated. "Yes."

"Well, what is it, then?"

"They found a body, here at Belle Vie. It was way out on the edge of the property line, by the fence and the cane fields out back. She was half-buried in dirt."

"Someone died."

"Someone was killed."

"Out there?" he said, in some disbelief. "Who?"

Caren pushed the woman's face out of her mind.

"I don't know. It looks like it was a woman from the fields."

"Oh, man," Eric said, taking a slow, leveling breath. "Does Morgan know?"

She was getting to that.

"They've talked to the whole staff, trying to find out if anyone saw or heard anything. I don't even know how someone got on the property, the woman . . . or whoever it was that did this to her." She looked out the window where the world of Belle Vie had gone black. She could hardly see more than a few feet beyond her office window, a fact that had never bothered her before. But suddenly she was aware of feeling afraid and alone living out here. "I don't know, Eric, the whole thing is creepy."

"Is the plantation looking to protect itself from liability?" he said, completely misunderstanding her reason for calling. "I'm sure Clancy's firm can handle it, but I still know some folks at DeLouche & Pitt in the city. Bob Klein is still convinced I'm coming back to work any day now." There was a faint chuckle in his throat that faded almost instantly, as he realized, too late, that he'd stumbled into tender territory. They were both silent for a moment. Caren said, "The detectives also spoke to Morgan."

"Why?"

"She lives here, and they wanted to know what, if anything, she knew about it."

"She's just a kid."

"I was with her the whole time," she said, trying to keep her voice steady, the facts laid bare. "They asked her if she had seen or heard anything strange on the property in the last few days. I was right next to her when she told the cops no."

"She must have been terrified."

"She was lying."

"What?"

"I found blood on one of her shirts, Eric."

He was quiet, his breathing momentarily halted.

"I don't understand."

"In the laundry, on the right-hand sleeve of one of her shirts, I found blood."

"So you think she killed someone?" he said, sounding amused and also vaguely relieved. The idea was so preposterous that it seemed to lighten things on his end. Caren said, "No, I don't think she killed someone," adding, "She's left-handed."

The silence returned.

"Jesus, Caren," he mumbled.

Then, more sternly, he said, "You're not serious, are you?"

"How did she get blood on her shirt, Eric?"

"Oh, Caren," he said, his tone warm, almost playfully admonishing, treating this like the time Morgan was six months old and Caren was sure she'd stopped breathing until Eric put a mirror to her nose, or when she was convinced the women at the day care center were secretly feeding her newborn daughter bottles of whole milk.

"She probably just fell down and scraped herself at school or cut her hand or something," he said.

"It was too much blood."

The words painted a picture, one that gave him pause.

"And you asked her about it?"

"She's *lying*."

"How can you know that?"

"What do you want me to say, Eric? She's my kid."

Eric let out a short, bullish sigh.

She knew the sound. It meant he was thinking.

"Blood?"

"Yes."

"All right, let me talk to her, then," he said.

"She's home right now."

Before hanging up, she told him she'd be waiting for his return call.

Outside, the wind had picked up, snaking in ragged coils through the dark and shaking the trees against the window. The branches were like fingertips on the glass, tapping for her attention. She walked around her desk to the window. As she bent to remove the phone book on the ledge, she swore she heard voices, coming from the direction of the quarters. She swore she heard . . . *singing*. It was faint, and she thought she was imagining things, but when the wind picked up, it delivered the sound right to the window's ledge. Caren took a step back, thinking that someone was out there.

When the phone rang, she actually jumped.

On the other end of the line, Eric repeated the same story Morgan had told her earlier, that the shirt was probably not even hers, the whole thing likely a mix-up at school, and Eric still didn't think any of it added up to much; he still had a hard time believing it was blood on his daughter's shirt, or that Morgan would lie. Caren bit her tongue rather than point out the ways she felt she knew her daughter better than he did. It seemed mean-spirited. It was never his idea for Morgan to stay in Louisiana.

She reminded him of the amount, the odd placement on the sleeve.

"I wouldn't worry about it," he said, sounding suddenly very far away. For the first time, Caren wondered what he was doing when she called, if his dinner was getting cold, if Lela had been waiting this whole time, alone at the table.

"They're getting a search warrant, Eric."

"The cops?"

"They'll be here in the morning," she said.

Something shifted in Eric's demeanor.

He was a trained lawyer after all, and Morgan's father.

He was quiet a good, long while.

Then he said, "I honestly wouldn't worry about it, Caren."

"Okay," she said, because she wasn't going to worry about it. She was going to get rid of it.

Her first thought was the river. But there was, of course, the issue of weight, of how to keep the thing from merely skimming the surface of the water and floating along in plain view. She could just imagine someone finding her daughter's shirt tomorrow morning, tangled in a thick of weeds along the riverbank, having traveled barely a mile by sunrise. And anyway, the levees in this part of the parish were eight feet and a challenge to navigate even in broad daylight. Nor could she come up with a convincing enough story to tell Gerald that would explain her stepping out on an errand in the middle of the night, after she'd made a point to put him on post, right outside her front door. Besides, she knew from experience that literal disposal was often tricky. That's where most people made their biggest mistakes. One of the first cases she'd assisted on, a kid had tossed a knife in a Dumpster, mere feet from his apartment; it was city property by morning, as soon as the trash trucks rolled past. No, it made more sense to keep any evidence close, within the bounds of a carefully laid argument about Fourth Amendment rights against improper search and seizure. She didn't know what was on the shirt or how it got there. But she knew Detective Lang would never lay eyes on it. Not until Caren had more information. The law, she knew, is a narrow little box, and it takes only a single misstep to find yourself on the outside of it.

It was after two in the morning when she came up with a plan.

Morgan asleep upstairs, Caren washed the shirt twice, both times using double the amount of bleach. She leaned against the stove, watching the swish and slosh of the machine, the violent jerk-and-pull of her daughter's white shirt. The plate of food from Lorraine's kitchen was still sitting untouched. Caren made a halfhearted attempt to eat. The fried 'gator was rubbery and cold and completely inedible. The greens were coated in white animal fat. The sight made her stomach lurch. She settled on a single lump of creamed potatoes, a small spoonful to dull the gnawing emptiness in her belly.

She swallowed, and she waited.

It was as calm as she'd felt all night.

The shirt, once out of the dryer, was startlingly white, everywhere *except* the spot on the right sleeve, where a ghost lingered. The color had faded to a muddy gray, but the half-moon shape was outlined clearly. Still, Caren felt relief. Who would make anything of this relatively small stain, the color and spirit drained to nothing, which, at this late hour, she was willing to concede might not have even been blood? Why would her daughter's rose-colored bureau ever make it within the bounds of a police search warrant? Surely, if she folded the shirt tightly, sleeves tucked in, and placed it in the back of some rarely used drawer, no one would ever notice. Upstairs, in her daughter's room, she watched Morgan sleep. It was almost ten hours she'd been out like this. Caren tried to wake her, gently shaking her shoulders. She heard her utter a sound, a faint hum that sounded a lot like *Mom*. But maybe it was only a wish, a whisper inside Caren's own head. Morgan's body remained motionless, save for the soft rise and fall of her breath. Caren pulled the sheets from the foot of the bed, covering Morgan's bare legs. Finally, she tucked the laundered shirt into the top drawer of her bureau before crossing the hall to undress for bed.

She lay down and closed her eyes, thinking of the strangeness of running into Bobby Clancy again, and the things he'd said about his brother, Raymond. She lay in the stillness with it. Only then, in the dead of night, her body on the very edge of surrender, did an image finally pop free: the dead woman, her face, the black eyes drawn in charcoal. She finally remembered where she'd seen her before.

7

It was a quarter after six when Donovan called, waking her.

She didn't remember falling asleep or how exactly she'd ended up face down at the foot of her queen-sized bed, her bare feet facing the headboard. The quilt beneath her was damp with sweat. The silk slip she hadn't bothered to change out of was like a sheet of saran wrap against her skin. The room was suffocating. She crawled toward the radiator. Her tongue was thick as carpet and tacky against the roof of her mouth. She turned the knob on the radiator. "What is it, Donovan?" she said.

"You called me."

Right, she thought.

She stood upright, mumbling a repeat of the earlier lie, the ruse to get him on the grounds of Belle Vie, though she mixed up a few of the details. This time, she invoked Raymond Clancy's name, suggesting *he* was the one with some proposed changes to the regular schedule. She told Donovan to come by her office by nine. He didn't ask any questions. "Yeah, all right," was all he said. The line clicked, and he was gone.

In a dim corner, the radiator rumbled and hissed as it cooled.

Caren propped open her bedroom window.

Dew sat on the chipped paint of the windowsill. The air outside was cool and wet, the plantation wrapped in a rolling, morning fog, the sky above still a blackish blue, barely a whisper of light on the horizon. In the dark of her small bedroom, she started to dress herself, sliding into jeans and a long-sleeve T-shirt.

She heard a sound coming through her open window.

In the early-morning hour, the wind was completely still, Belle Vie holding its magnolia-scented breath. Caren leaned her face into the fog, listening. The sound was faint, like a low whistle, a distant call. It was coming from the south, down by the quarters. From her second-story window, she could see only treetops, and even though it made no sense to her, she swore she heard voices . . . *singing*. It was the same floating sound she'd heard through her office window last night.

She stepped out into the hallway, peeking into Morgan's room.

Her daughter was still sound asleep.

Downstairs, Caren slid into her boots. The worn leather was cold against the soles of her bare feet. Outside, Gerald was sitting in his golf cart, a black windbreaker zipped to his chin. His hands were clasped, resting on the bulge of his midsection, and his head was thrown back against the headrest; he was fast asleep. Caren had walked out of the house without a jacket. She wrapped her arms tightly across her chest, trying to seal in her body's heat. "Gerald," she said, walking to the cart, parked just a few feet from her front door. Gerald stirred, opening his bloodshot eyes. He was in his late thirties and built like an NFL lineman. It took some effort, but he slowly pulled himself upright, wiping ashy, dried spit from the dark-brown skin around the corners of his mouth. "I was just resting my eyes for a minute, ma'am."

She asked him to stand, to please give her the keys to the cart.

"Everything okay, miss?"

She took his place in the driver's seat, feeling his lingering warmth through the thin cotton of her clothes. She told him to wait by the front door, reminding him, as she started the cart's engine, that her little girl was upstairs. "Yes, ma'am," he said.

Behind the wheel, she took off to the south, the cart's tires bumping against wet grass.

By the time she was past the guest cottages, the light had begun to change. The rising sun had whitewashed the horizon, burning through the moisture in the air and parting the fog just as she arrived at the mouth of the slave quarters.

Near the village, she slowed as she always did.

The cart's engine sputtered . . . then fell quiet.

Caren stared at the dark, empty cabins, their sagging porches facing one another. She felt the familiar chill in the air. And she heard the voices again, layered one on top of another, woven into a solemn chorus. It was a melody she recognized at once.

> *'Twas grace that taught my heart to fear,*
> *And grace my fears relieved . . .*
> *How precious did that grace appear,*
> *The hour I first believed . . .*

Caren held perfectly still, listening to the old church hymn. It seemed to be coming from the far end of the village, from all the way down the dirt road, all the way down to the last cottage on the left, the one her mother called Jason's Cabin.

She felt a soft wind at her back, cold and wet, like a spook's breath.

It quickened her pulse.

She stepped out onto the dirt road and started the walk, wondering if, in this early morning light, she was bearing witness to an actual haunting, the quarters come alive right before her eyes. The music grew stronger, the voices more fervent, the closer she got to Jason's Cabin, the one set nearest to the cane fields. Their sweetness was as sharp as needle points, leaving tiny pinpricks along the surface of Caren's bare skin. She got as far as the gate when it stopped suddenly, the sound fading as mysteriously as it had started. She paused at the gate, remembering the cold dread that had come over her yesterday morning, when she had, for no good reason, cut her inspection short.

She remembered Bobby's ghost stories, too.

Jason's Cabin, he'd always said, was haunted.

Inside, the place was cloaked in shadow, the room even darker than it had been yesterday morning. She took a few steps, making a few tentative stabs in the air, feeling her way around the small shack, patting the raw wood of the walls. And that's how she found it, the first real clue in the cops' case. Caren stopped short, waiting for her eyes to adjust. When the light finally came, she was staring at an empty space on the wall. She could see the outline still, the blank shape of an antique cane knife, with its long blade, flat and wide like the head of a hoe, and a handle of curved wood. The knife itself was gone. Someone had stolen it, within days of that woman's throat being cut.

The voices started again, like a whisper at her back.

Caren swung around but saw no one.

Yea, when this flesh and heart shall fail,
And mortal life shall cease . . .
I shall possess, within the veil,
A life of joy and peace . . .

The singing, she realized, hadn't been coming from the cabin at all. She walked back outside and the sound grew louder. It appeared to be coming from the cane fields.

Caren drove the cart around to the back side of the quarters, down the drab hill where no grass would grow. When she got within thirty yards of where the body had been found, she saw them out there. They were on the cane side of the fence, a small crowd standing in the dirt by the fields. One of the women was holding a candle, burned down to within an inch of her fingertips. The others were likewise facing in Caren's direction, their heads bowed solemnly toward the open grave on the other side of the fence. They were women mostly, six that she counted at a distance, all white and middle-aged and thick through the hips. Their voices were high-pitched and sweet, anchored by one lone tenor. At the center of their group stood a black man with round, almost cherubic, features. He was wearing black slacks, a black shirt, and a clerical collar, the cuff of white stark against his dark, coffee-colored skin.

Behind them, the field-workers were gathered. The men were small and compact, their skin tanned to a reddish brown, their dress nearly identical: sleeves of their works shirts secured with rubber bands at the wrists, the legs of their pants tied at the ankles with strips of cloth. They and a few women pressed straw hats against their chests, listening in silence, holding tight to the bittersweet melody, if not the words themselves. There was one man with his head down. He was leaning against the fence. With the back of one hand, he wiped at tears in his eyes. The black priest glanced in Caren's direction. He nodded kindly, but didn't smile. He held up his hand, signaling the group, and together they started the hymn all over again.

Amazing grace, how sweet the sound . . .
That saved a wretch like me . . .

Deputy Harris, who was coming up on his twenty-fourth hour on duty, had his backside leaned against the fence railing. He was smoking a cigarette, chewing on the fingernails of his left hand between frequent puffs, his nerves seemingly shot to hell. He looked over his shoulder at the singing Christians and the black priest and rolled his eyes, flicking cigarette ash within a foot of the mouth of the ragged, open grave. There were four short stakes in the ground around it, strung together with flimsy yellow tape.

Over the gospel melody, Caren heard the kick of a truck's engine.

Behind the workers, a Chevy pickup, the name GROVELAND stenciled in sunny yellow across its side, pulled to a stop on a strip of raised land between the fence and the rows of cane. Hunt Abrams was behind the wheel. From the cab of his truck, he stared at the scene: his workers standing idle and more than a half dozen strangers singing church music at dawn. His left arm was hanging out of the driver's side window. He stabbed a finger in the air, trying to get the young cop's attention. "Hey," he said. "You want to tell them to get the hell off my farm?"

Deputy Harris barely stirred. "My deal is on *this* side of the fence." He took another puff of his cig. "Long as they not disturbing the scene, it ain't my problem."

"Is that right?" Abrams said tersely.

Deputy Harris shrugged.

In the cab of his truck, Abrams paused for a moment. His eyes skimmed past the deputy, taking in once more the priest and the churchwomen. Then he rapped his knuckles against the side of the truck, nodding his head to get his workers' attention. "*Vamonos*, people," he said, his Spanish as dull as dry clay. "Let's go. *Trabajamos.*" Caren could see the nose of his shotgun resting beside him on the truck's front seat. The workers, all ten or so, returned their hats to their head. Moving wordlessly under a newly rising sun, they disappeared into the fields. The last man, his cheeks still damp, wouldn't move until one of the other men called his name. "*Gustavo, no puedes quedarte aquí,*" he said. The one named Gustavo wiped his tears. He made the sign of the cross before turning to follow the others. "Y'all need to get on away from here," Abrams said to the women. "We're running a business, not a prayer group." And when they didn't immediately move, he spoke louder. "I know you hear me. You're just making trouble for yourselves every minute you're still standing here."

The shotgun was still within arm's reach.

One of the church ladies, her face plump and heart-shaped under a mass of sagging curls, pleaded with the boy cop. "Did you see that? You hear the way he's talking to us?" But Deputy Harris was as unmoved by their complaint as he had been by Hunt's. Like he said, it ain't his deal. Though he did watch with some curiosity one of the churchwomen pulling a spiral note-book from her purse and making what seemed like copious notes about every detail of the scene on Groveland's sugar farm, even taking the time to jot down the truck's license plate number. Abrams glared at the lot of them. The priest, through all this, hadn't said a word, not to the cop and not to Hunt Abrams. He motioned to the women, signaling an end to their vigil. As the group began to form a line to take them out of the fields and toward the farm road, the priest, his English sharpened by an accent Caren couldn't immediately place, looked lastly at her. "Good day, ma'am," he said, as polite as she'd ever heard the words.

Hunt Abrams was still sitting in his truck when they'd gone.

He stared across the fence at Caren. "You got something you want to say about it?"

By the time she returned home, it was well past seven, and Letty was already at the kitchen stove, making eggs. Morgan was sitting at the round, two-seat table opposite the stairs, dressed for school. She was wearing another of her white oxford shirts, under the straps of a plaid smock dress, her head down in a math textbook. She appeared to be doing fractions. Caren kissed the top of her head and went to finish a single braid Morgan had started at the back of her head. "Don't," Morgan said, pulling away and brushing pencil-eraser shavings from her lined notebook paper.

"I thought you said you did your homework."

"I did. This is for tomorrow."

At the stove, Letty smiled. "Smart girl."

Morgan closed her math book, shoving it into her navy schoolbag, then stood up from the table and announced to Letty that she would wait for her by the car.

"She's in some hurry today."

"Sit down, Morgan," Caren said.

It was the first they'd seen each other since last night, since the heated talk in Morgan's bedroom. Caren wanted her to know they weren't finished. But she also didn't want to get into it with Letty in the room, the business of the blood and the police. "It's terrible what happened to that lady, isn't it?" Letty said, correctly reading the topic on everyone's minds. "*Pobrecita*, eh? Makes you wonder if half of them wouldn't do better just staying right where they are. It can be hard over here, you know. I know girls like that. I got people like that in my family. They come from these little towns in Mexico, and they don't know what they're going to find, what it's really like here." She had her head bent over the stove and seemed almost to be talking to herself. "I lit a candle for her last night. Me and Gabby, we prayed for her."

Caren had been up with her, too, the woman, her face.

And the memory of where she'd seen her.

It was in town, not even a week or so earlier. Caren had

been standing in the middle of a long line at Brandy's Grocery on St. Patrick, picking up a few things Lorraine had sworn she needed first thing in the morning. There was an eighteen-year-old girl working a single register, a black girl identified as FAYE by her name tag. She had rhinestones on her fingers and glitter polish on her nails, and her station at the cash register sat just high enough off the ground that it allowed her to look down on the rest of them. The line had come to a halt, and Caren craned her neck, trying to see what the holdup was at the front of the line. Some argument was brewing, between the cashier and a customer . . . and it was her, Caren now realized, the woman from the grave. She could see those same sharp black eyes, even now. The cashier, Faye, was on the verge of calling over the store's manager. The problem, as Caren overheard it in bits and pieces, was over the purchase of a money order. Faye was demanding to see some form of identification to run the transaction, and the woman was saying *No, no, no,* the only word of hers that Caren could make out. The accent was unmistakable, though. It was an easy enough guess that she wasn't born and raised around these parts. She had a basket full of items, and all she wanted was to pay for them and for the money order.

"Huh-uh," Faye said, shaking her head. "I can't let you do that. We not doing no money orders anymore, ma'am, not without some form of picture ID."

There were groans in line.

To the cashier, the woman made her case, pulling out words, one by one. She took great care with the foreign language, telling the cashier in English that no one had asked for any identification when she bought a money order in the store last week. To which, Faye merely shrugged, saying, "I'm just doing what they tell me. You don't have a driver's license? A state ID?" Her tone was terse and impatient. She had grown tired of the whole thing, the back-and-forth. And in response to whatever the woman in line said, Faye pressed a call button at her station. The manager was now officially on the way.

Caren stepped forward.

She was just about to make an offer to help, to take the woman's crumpled bills and purchase the money order for her, using her own valid driver's license . . . when she heard a familiar voice behind her.

"I thought that was you," she heard a man say.

When Caren turned, she was standing face-to-face with Bobby Clancy. He had a six-pack of beer in one hand and a couple of oranges in the other.

"Well, this is a surprise," she said.

He blushed at the sight of her, the lines around his eyes crinkling softly when he smiled. At the time, they hadn't seen each other in nearly twenty years, and Caren smiled, too, warmed by this unexpected reunion. She couldn't look at him without thinking of her mother, the whole of her childhood. He mentioned Helen's funeral, reporting that he had come back to the parish for the service, to pay his respects, but especially to see her, to see Caren. "I guess I must have missed you, though."

"I guess so."

She left off the fact that she'd actually missed her mother's funeral. Helen Gray was dead and buried before anyone tracked Caren down or found a current phone number. It was Lorraine who ultimately made the call, catching Caren as she was walking out the door to work. Caren had had to ask her to repeat it twice. Lorraine got her street address, and three days later a box of her mother's things showed up on her doorstep. *She wanted you to have these, baby*, Lorraine had written in pencil. Caren had opened the box only once. She caught a lingering whiff of her mother's scent, rosemary and lavender and cigarette smoke, and she'd closed it at once and put it away.

Standing in line at the grocer's, Bobby said it was good to see her.

He said it more than once, in fact.

And there were promises to get together sometime, to catch up on old times, though no contact information was exchanged. She supposed he knew where to find her. He slipped out of the still unmoving line, passing her with a pat on the shoulder, abandoning the beer and the oranges, as others in line were fleeing in frustration, too.

"Is there some kind of a problem here?" the store manager said.

"No, there is no problem," the young woman said.

She quietly turned and walked out, the bell on the store's door clanging behind her. When Caren finally reached the front of the line, she saw the items the woman had left behind. Shoved behind the cash register was the small basket she'd been carrying. Inside: a pint of milk, a bag of white flour, a gift box of pralines, a hairbrush and pink ribbon, and a white teddy bear with a red bow tied around its neck. Caren had completely forgotten about the run-in, the close encounter with the dead woman, until last night.

Letty asked her if she wanted anything to eat. "You hungry?"

"I'll take coffee, if you made it."

Letty nodded toward a carafe on the countertop. "You're out of milk, though."

Caren thanked her, rifling through the cabinets for a mug. Letty was shaking salt and pepper into the hot pan. "Make a list if there's anything else you need."

"'Preciate it, Letty."

She couldn't do any of this without her.

The coffee was hot and thick and perfect.

"How's Artie?" Caren said, asking after Letty's son.

"That boy," Letty said, sucking air through her long front teeth.

She was a third-generation Mexican-American and locally born, south Louisiana through and through, sometimes mixing in grits with her eggs and chorizo. "Don't you know by the time I got home yesterday he's got his feet up on my sofa, playing Nintendo or PlayStation or Xbox or whatever in the world it is, like nothing's wrong? No fever, nothing," she said, rolling her eyes. "Bad, bad, bad," she said playfully. "You just wait till this one gets to middle school." She motioned across the kitchen to Morgan. "All of a sudden you have to watch them like crazy."

"I'll bet," Caren said, smiling tightly.

Letty set a plate of steaming eggs in front of Morgan. She put one hand on the girl's shoulder, leaning down to kiss the top of her head. Morgan didn't flinch or move, so welcoming of another woman's touch that Caren felt a flash of envy and an irrational impulse to separate them. Letty stood for a moment over the table, watching their girl eat. Then she snapped her fingers in the air, the line of gold bangles on her wrist chiming softly. "Oh, and bleach!" she said suddenly, opening a drawer for a pencil. On the back of an old Belle Vie brochure she started the grocery list. "It was nearly half a bottle in here yesterday," she said, shaking her head. "But now it's completely gone."

Morgan finally turned to look directly at her mother.

The emptied bleach, the questions last night about a bloody shirt. She put the two together as easily as the math homework she had been doing when Caren walked in. Caren told Letty, "You know, I think I'll pick up Morgan from school today."

"You sure?" Letty said, excited by the prospect. "'Cause you know Gabby's got midterms coming up, and I got laundry piling every which way around my house."

"I'm sure."

Morgan put her eyes down on her plate, pushing eggs around. The conversation with her mother was far from over.

Letty folded her impromptu grocery list, tucking it into the cotton cup of her peach-colored bra. She glanced back at Morgan, before leaning in Caren's general direction, her pencil-thin eyebrows raised.

In a whisper, she said, "*La policía llamó.*"

8

Donovan didn't seem particularly surprised to see two police officers in Caren's office. He paused only briefly at the threshold, just long enough to unzip his gray hoodie. He looked first at Detective Bertrand, who was standing just beside her desk, before glancing at Detective Lang, who was by the window, his hands on his hips.

Donovan looked at Caren last.

His expression was a mix of bafflement and disappointment—in *her*, a woman with no loyalty apparently—and he said nothing as he took the seat directly across from her desk, shoving his hands into the front pouch of his sweatshirt. He looked like a kid called before the principal. He reminded Caren of young men she'd met, clients whose cases she'd assisted on. Twice she thought to tell him to sit up straight, to not make this any harder on himself than it had to be. But she sat silent at her desk. She'd been instructed that the cops would do all the talking. Donovan was not her client. He was not her responsibility. He shook his head to himself, muttering, "This is bullshit, man."

"We just want to ask you a few questions, Mr. Isaacs."

"Yeah, all right," he said.

"I'm Detective Jimmy Bertrand," the big one said. "And this is my partner, Detective Nestor Lang." He nodded across the room at Lang. "We're with the Sheriff's Department, the Criminal Investigation Division. You understand what that is?" Donovan

112

looked at the two cops, his expression that of a man who didn't like being made a fool of. "Well, if you already got my name," he said, moving things along, "I'm going to guess you already know I'm well acquainted with the Sheriff's Department."

"That's right," Bertrand said.

Lang finally spoke up. "We're not here to talk about your rap sheet, son."

"Yeah, sure," Donovan said, rolling his eyes. "Whatever you say."

Detective Bertrand lifted a photograph that had been resting on the corner of Caren's desk since they arrived, only a few minutes before Donovan. The cop held it in front of him, and Donovan pulled his hands from his sweatshirt's pouch, rubbing his damp palms on the front of his loose-fitting jeans. Then he took the photo of the dead woman into his hands. "Do you know this woman, Donovan?"

They'd shown Caren the picture, too, just moments before Donovan walked in. Unlike the somber police sketch, it was a candid photo—the dead woman in a flowered dress that hung past her knees, the layers of her dark hair dripping into her eyes. It was the same woman Caren had seen in the grocery store, just over a week ago. She was smiling in the photograph, an expression that caught Caren off guard. It cut lines into her face, deep as dry creek beds along the sides of her mouth. She had a dark mole above her right eye, and two of her front teeth were capped in gold. And she was wearing those star-shaped earrings, one in each lobe. The photo appeared to have been taken on the front lawn of the Catholic church on Lessard Street in Donaldsonville. Caren recognized the priest standing with the woman, a hand on her shoulder. It was the black man who had led the candlelight vigil just this morning. Donovan hardly glanced at the picture for more than a few seconds. "Naw, man," he said. "I don't know her." He set the photo back on the corner of Caren's desk. She was studying the blank expression on his face, almost as closely as the two cops were.

"Where were you Wednesday night, Donovan?" Bertrand asked.

Donovan shot a glance at Caren, something that didn't go unnoticed by either detective. "School," he said curtly. He'd had enough experience in this area to know that the less he said the better. Of course, the word *school* out of his mouth only served to stoke the cops' suspicions. Just yesterday, Morgan had reported to all of them the latest plantation rumor going around—that Donovan had actually quit school.

"River Valley Community College?"

"Yeah."

"Where you're a student?"

Donovan hesitated for half a second. "Yes."

"Okay, Donovan," Bertrand said. He shot a glance at his partner. Lang stepped forward, clearing his throat. "Do you remember what time you got in, son?" he said.

Again, Donovan looked at Caren.

"Wednesday *night?*" he said, repeating the cop's question and seemingly stalling for time. "I may have to ask my grandmother about that," he said shrewdly, both avoiding the question and invoking, in his grandmother, a ready alibi, should he need one. Betty Collier would say just about anything to protect her grandson.

Watch yourself, Caren almost said.

Be careful, Donovan.

"Actually," Bertrand said, "we already talked to your grandmother."

"You did?"

Bertrand nodded. "We have two officers over to her place right now."

"She said you were at work on Wednesday night," Lang added.

Donovan looked confused at first, then nervous. He rubbed his palms on the front of his jeans, shifting his posture to a more erect, attentive posture. "She did?"

"Betty Collier is in her eighties now, I believe," Caren said suddenly, breaking Lang's one rule. She wanted to throw Donovan a lifeline. "Perhaps she got confused about which day you were speaking of." Donovan was not here on Wednesday night, none of the staff was. She'd already told the cops as much yesterday. "He wasn't on the schedule."

"That right?" Bertrand asked Donovan.

"Yeah, that's right."

"Which means you had no reason to be here that night, right?"

Donovan nodded.

There was a next question that naturally followed, and they all waited for it. Bertrand looked at his partner, who was clearly the one running things, no matter that he'd said very little during the interview. To his partner, Lang gave a small nod.

"*Were* you, Donovan?" Bertrand asked. "Here on Wednesday night?"

Again, Donovan looked at Caren, as if she were somehow behind the policemen's questions, their presence in her office, as if he thought she could make this whole line of inquiry go away with a nod of her head. It was a look of helplessness that Caren recognized from her days sitting across the table from scared clients.

She swiveled in her chair and looked at Bertrand.

"Asked and answered, Detective," she said.

"What was that?"

"You asked him the question, and he's already answered it."

She looked at Donovan. "You don't have to say anything else."

Bertrand looked at his partner. "What the hell, Nes?"

Caren could feel Lang's glare at her back. Donovan was staring, too.

He wasn't sure either what had just happened, if this was choreographed, some kind of a trick. He wasn't sure he could trust her. He took a gamble and ignored her advice. He opened his mouth anyway.

"Naw, man," he said. "I wasn't here."

Lang slid his hands into his pockets. "Son, why don't you take a ride with us down to the station? We have a few more questions for you, and it might be more comfortable down there than in here." He nodded at the surroundings, Caren's overstuffed office. But she knew the idea was to get Donovan away from *her*. Lang was gentle with it, exceedingly polite, as if Donovan would be doing him a huge favor if he said yes. "We could get you something to eat, some decent coffee."

"I'm not hungry."

Lang smiled. "Son, we think we can get this all cleared and squared away in short order. You let us borrow a little more of your time, and you'll be on your way."

Caren looked at Donovan. She shook her head.

Don't, she thought.

"So what do you say?" Lang asked.

To the cop, Donovan shrugged. "Yeah, all right," he said. He stood, hiking up his sagging jeans. Bertrand walked out the door first, Donovan skulking along behind him. He stopped at the door, just long enough to turn and look back at Caren.

"You ain't have to call the police," he mumbled.

It was an odd comment, one the cops seemed to ignore.

Lang was still standing in Caren's office after Bertrand and

Donovan had gone. He lifted the photo from her desk and tucked it into the pocket of his gray suit jacket.

"Who was she?" Caren asked him.

Lang pressed his lips together, deciding how much he wanted to share. "Well, it's not like we got any real papers on these folks, no fingerprints on file." He reached into the same pocket, pulling out what appeared to be a torn-off piece of a church program, where a few notes had been scribbled in pencil. "All we've got right now is the woman's name . . . Inés Avalo." He tucked the church program back into his pocket, his manner somewhat distracted, his mind already somewhere else. Pulling his cell phone from his waist, he checked an e-mail or a text message, reading silently, before returning the handheld device to its case. "You know, Donovan's grandmother swore her grandson was here on Wednesday night. She said *you* could vouch for that. She made a point of saying we should ask you about it." He lifted his tie, smoothing it down the front of his shirt, a thing with him. "Which means I've got Mrs. Collier saying he was at work that night, and you saying he wasn't, and Donovan swearing he was at school," he said. "Now, there's no way all three of you are telling the truth. I can't see how that's possible, can you?"

The phone on Caren's desk rang twice. She let it go to voice mail.

She'd had five messages from reporters on her office line this morning, and two more calls on her cell phone. The *Donaldsonville Chief* and the *Times-Picayune* in New Orleans, even the *Morning News* in Dallas. She'd ignored them all.

"The night that gal was killed, you told us none of your staff was on the premises."

"That's right. None of the staff was on schedule. I believe I said that, Detective."

"'Asked and answered,' yes," he said.

117

He didn't like her, she could tell. He didn't think she was on his side. "This isn't a courtroom, Tulane. And this ain't New Orleans. You remember that," he said.

"I know where I am."

"You told me no one was *on the property* that night. You were very clear on that," he said. "Near as I could tell, we weren't having a conversation about who was *supposed* to be here on the night the Avalo woman was killed. That's not what I asked."

"Donovan was not here. I don't care what his grandmother said."

Lang nodded, glancing down at his watch, pausing, as if he were giving her a minute to correct herself or change her story while there was still time. Outside, the cops in uniform were still fanned out across Belle Vie. She could see them through the window, running cameras over the ground, past a curious and rather confused-looking tour group led by Bo Johnston in costume. One of the tourists, a man in khakis and a ball cap, was snapping photos of the police activity with the camera on his cell phone. "You know, if there's anything else you want to tell me . . ." Again, Lang paused, offering one last chance. "Now would be the time," he said.

She thought about the stain on her daughter's shirt.

She thought about the dead woman in the supermarket, the fact that she'd inadvertently lied to detectives when she said she'd never seen her before.

Neither of which would be easy to explain away.

So instead she offered up the one thing that would shift his piercing gaze in a different direction. There was something he should know, she said, something she'd discovered just this morning, down by the quarters. "There's a cane knife missing."

Detective Bertrand was instructed to travel ahead of Lang to the police station.

Lang stayed behind, watching two uniformed officers at work inside Jason's Cabin, the last one on the left. The men had heavy flashlights in hand, their beams crisscrossing the black, dusty air, shining hazy light on the insides of the ragged shack: the rusted sugar kettle, the tattered quilt folded beside the straw bed, and the small tin cup waiting on the pine tabletop, as if Jason had just stepped out for a few minutes, instead of a hundred-plus years. The place felt strangely lived in. Caren felt a human presence here, where her great-great-great-grandfather had lived a life of labor, had raised a family within these four walls. She wondered if the cops could sense it, too. She was hanging back, standing in the doorway. It seemed impossible for more than three of them to be in the small shack at the same time. One of them was taking pictures, noting footprints on the ground, many of which Caren recognized as her own, the mark of her boot heels in the dirt. "How long has it been gone?" Lang asked.

He was pointing to the empty space on the wall.

Caren had provided him with a picture of the missing cane knife, torn from one of the coffee-table books they sold in the gift shop. It was a photograph of the exact same slave cabin. In it, the antique tool—a relic from the days when all sugarcane was cut by hand, by men like Caren's ancestors—was hanging on the wall, in the very spot where Lang was standing now. The cop with the camera took his shot. The flash lit up the blank spot on the wall, shooting like a bolt of lightning through the room, and then everything went black again.

"I don't know," she said.

"But it's recent?"

"Yes."

"And Donovan would have had access to this cabin?"

"As would any member of the staff, or Danny for that matter, or any of the tourists who come through. We get over a hundred people here a week, Detective. No one is supposed to be back here unsupervised, but it happens." For all kinds of reasons, she thought. She'd known lovers to hide away in Belle Vie's most private corners—stealing kisses, and much more, in the cottages or the storage shed and, yes, even the quarters—which she'd always thought a strange and twisted choice, but perhaps no stranger than choosing to marry, to seal a hope, on the grounds of a plantation. Belle Vie was a cipher, really, a place in whose beauty one might find pleasure or pain, leisure or labor. People saw, in its iced columns, in the magnolias and aged oaks, what they wanted to see, what their own history told them to. She had answered the cop's question honestly, but Lang seemed to regard this as further evidence of her taking sides. He let out a small sigh, made a note in his pad, clicking his ink pen two times.

"You think that's what killed her?" Caren asked.

"It's a potential match for the wounds on her neck, yes, ma'am," he said. "Would have been nice to have had this information in hand when we were here yesterday morning. Thought you said you did a full inspection of the property."

"I brought it to your attention as soon as I noticed it."

Then she told him, "That's new, too."

She was pointing to something else odd.

On top of the wooden table, there were globs of milky white candle wax and the burnt wicks of cheap votives. It was yet another thing she'd missed when she'd been too spooked to stick around yesterday morning, too scared to stay in the cabin alone.

Lang noted this, too.

The cop with the camera took a few shots.

And then Lang glanced around the small cabin one more time, his eyes sweeping nearly every corner. He seemed puzzled. There was no blood in here, no sign of a struggle, and he was no closer to understanding where Inés Avalo was killed.

He clicked his pen closed, tucked his pad in his suit jacket.

He was heading to the station, he said. His officers would be on-site for at least another hour or so, combing the grounds, the open fields. Caren knew the limits of the warrant, which was signed late last night by a parish judge. She'd read it carefully this morning. The uniformed officers had arrived first. They'd gone through the schoolhouse and the employees' greenroom. She'd led them to the main house and the guest cottages and the groundskeeper's shed. The gift shop and the library were off limits, at least according to this warrant. They were the two buildings farthest from the grave site. She'd made that point several times during her interviews. She knew the detectives were free to return to the judge at any time, as the case progressed. The more information they gathered, the wider their scope of authority, their power to open any door. Lang was on his way to the station now, where Donovan had been taken in a cop car.

You ain't have to call the police, he'd said.

Caren was still bothered by it, those strange parting words.

9

Staff meetings were held twice weekly, on Wednesdays and Fridays, always promptly after the 9:15 show—and the one scheduled for this morning had been on the books long before the presence of law enforcement on the property. They met in the old schoolhouse usually, but some days they would gather on the south lawn, the wide swath of shaded grass between the schoolhouse and the parking lot, if the weather held. By midmorning, it looked like rain again. The sky had clouded over, and so after the morning's performance, Caren brought everyone together right there in the old schoolhouse, in front of the stage. Lorraine and Pearl, Val Marchand and Kimberly Reece and the other Belle Vie Players. Shep and Ennis Mabry, Dell and Shauna. And Nikki Hubbard and Bo Johnston, who were sitting next to each other in the first row of folding chairs. Eddie Knoxville was holding a plastic Saints cup, his cheeks flushed a drinker's pink. He had his black riding boots propped on the edge of the stage, where Cornelius McCrary was sitting, his Air Jordans dangling. Luis, now the sole member of the maintenance crew, was standing solemnly near the back wall. Danny Olmsted was here, too, though he had no real reason to be. She could have made an issue of it. But Danny, for better or worse, was a part of this family, too, and she wanted to hear what he had to say. Lorraine had her arms folded across her bosom, waiting. Pearl was sucking on the stone of a peach. The only people missing were Gerald, whom she'd already given the morning off, after he'd stood watch through the night, and the high school girls who worked part-time in the gift shop. And Donovan, of course.

She wanted to start there.

"Any of you talk to Donovan?"

Bo Johnston, who'd been cast as the overseer for his height and the strength implied by the broad span of his shoulders, raised a hand. "I saw his car in the parking lot this morning." Nikki, sitting close beside him, nodded. "Me, too," she hummed.

There were a few curious looks around the room.

"So where in the hell is he?" Cornelius said.

He had an afro pick sticking out of his uncombed hair, and he was wearing too much cologne, something Caren had previously made a note of in his personnel file.

"He's with police detectives," she said.

"Oh, good lord," Ennis said. He shook his head gravely, twisting the brim of his felt hat in his hands.

Lorraine sucked her teeth in disgust. "I told you," she said to the rest of them. "Didn't I tell you?" She pulled a cigarette from behind her ear and set it between her lips, even though she knew good and well she wasn't allowed to smoke in here.

"Tell them what, Lorraine?" Caren said.

"I told you they were going to try to put this on one of us," Lorraine said, preaching to her own choir. Pearl nodded. "Yep, that's just what you said." She pulled the peach pit from her mouth and stowed it in her apron pocket, saving it for later.

"No one here is a suspect," Caren said, though she wasn't sure she believed that. She was present during Donovan's police interview, and they were sure treating him like a suspect.

"But just so I'm clear," she said, "none of you have talked to him?"

There were head-shakes among the staff.

"Huh-uh," Cornelius said.

Danny Olmsted cleared his throat. "I left three messages."

Shauna said she'd left messages as well. "I told him something was up, but he never called me back." Between shows, she'd slid on a pair of black jeans under her slave costume to keep warm. On her feet were sheepskin-lined boots, a pair of pink Uggs.

"Me neither," Cornelius added. "Not a text, not a word from the dude."

"Since when?"

"Saturday."

He looked around at the others, pushing for consensus.

Shauna nodded. Dell, too.

Danny Olmsted was the only one not looking Caren in the eye.

"Saturday?" she repeated.

Cornelius said, "Yeah." Nikki said she'd last seen him leaving work.

So, apparently, not a single one of them had had any contact with Donovan for days, and certainly not since that woman was killed. It was the very thing that had been bothering Caren since he'd been in her office this morning. The more she thought about it, the more the whole interview seemed peculiar to her, starting with Donovan's demeanor. He frankly didn't appear to be taking it all that seriously, displaying little solemnity or alarm over the policemen's questions. He hadn't been on the grounds the morning the body was discovered and no one had spoken to him. It was at least plausible, she thought, that Donovan didn't even know a crime had occurred.

"Does Donovan know what happened?"

"You mean the dead girl?" Val said.

"I sure *hope* he don't know nothing about it," Ennis said.

"Aw, hell, Ennis," Lorraine said. "You know Donovan better than that."

Eddie Knoxville, sipping whatever concoction he had hidden in his black-and-gold Saints mug, shrugged; he wasn't so sure. Kimberly Reece was clutching a cup of coffee she'd somehow talked Lorraine into hand-delivering. She was as indulged and pampered as the character she played, Manette, the planter's daughter. "I always kind of liked Donovan," she said, sounding as if she might never see him again, as if Donovan's presumed involvement were already a done deal. Behind her, Dell rolled her eyes.

"Look," Caren said, because she didn't think it would do any good to scare them, "the detectives just want to talk to him. They just have a few questions, that's all."

"Questions about the murder?" Danny asked.

Caren stared at him for a moment. "Well, what else would they be asking about?" He opened his mouth to say something, then clamped it shut. She thought again of Donovan's parting words in her office. *You ain't have to call the police.* If Donovan didn't know about the murder, the body of Inés Avalo on the grounds, then what did he mean by that? What other reason would she have had to call the cops?

"Danny?" she said, waiting on an answer.

Cornelius was eyeballing Danny, hard.

Lorraine was shaking her head at him, slowly, back and forth.

Caren guessed something was up. She had long known there were things they didn't tell her, as a rule. She'd known that since she started here. They didn't consider her one of them. Apart from Lorraine, Ennis, and Luis, they didn't know her personal history, her upbringing as the daughter of the plantation's cook. To them, she was management, with a capital M, the eyes and ears of Raymond Clancy. It drew a line between them, like the fence between Belle Vie and those workers in the fields. She worked in the big house now, an ascension of class and station that alienated her from everyone around her, people she worked with every day, even people like Lorraine, whom she'd grown up with, people who were, for all intents and purposes, family. They didn't trust her, any more than Donovan had in her office. They didn't believe her when she said, "If you know something about Donovan, something to do with this investigation, I promise it'll be better for you, and for him, if you speak up now."

Danny didn't say anything more.

Ennis and Lorraine exchanged looks, but they too were awfully quiet.

Pearl let out a low, rolling whistle.

"Fine, then," Caren said.

"Something wrong, Miss C?"

She looked down at her clipboard, shuffling papers back and forth. She didn't want them to know how it cut, the way it seemed they didn't really *see* her. Besides her relationship with her daughter, Morgan, some days Caren felt totally alone out here.

"We'll run the eleven-o'clock show on schedule," she said, sticking to her talking points, the meeting's agenda. "Ennis, are you still okay taking over Donovan's part?"

Ennis stood, pressing his felt hat against his breastbone. In a god-awful dialect, something right out of *Uncle Tom's Cabin*, he ducked his head and repeated a few lines of Donovan's big speech near the end of the play. "Dem Yankee whites can't make me leave dis here land. Dis here mah home. Freedom weren't meant nothing without Belle Vie."

Eddie Knoxville cracked a smile.

Nikki Hubbard snickered. She nudged Shep, sitting to her left, who, Caren realized, had been asleep this whole time. "That's fine, Ennis," she said. She glanced at her clipboard, scanning the week's schedule. "Lorraine, I'll need you to prepare a tasting menu tomorrow for the Whitman wedding. They want to finalize the food as soon as possible. And, Luis, they'll probably want a look at the cottages, since I believe they're planning to have the bridesmaids and the groomsmen dress and wait in there before the guests arrive for the ceremony." She tried to catch his eye. "So if you could just take a second to look at the grounds out there and replace any wilted flowers and clip the hedges." Luis nodded, still looking somber, and Caren felt another wave of guilt about firing Miguel. "*Gracias*," she said, wishing at once she'd said it in English.

"Okay, then," she said to the others. "We'll try to stay on schedule as best we can. Mr. Clancy was very clear that we should go about our business as usual."

"Hmph."

"You have something you want to say, Lorraine?"

"Is that all he said?"

"Well, of course, he's upset that someone died," Caren added charitably.

"What about the sale?" Val asked.

"What sale?"

Val shot Lorraine a look.

Eddie, too. "Go on," he said. "Tell her."

"Tell me what?" Caren said, looking around the room.

"So you ain't heard, then?"

"Heard what?"

Lorraine smirked, drawing it out.

Pearl shot up a hand. "Clancy's going to sell the plantation."

Lorraine glared at her line cook, irritated at having been robbed of her chance to impart this big news, to Caren especially, who was frankly stunned by what she'd heard. She didn't say anything right away. She couldn't, really. She grew so still and quiet that she could count each breath in the back of her throat. When she finally spoke, her voice came out thin and dry. "Where did you hear this, Lorraine?"

"We don't know anything for sure," Dell said.

"Oh, it's something going on, baby."

"What are you talking about?"

Lorraine sighed, gracefully moving her heavy weight as she walked across the schoolhouse toward Caren, lowering her voice, selling the conspiratorial nature of what she was about to say. "I was out to Leland's place this morning, up in Baker, and Raymond come by to see his daddy. He had papers on him, a *lot* of papers. And he wanted Leland to sign. Bobby also called over to the house, twice, only Raymond wouldn't put him on the phone, hushing the day nurses and pushing them out of Mr. Leland's room. I was in the kitchen mostly, but I swear I heard them talking about selling Belle Vie. Raymond was trying to get his daddy to agree to it."

"You know anything about this, Miss C?" Ennis said.

Caren swallowed and said, "No, I haven't heard anything like that."

She couldn't imagine it was true. She could hardly imagine a world without Belle Vie, the way she'd always known it, with the Clancys and Luis and Lorraine, the kitchen where she'd spent her childhood. It had always been the same, even and especially in the year Caren had returned, waiting for her when she needed a place to stay and a way to start over. She thought of her mother, too. She couldn't help it. The last time she'd seen Helen was here, at Belle Vie, an argument that began and ended in the stone kitchen.

Val leaned back, folding her long, manicured fingers around a bony knee. Like the delicate Madame Duquesne, the character she played, she had a kind of timeless beauty, pale skin and red lips, all of it well preserved. "Well, I'd sell it," she said, waving away the disapproving looks popping up across the room. "This is riverfront property here, prime real estate, and worth a hell of a lot of money."

"Yeah, but what about us?"

"I've been here going on eight years," Ennis said. "What am I supposed to do if all this is just up and gone? I'm near sixty-four. I can't make it on no Social Security."

"It's a mistake," Danny said, shaking his head.

"Sure it's a mistake," Lorraine said.

Nikki was running her fingers through a chunk of processed hair, holding it out in front of her eyes, checking for split ends. Her red-and-black Donaldsonville High School letterman's jacket (class of '06) was draped across her shoulders. She and Shauna, Bo, and Eddie Knoxville had, so far, remained point-edly silent on the topic.

"I mean, if Raymond Clancy is serious about this, then he's making a huge mistake," Danny said. "This is a piece of history of major significance. It's been preserved almost better than any like it in the state, or in the country for that matter."

"He can't just close it down like a Holiday Inn, a rent-a-hall, or something," Lorraine said.

"It's his property, he can do whatever he wants with it," Dell said sourly.

"Danny's right, though," Lorraine said. "This is history."

Here, Shauna spoke softly. "I never knew even half of this stuff before I started working here . . . the way the slaves worked the fields, cutting all that cane by hand. I never really seen it up close like this, not before I got a job here. The way they lived and stuff, people like us. I mean, black folks really did something here. There wouldn't have been no sugar hardly anywhere if it weren't for what we did out here."

"That's why this don't make any sense," Ennis said. "It ain't like the Clancys to just up and sell all of a sudden. They've always been good about keeping all this open, keeping the history for the kids. You know, so people don't ever forget."

"It ain't like *Leland* Clancy," Lorraine corrected. "But this is all Raymond, and that one don't give a shit about nobody and nothing that don't line his pants pockets."

"I know the university would love to get its hands on some of the research materials housed here," Danny said, scratching at his chin. "It would be a real score."

"I bet it's Merryvale Properties, Giles Schuyler's group," Val said, still playing the game of real estate speculator. A one-time agent herself, she got out of the business the previous year when the market imploded and several properties she was planning to flip were put in foreclosure by out-of-state banks. "He and Clancy are friends, you know. I bet he's going to turn the whole thing over for development, another one of those high-end subdivisions." She was already allowing herself to get excited about the idea.

Bo Johnston shrugged. "That might not be so bad."

"That's some good construction work," Eddie Knoxville added, even though he was way too old, and too drunk, to do anybody any good on a construction site.

"Aw, hell," Cornelius said, scratching at his 'fro. "We ain't getting no construction jobs in this parish. Ain't no contractor gon' pay us fifteen an hour if he can pay some Mexican nine, hell, eight an hour, you feel me? Shit, we'd be lucky to work security out there, lucky to get a gig mowing lawns or some shit. No offense, Luis."

Luis, in his grass-stained khakis, hooked his thumbs in his pockets.

He hadn't said a single word during the entire staff meeting.

Caren looked over at Lorraine and told her there was no way Raymond Clancy would sell something that had been in his family for generations, going all the way back to the years after the Civil War, not without saying something to her about it. She found it unbelievable that Raymond would keep something like this from her, the general manager and the only person living on the place—to say nothing of her own personal history here. Members of her family had worked at Belle Vie, in one capacity or another, for as long as the Clancys had owned the plantation, longer even. She'd known Raymond her whole life. Her mother had cooked his every meal for most of his childhood.

"I'm sure he would have said something," she said, only just then remembering Bobby's sudden appearance in the parish, his sly report that he was keeping an eye on things, most especially what his brother might be up to. He'd made the same complaint as Lorraine, the bitter observation that his brother, Raymond, was all about money.

"Ask him, then," Lorraine said, hands on her hips, as if she were daring Caren to do just that. "Go on and ask Raymond what he and his daddy were talking about today. I'm not stupid, baby. I know what I heard." She tucked the unlit cigarette back behind her ear. Pearl, standing a full foot below Lorraine's chin, nodded her support.

"Yeah, you ask him," Ennis said. "We got a right to know."

"Shit," said Cornelius. "I need to know if I need to be looking for a job."

"Slow down, y'all," Dell said.

Dell, the third-oldest among the cast, behind Ennis and Eddie Knoxville, was wearing a red jogging suit and white sneakers, Keds knockoffs from Walmart or the Family Dollar. Caren had always appreciated her practical, no-nonsense manner. "Let's just wait and see what she finds out," Dell said. Even she seemed to demand an answer, one way or another. And it fell to Caren, their boss and the only one on the plantation besides Lorraine who'd ever spoken two words to Raymond Clancy, to find it. "Would you?" Ennis asked. "Would you talk to him, Miss C?"

Outside, the line for the next show was already forming.

She heard voices, women mostly, a sorority, or a book club maybe.

"I'm sure it's nothing," Caren said, urging them to get back to work, even as she felt her own legs unsteady beneath her. What *was* Raymond up to? She, too, thought she had a right to know.

Within minutes, the audience members were filing in. Caren hung around just long enough to introduce the play, slipping out quietly at the start of Monsieur Duquesne's first lines, words to his new bride upon arriving at their new homestead. "Ah, *ma chère*," he says, "we shall make a fine life here indeed."

The same lines, three days a week.

The whole thing was on a continuous loop, had been for years.

She walked to the main house and placed a call to Raymond's office. Joyce, his secretary, was unable to produce her boss or be in any way specific about when he might be available. Not once, but three times Caren called, trying to get a hold of him. By lunchtime, she'd already decided on a more direct approach. She left early to get Morgan from school, planning a single stop along the way. On the highway, she passed the exit for Laurel Springs, heading straight for Clancy's law office in Baton Rouge.

10

She'd never taken to the city. Nor did she have any deep love for sleepy Donaldsonville, the town where she was born, where she'd gone to grade school and high school, her mother driving her to town every day before she went to work in the heat of Belle Vie's kitchen. It was New Orleans that had always held Caren's imagination, held her heart in the palm of its jeweled hand, in the breath of every blue note creeping out of somebody's window, down streets glowing coral and pink, where folks drank French coffee and bourbon on their porch steps, chatted up their neighbors through the night. She was twelve years old when she first laid eyes on it, a city that never lost the luster and magic she affixed to it in girlhood, the lens through which she first viewed it, one warm day in March. She'd been pulled out of class unexpectedly, her mother making a rare appearance at school midday. Helen Gray wasn't dressed for work, had at some point taken the time to go home and change. She was tall and slim, Helen, possessed of the same sharp features as Caren, cheekbones cut into the putty of her nut-brown skin and a mouth set in a tight line, softened only by sudden laughter, when she would throw her head back, showing the tiny gap between her two front teeth. She was wearing a long skirt that day and a blue sweater set, had slipped on a pair of heels, and on her neck set a circle of pearls. She was dressed for church, it seemed, for some solemn task that lay ahead for both of them.

She nodded toward the passenger seat. "Get in," she said.

Caren slid in without a word and rode the first fifty miles in silence.

She fiddled with the radio until the signal gave out. And only once did she trouble to ask her mother, "Where are we going?" Helen stared at the road ahead.

They came into the city from the west.

Helen rolled down the window at a certain point and lit a cigarette.

She was tense, Caren could tell, but also loving and openly solicitous the further east they got, reaching across the upholstered front seat from time to time to pat Caren's leg. She wanted her daughter to know she was on her side, no matter what came next.

Caren kept her face pressed to the passenger-side window, taking in the suburban sprawl of Kenner and Metairie, the flat, gray strip malls and big-box stores and houses made of cheap wood, their back sides pressed up against the interstate, all the while catching glimpses of her reflection in the glass. She hadn't combed her hair, hadn't bothered to smooth the kinks along her hairline or change her clothes. She was still in her school jeans, her green-and-white gym sneakers, and a worn T-shirt. This, too, she would come to hold against her mother. She'd never been given a chance.

He lived in Uptown, on Chestnut Street.

He was a doctor, a specialist of some sort, one of the few blacks who'd been welcomed into the oak-lined neighborhood of colonials and Victorians, of bankers and lawyers and retired businessmen. Even as early as the 1970s, Glenn Carle was a respected member of that community, a family man, with a wife and two kids.

They were in the front yard that day, all of them.

Helen parked their white Pontiac across the street.

The house was only a few blocks from Napoleon Avenue. Caren could hear music from a nearby restaurant—not ragtime, but something like it, something bluesy and full of long notes, wafting from two streets over. The sun was almost setting. She asked her mother why they were here, and Helen nodded to the man in the yard of the butter-yellow house. He was sitting on the porch steps with a newspaper folded into a tight square, slippers on his feet, looking up from time to time to watch his kids playing . . . which is how he saw them, parked across the street, hidden in the shade of an old oak.

"That," her mother said matter-of-factly, "is your father."

He stepped down from the porch, suddenly ushering his family inside for the evening, the wife and his two kids, a boy and a girl, the girl not that much older than Caren. He waited and watched them gathering balls and books and a folded-up lawn chair that, in this neighborhood, would have been gauche to leave sitting outside overnight. He waited until his whole family was inside the house before crossing the street. Caren was slouched in the front seat of her mother's car, feeling her stomach lift and then sink, feeling a clammy sweat across her back and chest. He didn't look anything like her, she thought, with his thick arms, his dark skin, and narrow, almost delicate features. He put one hand on the roof of the car, the other on the window frame, leaning in, addressing her mother first. He didn't seem angry, or even exasperated. Still, there was no joy in his face, no pleasure in their sudden appearance here, outside of his home. Looking at Caren's mother, he sighed and shook his head.

"Come on, Helen," was all he said.

Then he looked at Caren, for a long time actually, the corners of his mouth turning up, not so much into a smile as an expression of marvel, wonder, and what-if. Caren felt her cheeks burn.

He reached into the car, reached all the way across the front seat for her left hand, his skin incredibly soft. He held her hand, gave it a squeeze, then nodded to Helen and turned and walked back across the street to the front steps of his house. Years later, when he thought Caren was old enough to understand, to accept his version of an apology, he would say he felt he owed something to the people with whom he had set down roots. Family is fate, he'd said; but it's also a choice.

Her mother seemed to think this would finally put the whole ugly thing to rest, this question of where and to whom Caren really belonged. The facts about her father had been made plain, hadn't they? He was a man neither one of them could have. "I'm your mother," she'd said on that long car ride home. "I'm your family." But a seed of resentment was planted that day, one that grew through Caren's teen years. Up till then, she had only ever known herself as a Gray, as the daughter of a woman whose whole life had been spent in Ascension Parish, whose very identity had been formed around a legacy of labor on a plantation. And now Caren wanted something more. She peppered her mother with questions about her dad, finally in her seventeenth year getting the barest of details, including the story of her parents' meeting at a wedding reception at Belle Vie, where her father was a guest. He'd ended up hanging around the kitchen after hours, a doctor with his tie hanging loose, looking for the pretty girl who'd served him earlier. She came down the steps with a smile. They were, both of them, testing out a mutual attraction that had come on strong and unexpected. It was an affection that held on for a few months, actually, with Caren's father making the nearly hundred-mile drive at least once a week, until he just didn't anymore, until he went back to his wife and his doctor's life and the butter-yellow house in Uptown—an outcome Helen swore she saw coming. She was a country girl, after all, a cook, and a woman men like Caren's father just didn't marry. Helen said she knew he would never leave his world in New Orleans. But what Caren could never understand is why they didn't leave theirs. She couldn't understand staying at Belle Vie, in the tiny world of Ascension Parish, when just down the highway there was a father, a man, and a life that Caren imagined was far better than the one her mother had given her, a childhood spent on a plantation, in the shadow of the big house. She started to hate her mother a little after that, for not wanting more. And she started dreaming of a way out.

Raymond Clancy's office was on Third Street, not far from the capitol building. Caren could see the octagonal tower from the twelfth-floor offices of Clancy, Strong, Burnham & Botts, where she was waiting now, looking slightly out of place among the well-heeled clients, men in fine-stitched suits and women in designer boots. Caren was still in jeans and her ropers, which were dotted with mud, having bothered only to change her shirt and tie up her hair with a rubber band before heading out.

When Clancy came out to greet her, she stood, smoothing the line of her jeans. "Gray," he said. "You must have read my mind." His smile was broad and tight. He had large, white, capped teeth and his breath smelled of licorice, or else gin. He gripped her hand while patting her on the back. "I've been meaning to call you," he said, somehow ignoring the fact that she'd phoned his office three times today. He led her down a long, overlit hallway, the walls of which were lined with photographs of partners, past and present, including a large portrait of a young and handsome Leland James Clancy, Esq. It was Bobby, Caren noted, who looked most like his father.

His office was the last one on the right, large and professionally done, with floor-to-ceiling drapes of heavy brocade that framed his view of the Mississippi River, and a credenza that Caren happened to know he'd had his decorator pull from one of the cottages at Belle Vie. The guest chairs in his office matched the carpet, which matched the buttered-beige color of the walls. The décor was attractive and strong, but blander than she would have thought his wealth and position afforded him. Caren couldn't see the point of having that much money if all of it led to beige.

It wasn't until Clancy closed the door behind her that she realized they weren't alone. In a rear corner, on the left side of Clancy's desk, two men were hunched over a laptop computer, the young one, a white guy in his thirties, sitting on a backless ergonomic chair, typing. Someone might have taken him for a young lawyer or a legal aide at the firm, but Caren didn't think so. She'd gone to law school, for a while at least, and she'd lived with a lawyer once, one who had worked in an office just like this one—six, sometimes seven days a week. These two just didn't look the part. The older gentleman was wearing a navy sports coat and no tie and Rockports on his feet. His arms folded across his chest, resting on the rounded topside of his middle-aged belly, he looked like a consultant of some sort, Caren thought. The man's eyes were sharp and blue, and they were unapologetically trained on her, had been since she walked in.

"I hear they got a kid in custody," Clancy said.

"Well, not exactly."

"One of ours, right?"

"Donovan Isaacs. He's one of the Belle Vie Players."

"So he's the state's problem, on paper at least." He looked at the older man, the consultant-type, and directed this last bit toward him. "That's good for us, Larry."

Caren looked back and forth between the two, not understanding the exchange or what Donovan's legal troubles had to do with this man, Larry. "My understanding," she said, to be clear, "is that the detectives from the Sheriff's Department are just asking him some questions, Raymond, same as they did with the rest of the staff. Even me."

"Oh, yes," Clancy said. "They mentioned you."

She started to ask what he meant by that, but he seemed distracted by the other action in the room. The younger aide-type had a BlackBerry that hadn't stopped ringing since she'd walked into the office. He turned away from the computer to answer it, cradling the phone against his shoulder, unbuttoning and rolling his sleeves.

"Yeah," he was saying into the phone.

Larry was listening, resting his chin in his hands.

"Raymond," Caren said.

He turned to her, looking briefly as if he'd forgotten she was there. He slid his hands into his pockets. "Well, I sure hope they catch him, whoever did this thing. They're saying that gal got her throat cut."

I'm here about the case, she told him.

"I need to ask you something."

He was staring again at the two men, but he nodded. "Yeah, sure."

"Are you making plans to sell Belle Vie?"

Raymond turned, his brow wrinkled. "What?"

"Lorraine Banks, from the kitchen staff—"

"I know who she is, Gray."

"She says she was at your father's house this morning."

She paused here, feeling awkward about relaying this second-hand information, gleaned from a woman who fully admitted to eavesdropping on a grown man speaking with his father. "She was at the house this morning, and she said you and your father were discussing a sale. She said you were talking about selling the plantation."

Raymond glanced briefly out the window at the Mississippi River, his expression as murky as its waters. "Well, Lorraine, of all people, ought to know Daddy's not going to live forever. You, too, Gray," he said. Then he turned, looking directly at her. He was being careful with his words, she thought, giving the impression that this whole line of talk was a rehearsal, a trial run. "Look, I don't know what all Lorraine thinks she heard, but it's no secret that Daddy's getting on and my family and I are in the uncomfortable position of having to make decisions about his estate. I mean, the age he is now, I ask him at least a few times a month what he wants to do with all of it. The house in Baker, Belle Vie, even this building we're standing in. Daddy owns this, too."

"I didn't know that."

"And if I'm for real about 2010, then I think—"

On the other side of the room, Larry cleared his throat.

It was the first and only sound he'd uttered.

Raymond nodded in his direction, but continued his remarks to Caren. "In the long run, I think it's clear that I can't keep up the day-to-day of the thing," he said, and Caren nodded, as if this were perfectly understandable, even though she thought the whole day-to-day of Belle Vie was the reason he'd hired her. "And my brother Bobby can't handle that kind of stress. As it is, Bobby is just one more thing for me to worry over since he's nearly forty-five years old and can't be counted on for shit. No job, no home, no family, nothing that would ask him to work hard. He's a goddamned scientific experiment, is what he is. Ought to turn him over to the nearest university, let 'em run whatever kind of test can tell me if he drank himself stupid or was born that way." He sounded so harsh and agitated that Caren couldn't imagine what had happened between the two brothers over the years to make them each speak so unkindly about the other. She made a quick decision to keep to herself the fact that Bobby had dropped by Belle Vie unexpectedly, checking on his brother's handling of things.

Raymond caught himself, softening his language.

"It's just . . . a lot of this stuff falls on me, making family decisions. And I got a lot to think about in the coming months, some opportunities that have come my way." By this point, Larry was eyeing Raymond closely. His brow was arched, and Clancy realized he'd said enough. "I mean, that's even *if* I'm running," he was quick to add.

Larry shook his head, a warning, it seemed.

For some reason, this made Raymond smile.

"Oh, hell, Becht, it'll be in the papers tomorrow," he said. "The guy is toast."

He looked back at Caren, his mood measurably brightened. He put a hand on her shoulder, leaning in conspiratorially, enjoying the moment, the telling of another man's misfortune. "Look, something's opened up for me, Gray, something big. You know Fred Dempsey, that Republican rep from the Seventh District, down to Lake Charles? Well, the man is getting himself a divorce from a bitter, bitter woman, and his whole life story is about to be laid wide open. We're talking sex clubs and pornography," he said, delighted. "And, even worse, it turns out he's been paying all his house staff in cash. I mean, it's going to get ugly. That shit just won't fly, not in a Senate race. And it could open up the field for a guy like me. There's no real contender in the Democratic primary. I could take the whole thing." He smiled, and then caught himself, trying to tame his excitement, to find a note of humility. "People in this state know what we're about, the Clancys. Daddy put his money where his mouth was, donating to the schools and such, scholarships and all that. Even way back when, when it wasn't popular at all, he made sure that black kids got as good as whites. I mean, that's just the kind of good public service that folks associate with a Clancy. And I could really do something with that." In other words, Caren thought, Raymond had rightly calculated the impossibility of winning so much as a PTA seat in the state of Louisiana without the black vote, and this Larry Becht—whom Caren now understood to be a consultant hired not by the firm but for Clancy's own political ambition—was here to help him turn the family name into political capital. Larry did not look the least bit pleased with Raymond's lack of discretion. He didn't look pleased with Caren, either, or her presence here. "But this is all down the line at this point," Clancy said. "You can tell Lorraine nothing's happening. Tell her to stop being so goddamned nosy for once."

"I'll let you tell her that."

Raymond laughed out loud. "I will, I swear I will, Gray."

"So you're not planning to sell?" she asked, because it still felt unclear.

"We don't know what we're going to do, Gray, not at this stage, no. But I promise you'll be the first to know whatever we decide to do with the land out there. Daddy and I know what you've done for Belle Vie, you and your mother."

Caren nodded, but she sensed there was more he wasn't saying.

"Is that it?" Raymond said, smiling, openly relieved, it seemed. "Is that what you drove all this way to ask me?"

"I was hoping to put everyone at ease. They're getting kind of nervous out there," she said, meaning the staff. "It's been a very difficult couple of days."

"Oh, of course, Gray."

"I just thought it would mean a lot if I could tell them their jobs were safe."

"Well, I'll count on you to do just that. We need stability right now, more than anything. It's a mess, this thing that's happened. Makes me sick to my stomach."

His desk phone beeped, followed by the sound of Joyce's smoker's voice.

"Tom Hinman, Mr. Clancy. He's retuning on the state matter."

"Tell him to hold."

"Yes, sir."

The line clicked, and Clancy looked at Larry, who was motioning in Caren's general direction, offering Raymond some silent instruction, some last piece of business to handle. Raymond nodded at him, and then Caren felt his hand on her back. He leaned over her, awkwardly shrinking his normally impressive height and making her feel as if she were under the weight of a massive shadow, a fast-moving rain cloud. "Look, Gray," he said, in a whisper both husky and strong. "We just want to reiterate the importance of not speaking with the press about what's happened out there, that gal killed and all. Now, they'll try to put a story together anyhow, but the less we give 'em, the better. You understand? No reporters, hear? Not a word about a body at Belle Vie or that it was a Groveland worker who was killed. In fact, nothing at all about the Groveland Corporation, okay?"

They'd already gone over this.

She didn't understand the need for a second instruction about his call for silence on the issue, and she told him so. His eyes narrowed a bit, and the grip on her shoulder tightened. "I just want to make sure we're clear, Gray. I wouldn't want to invite any trouble, for my family or yours. We've been good to your family, haven't we, you in particular, Gray?" She knew where he was heading. They had an exchange like this at least once a year, Raymond reminding her what all he and his daddy had done for the Grays. "I think you owe us a little of your trust on this. We wouldn't let you down, wouldn't leave you hanging, no matter what we decide about Belle Vie." His breath was warm, suffocating, really. She tried to understand how they had somehow made it back around to the subject of a sale that supposedly wasn't even happening.

The intercom beeped. It was Joyce again. "Tom Hinman holding, sir."

"I need to take that, Gray."

"Sure."

She was escorted out by Joyce, a middle-aged black woman with impeccable taste. Her hair was stylish and short, and her clothes, silk separates of olive and gold, were cut close to her petite frame. She saw Caren all the way to the bank of elevators in the firm's lobby, holding open the doors when a car arrived and seeing to it that Caren and her muddy boots made it all the way inside and on their way out of the stately building, even going so far as to reach inside the car and press the ground-floor button herself.

Caren arrived at Morgan's school a little before the final bell. She signed the visitors' sheet in the main office, where the receptionist, upon seeing her name and that of the fifth-grader she was there to pick up, stopped her just a few minutes later. Caren had already made her way to the east hallway, which was painted yellow and decorated with a mural of fleurs-de-lis in shades of purple, green, and gold, a different fifth-grader's name written in script inside each lily-shaped symbol. Her daughter's name was near the top: *Morgan Ellis, 9, Rm 112,* Ms. Rivera's homeroom class. She heard a woman behind her, calling her name. Caren turned to see the school's receptionist, her low heels clicking on the tiled floor. Catching her breath, she informed Caren, without any hint of alarm, that a man had been by the school early that afternoon, asking to see a Morgan Gray.

"Morgan?" Caren said. "*My* daughter?" The receptionist, a woman with big, round glasses and tight plum-colored sweater, nodded. It was an older gentleman, Caucasian, she felt the need to add.

"We don't get that a lot," the woman said. "Usually parents alert us if a visit is planned." She offered this last bit as a soft reprimand, scolding Caren for not following the rules. But Caren had planned no such visit, and she couldn't imagine who would have come by the school, asking after her daughter. "Was it a cop?" she said, though she had a niggling feeling that this couldn't be so. She certainly didn't put it past Lang to try to get Morgan away from Caren, to speak to her alone. But Lang, or any cop associated with the case, knew her daughter's last name was Ellis, not Gray.

"No, ma'am," the woman said. "He didn't look like any police officer I've seen." He was wearing jeans, she said, Wranglers, and he just, well, he just didn't seem like a cop. And he wouldn't leave his name when she asked. He'd turned around and walked out of the school's office without saying another word.

"Thank you," Caren said, feeling her mouth go dry.

By the time she made it to the door to Ms. Rivera's classroom, she felt fairly certain it was no cop who'd come by the school. The more she thought about it, the sicker she felt, a breathtaking fear that made her head hurt, made her chest feel cold and hollow, a small cry of panic echoing in the dark. The school bell rang, startling her, and she was quickly pushed back by a stream of fifth-graders spilling out into the hallway. The boys pushed and shoved each other, teasing and laughing. The girls moved more slowly, in groups of two and three, their small heads pressed together, their bell-like voices quietly intense. Inside the classroom, Morgan was still at her desk when Caren entered. She was shrunk down in her chair, wilting under the gaze of her teacher. Donna Rivera was standing over Morgan with her arms crossed and her behind leaned against one of the school desks. She was a dyed blonde in her twenties with a voice like spun cotton and a tendency toward brightly colored sweaters with appliqués of apples or trees or napping cats. She wore a pen on a chain around her neck. "Caren," she said, calling her by her first name, part of a culture of equity and free exchange between parents and teachers that was greatly encouraged by the Laurel Springs School District. It was meant to suggest that she and Caren were in this together, that they had the same investment in the raising up of this child, when, really, nothing could have been further from the truth. "I'm glad you're here," she said. "I was just taking a moment to speak with Morgan here about the need to follow rules." She looked down at Morgan, pausing briefly to give her wayward pupil a chance to agree. "And we've decided she will no longer read unassigned materials during science class or social studies or any other time except what has been set aside as an accepted time for reading. Isn't that right, Morgan?"

"You don't want me to read, got it."

She stood up out of her desk, ready to leave.

"Sit down, Morgan," Caren said, more sternly that she might have if they were alone, because she wanted Ms. Rivera to know she wasn't responsible for everything that came out of her daughter's mouth. "I don't believe Ms. Rivera said she was finished talking." The teacher, perhaps reassured by this show of force, said, "No, she can go."

Morgan practically sprinted out of the classroom, dragging her backpack. Caren was only a few steps behind her when she felt a cool hand at her elbow. Donna Rivera was motioning her away from the classroom door. "May I speak with you a moment?"

"Of course."

Morgan's locker was directly across from the open classroom door, and Caren could see her pulling out her schoolbooks and loading them into her backpack. Inside the locker, she saw several of Morgan's white school shirts, balled up on the shelf.

"Is everything okay at home?"

"Why? Did Morgan say something?"

Donna smiled reassuringly. She tapped her index finger against her lips, trying to find the words, the right way to put whatever it was she was about to say about another person's child. "Well, I think you know we've had some concerns about Morgan's . . . social spirit. I know I've mentioned it before. I'm sure you remember." Caren remembered a single sentence scribbled at the bottom of one of Morgan's report cards, a note about her daughter being very shy, presented then as a character trait and not pathology or anything that would warrant the serious tone of this conversation. "It's just that we're nearing the end of the first semester, and I can't say that Morgan has made a single friend this year. She eats lunch alone, reads during recess, and I never hear her talking with any of the other girls about sleepovers or parties or any activities *outside* of school."

"Well, we live a ways outside of the parish."

"You're out on the plantation, right?"

"That's right."

"Hm . . ."

She nodded to herself, thinking. "I guess I just thought she would have opened up by now," she said. "Sometimes we see this kind of withdrawn behavior with kids who have some personal stress at home." Her voice ended on an up note, and

Caren realized this was meant as a question. She was staring at her, waiting.

"Well, her father's getting married."

"Oh?" the teacher said, though Caren got the sense this was not news to her.

Treading carefully, she said, "And how does Morgan feel about that?"

"She's excited to see Washington, D.C."

Which didn't answer the question, and Caren knew that, but she suddenly wanted out of this impromptu meeting in Ms. Rivera's classroom. Morgan's social spirit, as the woman put it, was about the least of her concerns about her daughter right now. "Well . . . we've got a long drive back." Donna held up a single finger, signaling her to wait for just one more moment. She crossed to her desk and opened the top drawer, from which she pulled a stapled stack of papers that were well-worn and curling at the edges. She walked the papers over to Caren, holding them out. "This is what Morgan was reading in class today," she said. "It's very . . . advanced."

Caren glanced at the top page, taking in the title: "Recovery and Reconciliation and the Emergence of a Free Labor System in Ascension Parish."

But it didn't really register.

Something in the school hallway had caught Caren's attention.

Outside the classroom, Morgan had dropped her book bag at her feet. She was staring, gape-mouthed, at something in the distance, well out of Caren's line of sight.

"Another possible explanation for Morgan's behavior in the classroom is that she is simply too bright for this environment," Ms. Rivera was saying, speaking over Caren's shoulder. "There are some excellent advanced programs at other schools in the state. They're worth looking into. It might be a better fit for someone like Morgan."

In the hallway, Morgan broke into a huge grin.

"Daddy!" she screamed, running down the hall.

Stunned, Caren walked out of the classroom, turning to her left, where she saw her daughter pushing through the crowd of students, racing to the waiting arms of her father. He swept her up, lifting her. Morgan laid her head on his shoulder, a place where she had always felt safe. Eric looked down the length of hallway to Caren. He was wearing a light-gray suit, looking as if he'd just come straight from work, as if he'd decided at his desk, just a few hours earlier, to catch the next flight to New Orleans. The tail of a paisley tie was peeking out of his side pocket, and his shirt collar was unbuttoned. Holding his only child in his arms, he gave Caren a small shrug that suggested he couldn't help himself: *I'm here.* She was struck by how thin he looked. He'd changed his glasses, and his hair was shorter. But it was Eric all right, and Caren felt at once the regret, cutting and familiar, but also, as their eyes met across the noisy school hallway, a sense of joy, relief almost, that this man was Morgan's father.

11

She's not talking," he said.

Eric folded his arms across his chest and leaned back against the cheap Formica countertop of Caren's small kitchen. His suit jacket was in the other room, along with a small overnight bag, set at the foot of the parlor's leather couch. Morgan was upstairs, changing out of her school clothes and washing up before an early dinner. She'd chosen to ride home in her dad's rental car, just the two of them, and he'd again tried to get her to open up, expressing to her the gravity of the situation. "She swears she doesn't know anything about it, that she never even left the house that night," he said wearily. "And she's sticking to her story that the shirt probably isn't even hers. She doesn't know how any blood got there." He shrugged his shoulders, not sure what to make of this entire situation, the very fact that he was standing in her kitchen. He was looking right at her, and Caren felt shy all of a sudden. She felt his eyes on her back as she turned, standing over the hot stove, stirring an array of steaming pots on the burners. Letty had left a chicken casserole in the fridge before leaving work, but Caren had taken one look at it and decided against it. Eric hadn't been in Louisiana in a long, long time, and she wanted him to have the real deal. So she'd borrowed the golf cart from security and driven over to Lorraine's kitchen, begging off bits and pieces of the menu she was working on for tomorrow, and grabbing a bottle of

Bordeaux from the wine room. Lorraine had kindly asked few questions, but was plainly enjoying Caren's nerves. "Word is you got a visitor out there, baby," she said, smiling big.

At her own stove now, she heated Lorraine's food: shrimp fritters; steak *grillade* over sticky rice, roasted cauliflower brushed with salted butter and coriander, and butternut squash mashed with candied yams and ginger. Smoke and steam filled the kitchen, and Caren thought to open a window. The heat was starting to get to her.

Carefully, she said, "Someone came by Morgan's school today."

Eric looked up at her. "What?"

"I thought it was a cop . . . but maybe not."

It was a man in Wranglers, the woman in the front office had said.

Caren had a sudden memory of that red pickup truck on the highway, the one that had tailed them from Laurel Springs the day before, the same truck she'd seen on the farm road by Belle Vie, circling and doubling back, a white man behind the wheel.

"How scared should I be, Caren?"

"I don't know."

"And you're sure it was blood?"

"Yes," she said, hearing aloud the kernel of doubt in her mind. Now, with Eric here, standing in the same room, she wasn't feeling sure of anything, could hardly think straight. "And, anyway, she's acting weird. She's acting like she's hiding something."

She left out the rest of it.

Her panic Thursday night, what she'd done with Morgan's shirt.

She was hiding something, too.

Eric shook his head. "I don't understand. Why would she lie?"

The heat in the kitchen swelled. Caren felt hungry and

light-headed. She started for the small casement window next to the washer and dryer, turning her body sideways to pass Eric. Cracking open the windowpane let in a cool stream of air that shot down the length of the kitchenette, parting the heat and steam. She wiped a film of sweat from her forehead, drying her palm on the front of her jeans. When she crossed from the window back toward the stove, again turning sideways to pass Eric, they came face-to-face for the first time, and he reached for her arm. It wasn't an embrace exactly, and yet the touch paralyzed her, pinning her in place, so close to him that she could feel his breath against her cheek. She could smell his aftershave, a sweet, musky scent that made her think of summer, nights he used to sit out on their old porch. She wondered if Lela let him smoke—or if there were parts of his life, this trip even, that were outside of her authority. "If Morgan saw something . . ." he whispered, his voice trailing off at the mere suggestion of what that could mean for his daughter. He could hardly tolerate the thought and backed away from it almost as quickly as it had come to him. He was trying to stay levelheaded, to be practical about this. "What are the cops saying?"

"They think the woman was killed over here, somewhere on the plantation. There was a knife missing from one of the slave cottages, an antique cane knife."

"A what?"

"It's a knife for cutting sugarcane," she said, holding her hands a foot or so apart to offer some idea of what she was talking about, a knife capable of cutting through a stalk of cane in a single swipe. "The thing might have been over a hundred years old."

"And they haven't found it?"

She shook her head.

"Well, who all have they been talking to?"

"The staff mostly. They took Donovan Isaacs to the station this morning."

"Why him?"

"He didn't come to work yesterday morning. And I get the sense they don't think he's being completely truthful about where he was the night she was killed."

"What do *you* think?"

"I'm not entirely convinced Donovan knows there's been a murder at all."

Eric sighed, shoving his hands into the pockets of his now wrinkled slacks. He looked exhausted. Standing this close, Caren could see gray hairs creeping in at his temples. That's new, she thought.

"Who was she?" he asked. "The dead woman."

For some reason, it made her sad to say her name out loud. "She was a planter out in the cane fields," Caren said, and left it at that.

"They talk to any of the crew out there?"

"Yes," she said with a nod. "But I don't know much more than that."

Eric folded and unfolded his arms again, as if he couldn't decide what to do with his nervous hands, finally resting them in the damp pits of his dress shirt. "What I don't understand . . .if she was a field-worker, what was she doing on this side of the fence. Why was she over *here* . . . on the plantation?"

Caren shrugged.

She'd been wondering the same thing.

There were soft footsteps on the stairs, which she noticed before Eric did because she had lived in this apartment for four years and knew the sound of her daughter's movements. She had some vague sense that it was a mistake for her and Eric to be caught standing together this way, so close that their knees were touching, that it might confuse or upset Morgan in some way. But she didn't move right away, and soon it was too late. Morgan was standing with them in the kitchen. She'd changed into a jean skirt and a long-sleeve purple T-shirt, and she'd borrowed one of Caren's leather belts, which hung loose around her girlish hips. She stood still for a moment at the foot of the stairs, staring at the rare sight of her mother and father, together in the same space. She looked at both of them and smiled brightly. Eric turned and saw her then. He had the same conservative impulse Caren had had . . . only he didn't hesitate to put distance between the two of them, dropping her arm at once.

They took a walk after dinner, under the willows at dusk.

Eric, in all the years Caren had lived here, had been to the plantation only once before, and even then he'd hardly left the main house, playing with Morgan for an hour or so on the front lawn before taking her to the zoo in Baton Rouge. And the whole time they were dating, even after Morgan was born, Caren never once brought him home, to Ascension Parish; it was years before she told him what her mother did for a living, or described the grass behind the plantation kitchen where Caren had played as a child. He'd never crossed Belle Vie's green fields or walked the main road at dusk or paused before the garden to take in the autumn crocus and white hydrangea, or the bed of pansies planted in a rusted, three-foot-wide sugar kettle, once used for boiling cane into molasses. She could sense Morgan's delight in showing her dad where she lived. Eric was holding her hand while craning his neck, glancing up at the arch of magnolias overhead. It was a beautiful evening, cool and moist and nicely lit by the setting sun. But it would be dark soon, and Caren wanted everyone home, behind closed doors.

"Let's start back, guys," she called.

Eric held out a second hand for Morgan, who took a large knee-bending jump in his direction. They'd gone as far as the guest cottages, Manette and Le Roy, and Caren thought it just as well to avoid the quarters at this hour. She turned and led the way back to the library. She could hear them behind her. Morgan was telling Eric about a book she'd read for school, about a girl who had a magic coat made of colorful scraps of cloth. Skipping a few feet ahead, she tried to describe for her father the kind of dress she wanted to wear to his wedding. It involved rhinestones and lots of tulle.

At the house, Eric supervised homework and bedtime, while Caren cleaned the kitchen and made a bed for Eric on the couch out of blankets and flannel sheets. He came down as she was tucking the sheets underneath the couch cushions, smoothing the cotton with her hands. Her skin was rough—puckered on one side from dish-washing, and dry and ashy on the other. She wished she looked better, well-rested and fresh, that she'd prepared for this moment, Eric in her home. She knew it wouldn't change anything, for either one of them. Still, it mattered to her in some small way.

"She's sleep," Eric said.

"She didn't ask for me?"

"She's tired, Caren."

Caren nodded and said, "I know."

"What time is it, anyway?"

She looked at her wristwatch. "It's a little after eight."

"Can I use your phone?" he asked. "I never charged my cell before I left."

"Of course."

She brought him the cordless from the kitchen, then closed the door to the parlor, giving him some privacy. Alone in the kitchen, she finished the bottle of wine from dinner, eventually heading upstairs when she realized she could hear Eric's voice through the wall, when it became clear, by his gentle tone, that he was talking to Lela.

In her room, she changed clothes, then fished through her leather tote bag for a tube of plum-colored lip gloss, the last of her beauty rituals to survive motherhood. There, in the bag, she found the stack of photocopied pages she'd thrown into the bottom of her purse hours ago; it was the typed report that Morgan had been reading in class. Curious, she glanced again at the title: "Recovery and Reconciliation and the Emergence of a Free Labor System in Ascension Parish." Looking at the author's name, she made a face. The paper was a copy of Danny's unpublished dissertation.

RECOVERY AND RECONCILIATION AND THE EMERGENCE OF A FREE LABOR SYSTEM IN ASCENSION PARISH

Daniel K. Olmsted
Louisiana State University
Department of History
Doctoral Program

Abstract:

In the fall of 1872, the election of Aaron Nathan Sweats as the first black sheriff of Ascension Parish marked the zenith of a period of racial reconciliation in a parish and a nation still wrecked socially, politically, and economically by the Civil War and the formal government-rebuilding program known as Reconstruction. A free man of color from birth, Sweats was a Boston native, transplanted to Louisiana in his formative years. It can be, and has been, argued that he was ill-prepared to pioneer for his race as the chief law enforcement officer in a sugar-rich parish that had known Negroes as chattel property for over one hundred years. But Sweats proved his presence as more than a token sign of progress. He was not two weeks in office when a cane worker, an ex-slave and a cutter in the fields behind the historic Belle Vie plantation, went missing and was believed to have been the victim of foul play. It is precisely the type of crime that would have gone unprosecuted, or outright ignored, in the days when slavery was legal. But Sweats's determination to find the killer and prosecute the crime is a study of the ways in which both the region and the country's relationship to black labor were profoundly altered for generations to come.

The paper was dated May 26, 2001, and stopped midsentence on page 25:

According to the only remaining records of the investigation, blood was discovered in the cane fields, but the victim, an ex-slave called "Jason" was never found

Caren paused over the name.

She thought by now she'd heard all the stories, the legends and tall tales. But she had never heard anything about an investigation into Jason's death, and by a black sheriff no less, just a few years after the Civil War. The suggestion here, in print, was that Jason, her great-great-great-grandfather, had been murdered.

She couldn't understand how she'd never known about this.

And what's more, she couldn't understand why her nine-year-old daughter was reading a graduate-level thesis on the subject . . . or how she had gotten her hands on it.

She sat on the edge of her bed, skimming the pages.

There was a soft knock on her bedroom door.

At her invitation, Eric leaned his head over the threshold.

"I just wanted to say good night," he said, hanging behind the door, kind of, careful not to make any assumptions about where he was welcome in her home.

She turned Danny's manuscript face down on the bed.

"It's okay," she said. "You can come in."

He stepped over the threshold in his bare feet, stopping just a few inches beyond the door, determined to put limits on the situation, for both of them. He leaned against her maple chest of drawers, the one by the door. She felt a hot batch of nerves, pinpricks down her spine. She hadn't had a man in her bedroom, or her bed, in years.

"How is she?" she asked. "Lela."

"Worried."

"About you being here with me?"

They were the first words out of her mouth, and she regretted them immediately.

Across the room, Eric smiled.

He adjusted and readjusted his glasses, grinning to himself, tickled in some way he did not choose to share with her. "No, not that," he said, making her feel foolish for presuming to know anything about Lela's feelings or her faith in her future marriage. "It's just that I left so suddenly," he said. "She's as worried about Morgan as I am."

"You told her, then?"

"Well, yes," he said, a peculiar look on his face, as if he just now realized how little she understood about his life anymore. "She would have come down, too, but . . ." He wisely let the rest of that thought, and all its uncomfortable social implications, wilt away. At that moment, Caren felt she could go the rest of her life without ever meeting Lela Gramm. "Listen, Caren," Eric said, getting back to the issue at hand. "I'll talk to Morgan again in the morning. I'm sure it's nothing, just a bit of confusion is all. We'll get it all figured out, I promise."

"Okay," she said.

"Okay, then."

He lingered in the doorway, rolling something around in his mind. He was biting his bottom lip, chewing a corner of his own flesh, eyeing her on top of the bed. She was wearing one of his old Tulane T-shirts, faded and torn. He tapped his fingers on the dented wood of the door's frame. "It's good to see you again," he said quietly.

As he started out the door, she called his name. "Eric."

She didn't know why she was about to tell him this, except that she didn't have many people in her life she could talk to anymore.

"I think Raymond is going to sell the plantation."

Eric paused, his hand on the door. "When?"

"Soon."

The conversation in his office had done nothing to clear this notion, and it suddenly occurred to Caren that if she were forced to choose between Raymond and Lorraine as the one most likely to tell her the truth, she would pick Lorraine every time.

Raymond is definitely up to something, she thought.

"He had a guy in his office today," she said. "A Larry Becht, I think. They were talking politics, and they were both telling me over and over not to talk to the press about what happened. There was definitely an air of damage control in the room."

"Larry Becht? Are you sure?"

"Pretty sure."

"That guy's a Republican strategist. He runs an office out of Alexandria, Virginia."

Caren shook her head. "No, they were talking about the

Democratic primary."

"Caren, Larry Becht is part of that whole take-back-the-country crowd. He definitely swings hard to the right. If he's down here to launch a campaign, then Clancy is planning to run as a Democrat in name only, some kind of bait-and-switch."

"He's trading on his family name is what he's doing, the way black people, in particular, feel about the Clancys," she said. "It's his ticket to the Senate, he thinks."

Eric made a humming sound. "No kidding."

"You know, Leland was the main one pushing to integrate the public schools in this state, way back in the late fifties and early sixties. When every other businessman and politician in power was dragging his feet or just out-and-out swearing against it."

"And now Raymond's claiming it as his legacy? To court the black vote?"

Caren nodded. "The Clancys have always been big on 'Negro education.'" Her tone was not bitter, but there was something dry and distant there. Eric was scratching at his chin. She knew this information was of a more than casual interest to Eric, himself a political player. "I wonder why he would sell his place now?" he said. "Hasn't it been in his family for generations? I thought you Southerners liked all this Civil War shit."

Caren shot him a dirty look.

Tulane or no Tulane, what Eric didn't know about the South could fill several shelves of his office in Washington. But she didn't say anything. She didn't want to give the impression that she was in any way defending Belle Vie or what it stood for.

She wasn't.

"That ought to be Becht's pitch," Eric said. "Positioning Clancy as a legacy, a keeper of America's true heritage," he said. "That's how I'd do it, anyway."

"I don't really know what he's thinking or what he plans to

do with the land." She pulled her knees to her chest, wrapping her arms around her legs the way Morgan sometimes did when she was feeling particularly insecure. "This place is over a hundred and fifty years old. I guess I just thought it would always be here."

"You think someone would tear it down?"

"I think if Raymond and his brother let it go, anything could happen."

"So what are you going to do?"

She looked down, fingering a knot of thread on the bed's quilt. "I guess I need to start making some contingency plans. I have to start thinking about where we would go. I could get a place in Baton Rouge, I guess, start over there. It's not far from her school." When she caught Eric's eye again, she could see he was frowning. He grew quiet, pensive, his mouth turned down in a way that made him look sad.

"They have good schools in D.C., too, Caren."

Here we go, she thought.

"I'd love to have Morgan in Washington," he said. "You know that."

"And, what, send her to Sidwell Friends with Malia and Sasha?" She was teasing him about his social connections, his new life inside a White House administration. He'd been working in Obama's Office of Urban Affairs for the past ten months, one of the very first hired.

"Maybe," Eric said matter-of-factly, as if a spot in a private school were the very least of what was available to him in D.C. "I mean, I could make a call."

"You're serious?"

"We'd love to have Morgan in D.C."

The word, *we*, cut a little.

He slid his glasses along the bridge of his nose. "Well, at least

162

think about it," he said, and she nodded, feeling a queer warmth at the back of her throat, a vague sense that she might cry. For a moment, she actually wished she'd never called him at all.

"I will," she said.

"Well," he said. "Goodnight, then, Caren."

She could still smell him in the room, long after he was gone.

She lay awake in the dark, unable to sleep, seeing his face every time she closed her eyes. Restless and agitated, she rolled over onto her left side, feeling the cool, empty spot beside her. She squeezed her eyes shut, trying in vain to push him out of her thoughts . . . until finally, alone in the dark, she surrendered. *Eric*, she said, whispering his name and letting her mind drift all the way back to their beginning.

It was an unlikely and unexpected romance. They hadn't actually started dating until long after they'd met, almost a year after she'd walked out of Tulane; it was, not coincidentally, around the same time she'd asked her dad, one last time, for help with school. There had been checks here and there during her undergraduate studies, but now, trying to finish law school, she told him she needed something more.

He asked after her mother.

She didn't mention their falling-out.

Instead, she told him that if she reenrolled in law school now, full-time, she could still catch up. She could still graduate on time. She just couldn't do it on her own, she said. But her dad said no. His daughter, the real one, she guessed, was getting married the following spring. There was simply a limit to what he could do, he said. Caren had left his office in the Seventh Ward and walked back to work empty-handed. She had a full-time job by then, at the Grand Luxe Hotel on Poydras, a few blocks from the convention center, where she managed the bar. She was good at it, the managing of other people's problems, staff quibbles, and guest complaints. She liked even the smallest, dullest tasks. It passed the time, and kept her mind off other things.

She was doing a sweep of the floor, checking in with the night staff, when Eric Ellis walked in. He was wearing a trim, dark-blue suit, his shirt unbuttoned at the collar. He was there for happy hour with a handful of third-years from Tulane, two of whom Caren recognized. They'd all worked in the same law clinic the year before.

A year earlier, she and Eric had worked their very first case together, a simple battery charge that Professor Kazari let them take a crack at, leaving them alone in his office. Eric took one look at the file photos—the victim a white woman who'd been jacked by a lead pipe, both her eyes swollen shut, and the defendant, smug and indifferent in his booking photo, his black hair braided on one side and flying loose on the other—and announced he was going into politics, public policy maybe. Criminal law just wasn't his thing. He did his work, though, was too much of a gentleman to let it all fall on Caren. He transcribed police interviews, watched hours of security-camera footage from a liquor store on the corner of Lombard and St. Anthony. And he made sure all of their paperwork was filed on time. But it was Caren who spoke at the arraignment; she was the only one the defendant trusted; and she was the one who, during a long cross-examination at trial, put the victim at a bar in the French Quarter from the hours of two o'clock in the afternoon until midnight the day of her assault. She was quite drunk, Caren got on record, and unable to walk straight by the time she made it to the liquor store on Lombard, picking up a nightcap on her way home. Their client, the defendant, had offered her a hand when she'd stumbled off the curb, had even offered to call her a cab. But he was *not* the man who assaulted her, was in fact already a block away, on Sumpter, when the assault occurred. The woman had simply made a mistake. Caren liked the work, being inside a court of law. She liked the order of it, the hope implied, that we might get something right in this lifetime. At the defense table, Eric leaned in and whispered in her ear, "You just saved that kid's life."

She hadn't seen him in nearly a year, not since she'd left school.

He stopped in the middle of the bar, saw her, and smiled.

"Caren Gray," he said. "I was wondering where the hell you went."

She smiled.

It meant something that he'd thought of her, that he'd noticed she was gone. But she was not otherwise enthusiastic about the encounter, or the need to explain her life, her job in a hotel bar—not with two of her ex-classmates nudging each other, eyeing the cheap blazer she was wearing, the name tag on the lapel. She quickly sat them at her best table, the one across from the piano, with a view of the wharf. And she set them up with a bottle of Brunello, on her. Then she turned and walked through the kitchen to her small office and shut the door, hiding out until she thought they were gone.

Eric found her anyway.

About a quarter to closing, he knocked on her office door.

He was in jeans and a thin, cotton sweater. He'd gone home and changed clothes, and then come all the way back, he said. He wanted a chance to see her one last time. Caren sat behind her desk, fiddling with a paper clip, bending and twisting the silver metal, turning it over and over in her palm. She didn't want him to leave. She didn't want him to leave her *behind*. But she couldn't get the words out.

"Hey," he finally said. "You want to get out of here?"

She nodded. "Yes."

It turned out they had the same taste in music and a low tolerance for the French Quarter. Eric found the tourists loud and tedious, and Caren was a single woman who'd learned to avoid it out of a concern for basic safety. That night, they went to a blues club in the Seventh Ward, a dive joint that let you bring your own liquor, charging $1.50 for a setup—a plastic cup of ice and 7-Up or Coca-Cola, whichever you wanted. They sat close to each other in the dark, smoky bar, Eric resting one knee between hers, so that their thighs were touching. He cracked roasted peanuts in his hands, carefully peeling the skins before offering some to her. They drank a lot, beer and whiskey, and talked for hours—about school, Eric's family in Chicago, and what she wanted to do with herself, why she'd walked out on law school. Eric took her job at the bar as a lark, a break from the pressures of middle-class expectations, like the time he'd cut out of undergrad for a year to work at a fish cannery in Oregon, a summer job that he'd held on to for months, living out of a duffel bag. It was always understood that he would come back, that he would finish school. Eric's family background was not unlike her father's. He came from a long line of doctors, had two brothers who were professors, one at Loyola and the other at the University of Chicago. She didn't point out their differences, didn't tell him who she really was, a cook's kid from rural Louisiana who was lucky to have made it this far. She didn't tell him she'd run out of money, that even with student aid she couldn't pay her tuition, couldn't eat and pay rent at the same time. She couldn't stay in school without a job—and a job, a real one, meant she couldn't study, which meant she couldn't keep up her grades, or her scholarship. It was an impossible dance, one she'd been tripping over for most of her time in law school, ever since she'd stopped taking money from her mother, ever since they'd had their big falling-out. She didn't tell Eric any of this, the messy details.

Instead, she looked across the sticky vinyl tabletop and lied.

"I guess it just wasn't my thing," she said about law school.

Eric fell curiously silent, staring at her.

Then he said dryly, "Well, if it's all the same to you, I'd still very much like to have sex with you." He was teasing her, of course, knocking his knee playfully against hers under the table, letting her know that he didn't, in this moment, care a whit about law school, or anything outside of this room. She wasn't laughing, though. Instead, she asked him what he was waiting for. And Eric leaned across the table and kissed her.

They were at his apartment within the hour.

It was a tiny flat near Tulane's campus, just one room and a kitchen, a place much smaller than hers. Eric's bed was the centerpiece of the room and the thing on both their minds. She undressed him first, her fingertips grazing his warm, dry skin. He moaned like a wounded man, a man coming undone. He put her on her back and held her hand all the way through to the end. She was dizzy after. Her skin was on fire, and on her bottom lip she tasted blood. Eric buried his head in her neck. The union needed no more preamble than this. They were *Eric and Caren* at once. He thought she was smart and capable, he said. He told her he loved her after only a few weeks of dating. She thought him unconscionably beautiful, a deeply moral man with a sense of humor. They got a place together, not far from school. Eric still had a few months before graduation. He studied at night while she read books—short stories mostly, or business texts, the kind people leave behind in hotel bars. Or she would help him with his class outlines, criminal law still a sticking point for him. He liked to lay his head across her lap while she read his messy handwriting, making notes of her own in the margins.

It seemed to both of them that marriage was next. They talked about it quite a bit, in fact, often playfully disagreeing about the merits of a snowy Chicago wedding versus something reasonable, like New Orleans in the spring. She even met his family once, one cold winter when they went up to Chicago for his mother's birthday. Caren's mother, and the involvement of her parents in their lives, was never mentioned. There'd be time to explain, she thought. Neither one of them was in any particular rush. Eric had school, after all. And, anyway, Caren believed she had found, in Eric, her real family, and that nothing would ever change that. She was happy to wait.

12

Caren woke to the sound of crying in the fields.

She pulled herself up out of bed, stumbling toward it.

In the walking haze of her dream, they were right outside her front door, the swaying fields. She stepped barefoot into a jungle of sugarcane, the pointed tips of their leaves scratching the sides of her face. It was cold, the light pearl gray and brand-new. Daybreak meant work, and work meant faces in the fields, men handling cane. And somewhere in this maze, someone was hurt. There were moans, then a low whimper, coming from the south, maybe only a few feet in the distance, if only she knew which way to turn. The ground suddenly softened. Caren felt her toes sink in. She looked down and saw blood, a stream of it that cut the earth and curved like a scythe to the right.

She thought of Jason then, the blood and the mystery surrounding his disappearance. She worried what she would find here in the fields. She reached out and parted the cane . . . and then held her breath.

It was Helen on the ground, her mother. She was holding the torn and bloody body of Inés Avalo, had laid the small woman gingerly across her lap. She was covered in it, whatever had happened to the dead woman. There was blood on her mother's hands, on her clothes, down the front of her blue-and-white apron, and she was hollering for Caren to run back, to turn around and run and get somebody to help this girl. Caren heard the words, but she couldn't move. She hadn't seen her mother in years, and she was too scared to walk away, to miss her last chance. "I'm sorry," she said to her mom, feeling sick with grief, hot, salty tears pooling in the back of her throat.

Helen hushed her and told her to run back. "Hurry!"

Caren shook her head. She wouldn't leave her.

"Mom," she heard, in a voice that sounded small and not her own.

She heard it again, more urgent this time. "Mom!"

Caren woke in the dark to see someone standing over her. She didn't know what time it was, only that it had to be past midnight. The room was cold and dark, the curtains drawn. Morgan was standing at the foot of the bed, arms stiff at her sides.

"What is it, 'Cakes?"

"I heard something."

Caren reached over and turned on the bedside lamp. "What?"

Her head was foggy from the wine and she didn't immediately understand what was happening. "I heard somebody walking outside my window," Morgan said.

Caren quickly threw off the covers.

Morgan followed behind her as she walked across the hall to the other bedroom. She snapped open the curtains, her breath fogging the glass, and stared into the darkness. The library, by design, had a two-foot-wide path around its periphery, filled with the same fine gravel that lined the circle drive behind the main house. If someone or something was moving around out there, Morgan could have easily heard it from her bedroom window, which faced out toward the river. "Are you sure?" Caren said, thinking that maybe Morgan had been woken by the scuffle of a raccoon or a rat scooting around on the ground below. No, the girl said, this wasn't an animal.

"Someone was walking around outside."

Caren closed the curtains and said, "Come on." Half-dressed, she started down the stairs, Morgan behind her.

It was possible, she thought, that Eric had stepped outside for some reason and locked himself out. Or maybe he'd gotten turned around out there in the dark. But when she opened the door of the parlor, Eric was sleeping soundly on the couch, in a T-shirt and boxers, one naked leg slipping out from under the blankets. Caren peeked out of the library's front windows. She saw the back tires of the golf cart, which she'd left parked just outside the door. But it was all she could make out in the dark. She walked to the kitchen next and grabbed the telephone. She called 911 first . . . but she knew that the response time in this unincorporated part of the parish could be as long as twenty minutes, maybe even half an hour. So she did the only other thing she could think of, pulling Nestor Lang's business card from the antique desk by the front door.

A service picked up.

They wouldn't her give the detective's cell phone number, but the girl on the line promised a return call in ten to fifteen minutes. Caren hung up and then went to wake Eric, gently shaking his shoulders. His eyes, once open, were bloodshot. He felt along the couch's backrest for his glasses. He sat up, looking from Caren to his daughter.

"What's going on?"

Caren checked the lock on the front door, the bolts on all the windows downstairs, and then she closed the curtains. "Morgan heard something outside."

"I heard someone walking below my window."

"What?" Eric said, sliding on his glasses.

He reached for his shirt, his pants slung on a chair. He pulled them on, hopping on one leg at a time, his whole body

171

still sluggish and unsteady. He looked up at Caren, his eyes red and wild. The front of his torso rose and fell with each breath. He was still trying to take in what she'd said . . . to gauge the seriousness of the situation they were in.

"Should I go out there?"

"I've already called the police. There's nothing to do now but wait."

The three of them took up positions on the leather couch, Morgan sandwiched between her parents, leaning most of her weight onto her dad, burying her face against his bare arms. On the other side, Caren held her hand. They sat in the dark and listened to the wind, listening for any sign of trouble. Gerald was not on duty. Lang and Bertrand had pulled their uniformed officer late that afternoon. They were miles from their nearest neighbor or even a working streetlight. If someone was out there, roaming the grounds as a killer had done, they were, the three of them, helpless.

Caren thought about the guns in Luis's shed.

She should have taken them out of there a long time ago.

The wind brushed tree limbs against the side of the building. Morgan shivered. From outside, they heard a *pft-pft-pft* noise. It sounded like stones being thrown, like someone trying to break a window. Eric leaped out of his seat. Caren squeezed her daughter's hand, praying that it was only the black walnut tree on the north side of the building, raining shells across the rooftop. Eric walked to the front window, pushed back the curtains, and stared at a wall of blackness on the other side. It was impossible to see more than a few feet past the front door. "What's taking so long?" he said.

The phone rang.

It was Detective Lang.

He was on his own, without his partner, he said, and he was

waiting at the back gate . . . which meant someone had to go out there in the dark to let him in.

"I'll go," Eric said.

But they both knew he'd never find his way there and back, not in the dark.

Caren was already grabbing for her jacket and keys.

Morgan stood suddenly. "Mom?"

She was shaking her head, not wanting her mother to go, twisting and twisting the hem of her nightgown in her small hands, looking back and forth between her dad and her mom. "I'll be back in a few minutes," Caren told her. "And your dad's going to be right here." She turned and started rummaging through the drawer of the antique writing table, feeling around pens and paper receipts and stray coins for the small Maglite she kept there. She flipped the switch on the desktop lamp, searching inside the drawer for the flashlight. She tried to think what Letty might have done with it.

Morgan was watching her the whole time.

Caren heard her whisper, "I know where it is."

She looked up as her daughter slipped through the open kitchen door. She heard her small footsteps on the stairs. A few moments later, Morgan returned, the flashlight in her hand. Apparently, it had been in her possession, for who knows how long.

Eric said, "Are you sure about this, Caren?"

She nodded. "Lang knows I'm coming, and I have my phone," she said, patting her pocket. Outside, she slid into her boots. The golf cart was parked a few feet from the front door, the key still in the ignition, just as she'd left it hours earlier. Behind the wheel, she turned over the engine, looking ahead as two streams of light shot from the front grill. They revealed only the deserted main road and a swirl of gray fog.

The cart sputtered into gear.

She pressed her foot on the gas till she hit maximum speed.

Then she took off for the parking lot, cutting across the grass lawn, thinking it would be faster than staying on the main road. The cart bumped against the uneven earth, its two headlamps dipping and rising, throwing unexpected shadows across the landscape.

Lang was waiting by the main gate, standing in the parking lot.

He was, even at this hour, in a suit, and Caren wondered if he'd dressed for this. He unholstered his pistol as she drove them back toward the library.

The lights were all on, and Lang hopped out first. Caren went to unlock the front door for him . . . not fully realizing her mistake until it was too late. She'd just let a police officer investigating a homicide into her home without a search warrant. Her daughter's soiled shirt was still hidden away upstairs, the bloodstain still outlined in gray. Before she could stop him, Eric led the cop straight to Morgan's room.

Upstairs, Lang parked himself within a few inches of the bureau where her daughter's shirt lay. Morgan pointed to the window and tried to describe what she'd heard. "It was about half an hour ago, right?" Eric said, turning to Caren. She nodded, watching Lang. He was reading the room, collecting and indexing information: the call after midnight and the unexpected introduction of Morgan's father. He took a sweeping look around, at the twin bed, the bureau, the books and clothes on the floor. Then he holstered his weapon and made a slow walk across the carpet to the bedroom's one window. With a single finger, he parted the white curtains, glancing at the ground below. "She said it was coming from outside," Caren said, clearing her throat. She wanted this man out of her daughter's bedroom.

"Maybe we should take a look out there." Lang turned and looked at her, making some silent calculation. He looked back and forth between Caren and Eric. Then he looked at Morgan and smiled.

"Let's do that," he said to Caren.

Outside, Lang walked the grounds around the building, and she followed.

There was nothing wrong, nothing out of the ordinary. There were no new footprints out here that she could see, save for her own. Lang looked up from the ground, in a straight line, to Morgan's bedroom window. "Did *you* hear anything out here?" Caren shook her head no, and Lang offered to take another look inside.

"I don't think that's necessary," she said.

Instead, she took him on a ride around the plantation's perimeter, checking the fence line, making sure none of the locks had been broken, nor the fence posts disturbed, and when that revealed no signs of a security breach or a break-in, she took Lang all the way back to the main gate. He offered to send a squad car to patrol the area. Deputy Harris could sweep the farm road and the land around the plantation at least once an hour, but beyond that, the parish couldn't spare one of its handful of deputies for duty through the night.

That's fine, she said.

Exiting the golf cart, Lang said, "The knife is a match, by the way." Caren shut down the cart's engine, then turned to face the cop. "It's preliminary, of course," he said, "the coroner going by the photograph you gave." He smoothed his tie and buttoned the front of his jacket against a cool October wind. "I still can't imagine any reason why you would have kept something like that from law enforcement. Would have been nice to get a head start on the murder weapon."

"I wasn't *keeping* it from you," she said, to be clear.

Lang raised a hand to stop her, to let her know a protest was neither necessary nor of any interest to him at this stage. "I'm willing to give you the benefit of the doubt on this, I am. But that stops here. I imagine you've sniffed around enough law books to know a thing or two about obstruction. Last I checked, you can go to jail for that."

He was pinching his lips together, eyeing her.

She couldn't tell if he was serious, if this man was seriously threatening her, or if this was meant as a test, a way to see how badly he could shake her, and what might spill out in the process. Lang took a step closer to the front of the golf cart, the lights making shadows under his eyes. "You're running this thing, Tulane, you're the one in charge here," he said. "You give me every reason to trust you and that's what you'll get back. But if I think there's more you're not saying, I'm going to treat you like someone who's hiding something." There it was again, the ever-present sense with Lang that his mind was already made up, that he was merely filling in some image he was already carrying in his mind, like waiting on ink to dry. She knew not to give him more than he already thought he had on her. "Good night, Detective Lang," she said, locking the gate behind him. Then she drove straight to Luis's shed.

She wanted those guns.

The more she thought of how easily they could end up in the wrong hands—like the knife that cut that woman's throat, a murder weapon stolen right out from under her—the more she wanted them in her possession and not someone else's. She didn't tell Eric what she was doing. She didn't bother to call over to the library to let him know. She wasn't sure Eric had ever seen a gun, save for in a courthouse, or at a conference on gun control maybe. Caren could handle a .22 from the time she was eight or nine. She and Bobby used to pop off bottles with his daddy's pistol. She didn't mind guns. They had their place, like just about everything else. And she was not about to spend another night out here in the dark unarmed.

Luis's shed was on the other side of the main house, and she reached it in record time. She parked at the foot of a poplar tree, backing up the cart in such a way that its headlights shone on the front of the shed's wood door. Cradling the flashlight between her neck and shoulder, she fiddled with the lock on the door's latch, accidentally dropping her keys in the dirt more than once. She looked down and saw that her hands were shaking.

The door creaked when she finally got it open. She swung the Maglite, arcing its sharp white light against the shed's walls. Overhead, a frayed string controlled a single bare bulb. Caren gave it a good tug. The shed, she could see, was extraordinarily well kept. She had Luis to thank for the clear path through the shovels and brooms and coiled garden hoses resting on their sides. It made it easy for her to make her way to the locked cabinet on the rear wall. Inside, she found the two weapons: a .32 pearl-handled six-shooter and a 12-gauge shotgun. She grabbed them both, along with a box of shells and round-nosed bullets, pausing long enough to load six rounds into the pistol before leaving the shed. She shoved the handgun into her jacket pocket. Outside, she laid the long barrel of the shotgun across the front seat of the golf cart. Then she drove back to the east.

Somewhere on the drive, she reached into her pocket for her cell phone.

Eric would be worried by now, she knew.

Punching in the numbers, she looked down, briefly taking her eyes off the drive. When she looked up again, barely a second later, there was a figure staggering directly into her path. She slammed on the brakes. The cart screeched and bumped to a rough stop, and her cell phone went flying out of her hands, disappearing into the darkness. Her heart sank. Detective Lang was long gone. There were no cops out here. It was just her, the .32, and the man standing a few feet in front of her, bathed in the hazy light of the cart's headlamps. He was white and slender, with a mess of hairs scratched across his chin. The true shape and color of his eyes were hooded by a baseball cap, but he still looked awfully familiar. She hopped out of the cart, her hand shaking, the skin of her palm slipping against the handle of the pistol. "Hey, wait a minute!" the man yelled, waving his arms. He stumbled backward, tripping over his feet and falling to the ground. He held his hands in front of his torso in a gesture of surrender. "Hey, hold on a second!" he was pleading. "Aw, Jesus, lady, don't shoot!"

The sheer fright in his voice stopped her.

She lowered the gun.

He still had his hands up. "I'm just trying to find my way out of here, I swear."

"Who are you?"

"Lee Owens, ma'am. I'm a reporter."

Then, sensing that wasn't going to cut it, he added, "I'm with the *Times-Picayune*."

She checked his wallet, finding both an employee identification card for the *Times-Picayune*'s offices on Howard Avenue in New Orleans and a Louisiana State driver's license, both bearing the name Lee Owens. According to his license, Mr. Owens was thirty-nine years old . . . and lying about his height. He was no more than an inch taller than her, and she was just barely five feet seven inches. He was sweating openly, and the front of his khaki pants were stained with grass and mud, and he said very little as she drove them back to her apartment, keeping his hands visible in his lap. The shotgun was resting upright between them, the .32 still in her right hand. Up ahead, she could just make out the honey-colored light shining from the library's upstairs window. "How in the hell did you get in here, anyway?" she asked.

"I came in with a tour . . . and then I just never left."

Great, she thought.

That's just great.

She remembered the group this morning. He was the guy in the ball cap and khakis, the one who was taking pictures. "I guess I got turned around somehow," he said. "I've been walking around in circles out here." He looked up at the pale moon, the patch of stars behind the passing clouds, the only light this deep in the parish.

"What were you looking for?"

"Anything I could find about the girl, I guess." Caren felt him looking at her. But she didn't take her eyes off the road. "The Sheriff's Department isn't saying much, no more than the basic facts. I thought I'd come take a look around the place myself." He sighed, sounding frankly annoyed with himself, as if he'd only just now realized what a stupid idea this was. "This cloak-and-dagger, stakeout stuff, this ain't my regular deal. I'm not exactly a crime reporter. I cover the sugar industry at the paper. I've been on the Groveland beat for a while now. So, yeah, when I heard about the girl out here . . . it definitely got me to wondering if there was more to it, if the company was having problems again," he said. "I'm just out here chasing a story."

Caren slowed the cart to a stop, a few feet from the library's front door.

"You didn't know her, did you?" he said.

"No."

She cut the engine, grabbed the shotgun and the pistol, and

waved him out of the vehicle. Owens, confused, looked up at the building, unclear as to what was going on, why she'd brought him here. "What is this place?" he said, meaning the library, the cake-top miniature of the main house, dressed in the same white with black shutters. He seemed to genuinely not know where he was.

The library's front door opened and Eric stepped out, fully dressed now in his slacks and shirt. Morgan, still in her night-gown, was a small shadow behind her dad. Eric looked at Caren, the guns . . . and Lee Owens. "Morgan, get inside," he said sharply.

"Mom?"

"Get inside!" he yelled.

She quickly disappeared into the house.

Eric stood on the library steps, his eyes sweeping over this un-expected scene: a stranger, the guns, and Caren. "What is this?"

Again, she waved Owens out of the golf cart.

He slid out slowly, holding his hands out in front of him.

She gave him a slight shove, touching him for the first time. The back of his cotton shirt was damp, almost cold with sweat. She nudged him into the library, following a few steps behind. As she crossed the threshold, she turned and whispered to Eric. "He's a reporter."

Inside the front parlor, Owens removed his hat, as if he'd been asked over to tea, a gentleman caller meeting the family for the first time. He held out a hand to Eric, the de facto man of the house, making their acquaintance official. "Lee Owens," he said. "I'm with the *Times-Picayune*." Eric glared at him, keep-ing a protective hand on his daughter's shoulder. Owens gave Morgan a polite nod. By the door, Caren laid the two guns on the antique side table. The long barrel of the shotgun hung off the side. Then she turned to behold Owens in the light. Now that he'd taken off his hat, she could see his eyes for the first time. They were mossy green and clear as rainwater. His hair was a mess of sandy curls, pasted against his skin. "Look, I'd really appreciate it if you guys just let me out of here," he said. "I certainly didn't mean to cause any problems."

Flushed and overheated, Caren pulled off her jacket.

"He's just a reporter," she said to Eric.

"You don't know that."

Owens reached for his wallet, in an effort to clear this up.

The sudden movement was just enough to set Eric off. He lunged at the guy, covering the length of the room in a matter of seconds, until he was towering over him. Owens backed up quickly, defensively holding his hands in front of his chest. He shot Caren a look, begging for some help here. She sighed, feeling suddenly very, very tired. She walked up behind Owens and reached into his back pocket for his black leather wallet. From its folds, she produced the same bits and pieces of identification the reporter had shown her outside, including a credit card and a Subway sandwich card, creased and bent.

Eric scanned the information, his head down.

When he looked up again, he appeared not so much relieved as angry.

He tossed the wallet to Owens, hitting him in the chest. "I nearly had a fucking heart attack, Caren," he said, forgetting for a second their daughter standing just a few feet away. He slumped into one of the leather armchairs. Elbows on his knees, he buried his head in his hands. "Jesus fucking Christ," he muttered, and she finally saw how scared he must have been when she hadn't turned up again right away.

On the coffee table, the cordless phone rang.

"That's Lang," he said.

Eric, it turned out, had panicked.

When she hadn't returned, he grew concerned. Morgan was acting more and more skittish in her absence, swearing she'd heard someone outside their window, footsteps, she said. Eric had called the number on Lang's card, and now this was him calling back, checking to make sure everything was all right. Eric reached for the phone. But Caren got to it first. She let it ring two more times. "Answer it," he said. Owens was wearing an expression both sheepish and genuinely contrite. "Please," he pleaded. "I'll go, I swear."

Caren sighed and finally answered the phone.

"Sorry," she said straightaway, before reporting to Lang that the previous call was a mistake.

We're all fine, she said, before hanging up.

Eric shook his head in anger. "What is wrong with you?"

She didn't want the cop in her house, she said.

Which made no sense to Eric, who had no idea what was at stake.

He stood and stalked out of the room. Owens bent down to pick up his wallet, sliding it into his khakis, which were faded and worn. He set his ball cap back on his head and tipped the bill in her direction, a thank-you for the small act of kindness.

She drove him all the way back to the main gate, idling the golf cart while she unlocked the metal bolt. Owens stood directly behind her. When the gate creaked open, she turned to him and said firmly, "You never saw me, understand? We never spoke."

"Fine with me."

He slipped through the opening between the gate and the fence. The only cars in the parking lot were her Volvo, Eric's rental, and Donovan's late-model Acura, still parked in the same spot since this morning, before the cops took him away. Owens said his own car was parked on the highway, where he'd left it so it wouldn't be spotted anywhere near the grounds after hours. It was at least another mile and a half to walk, in pitch darkness, but he would have to navigate that on his own. Caren closed the gate, securing the metal latch.

There was one thing she wanted to ask him, though.

Through the white bars of the fence, she called out to him. "Hey, what did you mean back there, what you said about Groveland having problems *again*?"

Owens turned back to look at her.

The night silence between them was briefly filled with the soft rustling of cane leaves in the distance. Owens scratched the stubble on his chin. "Hunt Abrams, the farm manager over there, he's not local, so you know." He took a few steps closer to Caren, lowering his voice even though they were, pray to God, the only two souls out here. "They've moved him around a bunch of times," he said. "Bakersfield, California, their operations in South Florida. He was only six months at a fruit-processing plant they own in Washington State before they moved him out here, to this start-up." He nodded in the direction of the sugarcane to the south and west, swaying over the fence.

"I don't understand," she said, still not getting the nature of the company's "problems." Owens seemed initially inclined to leave it alone, to keep his mouth shut. But then, looking at her, he changed his mind, deciding to trade one act of kindness for another. A pretty lady out here, he said, you ought to know who your neighbors are.

"Word is, ma'am, he's got a bad way with his workers," he said, his breath visible and snaking through the bars of the fence, almost touching her on the other side.

"How's that?"

"Well, let's just say some of his people don't make it out of the fields."

183

Caren got a sudden image of those church ladies at dawn, the black priest, and the candlelight vigil, remembering how the women had taken note, literally, of Hunt Abrams's every move, documenting it, as if for some future purpose. Had they known then that there was more to this story, that Abrams was a man who ought to be watched closely? Owens seemed to think so. "But you didn't hear it from me," he said. He made a show of pressing his lips together, as if he'd already said more than he should have. Then, with a tip of his cap, he bid Caren good night, before turning and starting his long walk down the winding farm road.

13

"I want to see it," Eric said.

The rain had started in again, falling in black sheets against Morgan's bedroom window. He'd waited until she fell back asleep, watching from the doorway as Caren held her hand in the dark, as their daughter's breath deepened and she curled herself into a tight, soft ball. Caren kissed her on the forehead and then started out of the room. When she stepped into the hallway, Eric grabbed her by the wrist. "Caren," he said. His tone was soft and forceful and quietly intimate, so that she wasn't clear if the touch was meant to signal aggression or affection. His eyes were sunken and blood red.

"Where is it?"

"Where is what?"

"Morgan's shirt," he said. "What did you do with it?"

She stared at him for a moment.

"I got rid of it," she said, meaning the bloodstain. The light from her bedroom across the hall outlined the hard angles of his face, the tense, squared shoulders, but she could not, in shadow, read his expression with any precision. She heard the rain pattering on the roof and the bullish sound of his breathing. "I washed it," she said.

"I want to see it."

"I *washed* it, Eric."

"I want to see it!"

She sighed, glancing over her shoulder. The door to Morgan's room was still open. Eric made a move in that direction, but she stopped him. She knew where the shirt was, knew every detail of her daughter's room, even in the dark. He waited for her in the hallway, watching through the door as she went straight to the top drawer of the bureau beside Morgan's bed. The shirt was folded neatly. She walked it to Eric in the hallway. He unfurled it right away, snapping the fabric, holding it in front of his eyes. Dissatisfied with the light, he walked into Caren's bedroom. There, turning the cotton over in his hands, he asked her, "Where is it?"

"It was on the sleeve, on the left side."

Eric inspected the white sleeve, his eyes finally coming to rest on the grayish half-moon shape where the stain used to be. He studied it for a long time, and then looked up at her. This time, by lamplight, she could see his face clearly. He let out a long sigh. "You know what Morgan told me, when we were in the car today, when it was just the two of us? She told me she never saw any blood."

"What?"

"She didn't see any blood, Caren."

"I showed it to her, Eric," she said. "It was *on her shirt.*"

"Are you sure it was blood?"

His tone was gentle, an exaggerated show of patience for a woman whose motives it was clear he no longer trusted.

"You don't believe me."

"I don't know what to think, Caren."

"I know what I saw, Eric."

"But, Christ, if it really was blood on her shirt, why the hell did you *wash* it?"

"I just panicked," she said, which was a lie. But it was the only sentiment she thought he would understand. She knew exactly what she'd done, had handled the task with care and relative calm. There wasn't much in her life she could completely control, but her daughter's laundry was under her jurisdiction, she'd decided. Eric sighed again, sinking onto the side of the bed, Morgan's shirt still balled in his hands.

"I don't know what the hell I'm doing here."

"I didn't ask you to come."

"Yes, you did. You knew if you called me with this, if Morgan was in any kind of trouble, that I would come down here. You knew I would drop everything."

"You think I made all this up just so I could see you again?"

Eric looked up, his eyes meeting hers, but he didn't say anything, and his silence revealed his suspicions.

"A woman was murdered, Eric!"

"I know that."

"There were police here, and they were talking to our daughter. I was scared, Eric, and, yes, if I'm being honest, I'm glad you're here," she said, which, on its own, was hard enough to admit. "Why in the hell should I have to go through all this alone?"

"I have never asked you to raise Morgan alone. Let's be clear about that."

He stared at the shirt in his hands. "That was your choice, Caren."

Outside her bedroom window, the light was moving toward dawn. The sky was slate gray, and there were droplets of rain dotting the glass. Eric clasped his hands around Morgan's shirt. He leaned forward, elbows on his knees. He was momentarily lost in his thoughts.

Finally, he set the laundered shirt gingerly atop her quilt.

"This is weird for me," he said.

"What is?"

"Being here with you," he said. "I mean, I'm getting married in three weeks."

He glanced down at his hands, resting them as a set in the space between his bare knees. "You've been dragging your feet about getting Morgan's plane ticket for the wedding. You haven't made any plans to get her there. And I don't know what to think, what you must be feeling." He looked up, waiting for her to tell him what she was feeling. She didn't, however, and in the end Eric seemed to have expected this. He rose from the bed, leaving the shirt behind. "I just want to move on, Caren."

Fine, she thought.

"I'll buy her plane ticket tomorrow."

"Okay, then," he said, heading for the door. She could sense his dissatisfaction. But it was only long after he was gone that it occurred to her that maybe Eric had wanted something more from her, needed it even, especially now, on the eve of his marriage to another woman. Maybe, she thought, he had his own reason for coming all the way down to Louisiana, blood or no blood.

He had always said he didn't blame her for what happened.

And she supposed she was meant to feel grateful for that.

But, truth be told, she had always very quietly considered his lack of rage over her behavior, what she'd done, his own act of betrayal. He had not taken the news like a man so much as he had taken it like a lawyer, with a level head and a clear tone of voice. He asked few details but seemed comforted to know that it had happened only once, with a man she hardly knew, a guest passing through her hotel. Inside of fifteen minutes, he was holding her hand, owning up to his own bad behavior—the way he often used work as a shield, holing up in their extra bedroom with stacks of files most nights, just so he could have an hour or two to himself, something that, on the other side of becoming a father, he'd come to cherish more than sleep. Parenthood had turned out to be a costly miracle. It gave them a beautiful girl, yes, and a vaulted perch upon which to see the world, to sit and reflect on the nature of pure grace, the surprises life can bring. But it took from them, too. Eric was a new lawyer at a prestigious firm, working eighty-hour weeks; and Caren was by then managing most of the hotel's day-to-day operations, the dream of someday returning to law school having been laid aside by motherhood. Whatever of them was left at the end of the day went to Morgan first. She and Eric spent more and more time in their separate corners, their separate roles as her parents. Mothering, she learned the hard way, was about loss as well as love.

Those were rough years for Caren, right after Morgan's birth. She had taken Helen's death particularly hard, and having a child so soon after losing her mother had felt almost like a base form of punishment, pointed and cruel.

Eric repeatedly brought up Chicago as an option, a solution to their overworked lives and a place where they might settle down. His mother could watch Morgan some days. She might offer both of them, but Caren in particular, a guiding hand in parenthood. But the mention of his mother in place of her own only made Caren's grief thicker, hardening in places to an impenetrable crust. Eric told her almost daily that he hadn't meant it that way, but by then she wasn't listening. Any mention of Chicago and she would change the subject, sometimes walking out of the room. Eric grew irritated, then angry, repeatedly accusing her of making things deliberately harder on them, of having no real concept of family—which was as close as he would ever come to commenting on her background.

This from a man who had yet to propose marriage, she thought. She didn't think it was fair, Eric asking her to move across the

189

country without some kind of commitment, or at least a spoken promise to stay by her side. It was a kernel of resentment that grew into an irrational panic: he was going to eventually leave her, just like her father had left her mother behind. She and Eric were two people who had started out about as far apart in life as a man and a woman could have, and she started to wonder if Eric sensed it, too. The marriage talk had ended almost as soon as Morgan was born. She was starting to worry that her background mattered more than he let on.

She didn't even realize how angry she was.

Only how easy it was to act out.

Men came through the doors of her hotel every day, dozens by the hour, in fact. She found one from some far corner of the country, Seattle, or maybe it was Boston or Newport. She didn't remember. Nor did it matter, anyway. There was no way to soften it, to get around what she'd done. It was a stupid and impulsive act, a test with unseen consequences. And she, of all people, should have known better. One of the first things they teach you in law school, in the first week of any decent trial prep course: don't ever ask a question if you can't live with the answer.

The night she told him about the affair, they actually went to bed together, falling asleep in tandem for the first time in months. And then just before dawn the next morning, Morgan starting to stir in the next room, Eric whispered in her ear that *he* was sorry. It was obvious to him now, and he could finally admit to himself that there was a reason he had never proposed to her after all these years, why he'd never made it official. Lying half-awake in their bed, she listened as he told her that, deep down, if he was being honest with himself, he could admit that he'd always had doubts about whether she was the one. "I don't blame you, Caren," he said. "I really don't."

She was lying on her side, facing the wall.

She remembered feeling numb from the waist down.

"So that's it?" she said. "You're done?"

"I'm tired, Caren."

Morgan called out from her bedroom. She was still sleeping in Pull-Ups, even at five, and needed to be changed first thing. The morning duty was always Caren's, since Morgan was born, and so she alone walked down the hall to her daughter's room, helping her pick clothes for school and then starting breakfast. By the time she returned to their bedroom, Eric was already dressed for work. He kissed her, quite tenderly, his breath warm and sweet. It was the look in his eyes that finally broke her, when she finally started to cry. What she saw was relief. In the end, her transgression had cost him nothing. She had given him his way out.

That was August, 2005.

Within weeks, Eric, without telling her, went to Chicago for a second interview in the Economic Development Department of then-senator Barack Obama's hometown office. Eric had grown up in Chicago and had ties to the newly elected freshman senator.

He blew his cover that weekend, though, calling home to tell Caren he was not meeting a client in Tulsa, as he'd said, but was actually in Chicago. He'd been watching news reports about the hurricane, and he wanted her and Morgan to get out of the city while they still could. Caren, who had grown up near the Gulf (and slept through Category 3 hurricanes), would have stayed in the city, at the Grand Luxe Hotel, where some of her coworkers were bringing their families . . . if Eric hadn't insisted they leave.

Two last-minute plane tickets to join him in Chicago seemed extravagant and unnecessary, and things between them were still quite raw. She thought it was best if she stayed down south. She had wrongly assumed that getting a hotel room would be easy. But everything was booked, from the capital to Alexandria, even as far north as Monroe. In the end, they headed west. Caren pulled Morgan out of school and loaded up the Volvo with a single suit-case for both of them, plus a plastic bag with crayons and color-ing paper . . . grabbing at the last minute the paisley-covered box of her mother's things that Lorraine had sent her, setting it on the front seat beside her for the five-hour drive across the state line. They rode out the tail end of Katrina in a motel room outside of Beaumont, Texas, on and off the phone with Eric, neither one of them with any idea that the last evidence of their life together was being washed away as they spoke, Morgan reaching for the phone every few minutes to say hi.

Eric took that job in Chicago.

He wanted Morgan with him, but made no specific mention of Caren.

She asked for time to think about it.

They stayed in that motel room for days, she and Morgan, with its sage-colored curtains and thick, dusty carpet. Caren made the beds every day and cooked their meals on a small range stove in a corner of the room. A trucker's special, they called it, a place for people with no real home. They ate grits and butter, fried apples when she could find the right kind, and thick slices of ham on toasted bread—the sort of food her mother used to set aside just for Caren, nights she worked in the kitchen, nights Caren waited up for her. She felt a strange peace there, the whole of her life contained within the four walls of that motel room, her daughter napping on her lap some afternoons.

"I'm your mother," she said to her one day, a whisper in ear as she slept.

I'm your family, she said.

They stayed a few more nights, just the two of them, until

Caren was finally ready to go home, to the only one she had left. What they had, they packed into the car, heading out early, early in the morning, Caren with that box of her mother's things riding shotgun beside her. Interstate 10 will take you all the way into New Orleans if you let it, but instead they cut south from Baton Rouge, heading for Ascension and Belle Vie. She had steeled herself for the reunion. She'd prepared herself to hate the place on sight, pointedly refusing to be courted by a pretty picture, or its pretense of antebellum grace. And she made herself a single promise: she would not forget her family's generations of sweat here, and how trapped she'd felt by that very legacy, growing up in the shade of these trees. Her original contract was for one year. The job paid well and provided a roof over their heads. The plantation was furnished and populated, and she thought it might soften the losses they'd endured, for a while at least. The plan was to sit out for a few months, to stow away in a familiar place, until she could figure what she wanted to do next, what she wanted for her life and for her daughter. It was only supposed to be for one year. But the place got a hold of her, from that first day, the first hour even. And it surprised as much as it confused her to discover that she did not, after all these years, hate the plantation at all, that she *could* not hate what was now, and maybe always had been, her real home, the way she came into this world.

14

Things were tense between her and Eric the next morning, and he said very little as he waited for Morgan to get dressed, even eschewing Letty's hot, honeyed milk and French toast. Letty didn't seem to know what to make of them together, Caren and Eric. Each time she caught Caren's eye across the kitchen, she smiled knowingly, until Caren could hardly stand it anymore, eventually forgoing the idea of a formal breakfast and instead grabbing an apple on her way to work. Eric waited until she was halfway to the door before mentioning his return flight to D.C. that afternoon.

"You're leaving?"

Morgan had just come down the stairs. She was wearing jeans and a pink T-shirt and white socks. It was Saturday, and she didn't have school, and she'd had it in her mind that she and her dad would be spending the whole day together. Her eyes were doleful and wide, and she let a small leather purse fall with a thud at her feet. She looked back and forth between her mom and her dad, waiting on some kind of an explanation. Letty was bent over the stove, the bangles on her wrist tolling lightly as she stirred a pot of grits. Caren knew she was listening to every word. She wanted to ask her to leave, but had never once in four years made a similar request and to do so now would only draw more attention to the situation, or signal that something was wrong.

Eric said to Morgan, "I have to get back to work, honey."

Caren wondered if it was really Lela that Eric had to get back to.

"Did *she* ask you to leave?" Morgan said. She was looking at her mother.

"No, honey," he said. "This isn't about me and your mom."

Which, even to Caren, sounded like a lie.

He glanced her way before standing and crossing to his daughter. He lifted her tiny purse from the foot of the stairs. "I have to get back to Washington, Morgan. I kind of took off without telling anybody, and I need to get back to my work. Your mom's got everything under control here, and now that I know you're okay, I need to go home." Then he bent down, so they were somewhat eye-to-eye. "But, listen, if you need anything, anything at all, you know you can call me or Lela . . . anytime, okay?" Belatedly, he added, "We can still hang out this morning."

"It's not fair," she said.

"I'm going to see you in a few weeks anyway."

"Mom won't let me go."

"That's not true," he said, looking at Caren.

"I never said that, Morgan."

"She hasn't even bought my ticket yet."

"I'll take care of it today," Caren said. "I should have done it a long time ago." It was true. She had been stalling, and it wasn't fair to either one of them. "You're not going to miss your dad's wedding." That was all it took. Morgan broke out into a huge grin, showing the tiny gap between her two front teeth, looking, in the moment, just like Helen Gray, the grandmother she'd never laid eyes on. "Thanks, Mom," she said, leaping across the room to throw her arms around Caren's neck. She held her mother close and kissed her cheek, as sweetly as she did every year at Christmas when she discovered that, against all odds, she'd gotten exactly what she wanted. Letty likewise seemed pleased with the outcome. Caren caught her smiling to herself at the stove.

The tasting went off as planned at nine a.m., Lorraine having set an elegant table in the dining hall of the main house: china painted with gold and rose, silver flatware and taper candles and a shock of yellow chrysanthemums from the garden. And the food, of course, a five-course spread. The bride didn't touch a thing, letting her mother act as her surrogate. Caren had seen this many times, women who ceased eating in the days and weeks leading up to the big day. They were invariably the ones fuming on their wedding day because the food, the first they'd tasted in weeks, probably, was not up to their exacting standards, brides who ended up spending part of their reception in the ladies' room, crying. Miss Whitman's mother was a good sport, enjoying the food and the bottomless flute of champagne. The daughter, Shannon, was tense and brittle and far too young to get married, Caren thought. She made her mother describe, in detail, each and every forkful and mentioned at least three times that she wanted her own baker in Alexandria to do the cake. "Not a problem, baby," Lorraine said. She was wearing a white chef's hat today and a matching smock, for the full-service effect. She made sure to keep the older woman's throat wet, pouring the mother another glass of champagne. Mrs. Whitman giggled. Shannon, cranky and hungry, rolled her eyes.

On her laptop, Caren made a series of notes for their file.

Later, they took a ride across the plantation so she could show them every corner of the land. Shannon Whitman want-ed the doors and windows to the cottages open for at least thirty-six hours before her wedding day to get rid of the "old people smell." She also wanted to know what could be done about the bugs. Come sundown, they'd be nipping at everyone's ears. Caren made no promises, but said she could have Luis fog the front lawn on the morning of. Mrs. Whitman, still nursing a glass of bubbly, nodded agreeably. Caren ferried the clients along the fence line, out by the cane fields, and Shannon Whitman screwed her perfectly made-up face at the sight of all those machines and Mexicans sweating in the fields. "They're not going to be out there like that on my wedding day, are they?" Caren tried to explain that the cane farm operated separately from the plantation, and that she didn't imagine any of Miss Whitman's guests would venture this far out to the property line. But Shannon Whitman was unmoved. "Mama, can't they do something about this?" she said.

Again, Caren made no promises.

She had no contact information for Hunt Abrams, no cell phone or direct line, only a regional office number for the Groveland Corporation that was actually answered by a secretary at their headquarters in California. Getting in touch with the man meant a long walk into the fields. Abrams had certainly never expressed an inclination toward cooperation or neighborly consideration when it came to the aesthetic needs of Belle Vie's well-heeled clients. But she at least had to say she tried.

The back five hundred acres of the Clancy family property, and the whole of Groveland's cane farm, formed an L-shape around the south and west sides of the plantation, around the fence that secured Belle Vie. She drove her car along the farm road, toward the southernmost corner of the farm, where she knew there lay a short, dirt road that led into the fields. She would have to walk the rest of the way to Hunt's trailer on foot. She parked her Volvo and stepped out of the car, halting before a curious sight: there, along the side of the farm road, was a series of jagged holes in the ground where the earth had been pulled out in wide chunks, the ground hacked away by a shovel. There were a few wood posts strewn in the dirt, as if at one time a fence were being built here. It was an unsightly mess, a project abandoned and forgotten.

Abrams's trailer was a double-wide, stone gray and completely unadorned. It sat sandwiched between two uncut fields. The sign outside read: GROVELAND FARMS. Caren knocked on the door's metal frame and waited, listening to the mechanical cutters in the distance, the gassy *chug-chug* of their engines. She knocked a second time, this time pulling back the screen door. When her knuckles hit the surface of the plywood door, it popped from its frame and swung open. The trailer was unlocked.

"Hello?"

She stepped inside the stuffy room.

At first glance she spotted a television, but no computer. On the floor were a pillow and a sleeping bag, but no filing cabinets or fax machine, nothing that said this was a place of business. There was a coffeemaker atop a spare, uncluttered desk, and a cash box with a heavy, metal padlock. The trailer looked more like the hideaway of some illegal, cash operation rather than an outpost of a national corporation. Apart from a few cardboard boxes stacked with production reports, graphs, and charts, and a wall calendar, there was no evidence of anything that resembled a working office—no payroll cards or time sheets that Caren could see, no proof on paper that Groveland's workers even existed. In fact, she had to search for a pad and a pen just to leave Abrams a note, asking him to please contact her regarding the Whitman wedding. She was bent over and poking around, looking, when a line of clouds rolled past the trailer's one skylight, brightening the room. Something on the floor caught a wink of the sun's light. It was wedged between the flat carpet and the leg of Abrams's desk, a tiny thing, casting a glitter of light. Curious, Caren reached down to pick it up, not realizing until she had it in the palm of her hand exactly what it was she'd found: a single, star-shaped earring.

The trailer's door swung open.

She heard it slam against the metal frame.

She turned and saw Hunt Abrams, the top of his head almost touching the low ceiling, all six feet of him nearly hunched over in the trailer. He was wearing jeans and a black windbreaker and eyeing her with a bemused smirk. "You just stopping by to say hi?" he said. She was still holding the earring in her hand, the post cutting into the center of her palm. There was no getting rid of it now, not without Abrams knowing what she'd found in here, or making it seem like she'd come to his trailer specifically to snoop around.

On instinct, she hid her hand in her jacket pocket, realizing, almost immediately, the mistake she'd just made. She never should have touched the thing, never should have picked it up. It was in *her* possession now, and not his, and there would be no way now of proving it had ever been inside this trailer or anywhere near Hunt Abrams. Would Lang and Abrams even believe her if she told them where she'd found the dead woman's earring, now covered in Caren's sweat and fear?

"Might I ask what in hell you think you're doing in here?"

He took a step toward her. She felt the long shadow of his height creep across her chest, then up the sides of her neck, slowly enveloping her whole body. She mumbled something about the Whitman wedding, the client's concerns about production in the fields. She was already starting toward the door. Abrams reached out a hand to stop her. He grabbed her arm roughly. "The Whitman wedding, huh?" he said. He didn't believe a word of it. She mumbled something like, "Yes, sir," before pushing past him and out of the trailer, flying through the fields of cane.

199

* * *

Back in her office, she set the star-shaped earring on her desk.

It was identical to the one in the picture of Inés Avalo.

She found it odd that the cops had come through Belle Vie with a search warrant, but had apparently never thought to take a close look at the trailer of the dead woman's employer. At her desk, she Googled the words "Groveland and California." Then "Groveland and Florida." Then "Abrams and Groveland and Florida." She thought about what Lee Owens, the *Times-Picayune* reporter, had said last night, about Abrams having a bad way with his workers. Sitting stiffly, she watched the search results fill her computer screen. They were generic news articles about the company, its business dealings, and she skimmed through these rather quickly, not sure what exactly she was looking for. It wasn't until the second page of search results that she thought she'd stumbled on something worthwhile, a story in the Jacksonville newspaper about a woman who'd been hurt on the job, in a citrus grove near Lake City—and the fact that there had been whispers of a DA's investigation. The tagline told the basic story:

LAKE CITY, FL—HUNT ABRAMS, A PROJECT MANAGER FOR THE GROVELAND CORPORATION, MET WITH LOCAL LAW ENFORCEMENT TODAY, TO ANSWER QUESTIONS ABOUT THE BEATING OF ONE OF THE COMPANY'S WORKERS IN THE FIELD . . .

Caren clicked on the link to the article. She wasn't through the first paragraph when her desk phone rang. She ignored it at first, but it kept ringing, on and on.

"Yes," she said, picking up.

It was Betty Collier, Donovan's grandmother.

Right off she said she'd been calling Caren's cell phone non-stop for the past twenty minutes. The woman was beside herself with panic. But Caren no longer had her cell phone. After the strange run-in with Lee Owens last night she never found it, even after searching the whole northeast side of the property. "What's going on?" she said.

"I didn't know nobody else to call or I wouldn't bother you with it, God knows I wouldn't, but we got to get somebody down there right now, a lawyer or somebody who can straighten this mess out."

"Donovan?" Caren said, catching on. "Did something happen with Donovan?"

"Lord, if they ain't gone and arrested him."

"What?"

"They've got him down in lockup right now." She was crying by this point, her voice cracked and strained. "Help me, Lord, please," she said, calling on a power much higher than Caren. "Can you please help me get my boy out of jail?"

Caren called Eric because, besides Raymond Clancy, he was the only lawyer she had immediate access to. He answered his cell phone, somewhere between Belle Vie and Baton Rouge. He agreed to turn around and drop Morgan with Letty. He would meet Caren in the parking lot of the sheriff's station. "They probably won't let you see him, but if you do get in, tell him not to say anything until I get there." Eric had never met Donovan, and Caren couldn't help thinking that Donovan, were he to meet Eric under different circumstances, probably wouldn't like him very much, what with Eric's tailored clothes and his Tulane degree and the fact that he wasn't a Saints fan. The two men didn't know each other, and it was clear that Eric was doing this only as a favor to her. "I'll be there as soon as I can," he said. When she saw him later in the parking lot of the East Courthouse in Gonzales, his suit softly wrinkled, she was struck by how immeasurably kind he could be. "You don't have to do this, you know," she said.

He pulled his necktie from his pocket, sliding the ready loop over his head. "I'm just going to talk to him, get some information from the detectives," he said, adjusting the knot at his throat, above which dark hairs were coming in on his chin. He hadn't bothered to shave this morning, hadn't thought the day would lead to this. "I don't pay bar dues to the state anymore. I'm not licensed to practice here. But, hell, maybe they won't ask. Later, I'll make some calls, try to find him a real lawyer. If this is a murder rap, he's going to need a criminal lawyer, Caren, not someone like me."

He started for the doors to the station.

Then, he stopped suddenly. "You're sure about this kid?"

"Yes," she said, even though she wasn't.

It was only a strong hunch she had that this case was going in a wrong direction. She waited in the parking lot while Eric went inside. She was not family or counsel and was therefore not allowed to see or speak to Donovan. Instead, she sat on the hood of her Volvo, resting her boots on the dented bumper. Ten minutes passed, then twenty. Finally, she crossed to a pay phone outside the courthouse and called over to the kitchen at Belle Vie. The news about Donovan had spread, and Lorraine sounded alternately outraged and then helpless as she asked what they were doing with her Donnie. Caren related what little information she had, plus the fact that Eric was inside right now, talking to the cops. Lorraine seemed touched by Caren's willingness to help Donovan, impressed that she'd known just who to call, telling her for the first time in four years, "I'm glad you come home, baby."

Standing outside the courthouse, Caren smiled to herself.

"Thanks, Lorraine," she said, touched.

Lorraine promised to keep everyone there in line until she got back. This, too, made Caren smile. She hung up the line, then dropped a few more coins in the machine, checking in with Letty at the plantation's library. Twice, she tried to get a hold of Betty Collier, but there was no answer at her house at all.

Behind her, the doors to the courthouse opened.

Eric came out, breathless and worked up.

"They're holding him on a trespassing charge."

"What?"

"Oh, it's all bullshit," he said, walking toward his rental car, a blush-colored sedan that didn't suit him. "They don't have enough to hold him on a murder charge. They're just buying themselves some time. They're not setting a bail hearing until they can get an arraignment judge to the courthouse and that could be as late as Monday."

Caren was walking a few steps behind him. "Trespassing?"

Eric opened his driver's-side door. "Donovan seems to be under the impression that you were the one who called the police on him."

"*Me?*"

"He didn't even know they were Homicide. Before I got here, he had already told them he was on the plantation after hours the night that girl was killed," Eric said, shaking his head at Donovan's colossal stupidity. "He told them he'd copied a key, told them he was on the plantation without permission, working on some school project."

"A *school* project?"

"He was in there digging his own grave for hours," he said, nodding toward the courthouse and the sheriff's station inside. "He got scared and just started talking."

"Wait—Donovan said he was at Belle Vie on Wednesday night?"

She had been emphatic, indignant even, when she assured Lang that Donovan was most certainly not on the grounds the night Inés Avalo was killed. Donovan sat right in her office and told Lang and Bertrand that he wasn't anywhere near Belle Vie, and she had backed him up. It was one more thing likely to turn Lang against her.

"He told the cops he was at school," she said.

"He swears he *was* at school . . . at least by the time they think that woman was killed. He admits to being on the plantation but says he left before midnight and went straight to River Valley Community College, and he says he can prove it. He is adamant that he's never seen the Avalo woman in his life."

"I want to see the arrest report."

She wasn't sure they could get away with a trespassing charge, not without the owners of the property making some assertion that Donovan had indeed entered without prior permission.

"I don't have it," Eric said, arriving at his rental car.

"You didn't ask to see the cops' report?"

It came out rougher than she'd intended, as if she were challenging his skills, his knowledge of the very basics of criminal law. And it didn't go over well with Eric. "Jesus, Caren, I wasn't going to go in there asking for discovery items, and I'm not even the boy's lawyer. I'm not licensed to practice here, and last I checked neither are you." It was a warning to back off. Caren, stung, fell stone silent.

Eric stuck his key in the ignition. "That kid is in a lot of fucking trouble."

He cranked the car's engine.

Across the parking lot, Caren heard another car engine start in chorus. She turned to see a late-'90s Saturn four-door, marine-blue and dented across the front end. Lee Owens was behind the wheel. The *Times-Picayune* reporter had been sitting in his car for the better part of half an hour, she realized, the whole time she'd been waiting in the parking lot. He was wearing the same rumpled clothes from last night, the same ball cap with the name of a jazz club stitched in gray. SWEET LORRAINE'S in New Orleans. He'd been watching the doors of the courthouse this whole time.

Eric put his car in gear.

"Where are you going?"

"To check at the school," he said. "To see if he's telling the truth about any of it. If I'm going to call in a favor for him, then I at least want to know what the hell I'm talking about." He was about to close the driver's-side door. "You coming?"

She turned back to see Lee Owens leaving the parking lot. She saw the tail end of his blue Saturn pulling out onto Irma Avenue. "No," she said to Eric, heading toward her Volvo. "I'll meet you at Belle Vie later." Eric nodded without asking any questions. She'd seen him this way before, calm and focused, intent on getting his mind around some complicated puzzle. He didn't have all the wayward pieces at hand, but he seemed to grasp that something here was off. They pulled out of the parking lot at the same time, Eric turning left, and Caren heading to the right, pushing her eleven-year-old car up to fifty miles an hour, trying to catch up to Owens . . . just as the streetlight on Irma Avenue turned green. She followed him all the way out of the town of Gonzales. She wanted what Owens had, whatever secret knowledge about Hunt Abrams and Groveland's many "problems" the reporter was holding in his possession.

They crossed the Sunshine Bridge over the Mississippi, Highway 70 and drove straight into the town of Donaldsonville, Owens turning onto Albert Street, then again onto Lessard, just a few blocks from the town center. She lost sight of him along the way, when her car got caught behind a truck traveling with a haul from a nearby farm, its bounty hanging out on all sides. She could smell the cane, like cut grass and sweet milk, damp and terrestrial, the scent of southern Louisiana. The truck's tailwind blew through the open windows of her car. When she finally managed to pull around, she didn't see the reporter's car anymore. But by then, she thought she knew where Lee Owens was headed. She gunned her engine, trying to catch up.

15

The Feast of St. Joseph Holy Trinity Church sat on the south side of Lessard Street. Caren remembered it from the photograph, the one Detectives Lang and Bertrand displayed in her office, the snapshot of Inés Avalo and the dark priest, she in a bright dress, those star-shaped earrings catching the sunlight. She was smiling then.

The church was small and built of shale stone and painted wood. Its one front-facing window was a high arch of colored glass set in beveled panels, displaying the image of a cross beneath a yellow sun. Caren sat quite for a moment, staring at the color and light, the way the shifting clouds made play of the sacred scene. She didn't see Owens's car, not on the street or in the parking lot next to the church, which was paved with crushed oyster shells and outlined by a rusting chain-link fence, the gate of which was propped open with a loose brick. She'd lost him somewhere on the drive. He was nowhere in sight. But as she sat now, alone in her car, he almost felt like an afterthought. Strange as it seems, she felt as if the church itself had called her here.

St. Joseph's was not particularly pretty, but it was quaint and welcoming. The front lawn was dotted with wet, fallen leaves from a pecan tree overhead. The double doors were made of arched wood, with twin cast-iron knockers on either side. And just to the right, beside the church's two front steps, sat a tiny, bare-limbed birch tree, its branches adorned with glass bottles of cobalt and sea green, red and ginger brown, all of them in the shape of old soda bottles. It was an unexpected sight, nestled here at the threshold of a Catholic church; it was the kind of thing you could still find in the back swamps, in the desolate, rural haunts of deep Louisiana, parts of which seemed untouched by time and the march of history. The origins of the bottle tree were African, Helen had once told her; it was a folk tradition brought to this country by slaves, who, working with whatever materials were at hand, devised a crude method of catching and trapping malevolent spirits, to prevent their passage through human doors. The colored glass chimed in the light afternoon wind, its empyreal music calling. Caren answered the sound by opening her car door.

She crossed Lessard on foot, stepping into a cold wind that wrapped itself around her arms and legs. Her cheeks flushed, and she felt a dull ache in her chest the closer she got to the front steps. She hadn't been inside a church since her father's funeral—a cold February morning during Morgan's second year. After the church ceremony, she and Eric had stood awkwardly in the family home, where she finally met her brother and sister, and six of their kids, one of whom looked remarkably like Caren. They'd left before the food was served, when it was clear that her presence was making everyone uncomfortable. She had tried, at least. She had tried to do right by at least one of her parents. Missing her mother's funeral was something Caren never got over.

She was careful to wipe her boots before going inside the chapel.

The doors opened directly onto the sanctuary, so that there was no place for Caren to gather herself, to prepare for what she saw when she stepped inside. Down the center aisle, just below the velvet-draped pulpit was a casket. It was made of bleached pine, with rose stems carved on all sides. The coffin's top was open, and inside, peaceful as a sleeping child, lay Inés Avalo. She was in a white lace dress that buttoned to her chin, covering the injury that took her life. She looked stiff in white, like a nervous bride, unsure of what awaited her on the other side of this one life-changing day in church. She was nearly swallowed up by the layers of pale satin lining the casket. But even from here, Caren could see her naked earlobes. The sight of them made her knees weak. She reached for the nearest pew to steady herself. She lowered her body onto the wood, hearing it creak beneath her. She sat perfectly still, as if she were afraid she might wake her.

"I thought you said you didn't know her."

Caren turned sharply.

She saw Lee Owens, sitting in the pew directly behind her. Like a good Catholic, he had removed his hat in the church sanctuary. With his free hand he swept a rogue forelock of his sandy curls off to one side. He had a nice face, kind for the most part. At least she could tell he felt a tinge of guilt for sneaking up on her like this.

"I didn't know her," she said softly.

Not really, she thought.

"You want to tell me why you're following me, ma'am?"

"It's Caren . . . my name."

"I know," he said. "I was just being polite."

He leaned back against the rise of the church pew, smiling sociably, as if they were old friends. "Caren Gray, general manager and caretaker for the Belle Vie Plantation since 2005. Before that, you held a similar position at the Grand Luxe Hotel in New Orleans." Then he added, "I knew all this last night." He pulled an iPhone from his pocket, briefly checking the time before sliding it back into his khakis.

"Who's following whom?"

Owens smiled. "Aw, touché."

Then, sizing her up, he said, "You one of those who never went back?"

He was speaking of New Orleans, of course, and Caren sensed an unspoken criticism, a judgment that she, like so many others, was a fair-weather friend, a woman whose fidelity was only for the good times. He turned and stared solemnly down the center aisle.

Softly, he said, "She's pretty."

"What are you doing here?"

"Why? You're not armed, are you?" With a wry smile, he raised his hands in mock surrender, showing his open palms. Caren didn't think any of this was funny. "What happened in Florida?" she said.

She still had Inés's earring in her pocket, the one she'd found in Hunt Abrams's trailer.

Owens just sat there, chewing on his bottom lip.

"Last night, you said Groveland moved Hunt Abrams from Florida to Bakersfield and then Washington State. What happened in Florida?" she said, remembering what little she'd found on the Internet. "There was a girl who was hurt?"

"Wasn't 'hurt,' ma'am," he said. "She was beaten."

"By Abrams?"

"That's the way I heard it. He beat a woman for not clearing a row fast enough."

The thought made Caren's stomach turn.

"There were others, too," Owens said. "Was a field-worker in Bakersfield just laid down in a tangle of grapevines one day and never got up. He'd been working ten hours in hundred-degree temps without a water break." He glanced again at his phone, checking the time. "No one I talked to ever accused Hunt

Abrams of being kind. But the company looks the other way because he's made those guys a shitload of money. And, hell, he's never been charged with anything. So, you know, they just keep moving him around if they have to. It'll be interesting to see how they play this one, though. The problem for Groveland now is the timing," he said, shaking his head.

The words had a strangely familiar ring.

She'd heard Raymond Clancy assert nearly the exact same thing, the day the body was found. *The timing couldn't be any worse,* he'd said.

"I mean, they've got their eye on building a real deal sugar business for themselves down here. And I don't imagine they want a murder investigation cropping up right now. They've already successfully passed phase one, buying up nearly every sugar mill in Louisiana. I mean, they're about this close"—holding his right thumb and index finger about a hair's width apart—"from controlling all the cane manufacturing in the state." He sat forward then, rolling the bill of his cap between his hands. "Phase two, that's coming, you watch. It's all just a matter of time."

Here he'd lost her. "What is?"

He smiled, cocking his head and regarding her as a skeptic might, as if he thought she was putting him on. But she genuinely had no idea what he was getting at.

"What's a matter of time?"

"Oh, come on, ma'am," he said. "You telling me you never wondered why a big ag corp like Groveland is bothering with five hundred acres in central Louisiana?"

"No," she said flatly.

It was hard, actually, to imagine anything she'd spent less time thinking about.

"That farm back there behind your place, that's just the start."

"Of what exactly?"

"Well, ma'am, this parish sits at the center of a billion-dollar industry. That's the bare-minimum value of sugar in this state. And Groveland wants it. They've been looking for a way in for years now. But Louisiana ain't ever been too keen on corporate farming. That's Florida's deal, Texas and California. And so far, no family's ever been willing to sell to them. But then they took over the Renfrews' lease back there and pushed them out . . . and, see, that's how it starts. 'Cause wait, just wait, one of these days some other family that's broke and desperate, they'll sell their land to 'em, and then all the rest of the farms will start to fall like dominoes. It just has to start somewhere. But no one wants to be the first asshole to sell to a company from out of state."

Raymond Clancy, she thought.

A few moments passed before she realized she'd said the name out loud.

So it was true, she thought. She couldn't believe she hadn't put it together before. But now it seemed perfectly clear. Clancy was planning to turn Belle Vie over to the Groveland Corporation. That's why the repeated admonition that she was not to mention a thing about a Groveland worker being killed. Not a word to the press, he'd said. He was on the verge of a sale. Owen leaned forward in his seat. "I'm sorry . . . what did you say?"

He lied to me, she thought.

The son of a bitch lied to me.

"Raymond Clancy," she said. "He's selling the plantation."

"To Groveland?"

Owens already had a hand in his pocket, was already reaching for a pen and pad. He yanked off the plastic pen cap with his teeth, pressing her for more details. "Raymond Clancy isn't exactly hurting for anything. Why is he selling the plantation *now*?"

"Why don't you find out what Larry Becht was doing in Clancy's office yesterday?"

He lied to her.

Hadn't Bobby warned her?

She didn't owe Raymond any loyalty, she told herself. She didn't owe him anything. Owen was scribbling fast. "Becht?" She could tell the name meant something to him, had triggered some reporter's instinct. A political consultant would have only one reason to be in Raymond Clancy's law office. "Are you sure?" he asked, still writing everything down.

There were footsteps behind them.

She turned first, then Owens.

The black priest had emerged from a side hall, one that appeared to lead to the church's small suite of offices. He was walking directly toward them, a few loose sheets of paper tucked under his right arm.

"May I help you with something?"

Owens stood, holding out a hand. "Lee Owens, Father Akerele. We spoke on the phone."

"Yes, yes," the priest said, receiving the man's handshake warmly. "I remember, sure." He glanced at his wristwatch. "I have some time now. We can chat in my office. Ginny is not available, I'm afraid. She's the woman who heads our ministry for the farmworkers, the migrants and their families. She's been out in the fields, making rounds, checking up on everyone, the ones who worked the Groveland farm especially, the ones who knew Inés. A few of them are having a particularly hard time, as you can imagine. They come from all over, Oaxaca and Chiapas, Durango, even Zacapa, south of Mexico. But here, they're family. Ginny is doing what she can to help. There have been a lot of frayed nerves, and a great deal of fear. She's out this morning seeing about an attorney for some of the men on the Groveland farm."

"An attorney, Father?" Owens said.

Akerele gave the reporter a curious look, as if he wondered whether Owens was deliberately playing dumb, baiting him in some way. "Well, surely it comes as no surprise to a man who covers the sugar business for a newspaper that a good deal of the men and women in the fields out there are lacking proper immigration papers. We are keeping no secrets here. The men simply want assurance that they won't be put in jail just for speaking with the sheriff's men. The church has encouraged everyone to tell what they know. But they need protection, Mr. Owens, in every way. People take advantage, you know. We've had to consult lawyers in the past, even in regards to wage disputes, times the workers haven't gotten paid. It can be a danger for them to speak up." He shook his head to himself, bowing slightly, so that Caren could see a part in the center of his close-cropped hair, like the plow line of a well-kept field. "I've been in this country for almost eight years now, and in all the years I've been ministering to the migrants, I've never seen it like this. I am afraid for them in a way I've never been."

He sighed, shifting his papers from one arm to the other.

"Luckily," he said, "Mr. Orellana has been cleared. He was working in town that day, at a second job, cleaning up a construction site. He had a very strong alibi."

"Orellana?"

"Gustavo Orellana, Mr. Owens. He is a worker on the Groveland farm. I'm told that he and Inés had developed something more than a casual relationship." Akerele pressed his lips together, declining, without being asked, to say more on the subject.

Caren remembered the name Gustavo.

He was at the candlelight vigil, leaned against the fence, weeping.

Owens wrote the priest's words on his notepad, writing in the margins every detail he could gather about Akerele himself. "You're from Africa, Father?"

"Nigeria, son."

"You mentioned wage disputes and the like," Owens said. "Did Inés Avalo ever have any problems out on the farm, any troubles with the manager out there?"

Up to this point, Akerele had not looked directly at Caren.

But he knew she was there, of course, and he declined to say more in her presence. Remembering his manners, he finally turned to address her. He nodded his head and said, "Good morning," his accent like seashells on a string, sharp and melodic. "If you would like to pay your respects, there will be a memorial service here in the sanctuary this coming week. We welcome all who wish to honor her." He smiled warmly at her, and she felt strangely embarrassed. She was telling a lie, wasn't she? She didn't know Inés, she wanted to say. But even that no longer felt like the truth.

"She'll be buried here in town?" Owens asked.

"That has yet to be determined, I'm afraid," the priest said, his expression growing long. "We are still trying to locate her family in San Julián. We know she sent money home, at least once a month. She had two children, you should know."

The money order, Caren remembered.

The pink ribbon and the hairbrush and the white teddy bear with the red bow.

She'd been standing in that small grocery store, arguing with the cashier just to get these gifts, large and small, home to her kids . . . only to walk away empty-handed.

"We can't find a proper phone number for her family. I have sent two telegrams to the parish church nearest her village. But as of yet there's been no word, no way of knowing if her family there understands she's gone."

"That's in Mexico?" Owens said, still writing.

"El Salvador."

"Quite a long way from home."

Akerele nodded solemnly.

"Her husband was injured on a job some time ago, badly enough apparently that he can no longer work. And so I suppose she did what she felt she had to. She left her kids, a boy and a girl, the youngest not even two years old, with her mother's people and came north for work." He looked at Owens and Caren, as if they'd loved her, too, as if the three of them shared that much. "It was only meant as a temporary stay, to send money home, to get out of a hole. She was supposed to be going home."

He sighed.

"I have given myself until Monday," he said. "If I cannot find a relative, someone to claim the body, we will make a final home for her here. She will not be alone. She will have a proper resting place."

He neatened the sheaf of papers in his hands.

Then he looked at Owens. "Shall we, then?" he said. "We can speak more in my office." As they turned to leave, Akerele again smiled at Caren. "Good day, ma'am." Owens followed the priest to his office, leaving the two women alone in the church sanctuary. Caren stood eventually, walking the length of the center aisle to stand at the edge of the pine casket. From her jacket pocket, she pulled out the tiny, star-shaped earring, a thing she had no business holding on to. It would only cause her trouble every minute she kept it in her possession, the effects of a dead woman, a murder victim. She leaned forward and tucked the earring into the folds of satin.

She stood there for a long time, gazing at Inés Avalo, at the heart-shaped face and the half-moons of her sleeping eyes, the clasped hands still marked by work in the fields. Somewhere, Caren thought, there were two children, a boy and a girl, who nightly dream of that face, two kids who have no idea their mother is never coming home.

When Caren walked through the front door of the library, Eric was alone in the house. He had his back to the door, and he was on the phone.

She took off her jacket, left her keys on the antique writing table, and waited. "I don't know," Eric was saying into his cell phone. "I'll see what's available tomorrow." He turned, noticing Caren for the first time. "I'll call you as soon as I know when I'm coming home." He paused there, his voice growing soft. "You, too, honey."

He ended the call, shoving the cell phone into his pocket. He turned to Caren and said, "I missed my flight."

She was already walking toward him, her arms hanging helpless at her sides. She walked right up to him, standing so close that their torsos were almost touching. "What are you doing?" he said, sounding at first confused and then alarmed, as if he were retreating from an electric charge. She wanted him to touch her, for someone to please hold her. But she knew it was not her place to ask, not anymore. She simply stood there, pressing herself closer to him, until she could feel the heat coming through his clothes, until she could feel the outline of his body against hers. "Don't do this," he said. She wasn't playing fair, she knew. But she couldn't stop herself either. She laid her head on his chest, hearing his voice above her, whispering a plea. "Don't do this to me."

Finally, she cried.

For Inés, those two kids.

For Belle Vie, slipping away.

And for her mother, already long gone.

And she cried for this man standing in front of her, yet another loss. He finally relented and put his arms around her, holding Caren up in all the ways she no longer could. She felt a warm kiss on her forehead, and when she looked up, their eyes met, and it was Eric, she would always remember, who put his lips on hers. His breath was sweet and hot, his hands rough across her skin. She cupped his face in her palms, kissing him tenderly. Eric pulled away first, staggering slightly, like a drunk on two legs for the first time in as many days. He lowered his eyes, shaking his head in self-reproach, or else surrender. Then he took her by the hand and led her through the parlor and the empty kitchen and up the narrow stairway to her bedroom.

The
Olden Days
of Belle Vie

16

Eric got dressed first. He sat on the side of the bed, his back to her.

"Where's Letty?" he said. "Morgan?"

"The store, maybe," she said. "Plus, Letty said something about taking Morgan along to her son's softball game, down in Vacherie."

Eric stood, tucking his shirt into his pants. "I need to get some air." He walked out of the room without looking back, leaving Caren alone on the bed, the bunched-up quilt snaked between her legs. She rolled over onto her back, one arm curved above her head. She could see part of the sky through the trees outside her window. The clouds had briefly cleared, and the shard of blue was as startling as sunlight pouring into a dark cave. She lay perfectly still for a few minutes, then slowly roused herself from bed, slid on her clothes, and headed downstairs to face him.

Outside, Eric was leaning against a small pin oak tree, smoking a cigarette. She walked within a few feet of him, slowing as she neared, shoving her hands into the pockets of her jeans. Her eyes were red and puffy, the skin on her cheeks rubbed raw from the stubble on Eric's face. She had been turned completely inside out.

It was a while before either of them spoke.

"Eric," she said.

He sucked on his cigarette, the filter pinched between two of his fingers, not exactly looking her in the eye. "Donovan *did* go to school Wednesday night, by the way," he said, blowing smoke into the wind. "The night that girl was killed, he was there, long before the cops say the Avalo woman was killed."

She let out a sigh. "Come on, Eric."

But he just shook his head.

"I can't, Caren," he said, taking another drag. "I can't talk about this right now, okay. I just can't. You asked me to do you a favor and I did you a favor. The kid was on the college campus, just like he said. He needs a criminal defense attorney."

He reached into his pants pocket and pulled out a folded-up piece of paper. On one side, otherwise blank, he'd scribbled the names of several attorneys and their phone numbers, each with a 504 area code. On the other side of the paper was a messy table of handwritten names and dates and times in two columns, labeled "In" and "Out," next to lists of words she didn't, at first glance, understand. It appeared to be a sign-up sheet of some sort, with the heading: RIVER VALLEY COMMUNITY COLLEGE AUDIO & VISUAL ARTS CENTER. "I copied this myself," Eric said, tapping the paper with his index finger. "He checked in camera equipment to the school's video lab a little before twelve-thirty in the morning. I talked to a girl who works at the lab who's sure she was the one who signed in the equipment when Donovan returned it. She said he brought it all back himself."

Caren grabbed the paper from Eric, studying it more closely.

Donovan's was the second-to-last name in the far-left column.

According to this, at 12:22 a.m. he returned a Sony DSR DVCAM camcorder, an Audix miniature condenser microphone with a 50-inch boom arm and two sets of headphones, a Lowel two-light kit, four 25-foot extension cords . . . and a tripod.

Oh, God, she whispered.

She looked up at Eric, shaking her head in disbelief.

"What?" he said.

"He was here Wednesday night, that's what you said before?"

"He said he was working on some kind of a school project," Eric said. And then, clearing up an earlier misconception, he added, "It turns out he has not, in fact, quit school, but is on some kind of academic probation for carrying too light a load."

"And he was *here*?"

Eric nodded. "But he says he left a little before midnight, *before* the murder. He left Belle Vie and went straight to the River Valley campus in Donaldsonville. He didn't mention it when the detectives first cornered him in your office because he thought he could talk his way around it. I told you, I don't think he had any idea those were two homicide cops he was talking to. I don't think he really thought it was a big deal, him being on the plantation after hours."

"With *camera* equipment?" Caren said, repeating what she took to be the most revealing part of what Eric was saying. She had a pretty good idea this was another one of Donovan's stunts. Only this time he'd gone too far, landing himself in real trouble.

"I can't believe he did this," she mumbled.

"Did what?"

It would have taken too much time to explain the origins of her growing suspicion, her guess as to why Donovan had snuck onto the plantation after hours, with camera equipment no less. She would have to go all the way back to the summer, when Donovan came into her office with a handwritten script and a story he was dying to tell about life at a place like Belle Vie. "The truth is going to come out," he'd said.

Oh, Donovan, she sighed.

She turned back to the library. Inside, she grabbed her key ring and jacket.

When she stepped outside again, Eric was on his second cigarette.

"Are you going to be here when I get back?" she said. Eric, who was standing on the grounds of an antebellum plantation wearing the same clothes as yesterday, clothes that were only minutes before crumpled on the floor beside her bed, looked dazed. "Where am *I* going?" he said, shrugging at the absurdity of it all.

Caren started for the main house alone.

Upstairs, she tore through the drawers in her office, the mess of papers and files on the painted settee near the door, even lifting phone books beside her desk; she was looking for a stack of yellow legal paper. She couldn't remember if she'd kept the handwritten script or if Donovan had taken his copy back. This whole mess could be cleared up in an instant, she thought. The cops needed to know that Donovan had his own reasons for being on the grounds after hours on Wednesday night, and they didn't have a thing to do with Inés Avalo. When she couldn't find the script in her office, she left the main house and walked across the lawn, heading for the old schoolhouse.

They were all onstage for the eleven-o'clock show.

Which meant the greenroom was vacant.

She could hear their voices through the plaster wall as she snooped around the room—Bo Johnston and Eddie Knoxville, in character, were talking about the advance of Union troops on New Orleans. The place was littered with soda cans and used tissues and crumpled copies of the *Times-Picayune*, and somebody had left a half-eaten ham and onion sandwich in plastic wrap sitting out. Across the room, against the far-left wall, stood a column of twelve-by-twelve-inch-square lockers, none of which had ever been secured except the one belonging to Val Marchand, who brought her own padlock from home. Caren opened them one by one, picking through Dell's *Essence* magazines and romance novels and an open pack of Virginia Slims, Bo Johnston's tank tops and roll-on deodorant. Finally, she stumbled on Donovan's personal locker. The cops had been in here yesterday, as part of their search. And this is what they left behind: a hairbrush; a couple of unmarked CDs; a pair of rubber, open-toed slippers; a tourist map of the plantation; and, at the very back of the locker, a stack of white paper, bound by brass brads, which the cops must have mistaken for a copy of the plantation's official staged play. But Caren knew better. This script had Donovan's name on the cover.

RAISING CANE: A NEW SHERIFF IN TOWN, by Donovan James Isaacs.

And below that, the words: *Inspired by a True Story*.

It was a work in progress, maybe twenty or thirty pages long, with bits and pieces blacked out and handwritten notes scribbled in the margins. But the story was immediately familiar. The setting, as was noted in a surprisingly well-written opening, was 1872, three weeks after the election that put Ulysses S. Grant into his second term—the same election that, just a few years after Emancipation, put a black man in the highest law-enforcement office in the parish. There was, quite literally, a new sheriff in town, a man by the name of Aaron Nathan Sweats, a name Caren had seen once before, in the pages of Danny's dissertation. Sweats was the lawman who had investigated Jason's disappearance, who believed that he'd been the victim of foul play. Caren felt a tingle at the mention of the family name. *Jason*. A man missing one hundred and thirty-seven years, and yet here he was again, showing up in print right before Caren's eyes. She flipped through the pages of the script, trying to understand how Donovan Isaacs, the same employee who'd once asked her if slaves could talk, had put a story like this one on paper. She would have put her next month's salary on the fact that he'd had some help.

It was Danny she wanted to talk to.

Caren hadn't seen him all day, so she started the quarter-mile trek to the plantation's kitchen, to pay a visit to the eyes and ears of Belle Vie.

Lorraine was drinking a beer when she walked in.

The kitchen was unusually cluttered. There were torn sheets of notebook paper everywhere. Lorraine pulled a pencil stub from the front pocket of her soiled apron. She was making notes. "I'm going to need to order at least twenty pounds of crab legs for the Whitman gal. You can charge 'em what you want for it, baby. I don't care. I've got a theme in mind, and that girl is just going to have to trust me on this one."

"Lorraine," Caren said. "Have you seen Danny?"

"No, ma'am, baby."

"Pearl?"

She looked over at Lorraine's second-in-command, who had her size-five feet set atop an orange crate in the corner; she was eating sour cream straight from a plastic tub. Pearl shook her head no. Lorraine said, "I believe he stays in town on Saturdays, baby." She was still scribbling her menu notes. "You not likely to see him today."

Caren held up Donovan's movie script. "Did you know about this?"

Lorraine screwed up her face at the sight, scrunching up the puffy flesh around her eyes. Pearl, seeing the script in Caren's hand, froze, a cream-covered spoon a few inches from her mouth. She dropped the tub of sour cream, spilling it on the concrete floor, before scurrying out of the kitchen on her bare feet. Lorraine, watching her number two crumple in the pres-ence of modest authority, rolled her eyes. She slid the pencil stub into her pocket and wiped her hands on her apron. "Well, for the record, baby," she said to Caren, "I never approved of it. I knew it was going to lead to trouble, one way or another. But you can't be after these people all the damn time," she said, as if the very fact that Caren was coming to her for information was further proof that Lorraine was the one in charge here, the real lady of the house. "I firmly discouraged it," she said. She gathered her menu notes, stacking them in a messy pile.

Caren stood before her, dumbstruck.

"Wait, who else knows about this?"

"Well," Lorraine said with a sigh. "There's his cast . . ."

"*His* cast?"

"The *cast*," Lorraine said, as if this were obvious. "The Belle Vie Players."

"They all know?"

Lorraine nodded, and said, "Yes, ma'am, baby."

It was as if Lorraine had literally struck her in the face.

She hadn't realized, until maybe that very moment, the depths to which she'd come to think of them as family over the years, not just *a* family, but *her* family. Lorraine and Pearl and Luis, Nikki and Dell and Shauna and Ennis, Cornelius and Bo Johnston and the whole cast . . . even Donovan. "Why didn't you all say anything?" she said, raising her voice at Lorraine for the first time ever. She was angry, but also hurt. Why didn't *any* of them say anything to her? "Why in the world wouldn't you tell this to police?"

Lorraine gave a slight shrug, the gesture nearly lost in the rolls of fat on her neck and shoulders. Then, matter-of-factly, she said, "They didn't ask." She took her stack of handwritten notes to her "desk," the card table on which sat her television set, today's paper, and an open pack of menthol cigarettes. She shoved the loose papers into a grease-stained manila envelope. She didn't seem the least bit bothered by the implications of the information she'd been withholding, the fact that Donovan had apparently been coming onto the grounds after hours for some time now and was here on the night a crime was committed, a murder. "I'm glad he done it, though, tell you the truth," she said, meaning Donovan's movie project. She reached into her apron pocket for a Zippo lighter, a gift, Caren remembered, from the entire staff. They'd had it engraved for her sixtieth birthday last spring. Lorraine lit a smoke, sucking hard before exhaling. "If Raymond's gon' let this place go, there ought to be some way to know it was ever here. It's got to be some way to remember it."

Caren glanced down at Donovan's script.

Behind her, Pearl poked her head into the kitchen.

She disappeared just as suddenly when she realized Caren was still here.

"And just for the record," Lorraine said, again insisting that she be seen as an innocent party in this, "I told Donovan to leave the little one out of it."

Caren looked up suddenly.

There was a breeze blowing through the open door. It lifted the hairs on her skin, woke every raw nerve ending in her body.

"Excuse me?"

"Morgan," Lorraine said, surprised that Caren hadn't already guessed as much. "I told Donovan not to involve the girl, no matter how many different ways she asked."

"Morgan knows about this?"

For the first time, Lorraine sensed she had waded into real trouble.

She had no children of her own but had always shown great care where Morgan was concerned. "I made him promise, Caren," she said, her voice hushed but firm. "I told Donovan— under no circumstances was he to have that baby out after dark."

* * *

That night, after Letty dropped Morgan off and left for home, her baked chicken and rice sat untouched on the kitchen table. Upstairs, it was just the three of them. Eric and Caren told Morgan it was time to talk. It was time for her to tell them the truth.

"I did."

Caren shook her head. "No, Morgan, you didn't."

She held up her purloined copy of Donovan's script.

Morgan merely glanced at it and shrugged, the way only a child would, one who has no earthly understanding of the consequences of her foolish actions, who believes a lie will close a door instead of opening twenty. Caren didn't know if it was rage that gripped her . . . or pure terror. She grabbed one of Morgan's pudgy, soft arms, squeezing until she felt bone, squeezing as hard as she might have to stop her daughter from marching into oncoming traffic or walking absentmindedly off a cliff.

"Caren," Eric said, stopping her.

On the bed, Morgan started to cry.

Her father knelt before the small twin bed, turning his back to Caren. He reached for Morgan's hands, two small fists that completely disappeared into his own. This is why nature intended two souls to raise a child, Caren thought. She wanted to shake her daughter by the shoulders until all her secrets spilled out like marbles onto the floor. Eric, on the other hand, was calm in his approach. "We need you to tell us what's going on here, Morgan," he said. "I can't say enough how important it is for you to tell us the truth. *Now*, Morgan."

"Is Donovan going to prison?"

Eric glanced at Caren.

Alarmed, she asked, "Did you see him hurt someone?"

Morgan shook her head.

Caren repeated the old refrain. "How did you get blood on your shirt, Morgan?"

Morgan looked at her mother, her eyes like two polished stones, hard and cold. "You sent him away," she cried, pointing at her and blubbering through her fury. At first Caren thought she was talking about her father, accusing Caren of sending Eric away.

But Eric understood.

"Honey, your mother didn't turn Donovan in," he said.

Morgan wiped her nose with the back of her hand, smearing snot across her plump, brown cheeks. "It wasn't him," she said emphatically. "He didn't *do* anything."

"You need to tell us what you saw."

"It wasn't him," she kept saying, over and over.

Eric waited for her to add something more, to explain herself. "Come on, Morgan," he said, growing impatient. He looked at Caren at one point, his expression surprisingly helpless. "Morgan," her mother said softly. By now, the girl's bottom lip was trembling. She was looking at Caren, her eyes wide and pleading, waiting, maybe, for just the tiniest nudge. "What is it, 'Cakes?" Caren said. "Just tell us what you saw."

"The knife," Morgan said finally, her eyes welling up again. "I saw the knife."

17

Morgan had known about Donovan's history project for over a month. He'd started working on it at the start of the fall semester, dropping all his other classes so he could focus on the film full-time. He thought the project could earn him a solid A for his history class. But then the more he got into it, the more he decided he was thinking too small. The story was good, one that needed to be told, about life on the other side of slavery. He thought he might take it to New Orleans; they had an annual film festival, and those movies played in a real theater; some of them went on to make real money. He had the school's equipment, a ready cast of actors, and a location that was already perfectly set-dressed. He had no intention of letting a no from Caren stop him, so he never asked for her permission. Instead, he copied one of Gerald's keys and started casting the Belle Vie Players in his film. They would work at night, paid in cold pizza and warm beer and the promise of glory to come if the movie got picked up by a major distributor, or, failing that, found a life of notoriety on YouTube, Donovan's name going viral. *Raising Cane* would be groundbreaking, a story to put to rest that "Swing Low, Sweet Chariot" mess for good, he said. Donovan wanted to blow the world away with the story of a gun-toting sheriff who was kickin' ass and takin' names, just a few years after black folks "quit" being slaves. Donovan finally had a real story, one he could believe in, and he promptly cast himself as the sheriff.

All of this Morgan learned by hanging out in the kitchen after school, where the Belle Vie staff treated her like a cousin or a baby sister who was loved and tolerated, if not particularly taken seriously. And, yes, just like Lorraine said, Morgan had asked Donovan if she could be in the movie. But Lorraine, who wanted no part in this elaborate misadventure—Dell and Val Marchand had likewise opted out—put her foot down about the girl. Donovan, within earshot of Lorraine, had turned Morgan down. He wouldn't even let her on his crew, which consisted of him and Shep on camera and lights, respectively. Morgan backed off, making do with gossip and stories from the set. Her loyal silence and fervent avowal not to tell her mother bought her a ticket to the backstage drama. There were complaints about Eddie Knoxville's drinking and the fact that he could never remember his lines. Shauna complained about the bugs and wanted to know if they could move some of the scenes into the main house. Oh, and Nikki didn't like the fact that Shauna got to play the part of the pretty schoolteacher.

This went on for weeks.

But then came the rains and everything was shut down. Donovan said they'd pick up again when the weather got better, which it didn't for the longest time.

"Wednesday night, though," Morgan said. "It was supposed to be clear."

She had never been "on set," had never left her mother's house without asking. She looked at Caren as she said this, wanting her to know that this was a one-time indiscretion. Caren found herself nodding along encouragingly. "I just wanted to be part of something," Morgan said, speaking of Belle Vie's staff. She just wanted to feel like she was part of this group, she said. "I'm not like you, Mom," she said. "I don't like being out here all by myself. I don't want to be alone."

Eric looked at Caren but was kind enough not to comment.

"Go on, 'Cakes," she said.

Wednesday night it was all set, Morgan said.

Everybody was supposed to be there. It was going to be her big chance.

"Nikki and Bo, Shauna and Cornelius and Shep and Eddie . . . and Donovan. It was supposed to be everybody out that night. Donovan was all excited. They were going to shoot the big scene where the sheriff makes an arrest for the killing of that man, the one who went missing." Caren stopped her here. An arrest, she thought. She didn't remember seeing that in Donovan's script.

"You mean Jason?" she said.

Morgan nodded.

Eric, who was not following even ten percent of this, looked sideways at Caren.

She looked at her daughter and nodded. "Go on."

Morgan, who had finally stopped crying, wiped her cheeks with the seat of her palm. Her mouth had gone dry, and her lips were chapped. "I just wanted to hang out with Donovan. I just wanted to be friends with all of them. But he didn't want me there."

"Where?" Caren asked.

"The Manette house."

She knew they were planning to shoot there. So she waited until her mother fell asleep, then she took the flashlight from the top drawer of the antique writing table and walked across the plantation.

Donovan, it turned out, was the only one there.

"No one else showed," she said. "He had the camera, the

lights, and all that. But no one else was there. He tried calling a few people, but he couldn't get anyone on the phone. He was real mad. He said it was just because of a little rain. That's why no one had showed up. He called them a bunch of pussies." She looked at her parents, waiting for some reaction to the word.

"And then what happened?" Eric said.

"Donovan told me I had to leave, that he would get in a shit-load of trouble," she said, coloring the telling, emboldened by her success with the earlier vulgarity. "If anyone found out that he let me stay out there like that, he would get fired, he said, or worse. It was almost midnight by then, and he told me to go home."

"But you didn't," Caren said.

Morgan shook her head. "No."

She hid behind one of the magnolias, she said, the one that sat between the two cottages on the back side of the Manette house. Caren nodded; she knew the color and personality of nearly every tree and shrub on the property. "Donovan said he was going to wait around for them a little while longer," Morgan said. "He was going to shoot some background stuff in front of Manette, on the path, like pictures of the house and stuff, and I thought I could just wait, too. I thought when everyone got there, he might change his mind . . . or he'd be so busy he wouldn't even notice I was there."

Eric's cell phone rang.

Morgan was the only one who didn't jump.

Her father reached into his pants pocket. He glanced at the phone number. Caren wondered if it was Lela, if he'd told her what had happened between them this afternoon. He silenced the ringer without answering, without saying a single word.

"I think I must have fallen asleep," Morgan said. "The rain started. It was just a few drops at first. I felt it on my face, and it woke me up. It was quiet, real quiet. And I kind of, for a second, forgot where I was. I didn't see Donovan. I didn't see anybody."

Caren remembered that it was shortly after midnight, twelve-twenty in the morning according to the sign-in sheet, when Donovan checked in the camera equipment on campus, all the way in Donaldsonville. He was already gone by then, she realized, and Morgan woke up out there on the grounds after midnight, totally alone.

"I heard something," she said.

"Heard something, like what?"

"I heard somebody scream."

"Jesus, Morgan," Eric muttered. "Why didn't you say anything?"

He sounded exasperated with her, even disappointed, as if he'd forgotten she was only nine years old. Morgan shrugged, only this time the gesture seemed small and sad. "I didn't want to get anyone in trouble." Even at her age she seemed to grasp the supreme irony of this statement, what with Donovan sitting in a jail cell right now. "You have to help him, Mom," she said. "He didn't do this."

"Where was the knife, Morgan?" Caren asked, pressing her. She needed her to finish what she'd started.

Morgan paused, swallowing hard before continuing.

"The scream came from down by the quarters," she said. "Manette house was empty, and I thought for a second that maybe Donovan had moved everything down there. Maybe they were filming something down there. It was getting cold, but it was only drizzling at first, and I thought I might still get to see them doing the movie. I could get a blanket for Shauna or help Eddie with his lines. I thought they might let me help." She pulled away from her parents, bringing her knees into her chest and scooting her body to the center of the bed, so that she seemed alone on her own island.

"I got all the way to the dirt road," she said.

"In the quarters?"

Morgan nodded.

"Where is this?" Eric asked.

"The slave cabins," Caren explained.

Eric made a face but said nothing.

"There was light at the end."

"Light?" Caren said, confused.

"In one of the cabins."

Caren shook her head, thinking this couldn't be. Past the guest cottages, there was no electricity on the grounds. Sure, it was possible that Donovan had a small generator or a battery pack for his portable lights and equipment, but Donovan, Caren knew, was already either back on campus by then or on his way, and Morgan was out on the grounds, alone with Inés and her killer. It physically hurt her to listen to her daughter recount her slow march down the dirt road, through the shadows in the quarters, all the way to the last cabin on the left, Jason's Cabin. Morgan had still been expecting to find the whole crew out there, she said, Donovan and the cast.

She walked toward the light. It was dim and yellow, not like the sharp white light of the flashlight in her hand, but something soft and flickering. She got all the way to the gate, but then something made her stop. "I got kind of a funny feeling all of a sudden," she said. "There was no one out there." Not Donovan or Shauna, Nikki or Shep. There wasn't a single cast member in sight. Which made no sense to Morgan; she couldn't understand where the light was coming from. She thought of the plantation ghost stories and got very, very scared. It was when she turned to leave that her flashlight caught the shape of something on the ground, resting just inside the low-lying fence, the gate to which was wide open and swinging in the wind. "I just wanted to see what it was," she said.

"You touched it?" Eric asked.

"It was warm . . . and wet."

She pointed the flashlight on the ground and saw blood.

"I ran," Morgan said, sounding relieved to have this confession behind her. "I ran all the way home." She looked up at them. Eric was standing, hands on his hips.

"Show me," he said.

It was after dark when the three of them started for the quarters, Caren chauffeuring from behind the wheel of the golf cart. She stopped at the top of the dirt road, as she always did, idling the cart while Eric, who had never laid eyes on the slave cabins, was staring straight ahead. He'd never seen anything like it, and Caren found herself wanting to reach for his hand, because no person should experience this moment alone, this face-to-face meeting with one's own history, the family you never knew you had. The cottages were aligned in two rows, three on each side of the dirt road. Their spindly columns were like tired arms at the end of a long day's work, nearly crushed beneath the weight of what they were being asked to hold up. The plank porches sagged in places; each cabin, silhouetted by the newly set sun, was no more than a few feet wide, smaller than some of the SUVs riding on American highways.

Caren could hear Eric's breathing.

He was so quiet for so long that Morgan, sitting between them, whispered, "Daddy," while nudging him in his side.

He turned, looking first at Caren, and then his daughter. Then, facing the quarters, he put both hands on the cart's dashboard, as if he were literally bracing himself for what lay ahead. Finally, he stepped out. Caren shut the engine, and the two of them followed their daughter's small footprints in the dirt.

In front of Jason's Cabin, Morgan stopped.

She turned, looking over her shoulder at her mother and father, and, without saying a word, pointed to a spot just inside the gate: *It was right here.* Caren walked ahead of Eric, who was studying the face of each cabin he passed, the hollow windows like eyes behind which lay a glimpse of the soul of slave life; and they, in turn, seemed to be watching him, too, this black man in wool gabardine and dress shoes, a five-hundred-dollar watch on his wrist. The tiny square yard in front of the last cabin on the left was filled with dirt and patches of grass, all of which had been washed over by days of rain. Standing at the threshold of the gate's small wooden door, Caren saw no trace of blood. She pulled the black Maglite from the back pocket of her jeans and shone a thin stream of light on the spot where Morgan said she saw the bloody knife. She knew the cops hadn't found the murder weapon, which meant whoever left it there must have returned at some point to remove it, the same way they tried to steal off the property with Inés's limp body. Stopped by the fence, Lang had said. Eric was behind her. He nodded toward the cabin. "Is it okay if I go in?"

Caren opened the gate for him.

Morgan clung to her mother's side as she followed them into the cabin. Soon the three of them were crowded inside, a family barely contained by these four walls. It was hard to imagine Jason raising his own family here. Eric, who was nearly six feet tall, hunched over as he studied the artifacts in the cabin: the gathering of rusted pots and pans around a fire pit dug into the ground; the patchwork quilt and straw pallet on the dirt floor; and the unfinished table, which Eric stared at for quite some time. Morgan said, "I want to go back." Caren nodded, but she didn't move. Like Eric, she was looking for something, though what, exactly, she couldn't say. A clue, maybe, as to what went on in this one-room shack. "I'm serious, Mom," Morgan said. "I don't like it in here." Caren felt it, too, the air so still it cut, the feeling that you could never get enough breath, no matter how hard you tried. She'd avoided this cabin before. It had, even before Inés's murder, made her feel unimaginably sad. She was just about to leave when Eric pointed to something on the tabletop. She moved closer and saw those same drops of candle wax, milky white and fresh enough to peel with ease when Caren scratched at the wax with her thumbnail. She remembered Morgan's description of a flickering light coming from the cabin and had a terrifying thought that the killer could have still been inside the cabin that night, while her daughter was only a few feet away at the gate. Eric must have been thinking the same thing. His face was blanched with a look of horror. He shook his head slowly. *This is not good, Caren.*

He was right.

This was not good at all.

She made an instinctive turn toward her daughter . . . but Morgan was gone. Caren called her name calmly at first. But she heard no response . . . and her panic started to spread. She ran for the door. "Morgan!" she yelled. It was Eric who stopped her, grabbing her from behind and practically lifting her off the ground. He pulled the whole weight of her toward the front window, so that she could see Morgan was standing outside by the fence, waiting. This wasn't all Caren could see. What was also clear from this vantage point, this gaze through the cabin's front window, was the realization that if the killer was still inside the shack when Morgan stumbled upon the bloody knife, then he very likely got a good look at her nine-year-old daughter.

18

Caren wanted to go to the cops.

Eric reminded her that she'd destroyed DNA evidence, a felony.

Because neither one of them believed Morgan was upstairs actually sleeping, they were having this argument in the one room where she couldn't hear them, behind the closed door of Belle Vie's Hall of Records. It was a dark, windowless room the size of a walk-in closet. The floor was bare, and the walls were crowded, floor to ceiling, with half a dozen printer's cabinets, their slim drawers holding every piece of paper and every photograph that had managed to survive a civil war; the open contempt of Yankee soldiers, yeoman squatters and vagabonds; five different legal owners, three with the last name Clancy; and, for a brief time following the war, the United States Government— not to mention the coffee-stained hands of Danny Olmsted. There was a single sixty-watt bulb overhead, leaving the room dark and womblike. Standing at his full height, Eric's head almost touched the dropped ceiling, which was made of a cheap plastic that did not in any way match the colonial look of the rest of the building.

Caren had already peeled off several layers of clothing and was standing in a white undershirt and her grass-stained jeans. And still she was sweating. "Why can't we just tell Detective Lang what she told us without mentioning anything about the shirt?" she asked. She was testing the theory. She and Eric had been running through the merits of one strategy over another, the way they used to do when they were back in school together, working cases. Eric had his arms tightly crossed. He was shaking his head back and forth. "We tell them where she saw the knife," Caren said, trying to convince herself of her own line of reasoning. "We tell them she was scared and that's why she didn't tell them—or us—before. She's just a kid. They'll understand."

"It's a slippery slope, lying to a cop."

"How is it different from what you're proposing?"

"Not telling is not *lying*. It's withholding, and I for one can live with that."

"We can't hide this, Eric. Donovan is in jail. *Jail*. How exactly are you going to explain to your daughter that she should keep her mouth shut while someone, whom she *idolizes*, by the way, sits in jail for something he didn't do? What kind of message is that?" she asked, wondering just how deeply D.C. had changed him. "We can't do that to her, not over something like this. She has information that—"

"I don't care! I don't want my kid witness to a fucking murder!"

"She already *is* a witness, Eric."

"I don't give a shit."

"Better that we take control of the situation now."

"There's nothing she told us tonight that helps their case. She didn't *see* anybody. She can't give eyewitness testimony. And nothing she says puts them any closer to knowing where that knife is. My guess is that thing is long gone by now, sunk in the river somewhere. There's no reason to involve Morgan in any of it." He looked at her, the overhead light making deep creases of the lines around his eyes. "You think they'll protect her, but they won't. They don't give a shit. I don't want it known publicly that my daughter is a witness in a murder investigation. So far, we're the only three people who know she was out there that night, and that's enough."

"*Four* people, Eric. It's us, and whoever was in that cabin."

"You don't know that for sure, Caren. We don't know that anyone saw her at all. Which is why we don't need to go around advertising what she saw. We certainly don't have to put her name out there as a potential witness." He was so agitated he could hardly look at Caren, even though they were standing mere inches apart. She said his name with quiet care, reaching for his hand, which he, surprisingly, let rest in hers. The touch was real, sealing a connection that time and space had not undone. She wanted him to understand that she was scared, too. Her way was a risk, she knew that, but one that might ultimately protect their daughter. "If we just *talk* to the Sheriff's Department," she said, "we'll have a better chance of keeping her safe."

"Don't you dare, Caren," Eric said, seeming momentarily terrified that she might actually do it, that she might go behind his back even. "These backwater cops down here are just making this shit up as they go along, putting together a homicide case with spit and string. They put that kid in lockup based on total bullshit. You're not careful, Caren, and you're going to be looking at a charge yourself, for sitting on information in the middle of their investigation. Don't think they won't come after you."

"You sound like Lang."

"He threaten you?"

She hadn't told him that part yet.

Eric shook his head. "There is no way I'm trusting them with my kid."

Then, quite matter-of-factly, he said, "I'm taking her back with me."

"What?"

"She can't stay here, Caren."

She stared at him for a long time, trying to gauge how serious he was. "I trusted you," he said softly. He was rocking back and forth, chewing on his bottom lip, staring down at her. "You said it was safe down here, you said she'd be in a good school—"

"She *is* in a good school."

"You said she'd be happy."

Caren fell quiet then, looking down at the tips of her boots. Somewhere deep down she knew. Morgan wasn't happy here.

She could finally admit it to herself. Caren was the one who'd grown comfortable, feeling safe in the familiar, letting one year turn to two, and then three, hardly noticing when four years of her life had passed, right here on this same old plantation. "You said this would be good for both of you, and I trusted you, Caren. I don't understand how in the hell you let something like this happen."

"Oh, fuck you, Eric. Really."

"What the hell was she doing out in the middle of the night?"

"It's eighteen fenced acres. It's not like she was out at a nightclub."

"Still," he said. He was as angry as she'd ever seen him.

She sighed, feeling the weight of her own guilt, not just for this, but for all of it, every little thing that had led them here. "I'm raising her out here on my own, Eric."

"That was your choice, Caren." He wasn't giving an inch. She looked away, fixing her gaze on a shelf at her side, because she was afraid that if she didn't she might cry, and she didn't want that. "I'm doing everything I can out here, Eric. I hired Letty, I've got the staff, but it's not like I can watch her every minute of the day."

"If this is something you can't handle, Caren, raising our child, then I sure as shit wish you had said something sooner."

Softly, he said, "I'm getting her out of here."

"I can't just up and leave my job, Eric."

"This is not a job," he said. "I don't know what this place is, but it's not a job."

His tone was sharp and ugly, but not particularly unkind. If anything, she sensed in him a desire to rescue her along with Morgan, to tear them both away from the plantation. "You said Clancy is going to sell," he said. "You were going to have to leave anyway." He was still holding her hand. "You're better than this place, Caren."

She let go, pulling away to the farthest corner of the room.

She stared at the wall, the faded wallpaper in gray and blue, the lines of painted finches and jaybirds staring back. "I have a wedding here in a week. There are school tours scheduled every week for the next two months. I can't just *leave*, Eric. I walk out, and the whole staff, they don't get paid, not unless I process payroll. I owe them something more than that."

"I'm willing to give you some time, but I'm not going to wait around forever. My daughter is not staying here, Caren."

And then he turned and walked out.

A few seconds later, she heard him in the parlor, on his cell phone with Lela.

Caren felt trapped in this hot little room, unwilling or unable to run the emotional gauntlet that lay on the other side of the door.

It started as a way to kill time, picking through the plantation's records while she waited for Eric to get off the phone. The opening of drawers, leafing through the aging, yellowed papers, was at first mindless. In all the years she'd worked at Belle Vie, she'd never once come into this room to read through these documents, to touch the real history of Belle Vie, to hold it in her hands. It was obvious to her now that she'd been avoiding this quiet confrontation for years. There were no brides in here, no catered affairs, no twinkling lights on the north lawn. There was no spectacle, no scenery sure to charm. There was just history, naked and plain. It was right here, on the papers all around her, in flat text that belied the complicated nature of the narrative, the story of one American plantation.

She picked through the pieces.

One of the printer's cabinets—made of aged oak, the lacquer peeling in some corners—held farm records, arranged by decade, going forward into the 1930s. In each drawer, there were production records and bills of sale, registering the bounty of each year's harvest. Some eight hundred hogsheads in the good years, the years before the war, and down to as few as fifty hogsheads during the worst of it, the 1864–'65 season, when local planters had it particularly bad, when the ones who didn't abandon their land nearly starved to death. There were handwritten notes on loose sheets of coarse paper, marking, in great detail, the difficulties of finding hardy men and women to work the fields on the other side of Lincoln's war, when Negro labor was no longer the law of the land. Belle Vie had nevertheless survived, thrived even, in the hands of William P. Tynan, the former overseer for the Duquesne family who took it over after the Civil War. He eventually passed it along to his daughter and her husband, James Clancy, and then on to three more generations of the Clancy family.

All of this was recorded and stored in an antique leather portfolio that told the story of the plantation's chain of ownership, containing the various deeds to the property.

The organization was sloppy, which surprised Caren.

She noticed a serrated edge along the inside of the folder's binding.

She ran her fingers down the center spine. A few small, jagged triangles, dry flecks of old paper, fluttered to the carpet below. It appeared that some of the papers had been torn straight from the binding. She had a brief suspicion about Danny. She didn't put it past him to treat the plantation like his own private fire sale, lifting pieces from Belle Vie's historical records, which he clearly coveted. A real score for the university, he'd said.

There were many other documents in this room: Maps detailing the plantation and its many ornate structures, plus government documents, including one signed by President Ulysses S. Grant, sanctioning the transfer of title and deeding the plantation to the Clancys' ancestor, William Tynan, in the year 1872, eight years after the Union took possession of this stretch of Confederate land.

1872, Caren thought.

The same year Aaron Nathan Sweats was elected sheriff.

The same year he investigated the mysterious disappearance of an ex-slave.

What, she wanted to know, had really happened to Jason?

She wondered if some clue lay here, in this very room.

She poked through the slave accounts next, the records of every man, woman, and child born, bought, or sold from the estate. They were in a cabinet marked inventory, together with notes about farm equipment and supplies in the storehouse. There were pages and pages, listing every slave ever owned by Monsieur Duquesne before the war.

Margaret and Julianne, Charles and Henry, Mathilde and Sarah Anne. All listed as American-born Creoles, their values ranging from two hundred to one thousand dollars.

There were also a Doe and a Rosine, two house slaves.

And Paul, Leandre, and Emile, a cooper, a blacksmith, and a mason, respectively.

Under the long list of American-born Negroes, Caren ran her finger past the names Anthony and Augustine, past Delphine and Dolphus, all the way down to Jason, the only man so named. He was brought to the plantation in the year 1853, though no more information was given, nothing about who his parents were. He was granted permission to wed an Eleanor, another slave, in 1859, when she was seventeen years old. It had been an empty promise, though. Within months, Eleanor was sold to a trader from Georgia, just one year before the war. Jason was eighteen years old. Though he didn't know it at the time, he was a man on the verge of freedom.

What was most striking to Caren, of all the things she read, was the fact that he stayed on the plantation, long after the war. Jason *stayed*, right here at Belle Vie, in the shadow of the big house, working the same land he'd farmed since he was a child, since the first day someone put a cane knife in his hand. He could have fled the parish, of course. He could have moved to New Orleans, or sought work up north. His life and his labor now belonged freely to him, and for a brief, bewitching moment, Caren tried to picture how her life might have been different if her distant ancestor had, back then, struck a path for something wholly new, a way of life that led all of them out of the fields. She felt a sudden and peculiar sensation, a longing that gnawed at her and made her head hurt; it was a feeling akin to trying to recall a dream when none of the details were in color.

Jason had *stayed*.

He learned to read here, on the plantation, taught by a colored woman named Nadine, inside the walls of the old schoolhouse. And for the first time in his life, he earned a monthly wage. He lived and worked at Belle Vie until, as was noted in Tynan's diary-like notations, he went missing in the Year of Our Lord

1872. Of his best employee, Tynan wrote plainly that Jason had simply walked off the job one day.

Caren closed the drawer on the file cabinet.

She tried to hear her mother's voice, the stories she used to tell.

She stood among a virtual mountain of documents, the official history of Belle Vie, and tried to remember the parts that *weren't* written down, the pieces that had been passed on, in stories and songs, for generations. She tried hard to put herself back at her mother's feet, nights Helen used to braid her hair, nights they slept back-to-back on a shared bed, nights Caren should have paid more attention. She would never get them back now and could recall few of the details, only the memory of her touch, the smell of olive oil on her hands, which she rubbed onto her raw knuckles after work in the kitchen. She could only recall the soft whispers in her ear, nights her mother tried to tell her, over and over, that Jason's life mattered, that his story was in their blood.

19

Eric was not in the parlor when she emerged. Upstairs, Morgan was on the computer in the sitting room. Caren didn't know what, if anything, she'd heard of her parents' fight, and she told her to go to bed. In her own room, she smoothed the bedsheets because she couldn't bear to see them so tangled, the way she and Eric had left them only a few hours ago. He was outside right now, talking to Lela on the phone.

Alone, she lay on top of the covers.

He was right, she knew.

Clancy *was* going to sell Belle Vie, and she would have to find another place to live. It was only a matter of time. She rolled over onto her side, staring at the wall, when the phone beside her bed rang, startling her. She glanced at the bedside clock. It was late, well after eleven o'clock. She couldn't imagine who would be calling at this hour. She sat up, reaching for the cordless on the nightstand. But by the time she answered, whoever was on the other end of the line had hung up. She scrolled through the caller ID screen on the telephone . . . feeling a sharp jolt when she saw the last call received. It was a phone number she recognized immediately: her own.

Someone had just called her from her own cell phone.

She remembered losing it last night, when she'd been startled by the presence of Lee Owens on the plantation after dark, and she had a fleeting thought that he, the reporter, had gotten his hands on it somehow. When the phone rang again, as it did just a few seconds later, she actually said his name out loud. There was no response, no words of any kind, only a slow, steady breath, the sure presence of another person.

And then . . . the line went dead.

Maybe, she thought, someone had found her phone on the grounds and was trying to return it to her . . . though something about this seemed highly unlikely.

She hung up the phone and stepped into the hall. The door to Morgan's bedroom was closed. Caren stood and listened, making sure she was asleep. Then she went straight to the computer in the sitting room and turned it on. In minutes, she found a customer-service number for her wireless provider. At this hour, the girl on duty was not able to give her any information about where the last call came from. She was, however, willing to sell an add-on to Caren's service account, a navigator that would track the location of her phone or any of the family members on her account. The girl probably took Caren for a nervous parent, making a desperate call to a cell phone company after eleven o'clock at night, hoping to discover the whereabouts of her kid. She probably made a lot of sales 'round about midnight. "It's easy," she said repeatedly. She could set it up right now, right over the phone, for $9.99 a month.

"Okay," Caren said.

And just like that she was hooked up.

There was a special link, the salesgirl said, that would show the exact location on a detailed map, as long as the cell phone was in use. Caren hung up and made her first test. She dialed her cell number, holding her breath through three rings, exhaling when someone finally picked up the line. She heard music, voices in the background. "This is Caren Gray," she said, waiting. But whoever it was on the other end hung up.

Caren stared at her computer screen.

In less than ninety seconds she had it.

There was a flashing blue light blinking back at her, telling her the call was coming from a spot just off State Highway 1, between here and Donaldsonville, not even fifteen minutes away. It was quiet in the house. By the time she made it downstairs, Eric was lying on the couch, eyes closed. He was off the phone now, but she could tell he wasn't asleep. He was just refusing to speak to her. So be it, she thought. She went for her coat and car keys. "Stay here with Morgan," she said. Eric turned his head to look at her. What he saw must have caused concern. She had just slid the .32 into the pocket of her coat.

"Where are you going?" he said, sitting up.

"I lost my cell phone," was all she said, before walking out the door.

There are some places in rural Louisiana that are untouched, that have remained unchanged for the past sixty-some-odd years, only that somewhere along the way someone thought to add a satellite dish and wi-fi. Rainey's was just such a place. It was a proper icehouse, a one-room building, long and lean, made of corrugated tin and painted wood slats, with a front porch that went all the way up to the edge of the highway. Caren had been inside only once, sent in to buy her mother a pack of cigarettes, exactly $1.75 in her hand; she'd been told to come straight back out, no dawdling. It was a farmers' place mostly, though on game nights—LSU in the fall, Grambling and Southern, and the Dallas Mavs in spring—the place cast a wider net, attracting an array of folks from the river belt. Tonight, the parking lot was sparse. Caren drove past it twice, jackknifing the road to double back, making sure she had the right place. There wasn't a building for half a mile in either direction. The phone call, she thought, had to have come from Rainey's. She pulled into the gravel lot and parked.

Stepping out, she had a clear view across the land, the cars and empty beer bottles . . . and a red pickup truck. It was rusted on its sides, and had a dent across the front grill. It was in every way identical to the one that had tailed her on the highway.

"You following me, ma'am?"

Caren spun on her heels, reaching for the .32 in her pocket.

She came within a few fatal seconds of shooting . . . Lee Owens.

When she saw his face, she quickly slipped the gun back into her pocket. He was in the same ball cap and khakis, had likely not been home to change in at least a day, still pecking away at his story, his investigation into Hunt Abrams and the murder of the cane worker. "What are you doing out here?" he said. He was grinning, excited to see her. Caren glanced back at the rusted red truck. She had no clue as to the driver's identity, or if he and the cell-phone caller were one and the same. "Come on," Owens said. "Let me buy you a drink." He was already starting for the steps of the front porch, but Caren got cold feet, pulling away from him and the front door of Rainey's, her boot heels digging in the gravel. "Can I ask you something?" she said.

Owens turned. "Ma'am?"

"You didn't call me, by any chance, did you?"

He smiled, plainly amused by the idea and treating it as if she had actually made him an invitation. "And when would this have been?" he said with a smirk.

"Last night, you didn't find my cell phone?"

"You mean while I was being held at gunpoint? Did I find your *cell phone*?" He rolled his eyes, but he was smiling, too.

"No, ma'am, I did not find your cellular telephone." He started again for the slatted porch. She could hear the music inside, horns and guitar, the canned sound of blues from a jukebox, Johnnie Taylor, she thought, or maybe it was Bobby "Blue" Bland. She could smell beer and smoked meat. Owens stopped in the gravel, his sneakers shuffling up a curl of dust. "You coming?"

"What are you still doing out here, this far from New Orleans?"

"I got something out of that priest," he said.

He walked back toward her, coming so close she could see straight into his pale-green eyes, could see two days of stubble down his chin. "Apparently, Inés Avalo had some kind of an altercation with Abrams in the fields, about a week before she was killed. Akerele said she'd found something out there, something that shook her good."

"What?"

"A bone."

"A bone?"

Owens gave her a grim nod. "She found a human bone."

Inside, they got a table.

Per local custom, there were two metal drums filled with ice by the doors, each one loaded with about ten different kinds of canned beer. Owens reached in and grabbed two Buds, waving his purchase at the girl behind the bar, who nodded and went back to texting on her cell phone. Caren took the corner seat at their table, scanning the faces in the bar. It was dark in here, the whole place cast in a blue haze, the only light coming from a television screen and the neon beer signs around the room. There were two *Playboy* bunnies painted on the back wall, and across from the bar was a display of monthly calendars going all the way back to 1989, dotted with a few RE-ELECT JUDGE

ELMER B. HIMES flyers that had long ago been forgotten. There were maybe a half dozen men in Rainey's tonight, mostly drinking alone, two white and the rest black, plus two women in their fifties, who were drinking beer out of lipstick-ringed plastic cups, their feathered bangs pressed close together in heated conference. They were either in love with the same man, or each other. She didn't recognize a soul in here. Was it really possible that one of them had made that call from her cell phone? She found herself staring at the short hallway that led to the bathrooms. She remembered, too, that Rainey's had a back porch, out by the propane tank. She thought to get up and take a look when Owens dropped into the seat across from her.

He had the two beers and a bag of chips to share.

Caren didn't touch any of it.

"You were right about Clancy," he said first off. "The Groveland deal, all of it."

He popped open the bag of chips, shoving a handful into his mouth. "I talked to one of the political reporters at the paper, and from what they fished out and what you told me, we're able to put together an angle on Clancy's plans. It's smart, actually, what he's doing. Selling the plantation to Groveland gives the company a foothold in the state's sugar business, and that launches Clancy's platform. 'It's the economy, stupid,' or something like that. He gets to position himself as the man with answers, a plan to broaden the state's economy and take the pressure off the gas outfits on the coast. And Groveland ain't stupid. Their executives are already pouring donations into a political action committee run by a crony of Larry Becht's. And where do you think that money's going to end up?" he said, raising an eyebrow. "In thirty-second spots running every fifteen minutes all over the state. Your boy Clancy is not playing around about this Senate run. He's got the seed money, the platform, and a family history that plays well across color lines."

She knew all this last night.

"What about the girl?"

Owens nodded, getting to that, washing down salt and oil with his beer. "Which makes this whole thing a much bigger story. The paper's planning a feature to run in the front section. It's big-league stuff now. I mean, we're talking about a U.S. Senate seat. We might even beat his announcement. This business with the girl, a Groveland worker killed, it could really mess up Clancy's deal and derail his political plans."

"What did Akerele say?"

"Oh, God," Owens said, taking another swig. "That girl was terrified of him."

"Of Abrams?"

He nodded. "Apparently they got into it about a week or so back."

"She found something, you said."

"That's right," he said. "Abrams had a small crew digging a fence out there. Inés, her beau, and another man, and lo and behold she pulls a bone up out of the dirt."

"A human bone?"

"That's what Akerele said," Owens added, and Caren felt a strange chill. She wiped at the cold sweat across her forehead. "He didn't see it, of course, but Inés was supposedly pretty spooked. She's real Catholic, you know, from the old country and all that, and she did *not* like the idea of digging around a bunch of bones or disturbing a final resting place. To hear Akerele tell it, it was long, maybe a femur bone, and too big to belong to an animal. No telling how long it's been there or where it came from. It's the rain that brought it up, probably. I understand y'all had it coming down hard in the parish . . . plus al that digging in the field."

"And she told Abrams about it?"

"Later she did," Owens said. "First she tried to put it back, bury it under dirt, you know, make it proper. At first she was too scared to say anything to anybody about it. But it weighed on her, I guess, and she brought the news to her priest, and he's the one said she ought to tell her employer." He nodded toward her unopened can of beer. "You gonna drink that?" Caren shook her head. He reached for it, but didn't open it right away. "Father Akerele suggested it could be something serious, part of a crime scene or whatnot, and he said if she was too afraid to tell the police herself, then it was her employer's responsibility, at the very least, to alert the Sheriff's Department as to what she'd found."

"She must have been scared out of her mind," Caren mumbled, picturing this woman far from home, far from her kids, and stumbling onto something so vile.

"Oh, yes, ma'am."

He cracked the second beer open, emptying the can in two swallows.

"So she tells Abrams all right," he said, burping softly. "And he nods and says, 'Yeah, okay,' but then she waits a day or two and nothing happens. Abrams halts work on the fence but never says another word about the bone." Owens set the empty can on the table. "And who knows if there's more where that came from, if there's a body buried out in the fields."

"And the cops never came?"

"The cops never came."

Across the room, in the bubblegum-pink display of the jukebox, the record changed, one 45 lifted and set aside, and another laid down in its place. It was Irma Thomas, local

257

queen of soul, singing "Soul of a Man." Owens leaned both elbows across the plastic tablecloth, checkered in blue and white. "She waited and waited for something to happen," he said. "And all the while she's losing sleep over taking a shovel to somebody's grave. So finally she got up the nerve to confront Abrams about it, saying something about getting the police involved." The door to the icehouse opened and closed again, and Caren looked up, studying the face of a white man in his late forties, his hair cropped and gelled, new sneakers on his feet. He hardly glanced in her direction. Caren, out of nowhere, asked to use Owens's phone. He slid it across the table, and she picked it up and immediately dialed her cell. As she heard the rolling trills in her ear, she took a good survey of the slightly drunk patrons at Rainey's, looking and listening. She heard no sharp sounds, saw no visible movement. No one reached into a back jeans pocket, or seemed in any way to react to the vibration of a cell phone anywhere on his or her person. What's more, not a single person had come down the hallway from the bathroom, nor opened the door from the back patio. She was no closer to knowing who had her cell phone or who was driving that red truck parked outside. She handed the phone back to the reporter. Owens slid it into his pocket. He drummed his fingertips on the tabletop.

"That's when Abrams lost it, got pissy with her, screaming at her. At least three people heard the confrontation in his trailer, thought it had actually gotten physical."

Caren finally told him about the earring she'd found in Hunt's trailer. Had it somehow come loose in a tussle with Abrams? she wondered. Again, she cursed herself for being so careless. She should have led law enforcement *to* the dead woman's earring, instead of putting it in her own hand—muddying a chain of evidence and weakening any case against Abrams. It wasn't the smartest thing she'd ever done, and Owens didn't disagree. But he didn't dwell on it, or let it tear him from the story he had to tell.

"Abrams told Inés he didn't want to hear another word about it," he said. "Nothing about bones or a body in the fields. He had no intention of inviting scrutiny or having anybody come out and tear into his sugar fields. It was too much money on the line."

"And this was, what, a week before she died?"

"Something like that."

"So who the hell is buried out in those fields?"

"No, telling, ma'am," Owens said. He ran the tin tab of the beer can along the surface of the table. "But you've been working right next to the farm for years, see all the folks out there coming and going. You know of any other disturbances, another cane worker who might have been there one week, gone the next?" Caren shook her head. She'd never noticed anything like that. But there *was* something else she'd seen.

"Come on," she said, standing suddenly.

Owens followed.

Ever the gentleman, he walked her to her car outside.

Then, he climbed into his Saturn on the other side of the parking lot. As she pulled out onto the highway, Caren noticed that the red pickup truck was nowhere to be seen.

She drove north along the Mississippi, Owens following.

When they got within spitting distance of the plantation, she took a short detour, driving past Belle Vie's parking lot, passing the main gate. She continued on the old farm road, stopping at the head of the dirt path, the turn into Groveland's farm, where she'd been just this morning, before her walk through the sugarcane to Abrams's trailer. She parked her Volvo so that the car's headlights shone onto the open field nearest the road.

Behind her, she heard the driver's-side door to Owens's car open and close. Within a few moments, he was standing beside her. "Look," she said, pointing to the haphazard pattern of holes carved deep into the ground, where someone had clearly been digging. Sure, Hunt Abrams may have told Inés Avalo that he had no intention of tearing up his fields. But someone had, she said, turning to look at Owens. Someone had been out here searching for whatever it was that lay beneath the surface.

20

The following day was a Sunday, cold and cloudy. Caren made sure she was up and dressed by daybreak, in a solemn gray dress and dark tights. She braided her hair in the dark, as tightly as she could, before slipping downstairs in her bare feet. Only outside, having passed Eric's sleeping form on the sofa, did she slide on her black pumps, the heels of which clicked on the bricks along the main road as she crossed the plantation to the parking lot. She followed the hymn that was playing in her head, had been for days, as she drove to the south, all the way to St. Joseph's church.

The congregation was not very big.

There were the church ladies, the ones Caren remembered from the candlelight vigil, white women who sat together in the first two and three rows of the tiny sanctuary, elbows and thighs pressed together, seemingly bound together in fellowship and worship. And behind them were the field-workers from Groveland and other nearby farms, the ones who could get away for the day. The women wore ill-fitting dresses with satin ribbons in their hair, and the men sat with black cowboy hats resting in their laps, their starched cotton shirts buttoned to their necks, though not one of them was wearing a tie. This was Inés's family here, the people who loved and cared for her on this side of the border. Caren searched out a seat in the bank of pews on the left side of the church. She sat alone, surrounded by voices singing,

261

the congregation and Father Akerele, belting the words to "No Greater Love Than This." Caren sat through the whole of the service, through the first and second reading, following the lilt of Akerele's voice.

She didn't take communion.

She didn't know the words to the closing song.

And as the parishioners filed out of St. Joseph's, shaking hands with Father Akerele on the front steps, Caren waited until she was the last in line. The priest took her hand, too, just as he had the others, his touch warm and friendly, his grip quite strong. He smiled at her, his black eyes a mix of mica and coal. "We found them," he said.

Inés's family, he told her.

"We found them, dear."

At his beck, she followed him back inside the church, where he inquired about a small donation toward a fund to ship the body back to El Salvador. She emptied her wallet, forty-three dollars and a few quarters. There was a young church usher in the sanctuary, a teenage girl in a modest yellow dress with a lace collar, who was picking up discarded programs and replacing hymnals. But otherwise, Caren and Akerele were completely alone. "They're heartbroken, of course," he said. "But there is some peace in knowing she can come home." Caren nodded, saying absently, "I'm sure." The priest stressed that they were still planning a proper memorial service for her loved ones here.

He stared at Caren for a while, reading something in her expression.

He slid his hands into the hidden pockets of his robe.

"But that is not why you came," he said.

"Donovan Isaacs was arrested this week," she said, surprised at how quickly the words tumbled out of her mouth, how bothered she was by what had happened to Donovan. Akerele sighed wearily. He turned and asked the girl—Megan or Mary or something like that—to please excuse them. He and Caren both watched in patient silence as the girl shuffled her patent-leather flats down the center aisle, eventually disappearing behind a floor-length velvet curtain that led to the church's back offices.

The sanctuary was empty now, just the two of them.

Akerele said, "You work with him, yes? The young man they have in custody?"

"Yes."

"The reporter," he said, explaining how he came to know this particular news. "The day you were here, you and Mr. Owens, I made an assumption about the two of you, I'm afraid. But, no, he told me that you are not together, that you run the plantation . . . this 'Beautiful Life,'" he said with a wry smile. It was presented as an inside joke between two colored souls, separated by a continent and a few tricks of fate. "And, of course, then I remembered you from the prayer vigil in the fields," he said, his voice temperate and kind. "You were touched by Inés . . . I can see that about you."

"I don't think he killed her."

Akerele raised an eyebrow. "You and the reporter," he said. "Your *theories*."

Then he let out another weighty sigh, thick and morose, a sound all the more distressing for what it implied about the limits of what one man's heart could take, God or no God. "As if I didn't know," he said. "We have this in my country, too, you know. Anywhere there is work to be done, someone somewhere will be standing with a boot to the neck of the one who must get down in the dirt and do it. Cane, cotton, rice . . . it is all of it the same. I did not need a reporter to tell me that Mr. Abrams is not kind to his crew."

"She found something in the fields," Caren reminded him.

Akerele stared at her for a long time. Outside, dark clouds were circling 'round, blackening the stained glass and painting the carpeted floor a deep red. "Yes."

"Someone was buried out there?"

"That was her belief, yes," he said. "It was an unsettling experience for her, to say the least. It haunted her for days, in fact. I urged her to make a full disclosure, to tell her employer, Mr. Abrams. But he took no action, told no one, as far as she could tell. And he grew angry after her repeated questions about the matter. She was frightened. A manager wields a great deal of power in the fields. He can, and has, docked her pay." He shook his head slightly, remembering. "It was very upsetting for her, the idea that she had possibly disturbed a grave site. She only wanted to know that they were doing right by God." The clouds darkened further and the light changed again, throwing shadows over Akerele's round face. He pulled his hands from his pockets, clasping them behind his back. "The sheriff's men, they have made me to understand that the Isaacs boy has had troubles with the law, that he is not without some criminal impulse. He was on the plantation without permission, yes? He was there at the crime scene."

Caren wanted to get back to Abrams and the bone in the fields.

"Did *you* tell the police detectives what Inés found?"

Akerele nodded. "They did not seem to place much significance in it. It appeared to be very old, easily damaged. Inés and a small crew had been out on the edge of the fields, near the farm road, digging to lay posts for a fence, when the blade of her shovel hit the bone. The policemen seemed to make of it what Abrams had when he'd learned of it. It was an artifact of some sort, they assumed, nothing more. Certainly nothing connected to Inés's death."

"That's it?" Caren said. "They never investigated any further?"

She found this striking, this pointed lack of curiosity on the part of the cops about just what in the hell had been going on in the Groveland fields. "What about the other workers?" she said. "Did they talk to them? Were there ever any questions about Abrams and acts of violence or cruelty against the men and women working for him, stories of someone who may have gotten hurt . . . or gone missing, even?"

Father Akerele stared at her, a weary look on his face.

"The newspaper reporter, Mr. Owens, he asked me the same thing." He shook his head. "I can only say what I told him, that I have tried to cooperate and assist the police officers in every way I can. Their questions for me, however, had more to do with her last day, the last hours of her life. I told them what little information I had. Wednesday had not been in any way extraordinary. Inés was at work, and then she came by the church, as she often did in the afternoons, when she could get a ride."

"Wait—she was *here?*"

"Well, yes."

"Are you sure?" Caren said, confused. All this time, she had assumed that Inés had been taken by force as she was leaving work in the fields that day. But according to Akerele, Inés had left the cane farm . . . and then *returned* to Belle Vie, sometime that evening, after the sun had set. And Caren couldn't imagine why. It was a fact that had continued to nag at her. Why in the world, on the last day of her life, had this woman ended up on the plantation grounds after dark? It was possible, Caren thought, that somewhere in the answer to that question lay a path toward clearing Donovan's name.

Akerele, who was still thinking back to that last day, said, "We are a safe place for fellowship. Our doors are always open. Ginny, our secretary, she sets aside a few hours in the afternoons, when work in the fields is done, to assist the workers. We try to help with child care, for those who have their families with them, or we help them find a doctor if needed, one who will take cash and ask few questions. Inés spoke passable English. She could get by. The others need a lot of hand-holding. Finding a landlord or a place where they can wash their clothes or send packages home. There can be a lot of fear in a foreign place, especially if there's been any kind of trouble."

"Was Inés in some kind of trouble?"

The priest looked down at the tips of his shoes, which were not expensive dress shoes, she saw, but black sneakers. Then he patted Caren's arm and said, "Follow me."

Behind the velvet curtain there were two rooms, divided by a thin, cloth-covered partition that did not reach the height of the ceiling. On one side, Megan or Mary was sitting on the floor, reading a social studies textbook. Beside her were boxes of copier paper and colorful church programs folded and stacked in neat piles. The girl looked up as Akerele escorted Caren past, but she didn't say anything and quickly went back to her schoolwork. On the other side of the partition sat Ginny. She was the woman from the candlelight vigil, the one who had pleaded with Deputy Harris to do something about Hunt Abrams. Today, she was dressed in khaki slacks and a burgundy blazer, large curls framing her face. Her lips were pink and her eyes a pale blue. There were square, black reading glasses tucked into the front of her shirt. She looked up from behind her desk, which was covered in notepaper and letter stock and cans of Diet Coke. Father Akerele began introductions, realizing only as he turned to Caren that he didn't, in fact, know her name.

"Caren Gray," she said.

Ginny stood, smoothing her blazer.

The tiny room, no more than ten or twelve square feet, smelled of her perfume, Shalimar, and incense, small, black cones of which lay in open boxes on top of a filing cabinet behind her desk. Ginny took Caren's hand in her own, which was plump and baby-soft. "You're out on the plantation, right?" she said, as friendly as could be. "I finally took my daughter last spring. I've lived in Ascension Parish my whole life and had never been to Belle Vie, if you can believe." Caren remarked darkly that she felt as if she'd never left, stealing a look at Akerele as she explained that her family, in one form or another, had worked the land for generations. "It's beautiful country out there, just outrageously beautiful," Ginny said. "You should be really proud."

Across the room, Akerele pressed his lips together, keeping his feelings about the plantation to himself. He said, "Ms. Gray had some questions about Inés."

"Oh, honey," Ginny said. "Did you know her, too?"

She was still holding Caren's hand.

"Ms. Gray works with the Isaacs boy."

"Oh." Ginny let Caren's hand slide from hers. She scrunched the pad of flesh between her eyebrows and wrinkled her nose. She looked back and forth between Akerele and Caren, her priest and a virtual stranger. She seemed not to understand the turn this meeting had taken. "Well," Akerele said eventually. "It appears that Mr. Owens is not the only one who thinks the detectives do not have their man."

"Hmph," Ginny said, folding her arms across her chest, pushing the blazer's shoulder pads up toward her ears. Her painted mouth was pulled into a tight line.

She leaned in and whispered, "I never liked Hunt Abrams either."

Akerele shot Caren a look.

To Ginny, he said, "Ms. Gray expressed curiosity about the

fact that Inés had come by the church on the day she died."

"Did Detectives Lang and Bertrand ask you about that?"

"Only inasmuch as they were trying to establish a timeline. I told them exactly what I told you, Father. She was here on Wednesday afternoon, for about an hour, leaving around six o'clock. But they didn't get into it much more beyond that."

"And do you know where she went after she left?"

"Home, I assumed."

Caren nodded, but she didn't think this was true.

She asked why Inés had come to the church that day.

"She was hunting about a place to stay."

"Inés . . . was homeless?"

"Oh, no, she stayed out in town with her boyfriend."

"Gustavo?"

Ginny nodded. "That's right."

"Was there some kind of problem, between the two of them?"

"No, ma'am, that wasn't it at all," Ginny said, shaking her head. "She and Gustavo were a real pair. It was real for them. I wanted her to stay with him. He was good to her, you know, real kind. And any dollar she spent on renting a room somewhere else was money she couldn't send to her kids. Lord knows she was trying to get back to them. I mean, it's hell being away from your kids, you know. I told her to save her money, but she was serious about finding some other kind of living arrangement." She turned around to fish for something among the mess of papers and files and tattered periodicals on a table pressed against the wall behind her. "She wanted some place cheap and clean and close to work, she said. We went through some listings, friends of the church, you know. I really tried to find her something."

"We try to offer what services we can," Akerele reiterated.

"Here," Ginny said, holding out a stapled stack of apartment listings and room rentals. It was three pages, typed. Caren flipped through it, the words blurring from one line to the next. Then she looked up, searching Ginny's face, then Akerele's. "I don't understand," she said. "Why was she so determined to move?"

At this, Ginny pinched her lips together. It was a hesitation.

Akerele gave her a small nod. "It's okay."

"She thought someone was following her," Ginny said, finally spilling it. On the farm road, in town, even out near the trailer park where she lived, she felt she was being watched. "I told those two police detectives. She was scared to death."

Akerele added, "It had been going on for a week or so before she died."

"Around the time she discovered the bone," Caren said.

She looked at Akerele, wondering if he sensed a connection, too.

He made a face, considering anew this sequence of events.

"I told the sheriff's men to look into it," Ginny said. "But they said they had nothing to go on since Inés had never filed a police report or anything, which I had begged her to do. But she wasn't having it. Said she was cursed, had been ever since that bone came up out of the ground. She didn't want to get thrown in jail for not having any papers, not when she was so close to getting out of here. A few more weeks and she prob-ably could've made up the money they'd lost during the rains." Ginny let out a long sigh. "I wish to God she'd left when she had the chance."

Caren felt a wave of nausea.

It was the incense and the drugstore perfume, making her stomach turn. And this: she now thought she knew why Inés was on the plantation after dark. "And you never found her a place, did you?"

Ginny shook her head. "A few days before she died, she just

stopped asking, and I stopped looking. And, unfortunately, honey, that's right where we left it."

Some place cheap and clean and close to work.

Inés had been looking for a place to stay.

By the time Caren pulled back into the parking lot of Belle Vie, dark clouds had started a march overhead. Like chunks of ash after a steady burn, they crowded out any hint of light or color on the other side, the sun or blue sky. The wind had picked up, too, whipping cane leaves in the distance, the sound like the percussive whoosh of seeds inside a baby's shaker. There was a storm coming, for sure, rolling up the Mississippi from the Gulf, gaining strength, bringing thunder and lightning, too. The air was sharp with it, the acrid smell of electricity lying in wait for a single, lone spark. Caren was determined to make it to the slave quarters before the storm hit, borrowing the golf cart from security and speeding to the west. Gerald was not on duty today, not on a Sunday. Except for weddings or private parties, the staff was not asked to work on the Sabbath. Caren was out this far on the property line alone. The plantation was a chorus of whispered voices. The wind in the tree leaves, the wind in her hair, and the long, green fingers of weeping willows dusting the grassy groves. Overhead, the shrieking whistles of mourning warblers could be heard as the birds fled the low branches of a nearby oak, flying out ahead of the rain. The machines had stopped in the cane fields, and the pastoral music of Belle Vie was all Caren heard as she approached the quarters.

She parked the golf cart as she always did, at the head of the dirt path, uttering a prayer the second her feet touched the ground. Only today, when she made the offering, she was thinking not only of her ancestors . . . but also Inés. It wasn't Catholic, her prayer, but a hymn her mother used to sing, the lyrics to a Mahalia Jackson song, about somebody dying for your sins.

She wanted some place cheap and clean and close to work, Ginny said.

And just across the fence from the fields sat these six cabins, where sugarcane workers, enslaved and free, once lived and loved and raised families for generations, cabins that Inés had likely laid eyes on every day she worked at the Groveland farm. Six surprisingly well-kept cabins, their history foreign to someone like her. Each and every one of them sitting empty through the night. The last one on the left not even a hundred yards from the fields.

Jason's Cabin, Caren remembered.

There had been blood inside the gate, Morgan said.

And a knife just a few feet from the cabin door.

And inside, Caren had found candles, lots of them, votives burned to stubs.

Could Inés, she asked herself as she approached the cabin's low-lying gate, could she have stolen onto the grounds of Belle Vie, like Owens did the night he and Caren met, and waited until sundown to sleep here, in this little slave cabin, where Jason had once lived, the place from which Caren's whole family had sprung? Were they so different really, Jason and Inés, two cane workers separated by time and not much else?

As Caren stepped into the tiny yard where summer cabbage once grew, peppers and okra, where chickens pecked feed in the dirt, she thought how desperate Inés must have been to choose this, a home literally behind bars, behind gates locked each night.

She must have thought she'd be safe here.

But someone had found her anyway.

Inside, it took a while for Caren's eyes to adjust to the low light and the swirl of black dust kicked up by wind blowing through the open door. She tried to picture Inés here, the way she had many times tried to picture her own ancestors living within these four walls—with the candles and the tattered quilt and the straw pallet on the floor, the antique tools and, of course, the night she died, the cane knife still hanging in its usual place on the wall.

Beyond the cabin walls, Caren heard the first crack of thunder.

She felt the ground move beneath her, the earth shaking from the force of it.

It made her heart stop.

Is that it? she wondered.

Is that how it went?

Inés was out here all alone and something, someone, startled her?

Frightened, did she grab for the first thing at hand, the knife on the wall? And the killer took it away from her? It gave Caren the idea that the killer had entered the grounds without a weapon, that he maybe hadn't intended to kill her at all, but some struggle had nevertheless ensued . . . and something went horribly wrong. The police had found no blood, no real forensic evidence inside the doors of any building on the entire plantation. Caren thought the confrontation, the moment her throat was slit, had to have happened outside the cabin, out by the fence, where Morgan saw blood. She turned, walking the last steps she imagined Inés took, from the center of the cabin to the front door, Caren's right hand clenched around an imaginary weapon, the antique cane knife. She inched slowly toward the cabin door. But when she tried to imagine the last person Inés saw that night, the whole scene playing in her head simply faded to black.

She had no idea who had been stalking this woman, or why.

Outside, she felt the first drops of rain, cold water stinging her skin.

As she reached out to open the gate, it swung out on its own, clanging against the fence in the sweeping, blustery wind. The rain was coming down harder now, the clouds blacker than they were only minutes before. She turned to the dirt road and ran.

21

When she walked into her office the following morning, Hunt Abrams was standing over her desk, hands stuffed in the pockets of his jeans, casually studying the papers sitting out in the open on her desk. He didn't start at her presence, didn't inch away from her things. He was wearing a cotton button-down beneath his Groveland windbreaker. His hair was greased at the sides, and he smiled slyly in her direction.

"We meet again," he said.

They were alone in here, and the feeling Caren had, creeping from her navel and spreading hot across her chest, was fear. She had a sudden disturbing thought about those holes in the ground out by the fields, the story of Abrams's fight with Inés over what she had found. She swallowed hard. "Can I help you with something?"

"No, ma'am."

In deference to decorum, he smiled politely, but his eyes didn't move, and the effect was cool and masklike and wholly insincere. Abrams, it was clear, didn't give a shit about being discovered like this, in her office. He wanted her to know that he, too, was free to come and go as he pleased; two could play the snooping game. He pivoted on the heels of his leather boots, casually perusing the antique furniture in the office, the floral wallpaper, and the stacks of books on the shelves, which included everything from yellowing agronomy texts to bound commemorative copies of *The Olden Days of Belle Vie,* and photo albums documenting every debutante ball and wedding and catered event held in the ballroom since 1972. Abrams took in the scene as he might an exhibit at a small roadside museum full of curios and knickknacks, all of it quaint but of no real consequence. She didn't like his hands on everything, or the knowledge that he might claim all this one day soon. "The first tour starts at nine-fifteen," she said, the words coming out thin and strained. "You're certainly welcome to purchase a ticket. But otherwise I'm afraid I'm going to have to ask you to leave."

Abrams smiled, but didn't move.

He went back to poring over the items on the shelf, reaching up to take took down a photograph, framed in silver and black, a picture of the Clancy boys, Bobby and Raymond, the two of them in their early twenties. The photo had been there for years, beside tins of aged molasses and two ceramic mugs from the gift shop, inside of which stood dozens of pencils and pens. The photograph showed the two young men, darkly handsome, and long and lean as twin stalks of cane. Bobby, the younger, had the same intense gaze she remembered from when they were kids, cocksure and strong, the look of a young man standing cliff-side, sure he can fly. Thirty years ago, it was Raymond whose entire countenance appeared disjointed and fragile in some way.

How things have changed, Caren thought.

Abrams stared at the photo for a few seconds, then left it on top of her desk. Behind them, there were heavy footsteps on the winding staircase. Caren turned to see Raymond Clancy ascending the top steps in a suit and tie, a plush wool coat buttoned at his trim waist. He nodded in her general direction on his way into the office, turning sideways to pass her in the doorway. To Hunt, he said, "Sorry, I'm late," before removing his coat and tossing it onto a chair. He walked behind the desk, taking possession, and motioned for Hunt to have a seat. Only then did he turn and address Caren directly. "Have Lorraine send over a pot of coffee, would you, Gray?"

Before she could utter a response, Abrams crossed to the office door and slowly closed it in Caren's face, leaving her on the other side.

She could hear their muffled voices, the hushed, somber tone. But she had no idea what they were discussing in private.

Well, there was no way she was walking to the kitchen for Raymond. He should have known better than to ask. Instead, she stepped out onto the gallery to wait him out.

The balcony's lacquered floor was still wet with morning dew, and she could smell a loamy, damp wind coming off the Mississippi. In the distance, there was the low, steady hum of Luis's riding mower. And to the south, Caren had a clear view of the plantation's parking lot. Eric's rental car was gone. Letty's van, too. Caren and Eric had yet to come up with a game plan; they weren't even communicating, really, Eric exchanging no more than a few words with her this morning, telling her that *he* would drive Morgan to school. This left Letty with little to do, and Caren had happily given her the day off. The river breeze rolled over the treetops. A patch of blue sky closed over with clouds, and Caren felt a chill.

Staring across the grounds of the parking lot, she noticed something else for the first time: Donovan's car was missing. Detectives Lang and Bertrand must have come and grabbed that, too.

"Gray," she heard behind her.

Raymond was calling her name.

By the time she stepped off the gallery, Abrams was already making his exit, breezing down the winding staircase, leaving behind a scent of Brylcreem and damp leather. He was whistling, the notes blowing through the main house like a cold draft.

"Shut the door, would you?" Raymond said, as she crossed the threshold into her office. He was standing behind her desk. He was on his feet and in his hands was the framed photograph of him and his brother, Bobby. Raymond seemed distracted, preoccupied with the image, staring at it as if it were a found artifact, something that might take years to dust off and make sense of. Then, for whatever reason, he set the frame on the desktop, face down. He put his hands on his hips, looking at Caren. He looked tired, but in a good mood. She could see a hint of glee in his eyes, and he did a poor job of masking it with a hangdog expression of contrition.

"Well, I guess I can't put any damn thing past Lorraine," he started. "She was right, I might as well tell you. She was telling the truth about Belle Vie." He waited for some reaction, but Caren said nothing, forcing him to spell it out, to say the words out loud, here in his father's old house. "We're selling it," he announced.

"When?"

"I talked to Jack Beverly at the statehouse this morning," he said. "We'll bring our relationship with the Tourism Department to an official close by the end of this month. But I want to shut down all operations well before then. Groveland is taking over the whole place, and some of the corporate honchos from headquarters are coming out this way. They're ready to draw up plans as soon as possible. We're just waiting for this business with the girl to die down." He motioned toward the desk, on top of which Caren noticed he'd laid open the insides of several newspapers. She recognized the *Donaldsonville Chief* and the daily papers out of Baton Rouge and Monroe, even the *Dallas Morning News* and the *Gazette* out of Texarkana. Each contained a small post about the death of a migrant worker, a temporary employee with Groveland. Inés remained an unnamed figure in each story; it was Groveland that had made the headlines.

But Inés was no longer a nameless figure to Caren.

She felt oddly protective of her, even in death, keeping her secret from Raymond, the fact that Inés had been living on his family's land before she died. She didn't trust how he might spin the information, painting the woman as a criminal, a girl who was asking for trouble.

Raymond was rocking back on his heels.

"This is just a minor setback," he said. "This deal is going through either way, Gray."

"You're just going to let them tear it all down?"

He bristled openly at the suggestion that he was being careless with a legacy. "This was Daddy's deal, not mine. I did what I could with the place. I think you know I've tried my best to preserve every little bit of the history. But hell if I want to be tied to this thing for the rest of my life. I don't know what people expect from me." He wanted so badly not be seen as a villain in this; he seemed to so resent the power he held that Caren actually wondered about his fitness to hold political office.

"You know, we have the Whitman wedding next week," she said, because signed contracts were something she thought Clancy would understand. There was the staff to consider too. "They deserve some kind of notice, a chance to find other work."

They deserved something better, she thought.

"The Whitman deal, sure," he said. "We'll go out with a bang." He was smiling now, picturing it. "It'll be one to remember. You can tell Lorraine to go all out, on me."

He was trying too hard, she thought.

"Aw, hell, Gray," he said sheepishly. "I know I should have said something. I should have been up-front with you. But all the ink on this deal wasn't dry, and I didn't want to get out ahead of myself. You understand, don't you?"

She didn't, not really.

"When are you going to tell the staff?"

Raymond's posture sank, making him look like a sulky, difficult teenager. He picked up a pencil and tapped it against the desktop. "Actually . . . I was thinking you ought to be the one to tell them."

"Me?"

"The truth is, they don't know me from Adam, Caren, not really. I'm hardly ever out here. I just think it would go over better if they heard the news from someone they work with every day, someone they actually like." He dropped the pencil on the desktop and shoved both hands into the pockets of his wool slacks. He turned slightly, looking out the window at the grounds of Belle Vie: the rose garden and the old schoolhouse and the rows of sugarcane in the distance. Something in his posture told her it was already done, all of it. This had all been decided a long, long time ago.

"So you're really going to do it, then, make a run for Senate?"

Clancy raised up a finger, very nearly wagging it in her face, coming just short of a scold. "Now, wait a minute, Gray, just wait," he said. "There's nothing set, not a thing decided. Don't you go breathing a word of it, hear? Larry Becht's got a way he wants this done, a proper announcement and all that." He stopped here, catching himself. "I mean, that's if, Gray, *if* I'm even running. There's nothing set," he said again, trying to appear a good deal more relaxed than he was. He lowered his pointing finger and shoved his hands again into his pockets. "I'm just considering it right now, just trying to think of what's best for Louisiana." He turned and glanced once more out the window at the sugar-rich land, the lush landscape. "I mean, the

279

truth is . . . Katrina was a wake-up call," he said, playing with his words, the pace and cadence of his voice, as if he were writing a stump speech off the top of his head. "We can't ask the coast to carry the whole state anymore, not economically. Folks don't like to say it out loud, but that oil and gas thing ain't gon' last forever. The coast can't take it. And anyone who tells you any different is just selling snake oil. It's a way of life that's on its way out, no doubt about it. I mean, we're losing land mass down there at an ungodly pace. Another ten, twenty years and those wetlands, the whole coast, will be gone. But sugar, that's here to stay. Agriculture is good business, Gray, always has been. Cane, cotton . . . they built this state in the nineteenth century . . . hell, maybe they can *save* it in this one."

He paused, so caught up in his reverie and his ideas about how all this might play to a crowd that Caren thought he actually heard the applause in his head before he remembered it was just the two of them in this room. He took a long, deep breath. "It's just that we've got to broaden our thinking about what's possible for Louisiana. This deal is just a start. There's no telling what a company like that can do for the state's economy. And that's a hell of a lot more important than keeping another tourist trap open."

"What does your father say, about the sale?"

Raymond glanced over his shoulder at her, but never directly answered the question. It was the first time she saw any hint of regret.

"He'll come around," he said.

"Bobby, too?" Caren said, remembering his snooping around the place, his sudden interest in his brother's business dealings. "Did he sign off on this, too?"

Raymond waved away the thought.

"This doesn't concern Bobby," he said. "And I wouldn't let him influence any decision I make, anyway. He doesn't understand business, doesn't think about the future, what's best for everybody. Leave it to Bobby and he'd still be sleeping in his old bedroom, right down the hall," he said, pointing to the suite of bedrooms on the other side of her office door. "Bobby would put his feet up and live off Daddy's money for the rest of his life." Something seemed to occur to him then, and he swung around suddenly, startling Caren, and asking, "Why? Did he say something to you?" Caren stared at Raymond, wondering why the mention of his brother had got him so heated.

"You'd do well to watch yourself around Bobby," he said.

"Funny, he said the same thing about you."

Raymond rolled his eyes.

Caren again tried to appeal to his sense of loyalty, saying, "Lorraine, Pearl, Ennis Mabry . . . some on the staff have worked here a lot longer than I have. Luis was handpicked by your father years and years ago. Are you sure you don't want to speak to them on behalf of the Clancy family, to let them know their service has been appreciated?" Raymond had his back to her again, his gaze cast on the manicured grounds outside. "I just think they'll take it better coming from you," he said flatly.

And then she understood.

Raymond Clancy wanted a shill, a race-neutral messenger.

He wanted her, the black woman, to deliver the news to the plantation's staff.

"I think you owe me this much," he said. Back here again, she thought, twice in one week. "My family's been good to you, Gray. I gave you a job when you needed one, gave you a place to stay, and you and I both know the Clancys took care of your family in more ways than one. Now, I've never cashed in on any of it, made your mama a promise that I never would. But I figure you can do me at least this much."

Fine, she told him.

"It's not going to go down easy," she warned. "We're under a lot of stress out here. The staff is worried about Donovan. His arrest caught all of us by surprise."

"It's a goddamned mess, I know."

"It's a mistake is what it is."

Raymond shot her a curious look. He appeared confused at first, and then troubled, or else irritated by the fact that there might be any loose ends to this story.

"What do you mean?"

"Donovan told the police he was here Wednesday night—"

"The report I got indicated he *stole* a master key."

"Yes," she said. "But I swear it's not what it looks like. Donovan had been sneaking onto the grounds for weeks, but only so he could work on a school project."

"What kind of a 'school project'?"

Here, she paused.

She knew how this would sound.

"A movie."

"A *movie?*"

"A film," she said, thinking that sounded better.

Clancy was growing frustrated. "Gray, what in the hell are you talking about?"

"There's a story about this place, about the history, that he wants told."

Raymond made a face, and Caren added, "Look, he's not a bad kid," feeling as surprised as Donovan might have been to hear those words coming out of her mouth. "He's got a few misguided ideas about what to make of Belle Vie and what it means, but surely you can understand that, for a lot of people, this place is . . . *complicated.*"

"What in the world does this have to do with the dead woman, Gray?"

"Nothing," she said. "That's what I'm trying to tell you."

"I don't understand."

"The cops are making a big mistake."

"Well, I don't have a goddamned thing to do with that. I don't have any say over how the sheriff runs his department. I don't know what all you think I can do about it. The kid admitted to breaking and entering, for heaven's sake," he said. Then, wagging a finger again, he added, "And you ought to stay out of it, too, Gray. Don't involve yourself any further. Those detectives already have their eye on you as it is."

"Excuse me?"

"Lang was asking about you, how well I know you and all that," he said. "Don't you go doing something stupid trying to protect this kid, hear? He's not your problem. Take it from me, Gray, sometimes the only way to get ahead yourself is to cut your losses where you can. Don't let a kid like that drag you down. He's not family. You come from better people than that." He came around from behind her desk, reaching out to pat her on the shoulder, as if he'd just paid her a great compliment. She shook off his hand. He took no offense by it, was already reaching for his overcoat.

"Let me ask you something," she said.

Raymond nodded absently, slipping his arms through the sleeves.

"Your family ever find out what happened to Jason?"

At this Raymond looked up. "Jason?" he said, repeating a name with which she knew he was familiar. Of all the Belle Vie Clancys, he was the least enamored of its history, taking as an affront even the suggestion that the beautiful land on which he'd been raised had served any purpose other than a pretty backdrop for weddings and fancy parties. It was the elder Clancy who made preservation a priority, and Raymond publicly fell in line behind the family's deeply felt duty to the past, all the while holding his nose closed.

"He worked for your great-great-grandfather, William Tynan," Caren reminded him. "He cut cane as a slave and then worked the fields for Tynan after the war."

"For a wage, I'm told." He wanted that made clear.

Caren nodded. "That's right. He worked the farm after Tynan became the legal owner of the plantation. That is . . . until he disappeared sometime in the year 1872."

"What's this all about, Gray?"

"Did you know there had been an investigation into his disappearance?" she said. "There was a newly elected black sheriff digging into it, sure he'd met foul play."

"No, I never heard anything like that."

"Yeah," Caren said. "I hadn't either."

"Well, that was a long time ago."

"That's the story, anyway," she said. "The one Donovan is trying to tell."

Raymond sighed. "Look, I'll have a talk with Lang, make sure they're coming at this from all angles. We'll get to the bottom of it."

He started for the door.

"One more thing, though," he said. "When the Groveland brass comes through here, I want you to arrange a special VIP tour for some of their folks, let 'em see the plantation up close, see all the history and all that. I just want the execs to get a good look before they make any final decisions, one last pitch to see if they'll consider preserving at least part of the plantation—the main house, or the library. Daddy would want that." He buttoned his wool coat. "And you'll talk to the staff?"

She nodded.

Raymond looked deeply relieved.

"I knew you wouldn't let me down," he said. "I know you appreciate what all the Clancys have done for you and yours." He touched her shoulder again on the way out. She watched him go, grateful for the stillness that came in his wake. She stood alone in the office, hers for as long as Belle Vie stood. For one lonely moment, she tried to picture it all gone, the house and the garden, the kitchen and the cottages, the library and the schoolhouse and the hundred-year-old oaks, all of it razed to nothing. The quarters, too, all of it flattened into a grid of cane, stretching as far as the Mississippi River, with only the wind remaining. She wasn't sure what she was going to tell the staff, or when. One thing she did know: Leland Clancy would never delegate a good-bye.

There was one person she needed to tell first.

The Rose Hill Cemetery lay across the river, on the border between Ascension and Livingston parish. Helen always said she didn't want to be buried in a crypt. She wanted to rest on high ground, up north where her people lay. There was a place for Caren, too, she'd said, a spot beneath a line of pines, an open space to the right of her mother's granite headstone, which Caren had bought with her first paycheck from Belle Vie, replacing the one made of polished concrete that had been set up in her absence.

It's done, Mother.

They're shutting down Belle Vie for good, she said.

She didn't sit, didn't want to linger, afraid that if she got down on the ground she might never get up. So she stood over the gravestone, clearing pine needles, brushing dirt with her open palm. She told her what she came to say, what brought her out here at least a few times a year. She came to say, once again, that she was sorry.

285

She tried to picture Helen listening to all this.

She tried to picture her long, slim legs, the bony knees poking out from beneath her apron, the way she pressed her fingers into the small of her back when she was thinking about something, stretching the time between cigarettes. Caren would have given anything to hear a last laugh.

But almost always what came to her was their last fight, the last day they spoke. Helen was still in the kitchen, working for the Clancys. Caren was in her first year at Tulane, in law school, on her mother's dime, or so she thought. That's the way Helen sold it, of course, telling Caren that she had worked as hard as she had, spent a lifetime on the plantation, saving everything so that one day she could pay for Caren to go to school. She wanted her daughter to have that law degree, liked the idea of her flesh and blood being on the right side of things, putting the world back in its rightful order. She couldn't think of anything more important for black folks, she said, than to have somebody in the family who could navigate the pricks and thorns of a bunch of rules they'd had no hand in creating. "That's how they cheat you."

Every family needed a lawyer, she said.

And that "One day you'll understand why I did it this way."

"You lied to me," Caren said on their last day.

It wasn't Helen's money, she'd just found out. It never had been.

It was Leland Clancy's . . . and Caren was just another charity case.

Raymond, on a visit home, had finally let it slip. For years her mother had pressed Leland to pay for her daughter's school, making clear that he was the one who *owed* her . . . something Caren never understood. "You lied to me," she said again, standing next to Helen in the kitchen.

"Oh, girl," her mother said, waving off the very idea. She was standing over the table, a vinyl-top card table where Lorraine, to this day, cut vegetables and chopped onions. It was foolish, what Caren was saying, a splitting of hairs and wholly beside the point. "You're going to finish law school, Caren, and that's the end of it."

But Caren wouldn't have it.

The whole thing made her sick with shame, made her feel as small and worthless as the days when Bobby had stopped playing with her, had stopped seeing her as an equal, or the many times she'd not been allowed in the big house. She didn't want the Clancys' money, the benefactions of a plantation owner. It was no way to start what she considered a new life, one freed from the burdens of a legacy she never asked for, freed from the confines of a world that always put people like the Clancys on top.

"Listen to me, 'Cakes," her mother said. "Belle Vie is *yours*. It's yours, too."

Caren stared at her, not understanding.

"Them people ain't got no more real claim to this place than anybody in our family, and don't think Leland Clancy don't know it, either. He's not stupid, Mr. Clancy, and he knows good and well he came into this place on someone else's back, that it was a way that was paved for him to sit in that big house that had nothing to do with his labors. Now you go on and let him put back a little of what he took."

Caren shook her head.

She could make it on her own, she said. It was the blustery protestation of a young woman for whom it would take years to understand the true pull of family, and the impossibility of escaping our bonds, or ever truly forgetting where we came from.

That day in the kitchen she was harsh and childish.

She made it clear to her mother that she wasn't ever going to be like her.

She wasn't going to be attached to this place for the rest of her life.

"Yes, you are," Helen said, just before Caren turned and walked out.

22

The box had been resting on a top shelf in Caren's closet since she'd returned to Belle Vie four years earlier; she'd placed it there the very first day she and Morgan moved in. Helen had packed it neatly, securing the paisley-covered sides with a strip of purple ribbon, a spool of which, Caren remembered, used to sit in the bottom of her mother's plastic sewing kit, among loose buttons and beads. Helen had wrapped it just as she might have any other gift for her only daughter, and pressed it into Lorraine's hands, making her promise that it would find its way to Caren in the event that Helen didn't get to hang out in this world for quite as long as she had a mind to. Caren had received it in this exact condition and had preserved its contents, essentially by never opening it. She had tried only once before, and become so overcome with grief—all the more powerful for the words that could not be formed to give it proper shape. It simply enveloped her from all sides, lingering like the smell of her mother's perfume.

She'd closed it and put it away.

This was years ago, at their place in Carrollton.

The box eventually traveled with her to the duplex in Lakeview, and in the days before that brewing storm, the one that drove her out of New Orleans for good, it was one of the few personal items she threw into the back seat of her Volvo. She had carried it in her arms as she walked once again through the gates of Belle Vie. Her mother had, in that way, been by her side for years.

Upstairs, Caren shut her bedroom door.

She set the paisley-covered box in the center of her bed, tugging at the frayed edges of the purple ribbon and watching it unfurl and spill off to the sides. Then, slowly, she lifted the square lid. The air inside felt very cold, as if the memories stored there had been packed in ice. Caren felt her fingers stiffen as she reached in and pulled out the piece of paper that was sitting on top. It was a report card from her first semester at Dillard, when she still bothered to send them home, and beneath that was a clipping of a newspaper article about the law clinic in New Orleans and its partnership with Tulane University—a news story that had mentioned Caren's name in passing, which her mother had underlined in pencil. *Caren Gray*. Going back in time, there were high school football programs, even though Caren had neither played nor cheered from the sidelines; there was a card she'd made her mother in the sixth grade, and a school photograph for nearly every year Caren had ever spent in a classroom, her face growing longer with each passing year. Her senior class ring was there, and a pair of gold-plated hoop earrings, along with a swatch of fabric from a dress she and her mother had tried to make when Caren was just six years old. She'd picked the fabric herself. It was green with bright-yellow stars outlined in gold. They'd bought yards and yards of it.

Caren smiled.

The sudden movement loosened her tears.

They fell in large, cloudy drops, dotting the colorful fabric.

Caren set each item on top of the patchwork quilt, her life's history spread like puzzle pieces across the bed. Then . . . at the very bottom of the paisley box she found a Big Chief notebook, wide-ruled, just like the kind Caren had used as a child. The pages were nearly all blank, the notebook serving as a kind of accordion file folder; it was stuffed with dozens of loose papers and photographs, some wrapped gingerly in plastic sandwich bags to protect the thin, yellowing paper. Caren found pictures of her grandparents, a newspaper clipping announcing their marriage in 1938, and an envelope stub, on the back of which her grandfather had tried to make mathematical sense of his piece of the cane farm's sugar profits for the year 1946, his end-of-the-harvest pay based on the money the Clancys made out of the fields.

One by one, Caren flipped through the items in the notebook.

And again, she had the sensation of falling backward through time.

Somewhere near to the very back of the red Big Chief, she came across a single item that stole her breath away. It was an old newspaper clipping, as thin and fragile as a fall leaf, dried and nearly forgotten in the wind. It was from something called the *Negro Advocate*, and it was dated June 1871.

INFORMATION WANTED:

JASON, AGE 29, OF BELLE VIE PLANTATION, ASCENSION PARISH, LA., WISHES TO OFFER A REWARD OF $30 FOR INFORMATION AS TO THE WHEREABOUTS OF AN ELEANOR, AGE 27, WHO WAS SOLD FROM BELLE VIE ON AUG 4TH, 1859. LAST SEEN AT THE SALE PEN OF GEOFFREY PULLMAN OF BATON ROUGE. SEND WORD, ALL WHO HAVE INFORMATION, TO A MISS NADINE WOODS AT THE PLANTATION SCHOOL. THANKFULLY YOURS AND GOD BLESS.

Caren held the paper in her hands, feeling a stir in her chest.

So that's why he stayed, she thought.

291

For *her*.

For Eleanor.

He stayed on the plantation, long after the war, because it was the only place Eleanor would have known to look for him; he was, after all those years, waiting for his wife. She'd been sold, Caren remembered, just before the war, and Jason would have had no way of knowing to whom . . . and he would have had no one to ask. Monsieur Duquesne had dropped dead before Union soldiers even made it to Belle Vie; his heart gave out on word they'd taken New Orleans. Le Roy, his only son, was killed in the first battle at Donaldsonville, shortly thereafter. Madame and the Duquesnes' only daughter, Manette, fled the coarse and grotesque authority of the Yankee soldiers, abandoning Belle Vie for good, thus laying the way for Tynan, the Clancys' distant ancestor, to take over the land. There were records left behind, of course. Caren had held them in her hands. But she could read, and Jason couldn't. Not without help.

Nadine Woods was the colored woman who worked at the plantation's school for ex-slaves. She had been Jason's teacher.

It was a relationship that grew close over time, during those years Jason was waiting for his wife's return. This was made plain in dozens of letters Caren found in her mother's note-book—letters in which Miss Nadine expressed her fondness for her pupil, and admitted that she, too, would have liked to have known Jason under a different set of circumstances. She referred to him as principled and strong. He called her smart and kind on the eyes, in the only surviving letter written in his strained hand.

All of this, Helen had wanted Caren to have. Including her own handwritten jottings on a few of the notebook's back pages, places where she'd tried to get down on paper the stories she'd heard passed on and on, through the generations, all the way down to the last of the Grays. Jason, her mother wrote, had lived on at Belle Vie until the fall of 1872, until the cutting season, which is when he'd gone missing. Eleanor had returned suddenly and unexpectedly that spring, to try to rebuild a life with a man she hadn't seen in years. And when one night he didn't come home, she repeatedly told anyone who would listen that she was certain he wouldn't have just up and left her, not after all the time they'd been apart and all he'd gone through to find her. Whatever she knew of Jason's special relationship with the schoolteacher was unclear. But Miss Nadine likewise had no idea what had become of Jason. It was Tynan, his employer, who had been the last to see Jason, claiming the man simply walked out of the fields one day.

Caren ran her finger over her mother's handwriting, felt the bumps and ridges from where Helen's pen had pressed into the lined paper. Then she turned to the last page of the notebook.

There, pressed between two sheets of wax paper, she found a plantation map. Strange, she thought, as she studied the thin paper.

The thing had to be more than a century old, and parts of it were nearly unrecognizable to Caren. In the top-left corner was a crude rendering of the old carriage house, which had been torn down decades ago, and hadn't appeared on any plantation map after the Civil War. There were other parts of the map that she didn't recognize, either—specifically the hand-drawn image of a structure, twelve feet by fourteen, just behind the slave quarters. In a stiff hand, someone had written the words, *built by my hand, August 1872*. The map was signed in the same handwriting . . . *Jason*. According to this, the structure he built just months before he died happened to sit right on the patch of land behind the slave village, where, for years now, grass had refused to grow.

* * *

Danny didn't show his face at Belle Vie on Tuesday.

By Wednesday, Caren set out to find him herself, heading north in her car.

Louisiana State University sat along the Mississippi River just south of the state capitol building. Its handsome campus, manicured without being staid, was dotted here and there by aged oaks, venerable and strong, much like the ones that rose up out of the ground at Belle Vie. There were flat, green lawns and sidewalks lined with purple and rose-colored flowers and dozens of red-tiled buildings, plus a watchtower reaching a height of nearly two hundred feet. Driving through the school grounds that morning, Caren couldn't believe how long it had been since she'd been on a university campus. She parked her car behind Foster Hall—walking distance, she was told at the main gate, from the offices of the History Department, where she could find Danny Olmsted.

Himes Hall was a Spanish-style building with an open walkway on one side, separated from its nearest courtyard by a row of grand arches. And according to the lobby directory, Danny's office was on the second floor, room 209. The door was closed, but unlocked. It pushed open slightly when she knocked. Inside, Danny was standing behind an aluminum desk stacked with manila file folders, loose papers, and takeout menus. He was hunched over his laptop, staring at the screen. Behind him there were crumpled cigarettes on the windowsill. He looked up once, and then did a double take. Caren Gray was about the last person he expected to see in his office.

"Hey," he said—nervously, she thought.

Gingerly, she pulled out the map, still encased in wax paper, from her mother's Big Chief notebook. "You ever seen this before?" she asked. Danny hesitated a moment, not sure what this visit was all about. He glanced over her shoulder into the hallway, as if he was concerned about who might be watching, and then reached for the plantation map. He stared at it for quite a long time. Caren could hear the squeak of shoe soles on the linoleum outside his office door. It was dark in here, a gray haze in the air. Danny turned on his desk lamp before collapsing into the rolling chair behind him, his eyes never leaving the map.

"Where did you get this?"

"What *is* it?" she said.

He looked up. "Where did you get this?"

"It was made the same year Jason disappeared," she said, showing him the reverse side of the map, which had been stamped by federal seal at a Homestead Land Office in New Orleans in November of 1872, right around the time Jason went missing.

Danny was clearing space on his desktop.

He set down the map so that he could study it more closely.

"I'd like to hold on to this."

"No," Caren said, shaking her head.

The map was hers.

Her mother had made sure of that.

Danny bit his thumbnail, shaking his head. "No, I've never seen it before."

Caren stepped across the dull carpet to his desk, lifting the map and returning it to the safety of her own two hands. "I know about the movie," she said.

"Oh," Danny said, his lips curling into an impish smile. He looked somewhat sheepish, but also greatly amused, as if the whole thing had been little more than a prank. "I suppose people were bound to find out about it sooner or later."

"He's in jail over this mess, you know."

Danny's face blanched. "What?"

"The cops know he was at Belle Vie on Wednesday night."

"But they can't honestly believe he had something to do with that girl."

"He's in *jail*."

Danny fell silent a moment. "I had a bad feeling about this."

"You've gotten him in a shitload of trouble, Danny."

"*Me?*"

"You didn't write that script?"

"God, no," Danny said. "I mean, I supplied some of the re-search. I suppose that's fairly obvious. But this was Donovan's deal, from start to finish." He shook his head to himself. "I thought it was the wrong story to tell. I told him it was a mistake."

"Why?"

"Well," Danny said cryptically, "it doesn't end well."

"What do you mean?" Then, remembering his university pa-per, its abrupt ending on page 25, she asked him, "Why didn't you ever finish your dissertation?"

"I didn't *not* finish it," Danny said emphatically. "I merely shifted focus."

"But *why?*"

Danny sighed impatiently. "Look, Jason's story is a fascinat-ing one; at least it appeared so initially. My whole field of study is about labor issues, post-Emancipation. And here was a man who'd been a slave and then worked the very same plantation, under contract. There's even some evidence that he tried to organize the other workers into a labor collective, to up their wages. He was looking for a way to have more profit participa-tion, real ownership. He was ahead of his time in that way. And then all of a sudden he goes missing, is presumed murdered, and there's this black man, this newly elected sheriff charged to investigate, a man who is living evidence that the old rules don't apply, that a Negro's death won't go unpunished. It's a rich area, for sure," Danny said. "Donovan went crazy for it, the idea of a black man in charge—what, six years after slavery is declared illegal? It was a story he'd never heard before." He reached into the jacket of his trench coat, which was draped over his chair, and came out with a loose cigarette and a plastic lighter. "Though I wouldn't consider it a shining moment of African-American history."

The light outside the casement window changed color and direction, dark shadows rolling in waves across the flat carpet.

Danny lit his cigarette, blowing smoke toward the ceiling.

"I mean, the guy was run out of office."

"The sheriff?"

"Ran himself out of office, really, by pushing for an indictment."

"He knew what had happened to Jason?"

"Well, that depends on who you ask," he said. "I mean, it sure looks like he was on to something, like the story is going to go one way, but then it all turns out to be some messy business over a broken heart." He rolled his eyes, shaking his head at the operatic turn of events, as if the history had failed him personally in some way. "It turns out Jason was smack in the middle of a love triangle of some kind. His wife, Eleanor—"

"And the schoolteacher," Caren said, finishing the thought.

Danny nodded. "Not exactly my field of study," he said.

He glanced down at his laptop, responding to some prompt on the screen. "The general consensus in the parish had Jason running off with one or the other," he said. "Or that maybe one of the women got jealous and did him in."

"But Sweats didn't believe it."

Danny shook his head, puffing on the end of his cigarette. "And made a fool of himself in the process . . . left himself open to accusations he didn't know what he was doing, that he was unfit to serve in the office of sheriff," he said, exhaling.

"The thing is, Jason's body was never found. There wasn't

any proof that a crime had even been committed. And certainly no clear motive to support the sheriff's theory of the crime, which put the murder weapon in someone else's hand, someone other than the two women Jason was involved with. The sheriff swore that Jason had been killed with his own cane knife, one loaned to him in the fields by his employer. He was insistent. Stubborn, some said. He actually wanted to put Tynan on trial for murder."

Caren felt her stomach drop.

She wasn't immediately sure she'd heard the name right.

"William Tynan?" she said, and Danny nodded.

"Raymond Clancy's great-great-grandfather?"

"Yes."

23

Raymond had lied to her, she thought.

By the time she made it back to Belle Vie, made it all the way back inside the cramped Hall of Records, she had a sickening suspicion that he'd lied to her when he said he didn't know anything about an investigation into Jason's disappearance. The room was exactly as she'd left it. The papers were still there, laid out on the low wood table in the center of the room, right where she'd left them. Slave records and bills of sale, farm receipts and the creased, worn photos of harvests past, the blank faces of sharecroppers and field-workers. And as Caren searched the file drawers, the many folders and leather binders in the room, she was again struck by the feeling that papers were missing—not just land records and such, but also pages and pages of William Tynan's diary. Only now Caren suspected this was evidence of more than just sloppy record-keeping. It suddenly seemed to her that someone had been in here, removing, page by page, pieces of Belle Vie's history, excising the parts he didn't like—like the fact that Raymond Clancy's great-great-grandfather was a suspect in the death of one of Caren's ancestors. The thought was dizzying. What else, she thought, could Raymond be lying about?

Slowly, meticulously, she put the papers back. One by one, she refiled the documents and historical records, leaving them just the way she'd found them.

* * *

Eric was in the parlor when she walked in.

He was sitting on the leather divan, and he was holding Morgan's school records. He wanted her to know he was serious. He was taking their daughter away from here. He'd changed his clothes, out of the wrinkled suit and into khakis and a deep-blue T-shirt, both crisp and unlined and likely purchased in town. He was resting his elbows on his knees, leaning his weight forward. "Caren," he said softly. "Look, about yesterday, what happened between us . . ." The words registered somewhere in Caren's brain. It was an opening, she knew, if she wanted to take it. But now she was the one who couldn't talk about this. She was still reeling from the news of Clancy's possible cover-up.

There was a knock on the library's front door.

It was tentative at first, then loud and growing more frantic.

Eric stood, but it was Caren who opened the front door. Pearl was standing on the other side, panting and out of breath. She'd run all the way from the kitchen with an urgent message from Miss Lorraine. There was some movement down at the court-house. They were putting Donovan in front of a judge.

Caren turned to Eric.

"They're arraigning him," she said.

Eric nodded and grabbed his car keys.

The judge was a black woman, fair-skinned and heavyset, with a ring of pearls choked around her neck. Her traveling nameplate read JONETTA PAULS. She was a circuit court judge, one they'd brought in just for this, the formal reading of charges against Donovan James Isaacs. Eric and Caren were sitting in the front row. Lorraine had come on her own, taking a seat behind them. The room was small, like a miniaturized version of a courtroom scene on television. The wood was fake paneling, and the banker's lamps on the desks didn't work. They were all drowning instead under the sharp white of fluorescent lights buzzing overhead. Caren looked around the courtroom. Betty wasn't here, she noticed, a fact that spelled trouble. She couldn't think of any good reason that would keep Betty Collier from her grandson.

Donovan looked awful.

He was handcuffed when they brought him in, two armed deputies at his sides, and he kept his head down, his chin pressed against his sternum. He didn't look around the room much, didn't make eye contact with Caren or anyone else, just stood there, shaking his head every time his lawyer whispered something in his ear. He was unshaven, his hair in knots, and Caren had the awful thought that they'd kept him in lockup for the past few days for the sole purpose of aging him, curing him like a cut of meat, making him look more like the thug they were here to charge. It was a reminder of the ways an arrest can often work backward, making a criminal of any life it touches. It pained her to see him this way.

Eric nudged her, asking why she hadn't given Donovan or his grandmother the list of attorneys he'd suggested — and that was the first time Caren took a good, long look at Donovan's lawyer. She had initially taken him for a court-appointed attorney, but now she wasn't so sure. He was in his midfifties and nicely dressed, too nice, she thought, to be taking work from the parish. And he looked vaguely familiar to Caren, in a way she could not get her hands around. He seemed too tall, and too big in the way he carried himself, for this small, country courtroom. He kept a proprietary hand on Donovan's shoulder through the whole thing. Where had she seen him before?

Up first, there was the reading of the charge.

The court clerk stood and officially named the matter: "The

state of Louisiana versus Donovan James Isaacs, who, pursuant to Louisiana State Penal Code, Title 14, Section 30, is hereby charged with the crime of Homicide in the First Degree."

"What?" Caren turned to Eric and whispered, "Wait, what happened to trespassing?"

Eric shook his head. "They must have gotten something else on him."

"What is going on, Eric?"

She felt sick all of a sudden, a rush of blood heating her from the inside out. She unzipped her jacket, pulling it away from her damp skin.

At the bench, the judge asked, "How do you plead, son?"

His attorney squeezed his shoulder and tried to whisper something in his ear.

Donovan kept shaking his head. "I ain't kill nobody, judge."

Bail was denied, with little apparent argument from Donovan's attorney. Caren didn't think he'd have gotten bail anyway, but it bothered her the way the lawyer didn't even try. What kind of defense attorney was this? She sat through the various house-keeping matters that followed—the official filing of papers, the comparing of calendars to set a trial date—all the while think-ing of the mess this boy had gotten himself into, all over his plans to retake and retell a history with his movie project.

The thought nearly pushed her out of her chair.

That's right.

Donovan had made a movie. He had rented *video equipment*.

Just as the deputies started to escort him out, she stood up. He looked at Lorraine first, and then at Caren in the front row of the gallery. His eyes were puffy and red. Donovan, she real-ized, had been crying. "Miss C," he said, calling to her. "Tell my grandmother I didn't do this. Tell her I didn't have nothing to do with it."

Caren was still standing. "Where are the tapes, Donovan?"

The *tapes*.

She didn't know why she hadn't thought of them earlier.

They were a piece of evidence that had been at their fingertips this whole time.

"Donovan . . . where are the tapes?"

By now the two deputies were pulling him out of the courtroom. His lawyer had a hand on his back, nudging Donovan along. Caren called out again. He turned and looked once more over his shoulder. Their eyes met, and for a single second she thought he understood. "Go to my grandmama's house," he said, as the cops pulled him out of the courtroom toward a holding cell. "Tell her it wasn't me."

When Caren arrived at her house an hour later, Betty Collier was in the front yard. She was wearing a housecoat and slippers, and she was, despite her eighty-two years, on her knees in the dirt, patting soil around a small bed of primrose and sweet alyssum, shaking her head to herself as she worked. She heard the rental car's engine shudder to a stop and looked up immediately. But she was no more comforted by the sight of Caren than she was by the state of her garden. Caren told Eric to wait in the car while she got out on the passenger's side. She could hear Betty all the way from the street. The elderly woman was muttering under her breath, turning the black dirt this way and that. "Just look at this," she said. "Just look what they did to my yard. No home training, not a nary a one of 'em." She was speaking of the policemen, she said. The ones who had tramped through her house that morning, she said, waving a search warrant; they'd been careless and heavy-handed, tossing her things and crushing her flower garden. "Just look at this mess." Her voice rose into a high-pitched wail.

303

"Detectives Lang and Bertrand were here?"

Caren remembered Eric's courtroom observation, that the detectives must have gotten something else on Donovan to change the charge from trespassing to murder.

"I don't know who all it was," Betty said.

She tried to stand tall a felled stalk of yellow primrose, but when she gave the plant the tiniest tug, the whole thing came up in her hand, roots and all. Betty lowered her head and started to cry. "I'm so mad I could spit," she said, her dark eyes piercing from beneath the many folds of her copper-colored skin. "I'd swat his little behind if I could."

It was hard to know who had hurt her worse: the cops or her grandson, whom she seemed to blame for getting himself into this mess in the first place, and dragging her one good home into it. Caren knelt down beside her and put a gentle hand on her elbow, helping the older woman to her feet. Betty felt for Caren's free hand and, finding it, squeezed so tightly it made Caren wince. Betty was holding on for dear life, it seemed. Together, the two went inside. In the kitchen, Betty cleaned herself up at the porcelain sink, drying her hands on a faded yellow washcloth hanging from the handle of an old gas stove. Then she reached across the kitchen counter for an open bottle of Maker's Mark. "For my nerves," she said. She poured two fingers into a chipped coffee mug and sipped slowly. Twice Caren asked her why she hadn't come to court this afternoon, but Betty never answered her. She set the mug on the tiled countertop and reached into the front pocket of her housecoat for a handkerchief. She blew her nose and then pulled from the same pocket a two-page, folded document that bore a stamp from the parish courthouse. "Here," she said. "They came with this."

The warrant was signed by the same JUDGE JONETTA PAULS and, below that, DETECTIVE NESTOR LANG. Caren read the list of items authorized for removal by law enforcement from 168 Crescent Place, Donaldsonville, LA 70346. The very first thing on the list was a knife, of at least eight inches in length, with a wooden handle—known colloquially as a "cane knife." The warrant went on to list almost any and every article of clothing that might belong to a man Donovan's age, noting that detectives were limited to collecting bloody clothing or shoes or items soiled with dirt and grass. There was nothing in print about videotapes or even copies of Donovan's unfinished script, the school project, he'd told the cops, that had brought him to Belle Vie after hours. Either the detectives didn't believe him, or they'd missed the significance of his admission.

But Caren knew what *tapes* meant.

At the counter, Betty finished the glass of bourbon.

Caren asked her if she happened to see what the officers took.

Betty shook her head. "All this mess, and they walked out of here with nothing," she said. "Not a damn thing." Caren turned and looked around the inside of the one-story house, which was made up of just a few small rooms. The living room and kitchen were divided by an oval table with a crocheted tablecloth laid gingerly on top. The television was a big black box, as old and bulky as a steamer trunk, and in front of it sat a daybed, painted a glossy white and adorned with a mound of throw pillows, some cross-stitched by hand. Betty must sleep here, Caren thought. The back bedroom was for her grandson, the only privacy in the house reserved for him. Through an open door, she could see the disarray left by the officers' search. The mattress had been upended from its bed frame, and there were men's clothes and shoes strewn about the floor, plus magazines and books open everywhere. A basketball had rolled into the hallway. "What about tapes?" Caren said. "Did you see the officers carry away any videotapes?" Donovan had told her to get to his grandmother's house.

Tell her I didn't do it, he'd said. And when she'd asked about the tapes in open court, he mentioned Betty again. Caren felt sure the tapes were somewhere inside this house.

Betty shook her head, her rheumy eyes gazing off in the distance, across the poorly lit room, fixed on some far-off thought. Caren wasn't sure she was still listening.

"Mrs. Collier," she said gently. "Why weren't you in court today?"

Betty let out a teary sigh, shrugging her bony shoulders. "I've had him since he was eight. I did the best I could with him. His daddy was trouble, too, in and out of jail." She dropped her hands into the pockets of her housecoat, the posture of a woman resigned to her fate. "I'm eighty-two years old, and I'm tired," she said, as if Donovan's story were already written in stone, had been since the day he was born. "I did the best I could," she said, wiping tears that had settled in the deep creases beneath her eyes. There was dirt under her fingernails. She smelled of Dove soap and whiskey. Caren didn't want her to give up on Donovan. Betty was the only blood family Donovan had.

"That lawyer should have let you know about the court proceedings," she said. "He should have demanded you be there today as a show of support."

"I don't imagine it matters no way."

"It does, though," Caren said. "You're going to want the best representation you can get for Donovan. You need someone who's going to walk your family through the whole process, not just somebody punching a clock or trying to get in good with the judge."

"Clancy's got it all worked out."

"Who?"

Raymond Clancy, Betty said.

He'd sent Donovan that lawyer, right out of his firm in Baton Rouge.

Caren shook her head. She thought Betty must have gotten it confused.

"No, ma'am, it was Clancy, all right," Betty said. "He called the house this morning, said not to worry on it. He was gon' make sure Donovan was taken care of."

"Raymond said that?"

Betty nodded. "And I want to thank you for that, Caren," she said. She had assumed this was Caren's doing, getting Clancy to go to bat for Donovan. "I know they've been good to your family over the years. He's just like his daddy, that one," she said. "The Clancys, they've always looked out for black folks."

No, Caren thought.

Raymond was nothing like his father.

She wanted to tell Betty to be wary, but she didn't want to scare the woman any more than she already was, not until Caren had more information, not until she knew just what in the hell Raymond was up to. She asked if she could look in Donovan's bedroom, making up a story about needing his work costume and other such items returned to the plantation. Betty nodded without saying anything. In her slippers, she shuffled in the direction of the open bottle of whiskey.

They were not hard to find.

Two unmarked DVDs—not *tapes*, not literally—inside a shoe box on the right side of the bed, near a stack of books on editing and camera techniques that he'd checked out from his local library, books that had Post-it notes and scraps of paper marking passages inside. Caren made a quick and easy guess as to the content of the DVDs. Stuck to the front of the clear plastic case was a taped note that bore a list of scribbled scene numbers.

Back home, she slid the first disc into the open drive on her computer, the one upstairs in her apartment. Raymond Clancy had left by the time they returned to the plantation, but she didn't know when or if he'd be back and thought it best to view the footage here, the little part of Belle Vie over which she had sole, if temporary, domain. She was seated in front of the monitor, Eric behind her, watching as the disc loaded. The first image on-screen was a shot of the slave quarters.

Caren felt a flutter in her chest at the sight.

My God, she whispered.

She had never seen anything like it, had never seen the quarters so alive, populated by real flesh and blood. It took her breath away. She saw at once what he was trying to do, Donovan, the history he wanted to record, to hold in his hands, to make sense of. He was trying to put it down for posterity in the only way he knew how, with video cameras and microphones, the tools of his generation. And it broke Caren's heart, broke it wide open, in fact. She stared at the computer screen in awe. For there he was. There was Jason, her great-great-great-grandfather. And here was the schoolteacher, Miss Nadine. The scene was of a celebration, a cakewalk in the quarters, sometime in the years before Jason's wife, Eleanor, returned—when Jason and his teacher were unwittingly falling in love. There was a feeling of felicity as the men and women fell in line for the cakewalk, a playful and flirtatious dance that got its start in slave quarters on plantations across the South. It was a tradition that had taken on a special tenderness on the other side of Emancipation, black folks holding on to some of the old ways, even as they moved forward into the still unknown world of freedom. And when Jason took Nadine's hand for a dance, Caren, watching the scene unfold, felt her own heart skip a beat. It was just Cornelius and Shauna on-screen, playing the parts. She knew that. And those twinkling lights were not stars, but a string of ninety-nine-cent Christmas lights slung across the cabin doors and the wooden fences. That was just Ennis Mabry in a pageboy cap and Lee overalls, pretending to strum a string guitar, just Nikki Hubbard and a few of her high school friends filling out the cast of ex-slaves. But she didn't care. She was seeing her own story, her own history reflected back to her, rounded out and in full color, and the feeling it stirred was something she would not, in this lifetime, forget.

They watched for nearly an hour, scene after scene.

But it wasn't until the last recorded scene on the second disc that she understood the full significance of the evidence she'd uncovered. They watched the final scene, the last one Donovan filmed on Wednesday night, over and over, maybe a dozen times. The whole thing was one shot, less than thirty-five seconds long—the footage taken on the main road, outside of Manette cottage, just like Morgan said. Her report of the night Inés Avalo was killed had included this fact: Donovan said he would wait around for his cast and crew, passing the time by getting some extra shots outside Manette house. And that's exactly what was on Caren's computer screen now.

"Take a look at that," she said to Eric, pointing at the screen. She held a finger to the top left part of the monitor, clicking the mouse to rewind the shot from the beginning. The image was dark, almost ashy, the strained result of trying to register true black on digital video; the scene had likely been lit with nothing more than a small bulb mounted on the camera itself. Donovan, manning the camera, swept the lens from the front of the cottage—the clapboard porch, the railing made of whitewashed pine—all the way down the length of the main road, pointing south toward the quarters. It was here that Donovan's voice cut in. "What the hell is that?" he whispered. It was nothing urgent, his tone; in no way did he sound alarmed. The shot—an image of the main road all the way to the quarters—slipped in and out of focus as Donovan zoomed in on a white light off in the distance. "Look," Caren said to Eric. He squinted at the screen.

The closer the camera zoomed in, the greater the strain on the image. But it was clear that the light was coming from the cane fields, on the other side of Belle Vie's fence. Eric's eyes widened as something astonishing happened: the light, which at a distance seemed whole, split in two. And even though the digital magnification distorted the image somewhat, it was clear that the two white squares were headlights. Somebody was parked out there Wednesday night, out by the fields, twin headlights pointed toward the plantation, not even fifteen feet from where the body of Inés Avalo had been found.

24

Eric asked her to replay it.

She asked him if he was seeing the same thing she was.

There was only one type of motor vehicle that sits that high off the ground, and Caren was convinced that those were the headlights of a pickup truck. Eric shook his head; he wasn't nearly as certain. But it was an automobile for sure, and when she mentioned showing the disc to Detectives Lang and Bertrand, he, surprisingly, didn't resist.

They would not mention Morgan or the bloody shirt.

The rules were the same.

But even Eric couldn't deny the significance of Donovan's footage.

They rode together to the sheriff's station in Gonzales, Caren sitting beside Eric in his rental, the DVDs in her lap. At the courthouse, Detective Lang greeted them first, in the hallway outside the Criminal Investigations Division, having earlier received her call saying they were on their way. It wasn't until the first disc was out of its case and loaded into a DVD player in one of the station's two interrogation rooms that Lang finally understood the connection between Donovan's "school project" and the scenes playing out on the TV screen. The three of them, Caren, Eric, and Lang, watched the film's story in silence. When Detective Bertrand came in carrying a Styrofoam cup of black coffee, she told them both the image they needed to see was on the second disc. But Lang approached this with an investigator's pace, wanting to see each frame of each scene lined end to end, so that he could comprehend the whole of the discs' meaning in the context of his murder investigation—one he believed he'd already solved. And so Caren watched, for the second time, the story of Jason and Nadine and Eleanor, the mystery of his disappearance, and the black sheriff determined to find the truth. Bertrand stared at the screen and frowned, asking no one in particular, "What in God's name is all this?"

On the television screen, the roles were reversed.

Donovan, their suspect, was the lawman.

Having cast himself in the role of Sheriff Aaron Nathan Sweats, he was wearing a wide-brim hat and Eddie Knoxville's black knee-high boots. Bo Johnston was doing his bit as Jason's employer and the cane farm's manager, Mr. Tynan. The scene was shot in the old schoolhouse, which had been made over to resemble a country jailhouse. Tynan was being interrogated about the last time he'd seen Jason alive. The sheriff's investigation seemed to turn on a cane knife, one used by Jason in the fields. It seemed odd to Sheriff Sweats that the knife had been *returned* to Tynan at the end of the workday, when Tynan swore he hadn't seen Jason again after he walked out of the fields.

The television screen cut to black.

Finally, they were at the very last shot, in front of Manette house.

"Here," Caren said to the cops.

Lang turned up the volume, as if that might help him see the fuzzy image more clearly. Bertrand, whose coffee had turned cold sitting on the tabletop, had his arms crossed tight against his chest, the shoulder seams of his sports coat so strained that

Caren could see each mustard-brown thread. Eric watched from the back of the room.

It was all there: Donovan's whisper, the white light, the camera's long zoom.

When the light split, when it became clear that Donovan's camera had captured twin headlights parked in the distance, in the cane fields, Caren kept her eyes on both Lang and Bertrand. Bertrand's arms dropped to his sides. He bent at the waist, staring at the nineteen-inch screen, his thick hands on his hips. Lang hit rewind. He watched the shot two more times, in complete silence. When he finally turned away from the screen, he looked at his partner first, then Caren. "This was Wednesday night? You're sure?" She nodded, although at present her only way of proving this fact was the word of her nine-year-old daughter. There was no time stamp on any of the scenes on the discs, and she had no way of knowing where the originals—the digital videotapes from the camera itself—were, not without talking to Donovan first.

"We're going to need to keep these," Lang said.

She shook her head. "You can make a copy."

Lang nodded at Bertrand. "Jimmy, go get Tommy from across the hall."

Bertrand backed out of the room, still staring at the headlights on the television screen, until he was all the way on the other side of the door. Lang stood. "I'm not sure I understand why this wasn't brought to my attention earlier." He looked at Caren first, before leveling a vexing gaze on Eric. "Especially seeing as you were in here passing yourself off as the boy's attorney, Mr. Ellis, not to mention practicing law in the state of Louisiana without a bar card." Eric started to speak, but Caren stopped him. She didn't need him coming down hard with some Yankee attitude, speaking with anything less than the respect this small-town detective was sure he deserved. She would handle Lang.

"I don't believe Donovan killed anybody, sir," she said to the cop.

Eric jumped in impatiently. "Why in the world would she withhold anything that potentially exculpates him?"

"Is that what you think this is?" Lang said, nodding toward the grainy video.

"It raises the possibility that someone other than Donovan killed Inés Avalo. Someone else was clearly present at the scene. It's right there on the tape."

Lang nodded absently.

"Well, see, the problem with that is . . . Donovan has already confessed."

"What?" Eric said.

Caren was sure she'd heard it wrong. "What do you mean he *confessed?*"

"He and his attorney are already in the process of working out a plea deal with the district attorney's office. He'll admit to guilt, and if he's lucky get the charge knocked down to second-degree homicide, manslaughter even. But that's all up to the folks in the DA's office."

Eric was frowning.

"Wait a minute," he said. "A plea deal isn't necessarily a confession."

"It is in my book."

"So you're not even going to look into this?" Caren said, trying to control her anger, nearly shaking from the effort. Lang pointed to the bluish screen and the video image. Dryly, he said, "The Sheriff's Department thanks you for bringing this in."

And that was it.

Caren looked at Eric and said, "I don't understand. Why would he take a deal?"

Lang was damn near smiling.

Sheer arrogance was the only thing that could explain why he said what he said next, why he laid his whole hand face-up on the table. "We got the knife," he said.

Caren didn't believe him.

She was *at* Betty Collier's house. The police had been through with a warrant, but Betty said they'd walked out with nothing. Lang's whole case was bullshit, and they knew it. "I want to talk to him," she said suddenly. "I want to talk to Donovan."

"No, ma'am," Lang said, shaking his head.

Eric grabbed her arm. "Come on, Caren, let's go."

"He's not the boy's lawyer, and you're not family." Lang was treating them as troublemakers, involving themselves in something that had nothing to do with them.

But Donovan *was* family.

He was part of the extended family of Belle Vie, *her* family.

"He can't take a deal," she said.

Lang smiled broadly, as if he was expecting this. "Well . . . if he doesn't, you want to know what's going to happen, Ms. Gray? The district attorney is going to put this evidence to a grand jury, and you, ma'am, will be among those subpoenaed. I know you've been lying to us from day one. You were the main one vouching for the fact that Donovan wasn't on the plantation Wednesday night, and now you're hand-delivering a videotape you've had in your possession for who knows how long, hard evidence that proves you knew where he was the whole time."

"Caren, let's go," Eric said.

"You digging yourself a hole, Tulane," Lang said. "Don't look good, neither, you looking at plane tickets to Washington, D.C. You got some reason to be making a fast exit out of the state?" She started to say something, to ask how he knew about that. But Eric grabbed her roughly by the arm. "Don't say another word," he said.

"I want to talk to Donovan," she told Lang.

315

Eric reached for Caren's hand, just as Bertrand returned with a skinny kid in Levis and a black Eagles concert T-shirt. He had a second DVD player tucked under one arm and two slim black-and-red cables draped over his right shoulder. Eric, without being asked, held Caren's hand while copies of the video discs were made.

She posed it as a last favor, asking Eric to get her inside the jail. Donovan was officially a ward of the Ascension Parish Sheriff's Department, and they could pretty much do with him as they pleased, could withhold privileges such as phone calls or visits from family or friends. So Eric placed an urgent call to a friend of his in the U.S. Attorney's office in Dallas. And that woman, an old law school classmate of theirs, placed a call of her own, to the jailhouse in little Gonzales, Louisiana.

Less than an hour later, Caren entered the jail alone.

Her name was already waiting on somebody's clipboard.

She left her personal effects with a female clerk, a black woman with brandy-colored braids and gold hoop earrings who eyed Caren and her expensive Patagonia jacket and muddy ropers with no small amount of curiosity. She offered no pleasantries, no friendly comments about the weather. Instead, she pointed to where Caren should sign her name and the red plastic tray where she was to leave her driver's license and keys. Her escort was a young deputy with an ash-blond buzz cut and rolls of fat above the starched collar of his tan uniform. He led her down a hallway with cracked linoleum tiles and fluorescent lights to a plain door with a small window.

Inside, Donovan sat alone, uncuffed, in a dingy jailhouse jumpsuit, and Caren could tell from first glance that he was expecting someone else. He didn't stand or greet her in any way. The deputy asked if she wanted him to stay, and she answered no, that she thought they'd be all right. She watched the cop disappear on the other side of the door. She heard the lock click, and then it was just the two of them. Donovan didn't look good. His eyes were red, and his cheeks were dappled with tufts of unshaven hair. He had his elbows on the table and his head held down low.

Caren sighed and said, "What are you doing, Donovan?"

He shook his head at her. "Just go."

"You can't take this deal."

Donovan clasped his hands under the table, shrugging his shoulders. "I can do two and a half," he said. "I might have picked that up on the trespassing charge, anyway." Then, trying to convince himself, he said again, "I can do two and a half."

"You're not serious, Donovan?" she said. "You don't really think they're going to give you two and half years on a murder charge?"

"Manslaughter," he said. He tapped his index finger on the white tabletop, as if he were counting out the days. "That guy, my lawyer, he's saying it's all worked out. I plead guilty to a lesser charge, and it's two and a half, that's what he said." He kept repeating the words, as if he were hammering a nail, closing his own coffin from the inside. "He says it's a good deal for somebody like me. The cops, the DA, they all know I got a felony record. So, yeah, I can do two and a half."

He thrust out his chin, playing with the idea of himself as a soldier, a man who's learned to take his licks. Caren couldn't think of a more dangerous way to test one's strength. She pulled out the second chair, sitting down across from him. "Listen to me," she said. "That lawyer of yours works for Raymond Clancy, and he's doing what he thinks is best for Clancy, not you. You need to understand that before you agree to anything."

Donovan cocked his head to one side. "What's Clancy got to do with this?"

"He got you that lawyer," she said. "The man didn't tell you he works for Raymond Clancy?"

"I thought the judge sent him. I thought he was court-appointed."

Caren shook her head. "He's a private attorney."

"My grandmama know about this?"

Caren avoided mentioning her trip to Betty's house that afternoon. She didn't want him to know how broken the old woman was, how it seemed she'd all but given up. "You ought to know . . . that Clancy is selling the plantation," she said instead.

Donovan shook his head in disbelief. "No way, man."

"It's sold, Donovan. Belle Vie, the farm, all of it. He's selling it to the Groveland Corporation."

Donovan didn't say anything right away.

He wore the expression of a man who thinks he's being lied to.

"But what's that got to do with me?"

"Nothing," she said. "That's what I'm saying. This is Raymond Clancy's deal. And he needs it to go through without any problems. He's got big plans for his political future, plans that involve Groveland, and you taking the fall for this is something he's willing to invest money in. It's a setup, Donovan," she said. He shook his head, turning to look away from her. Caren grabbed his arm. The skin felt fevered and hot. "Look at me," she said. "Don't you dare do this, Donovan. Don't you dare let them put you away for this. You are not your past, understand? I don't care what you've done or how many times you've been arrested. Don't let them make you into something you're not."

"What choice I got?"

"Go back in front of that judge and *don't* lie." She knew from experience that he could get a hearing to change his plea. But he needed a lawyer who was on his side.

"Aw, I'm fucked anyway," Donovan said. "I put myself on the grounds the night of the murder, admitted I'd stolen a key to the property. A jury might make a lot worse of that than whatever this lawyer, Wilson somebody, can work out with the DA."

"Where was the knife, Donovan?"

"They saying they found it in my car."

"Well, then somebody must have put it there."

"You don't fucking think I know that!" he said, slamming his fist on the table so hard that it shook and skidded an inch across the floor. Caren waited for the door to fly open, for the deputy to come charging in. Donovan held his breath, waiting, too. But no one came. A silence settled between them. It felt as thick as the door that closed them in this room. Donovan broke through it first. "I never saw that woman in my life and what difference does it make?" He gestured to the jail clothes and the locked room with an armed guard on the other side. What did the truth have to do with any of this? He was in jail anyway. Caren stared at him for a long time. Outside, she heard car engines, trucks passing on the road. All of it seemed very far away.

"Those tapes are evidence," she said. "They're proof some-body else was out there that night. You saw it, and I saw it. The headlights out by the field. It's right there on the DVD. If you tell me where the originals are, if the tapes have some kind of time stamp on them, a date, something, then that information goes to trial with you."

"You think they give a shit?"

He looked at her, a sad, crooked smile on his face. "Come on, Miss C," he said. "You think I didn't even try? It was a truck, I said. I *told* them. It was parked out there by the fields. But it don't look like that's going to change a damn thing, does it?"

She asked him to tell her exactly what he'd seen, the make

and model. Donovan waved her off, mumbling, "Naw, man, I didn't see what it was."

He couldn't be sure of the color, or any details.

It was just another dead end.

"Two and a half," he said again. "I'd rather take the deal than gamble on a life sentence at trial." He stole a sideways glance at her. "I suppose you think that makes me some kind of a punk," he said, and Caren finally understood that it mattered to him, that it had, all along, mattered what she thought of him. He actually looked up to her. "Don't do this, Donovan," she said. She was out-and-out pleading now. He didn't respond, choosing now, of all times, to remain silent. When he finally spoke again, his voice was soft and dry. He ducked his head and asked her, "So you watched it?" he said, referring to the movie, the history project that meant so much to him. "Yes, Donovan, I watched it," she said, telling him finally, "I think you should finish it."

25

It was late by the time they left the station. So, together, Eric and Caren drove to Laurel Springs to pick up their daughter from school, arriving a few minutes before the final bell. Eric parked the rental car a few yards down the road from Morgan's school, beside a newly planted Japanese maple, held in place by rope and wood stakes in the bark-covered ground. The rain had stopped, and Eric shut the car engine and rolled down the windows while they waited. The air was warm and smelled of wet grass. Through her sideview mirror, Caren could see the redbrick schoolhouse behind them, the state flag flying atop the Stars and Stripes.

"Hunt Abrams met with Raymond Clancy this week."

"Who?"

"He's the project manager for Groveland."

"The cane farm?"

She nodded, adding, "He drives a truck."

Black, she remembered.

"What was he doing with Clancy?"

"I don't know," she said. "But all of a sudden Raymond gets a lawyer for Donovan, and he's ready to take a plea deal? Just days after I see Abrams go behind closed doors with Clancy?" She shook her head. "It stinks, the whole thing. This is Raymond trying to protect his deal. The sooner this murder investigation goes away, the better it is for both of them, Clancy and Groveland."

Eric made a face. "What's at risk for the company?"

"Inés Avalo had some kind of altercation with Abrams, not even a week before she died. She found something, Eric, something out in the fields," she said, turning to look at him across the upholstered front seat. "She found a bone," Caren said. "Human remains."

"Jesus."

"Apparently she told Abrams about it, and it caused some tension between them. There was talk about going to authorities, but, according to Owens, Abrams wanted her to shut up about it."

"Owens?"

"The reporter," she said.

Eric turned away from her then, looking out the window.

She couldn't read his expression.

"Abrams is a bad seed, and apparently Inés Avalo isn't the first one of his workers to never make it home. There was a worker who died in California, and there was another woman down in Florida, a girl he supposedly beat pretty badly," she said. "Owens thinks there's a connection, between what Inés found and her murder, something to do with the question of who might be buried out in the fields. He asked me if any other cane workers had gone missing since Groveland took over the farm."

Eric shook his head, visibly disturbed.

He tapped his fingers against the steering wheel.

"So, what? You think he killed this Inés woman to cover for something else?"

"I don't know what to think, Eric."

"Who's the lawyer for the kid?"

"Someone from his firm," she said. "Raymond set it up."

"*Clancy's* firm?"

322

"Yes."

"Caren . . . Clancy, Strong, Burnham & Botts is a corporate firm, specializing in real estate and banking. We used to send business to them when I was at Klein & Roe. I don't think they have a single criminal defense attorney in the whole building. It's not what they do." He undid his seat belt, shifting several times behind the steering wheel.

Something here was very wrong.

And it went beyond the cops' slapdash investigation.

"The Avalo woman, she worked for Abrams?" he said, repeating the facts in evidence, turning the information this way and that. Caren nodded and said she was a field hand hired on for planting. She went on to explain the basic arc of a year growing cane, what she'd learned from a near lifetime at Belle Vie. "Planting's in late summer," she said. "The cutting season, the harvest, is late fall, and goes until the first frost. It's been that way for hundreds of years." Since her own ancestors cut cane in the fields, she said. "But everyone's behind this year because of the rain, which kept the migrant workers around a lot longer than they would have been during any other season." It's the rain, too, she said, that likely brought the bone up from out of the ground, pushing it out, like a depraved and dirty birth.

Across Main Street, two crossing guards in bright yellow vests were taking up positions on the circle drive in front of the elementary school, where cars and minivans were starting to line up. "So that's it, huh?" Caren said. "They found the knife, and that's their whole case?"

"That's all they need," Eric said. He was still tapping his fingers on the steering wheel, the sound as precise as a metronome, or the tick of a clock. It made Caren's heart beat faster, made her anxious and unsettled. "He *did* admit to being at the scene."

"That doesn't mean anything."

"You can't dismiss it, Caren. If this was your case, if we were back in school together, you'd have to find a way to address it for a jury. And, again, they have the knife. If it has some physical evidence on it, something tying it to—"

"No." She shook her head, adamant. "There's almost no physical evidence in their entire case. The rain washed over everything Wednesday night. Lang admitted from the start that it was one of the biggest problems with their investigation."

"They found the knife in his car. That's kind of hard to get around."

"Someone planted that, Eric, come on." The car sat in the parking lot for days, she reminded him. "Anyone could have had access to it. Lang was out there. And Abrams is just over the fence."

"That reporter was on the plantation, too."

Eric turned and looked at her straight on. "You never asked yourself what the hell he was doing wandering around the grounds in the middle of the night?"

"I certainly don't think he was tampering with a murder investigation."

She didn't add to this the fact that she liked Owens.

She trusted him.

Eric stared at her across the front seat, his expression grave. "Listen to me, Caren, don't fuck with that guy Lang, okay?" he said. "For whatever reason, the guy's got it in for you."

"What was that stuff about plane tickets?" she said. "How did he know about that?"

"You checked about flights for Morgan, didn't you?"

She nodded. "Saturday morning. I called the airline from my office."

"You don't think your phones are tapped, do you?"

"On what basis would they have to get a court order to monitor the phone lines?"

"They wouldn't need a court order if Raymond Clancy gave them permission. It's his place. You're his employee. You said you made the call from your work phone," he said. Caren's mind went back to the day the body was found. If Eric was right, and it was even possible that Lang and Bertrand were monitoring her phone line, then it was likewise possible that they'd heard her on the phone with Eric, discussing the blood on Morgan's shirt. They may have actually known about it for days.

She felt herself start to panic.

"But why would Clancy do that?"

"You know any reason he has to want to keep tabs on you?" he said. "I mean, I know your families go way, way back, for generations. I can't imagine what that's like. Whatever it is with you and the Clancys . . . it seems complicated, to say the least."

"Raymond's the one I don't trust."

"The feeling's mutual, apparently."

He turned and glanced again out the window. "It certainly seems like he wants to keep you where he can see you, so to speak, to know what you're up to."

"I can't understand why."

"He's threatened by you, maybe," Eric said. "You're smart, and that guy's paper thin. He knows you see right through him." Then Eric shrugged, his voice growing pensive and soft. "Or, hell, maybe every time he looks at you, he sees your mother's face and her mother's face before that, your grandfather, and all the people who fed him and cut the very cane that made his life possible. Makes him squirrelly maybe."

Caren undid her seat belt, shifting her weight in her seat.

She opened the collar of her jacket, letting out a rising heat trapped inside.

"I think Jason was murdered," she blurted out.

"Who?"

"My great-great-great-grandfather."

There was a sheriff, she said, a black sheriff, newly elected after the war, during the heyday of Reconstruction, when slaves were suddenly free to work *and* vote. "The sheriff," she said, "he had a suspect."

She turned and looked Eric in the eye. "It was Clancy's people, his ancestor. And I get the sense Raymond's tried to keep that part quiet for years."

Eric shook his head at the whole mess of it, how deep the history went.

Then he turned and looked at Caren across the stillness between them. "Just be careful, Caren," he said. "If Raymond *is* working with the cops, I mean, if he let them put a bug on your phone line, if he's somehow helping them build a case against you, you're going to be in a world of trouble. If the DA ever put you on the stand in front of a grand jury, you'd have one of two choices, Caren, either lie about destroying evidence . . . or tell the truth and go to jail."

He was right, of course.

She knew she was walking a fine line.

"And I don't think I could take that," he said softly.

Caren heard the school bell ring. Within seconds, a steady stream of plaid and navy was pouring out of the redbrick building. She told Eric he would need to pull around to the circle drive where Morgan usually waited. He started the car but didn't actually put it in gear. He glanced in his sideview mirror at the schoolkids, their backpacks and lunch pails in tow. Soon Morgan would be in the car, and this moment, just the two of them, would have passed. "Caren," he said. He was resting an elbow on the window's frame, his left hand on the steering wheel, as he stared through the windshield. She could see the faintest sheen of sweat above his brow. He seemed shy and slow to gather his words. His discomfort was apparent, almost painful to witness. They were no longer talking about Clancy or Abrams or Inés Avalo, she knew. Finally, Eric sighed. It was a whisper of self-reproach, but also a kind of peace. "I'm not sorry for what happened between us the other day," he said. "If I'm being honest with myself." He tried to smile, but lost the gesture about halfway through. Caren knew better than to say anything. She was careful not to draw any open conclusions from his statement. She knew she couldn't afford to want this man, not again, and yet the wanting seemed to be happening all on its own and without her say-so, ever since he showed up at Belle Vie. She wondered, not for the first time, what it would be like to do 2005 over again, if there could ever be such a thing as a second chance.

What a fool I was, she thought.

She was on the verge of telling him so when he turned and looked at her again.

"I love her, Caren," he said quietly, stealing the moment right out from under her. It didn't hurt nearly as much as she thought it would to hear it said out loud.

Behind them, a white Laurel Springs security jeep rolled to a stop.

In her sideview mirror she saw a security guard exiting the car.

Eric had both his hands on the steering wheel now. His grip was so tight that Caren could see the veins in his arms rising up like swollen rivers. He was like a man holding on to a small stick in a strong current, resisting an unspoken pull. There was something he'd wanted to say to her since he came back to Louisiana, since he walked into her home. "But you, Caren . . ." he whispered. A knock on the driver's-side door stopped him in midbreath. The security guard leaned in to tell them that

327

there was no parking on any street in Laurel Springs—a bike- and pedestrian-friendly community, as the pitch went—and that they would need to take whatever it was they were doing in the car someplace else. "We're just here to pick up our daughter, man," Eric said.

The guard tapped the roof of the car and then pointed back toward the circle drive and the school complex down the road.

As the guard departed, Eric rolled up his window.

Putting the car in drive, he headed for the nearest break in the median, making an awkward U-turn as he turned the car toward Laurel Springs Elementary School. They pulled into the circle drive behind a Chevy Tahoe with a purple-and-gold LSU Tigers bumper sticker across the back window. Eric inched the car forward, taking extra care in the swarm of schoolkids weaving in and out of the cars in the driveway. Caren stole a glance at him behind the wheel. The tension was still there. She could see it in his jawline, in the knot above his brow. She wanted to pick up where they'd left off.

"Eric," she said.

"There she is," he said, pointing ahead.

Through the windshield, Caren spotted the short, round shape of her nine-year-old. Morgan was holding her backpack at her side. Under her right arm were sheets of colored construction paper, red and gold, the foundation of some art or social studies project, Caren thought. At the sight of her, the tortoiseshell headband and the school dress, the backpack and all that, Eric smiled, tickled by this moving image, what had before existed for him only in photographs, his growing girl in the fifth grade. It occurred to Caren how few times he'd been able to do this, to drive his daughter to and from school—a duty so commonplace it was one of the first she'd turned over to Letty when she'd hired her. Driving Morgan to Laurel Springs had been an easier task for her to relinquish than dressing her daughter each morning or making her food or washing and conditioning her hair once a week, combing it out while Morgan sat on the floor reading books. These tactile moments had meant so much more to Caren that it was a long time before she could see Letty's hands in her daughter's hair without feeling actual envy. For months she thought on a daily basis of firing Letty. A woman who had only ever tried to offer a hand, to help Caren raise this girl way the hell out in the country.

It had been the same with Eric's mother, hadn't it?

Wasn't that at least part of her resistance to moving to Chicago, his hometown?

It wasn't just the lack of a marriage proposal, she could now admit. It was the threat of another woman, always had been. Not just in Eric's life, but in *Morgan's*. Hadn't this, deep down, been her real fear of sending her only child to D.C.? That she would somehow lose to Lela twice? First Eric . . . and then Morgan, too?

She had walked out on her own mother.

And there was no promise that Morgan wouldn't one day do the same, walk away from Caren and never look back. She could now see how carefully she had built their lives around this single fear, so afraid of losing her daughter that she'd shut out any competition or interference, packing the two of them behind glass—in a museum, Morgan liked to say—where they lived alone on the second floor of a borrowed house, miles from the nearest town. It would be the end of them, she knew, if she kept it up.

She was going to lose Morgan this way.

Just like she'd lost him.

Morgan arrived at the car on her dad's side. "I made my dress," she said, slapping the yellow construction paper against the driver's-side window. In marker and pencil, she had drawn a gown of purple and rose; it had a sweetheart neckline and long, ruffled layers going to the floor. She had not drawn herself into the design, but rather outfitted the dress on a long, lean figure in pointy high-heeled shoes. The image saddened Caren, the fact that Morgan wanted to look so unlike herself at her dad's wedding. "I think I could make it," she said, meaning the dress. Caren happened to know for a fact that Morgan had never even seen a sewing machine, but she was careful not to point out this detail. Morgan, who once taught herself to make soap, was not easily discouraged, and Caren didn't want her to think she was blocking her carefully laid wedding plans. She knew what the day meant for her daughter, how excited she was.

Eric unlocked the car's back doors, and Morgan climbed in.

Because she was hungry, they stopped at a roadside café on the way, a small hut off the highway that served crawfish boiled over an open flame, in big, black pots behind the restaurant. Caren ordered Texas toast and a beer. Eric and Morgan went all out: crawfish and *boudin* with pepper jelly, and corn fried with *pasilla chiles* and sweet butter. Eric ate with abandon, savoring the pork-skin crackle and ordering a beer for himself and a second for Caren. Morgan shared her crawfish plate with her dad, showing him how to suck meat from the head, because she, at nine, was better at it than he ever was. Caren sat across the damp picnic table, watching the two of them, listening as Morgan told her father that Ms. Rivera was not a bad homeroom teacher, but that she lacked creativity when it came to discipline, which made Eric laugh out loud, throwing his head back. More than once, he glanced across the table at Caren, holding her gaze, smiling, his face flushed with heat. She would have done almost anything to hold on to this moment for a little while longer. She took a pull on her beer. It was sharp and cold going down. "Morgan," she said finally.

Morgan looked across the table, salt and grease all along the sides of her mouth. Caren offered no preface, no buildup, only the truth she knew no easy way around. She was going to have to let her go. "You're going back to Washington with your dad."

Morgan looked back and forth between her parents. "Why?"

It was not the reaction Caren was expecting.

She stupidly thought Morgan would ask few questions, that the same girl who'd been bugging her about a plane ticket to D.C. for weeks now would simply throw her arms around Caren's neck and whisper, "Thank you, Mom."

She was not in any way prepared for the wounded look on Morgan's face.

"But you said I didn't do anything wrong," her daughter whispered.

"Oh, 'Cakes, I'm not sending you away. I would never send you away."

And to her surprise, Morgan started to cry.

Caren stood and walked around to the other side of the picnic table. She straddled the wood bench and pulled Morgan against her, feeling the girl's warm tears through her cotton shirt. She could smell the shea butter in her daughter's hair. And it was all she could do to go forward with this plan. "The wedding is coming up soon anyway," she said. "It's just a few weeks away, and Daddy thought you might stay for Christmas this year." She tapped Morgan's shoulders until the girl looked up at her mother, until Caren could see her face. "There's snow there," she said.

"Are you coming?"

Caren shook her head. "Huh-uh."

Morgan looked at Eric. "Daddy?"

She seemed, at this point, more confused than anything.

331

"The plantation is closing, honey," Eric said.

"No, it's not," she said emphatically, turning to her mother.

Caren had never talked over her daughter's head or assumed there were things she wouldn't understand, had always been bothered by people who underestimated kids' native intelligence. But she also didn't have the energy to explain it all—the spread of corporate farming and Belle Vie's tenuous value at the dawn of the twenty-first century, or Raymond Clancy's political ambitions. In that moment, only the little bit that pertained to them mattered. "It is, 'Cakes," she said. "Belle Vie is closing."

"Because of Donovan?"

"No, honey."

On the highway, a pickup truck chugged past, close enough that Caren could smell its exhaust. Behind them, plumes of steam rose off the fat, black kettles of boiling crawfish. "You'll be with your dad for a few weeks, maybe until December. You guys can get a tree and decorate it," she said, trying to sell it to Morgan, but also to herself. "The thing is, I have some decisions to make about where we're going next, what happens for all of us. 'Cause right now it looks like I'm going to be out of a job."

Morgan stared at her for a moment, maybe not buying any of this.

She and her mother had never, for more than a day, been apart.

"But you love Christmas," she said, sniffling.

Caren smiled and kissed her forehead.

"What about school?" Morgan said.

Eric started to answer this one.

Caren gave him a look, shaking her head slightly. *Not now.*

"We'll talk about it," she told Morgan, patting the hair at the nape of her neck.

Eric told Morgan that Lela was excited to see her again.

Morgan shrugged, looking down at her plate, picking at a few stray kernels of corn. "I guess if it's just for a little while," she said.

Caren paid for their meal in cash.

On the ride back, heading south toward Belle Vie, she asked them both to make one last stop with her, directing Eric to the highway exit that led to Donaldsonville, to the tiny church on Lessard Street.

Final Tours

26

The casket was closed for the service. Morgan, who had never been to a funeral or a wake or memorial service of any kind— had never even known a person who had died—was plainly fascinated by the spectacle of the thing. The prayer candles and the spray of gladiolus and white carnations, and the short, black priest in his dress robe, a formal stole of red and gold draped about his shoulders and hanging near to his ankles. She sat on the edge of the pew, leaning forward, her elbows propped on the back of the bench in front of them, as if they were at a ball game or the theater, and twice Caren had to ask her to please sit up, to show Inés that least little bit of respect. Eric was appropriately solemn, but distant. He didn't know the woman, of course; he was sitting in this tiny, dimly lit church for Caren. From Father Akerele's opening prayer to his reading from the Book of Wisdom—*the souls of the just are in the hand of God, and no torment shall touch them*—to the congregation's whispered *Amen*, Caren was on the verge of tears.

Everyone was invited to speak.

Friends and loved ones.

The first to the lectern was Ginny, the church secretary, with her ruby-red curls and her graceful pear shape poured into a black pantsuit, a small pink flower in the lapel. She was holding a tiny, square piece of paper, her hands shaking slightly. The church was not full. But a good number of people had gathered

337

to honor Inés, more than Caren would have expected for a woman born and raised over a thousand miles away. There were the church ladies, of course, and also the Groveland workers, and a few field hands from other farms. One man was biting at his nails. Another, nearly as dark as Caren, had his head down in prayer. She remembered him from the candlelight vigil, when he'd leaned against the white fence in the fields, hardly able to tear himself away from the site, the shallow grave, the space that could not be filled. It was Inés's love, Gustavo.

There were others, too.

Lorraine had come to honor a woman she didn't even know, simply because she had walked among them, no matter how invisible. Dell and Pearl and Ennis Mabry had also come. 'Cause that's just what black folks do. Southerners, too. These were cultural artifacts that, God willing, would go untouched by time. Raymond Clancy was here. Caren had seem him in a back pew on her way in, seated next to, of all people, his brother, Bobby, who looked distinctly uncomfortable in a suit. Whether by coercion or his own free will, he had come to play his part: son of Leland James Clancy, a man beloved in this parish, who would have demanded his sons put aside their petty disagreements and show respect for the fallen, an innocent woman who'd been killed on the very land the Clancys had lived on and loved for nearly two hundred years. Caren caught Bobby's eye. He nodded at her, then turned his attention to the altar.

"Inés was warm and quick to smile," Ginny said.

At the pulpit, Father Akerele listened with his eyes closed, nodding.

"And she believed deeply in God."

Amen, someone called.

In the center pew, Caren felt a sudden motion on her left side. She turned to see Lee Owens sliding into the open spot next to her. "Guess who's here?" he whispered, leaning in so closely that she could smell his aftershave, a musky scent, like the dried leaves of bay laurel. He nodded over her shoulder, and when she turned she was surprised to see yet another familiar face in the back of the church. In the very back row, on the far-right-hand side, Hunt Abrams was sitting alone, arms folded across his wide chest. He was wearing the same black Groveland windbreaker, hadn't even bothered to change out of his jeans. "Paying his respects, I see," Owens said. He raised an eyebrow at the audacity of it, the sick act of a killer showing up at his victim's funeral. Caren felt Eric watching her, taking note of this whispered exchange between her and the reporter. But when she glanced over to meet his eye, he had already turned and was now staring straight ahead. He was holding their daughter's hand.

At the lectern, Ginny made the sign of the cross.

Then, in halting, high school Spanish, she said, "*Descanse en paz.*"

Rest in peace, Inés.

As Ginny started down the short flight of steps at the edge of the altar, Akerele held out a hand to escort her. Caren glanced again over her shoulder. Hunt Abrams was looking right at them, at Caren and Eric and Morgan—at her nine-year-old daughter, the girl who had first stumbled upon the bloody knife. *We should go*, she thought. *We should get her out of here right now.* Only she couldn't think of an easy exit out of the small church that wouldn't take her daughter within inches of Abrams's grasp.

There was a sudden rustling, a sober murmur in the crowd.

One man was walking to the lectern alone.

It was Gustavo, wearing a pressed shirt, black and red, his nerves plainly showing. Even from a distance, Caren could see his lips quivering, and there were dots of sweat across the leathered skin of his forehead. "*Lo siento,*" he said, trying to gather himself. He kept looking in the direction of the back of the room, where Abrams was sitting. Then he crossed himself and began again. He didn't cry, and he didn't say his name. There was just this, this one declaration, a mere whisper into the microphone.

"*Yo la amaba.*"

I loved her, he said.

He knew he shouldn't say that, not here.

He knew they weren't married.

And long ago they had made a pact not to speak of their families, the ones back home. "*De este lado,*" he said. "*Fuimos solo nosotros. Y era amor.*" On this side, he said, it was only us, and it was love. He knew there was a husband. There were kids. And he could speak to her love for her children, whom she'd hadn't seen in almost three years.

She sent money home each month, and she prayed.

She prayed for those kids.

She worked every day for them, even looking for day work when the rain pushed them out of the fields—cleaning houses or washing dishes at the VA center in Darrow or doing cleanup at construction sites, hauling trash, some of which she would lug home, to a small camper they shared. Books or used clothes or the base of a porcelain lamp or a piece of an old bed frame. She found a use for everything.

Here Gustavo smiled.

Inés was headstrong, he said, and sometimes stubborn. At this, one of the other field-workers smiled in kind. *Sí,* he called out, sharing this particular memory.

Gustavo glanced down at the casket, covered in flowers.

She didn't like it here, he said. She was trying to get enough money to leave, to go back home, or at least get as far as Texas. She thought, if nothing else, she could make more money picking grapefruit along the Valley. Gustavo lowered his head.

I wish she had gone, he said.

She should have gone home.

Por eso cantamos para Inés, he said.

So we sing for Inés.

We sing her soul home.

By now Caren was crying openly. Through the sting of her tears, she watched as Gustavo walked back to his seat, while some of the churchwomen stood to face the congregation, positioning themselves below the altar. Ginny was standing in front. In chorus, they began a hymn: "What Wondrous Love Is This." Owens, sitting next to Caren, mumbled the words in a soft tenor, speaking more than singing, and she was surprised that he knew each verse by heart. This close up, she could see his hair had been slicked back and combed. Out of his usual khakis and ball cap and into slim black pants, he'd clearly gotten dressed up for this, for Inés. And when Father Akerele asked the congregants to please join hands, it felt oddly comforting to hold his, Eric on one side and Lee Owens on the other.

Outside, she asked him to wait for her.

But somehow as they filed out of St. Joseph's with the rest of the congregation, Owens got ahead of them. Eric was close by Caren's side, ushering her along, but also keeping her and Morgan well within his sights. She could feel his presence behind her as they made it down the church steps. "Let's go," he said, holding tightly to Morgan's hand. She was still in her school uniform, her bare legs open to the night air.

Abrams was long gone, his black truck nowhere in sight.

Lorraine and Pearl, Ennis and Dell had already left in Lorraine's Pontiac.

Bobby Clancy was still lingering on the dewy lawn, beneath the low branches of the black pecan tree. He smiled when he saw Caren. He ambled over, both hands balled inside his pants

341

pockets. Beneath his dark suit, Caren noticed a pair of camel-colored boots. "Hey," he said. And Caren said, "Hey," back, introducing him to Eric and her daughter, Morgan. He nodded warmly at the girl, folding his tall height in half by bending at the waist, so he could shake her hand like a gentleman. "Lord, if she don't favor Helen," he said, glancing back at Caren. "And as pretty as her mama, too."

Caren caught the faintest smile on her daughter's lips.

"You don't remember me, huh?" he said to Morgan.

Caren thought he was drunk, or at least halfway there. Bobby had never actually met her daughter, not even as a baby. "Bobby and I grew up together," she told Eric.

Bobby smiled sloppily, swaying a little on the heels of his boots, and again Caren wondered how much he'd been drinking. "Wouldn't know it now, but we was real close," he said. "And I was way too shy to tell her I had something of a boyhood crush on her."

Eric looked from Bobby to Caren, who felt her cheeks flush.

She felt embarrassed, but also slightly angry with Bobby for finally saying it out loud, and here of all places. She felt she would have rather gone the rest of her life pretending not to know what she always had, that Bobby liked her and that he felt hemmed in by the proscriptions of his birth and name, the rules that he imagined kept them apart. Bobby basically said as much now, adding, "Yeah, well, times were different back then," while fiddling with something in his pants pocket. Through the fabric, Caren thought she spotted the outline of a flask. She wanted to change the subject.

"So I guess you know about the sale, then?"

Bobby looked back toward Lessard Street, where Raymond was sitting in the driver's seat of a late-model Cadillac, watching this little reunion between his kid brother and Caren. He tapped on the horn, letting Bobby know his ride was leaving.

Bobby turned back to Caren. "I'll talk to you about it later."

Then, he pulled out a silver flask and took an open swig in front of everyone, before tramping across the grass toward the passenger seat of his brother's Cadillac.

By now the crowd outside St. Joseph's had thinned. There were still a few lights on inside the church, but Ginny had already pulled closed the gate to the church's parking lot, which was now vacant. There was a rustle of tree branches overhead and a cool wind swaying the leaves. It was cold out here, and getting colder. The field-workers, everybody, was gone . . . except Lee Owens, who was waiting for her.

"I hear they charged the Isaacs kid," he said.

"Caren," Eric said, putting a hand on her elbow.

He was through with it, she knew, all of it. The plantation and the cane fields and the sloppy murder investigation. The rain and the muggy mess of Louisiana.

"Can you give me a minute?"

Eric looked at her, then at Owens. "We'll wait by the car," he said, tugging at Morgan's hand. Caren watched as he led her toward the rental car across the street.

"I have something," she said, turning to Owens. She still had the DVDs in her pocket—the headlights caught on tape. She pulled out the plastic case, the clear cover catching the light of the street lamp. The whole effect threw a yellow glow over the bottom half of Owens's face. Who knew what could happen, Caren thought, if a newspaper took seriously what the cops wouldn't?

Screw Lang, she thought.

Eric called out her name again. "It's late," he said.

"I could drive you later," Owens said. "I mean, if he needs to get her home."

When Caren presented this idea a few moments later, and

out of Owens's earshot, Eric lost the last of his patience. "What are you doing, Caren, you don't even know this guy." He had his fingers dug into Morgan's shoulders, keeping her close. Morgan was leaning her head against her father's torso. She was shivering.

"Take her home, Eric. I'll be fine."

He looked from her to Owens, then back to her again, rolling his eyes. "Caren and her many suitors," he muttered.

Now she thought he was just being mean.

"It's not a *date*, Eric," she said. "He's a reporter."

Eric let out a wearied sigh.

He stared at her for a long time, the amber street light softening his features. He was worried about her, that's all. "Just be careful, Caren."

Morgan was still standing between them, unsure in which direction she was meant to go, if she should stay with her mother or go with Eric. "Go with your dad," Caren insisted. "I'll be fine, 'Cakes." Morgan's eyes narrowed to slits. She looked past her mother, sneaking a peek at Owens. "Is Donovan going to be okay?" she asked.

"I don't know, 'Cakes."

Morgan nodded sagely, a kid getting an early, unwelcome lesson in the breadth of life's vast unfairness. She took a sideways glance, a second look at Owens. "Don't keep her too late," she called to him, before skipping off to catch up to her dad. Owens was highly amused. "What a great kid," he said, as Caren stood there, watching her go.

They sat in his car, in the dark, only the blue light of his laptop computer between them. Owens hit rewind and they watched it again, the last scene on the second disc. Caren could smell the soapy pomade in his hair, the hint of mint on his breath. He was

344

chewing his fingernails, utterly perplexed. "I don't understand," he said, staring at the headlights on the screen. "Why would he take a deal?"

"The whole thing started as a misunderstanding," she explained. Outside, the rain was misting, swirling about, like tiny seeds in the wind. "Donovan, the kid with a criminal record, admits to being at the scene of the crime the night she was killed, not knowing what he was getting himself into, and then the cops just kind of zeroed in on him and never looked back. And now they're saying they have the murder weapon."

"The knife?"

Caren nodded. "But his car sat in our parking lot for at least a day. It sat out there completely unsupervised for a whole night. Anyone could have put it there."

Owens was still staring at the computer screen, at the shot of the truck's white headlights, the visual fact of someone parked just over the fence in the cane fields.

"Abrams sleeps in his trailer, by the way, so he can be first in the fields at sunrise," he said. "That's not even five hundred yards from the grave site." He tapped his fingers on the steering wheel. The nails were bitten to the quick, gnawed and pink. Caren noticed he wasn't wearing a wedding ring. "There's almost no excuse for him not being a person of interest in this, especially in light of his past behavior," he said. "I tried to offer an affidavit, to tell Lang what I know, the research the paper has on file for the man right now, but they don't want to hear it. For them, this whole thing is solved."

She caught a note of something between heartache and rage behind his pale green eyes. She wondered what all this meant for him, why, beyond his job, his reporter's eye for a lie, he was so beset by this particular story, why he cared so much.

"Clancy got Donovan a lawyer," she told him.

"*Raymond* Clancy?"

She nodded, adding this to the growing list of his shady behavior of late. He wanted this deal with Groveland to go through, and Abrams getting arrested for murder, or even being under suspicion, would surely pour cold water on the plantation's sale, as well as the launch of Clancy's political career. Getting Donovan a lawyer was a sleight of hand, a trick, a cover . . . but for what exactly, she wondered.

Once more, she tried to walk through Owens's take on the case. "So Inés finds a bone out in the fields, a body part buried in the Groveland farm, and less than a week later she's dead," she said.

"Very rarely does one come across an honest-to-God coincidence in my line of work," he said. "If it smells rotten, it's usually 'cause it is."

"You think Abrams told Clancy what was buried out in those fields?"

"It *is* his land. Clancy's, that is."

Caren wondered how deep this cover-up went.

Outside, the wind lifted, swirling and shaking rain from the tree leaves overhead, drops as soft as water on wet cotton, a faint thumping on the roof of the car. Caren shivered. Owens, without comment, rolled up his car window, sealing the air between them. The church lights were still on, but the place was otherwise deserted, the bottle tree twinkling in the rain, doing its colorful best to protect the chapel and its last guest. Caren thought of her all alone in there.

"Inés was sleeping in the quarters," she said. "She spent the last nights of her life sleeping inside a slave cabin." Akerele and Ginny were right. She must have been terrified, Caren said.

She turned to look at Owens.

He was already turning his key in the ignition.

"Come on," he said. "I want to show you something."

* * *

They drove south on East Bayou Road, past the town center and heading into the ragged outskirts of the parish. About a mile past the high school, she asked him where they were going. Owens was hunched over the steering wheel, staring studiously at the unbroken lines on the asphalt ahead. And then, with no warning, he yanked the wheel hard to the left, the sudden move pushing Caren against the side of the door.

They had turned onto a short, red-dirt road, no more than an alley cut through a block of weeds. It was lined on both sides with trailer homes, double-wides and singles propped up on blocks and parked haphazardly on messy, trash-strewn plots of gravel and grass. Nearby sat a grove of rusted cars, made over for lawn furniture. A '76 Le Mans sat under a colorful blanket, its dirty fringe dappled with dried leaves and empty soda cans left on its hood. The place was a makeshift subdivision of some kind, a virtual tent city. "What is this?" she said, staring ahead.

"That one was hers."

He was pointing to a small camper, the kind of thing a suburban family might hitch to the back of a station wagon, a thing to sleep in for a night or two, not a life. But this, apparently, had been Inés's home. She had taken the care and time to clip the weeds out front, had doctored a large hole in the structure with an artful weave of black and gray duct tape, and had arranged a pile of broken concrete and rocks to hold up the camper's front end. It was not so far a leap from here to the quarters, Caren thought. She heard the punch and twang of *tejano* music. There was a television playing in a nearby trailer. A roll of canned applause blew across the night air. The terrain was rough, rocking the small sedan back and forth as Owens inched them forward. Rainwater swirled in open pockets in the middle of the road. Caren begged Owens to turn back before they got stuck out here in the mud.

Instead, he parked the car in a patch of weeds by the side of the road.

The sky was dark, a deep, midnight blue. Owens shut the car engine, undoing his seat belt and reaching for the door handle. "What are you doing?" Caren said.

"When we spoke, Akerele told me there were no other acts of violence that the church was aware of, or disturbances of any kind, and certainly no workers who went missing." Caren nodded. Akerele had reported the same to her. "But he also said those workers are like family," he said, cracking open the car door. "Maybe Gustavo, the guy she was living with, knows more than the rest of them are saying." He stepped out of the car, and Caren, not sure she could stand being left alone in this car, on the side of a dark road, got out and followed him. The heels of her boots sank in the mud as she struggled to catch up to him. Together, they walked in a line down the center of the dirt road.

In the distance, she heard a whisper of Spanish, the low hum of talk radio. A few feet away, two men were smoking cigarettes and sitting on top of the Le Mans, a Styrofoam cooler at their feet and a pile of ice and a fishing line dumped in the grass. One of the men was gutting a flathead catfish. The blade of his knife shone beneath a flashlight that was rigged to the roof of the car. The other man was drinking beer out of a can. He squinted in the advancing darkness, trying to make them out, two figures on the road. The one with the knife hopped off the hood of the car, walking toward them, the blade pointed down. There was blood dripping off the tip. Owens froze, staring at the knife. Caren stepped forward and told the man, "*No queremos problemas*," making use of the Spanish she'd learned on her first part-time job in New Orleans, waiting tables at a steak house. The man's posture softened somewhat. He gave her a curt but not unfriendly nod, before returning to his fish, looking up every now and then to stare at Owens. The man he was with threw his head back, draining his beer and staring at the night's stars. Across the road, a toddler was witnessing this whole scene. He was wearing a football helmet and a diaper, watching them from the doorway of a nearby trailer, the grill of his Cowboys helmet pressed against the mesh of the screen door. Behind him, Caren heard the faint sounds of a television game show playing low.

Finally, they made it to Inés's camper.

The front door was a thin black screen, framed in a cheap aluminum that rattled in its hinge when Owens knocked. Together, they waited to hear movement, some sign of life inside the camper. The man with the knife was watching them. In the other direction, down the main road, Owens's car was a silhouette in the distance. For a brief second, she thought she saw something, or *someone*, moving beside the car. Weeds, she told herself. Please, God, let it be the weeds.

"*No hay nadie allí.*"

Caren swung around.

It was the man with the knife. There's no one there, he was saying.

He tossed the filleted fish onto the pile of ice chips, then reached into the cooler for another, running the flat blade along the skin. "*La señora está muerta,*" he said. "*Y su novio, se ha ido. Se fue.*" The woman, he said, was dead, and her man was gone.

"What's that?" Owens said. "What's he saying?"

Caren shushed him.

"*Cuando?*" she asked the man.

"*Esta noche.*" Then, he shrugged. "*Agarró una maleta y se fué.*"

Gustavo's gone, she said to Owens.

He took a bag and fled.

"Ask him if he knew them."

"*Usted los conocía?*" she asked.

The man with the knife stared for a long time, looking between Caren and Owens, this white boy. Maybe it was the language, the ease with which he and Caren had fallen into conversation in his mother tongue, but he seemed to get no charge from her presence. She was a woman, *y una morena* at that, and he regarded her as more a curiosity than a threat. No, he said, going back to his knife and his fish.

Owens nudged her to keep it going.

Caren asked the man if he knew the Groveland farm.

"*Sí*," he said. "*Pero nunco he ido.*"

He's never been there, he said.

He was not a man for the fields. "*Me gusta el agua.*"

He slapped a fish on ice and reached for another.

Owens seemed lost without a working language. He was leaning on Caren, literally, pulling at her elbow and holding on way too tightly. "The field-workers, do they live around here, too?" he asked Caren, nudging her to turn and ask the man with the knife. She felt his insistent breath in her ear. She told him to stop and let her talk.

"*Hay otros campesinos de la granja que viven aquí?*"

"*No, no.*" The man shook his head. "*Solo ellos,*" he said, pointing to the camper where Inés and Gustavo lived. They were the only Groveland workers here.

"*Está seguro?*"

"*Sí*," he said. He was very sure. They didn't get many strange faces around the campsite, he said, a strange smile on his face, looking at Caren and Owens, as if to prove his point. "*Claro, la policía llegó.*" The police, of course. They were here.

His buddy, who had so far let nothing past his lips save for cold beer, nudged the man with the knife. "*Y el gringo,*" he said, his speech so slurred that Caren didn't catch it the first time. The man with the knife nodded. There was someone else who had come snooping around the campsite a few times, specifically looking for Inés.

"*Un gringo?*"

"*Sí,*" he said. The man was kind of dark, with black hair, and tall, very, very tall, the drunk man said, holding his hand a foot or so above the roof of the Le Mans. He had come around a few times the week before Inés died. "*En un troca rojá,*" he said.

"He was in a red truck?"

The man nodded.

She played his words back in her head: a man in a red truck stalking Inés . . . just like the man in the red truck Caren had seen in her rearview mirror more than once this past week. She heard Owens's words again, his pronouncement that true coincidences are rare, and for the first time she had a fleeting doubt about Abrams being the killer. Was there someone else out there? A killer who had gotten to Inés Avalo and was now following Caren?

She told Owens she was ready to go.

She wanted to get the hell out of here.

But Owens didn't see how he could get this close to Inés, to where she had once lived, and not go inside. "Just for a second," he said, as he reached for the camper's screen door.

Owens stepped in first, feeling along the buckled walls for a light switch. But there was no electricity in here, only an oversized mechanic's flashlight hanging on a nail by the door. Caren flipped it on and saw that there was no running water, either. There were bed sheets on the floor and stacks of folded clothes, plus a crate of dented kitchen utensils, a plastic holly wreath, ceramic bowls, and a rolling suitcase. She found a use for everything, Caren remembered Akerele saying. Among her things were a red plastic cooler . . . and dozens of votive candles burnt to stubs, just like the ones Caren had found inside Jason's Cabin in the slave quarters.

351

She felt a line of sweat down the center of her back.

There was no ventilation except for the screen door, and every step Owens took, the whole camper swayed and tilted to one side. Stop, she whispered. Just stop. She wanted him to stop moving, to turn around and drive them out of here. "Give me the keys," she said. She couldn't put words to it or easily explain it, but she felt, in that tiny camper, the same frank stillness, the breathtaking absence of anything resembling human life, that she felt in Jason's Cabin. Owens was oblivious. He was bending down to look through a pile of magazines and papers inside an old shoe box. Caren told him she felt she couldn't breathe. He looked at her, hearing for the first time the distress in her voice. But before he could get to his feet, there was a loud thump along the side of the camper, as if someone had taken a bat to the outside walls; it was forceful enough that the whole structure swayed from side to side.

"What the hell was that?" Owens said, reaching for something to hold on to. Caren turned and looked out the screen door, to the dirt road.

The radio, she realized.

She didn't hear it anymore.

Nor the television in the neighboring trailer.

It was as if she and Owens were the only two people left out here—them and who or whatever was on the other side of the camper's wall.

She heard a soft patter coming through the wall. Footsteps.

Owens must have heard it, too.

He pointed to the screen door and mouthed the word *Go*. They both turned and ran. Outside, the man with the knife was gone, and his friend on the hood of the Le Mans. The toddler and his blue-and-white football helmet were also gone. Everybody, it seemed, had suddenly hidden behind closed doors. Had they seen something, she wondered. Had something out on this dirt road spooked them good?

Owens told her to keep running.

She was comforted by the sound of his footsteps behind her.

The Saturn was where they'd left it, waiting along the side of the road. Owens clawed at the keys in his hand, trying to find the right one. He opened the doors, and they both slumped inside. When he finally got the car started, slamming it into re-verse and backing down the dirt road, Caren stared down the length of the alley and the broken-down trailers. She didn't see a single soul, but she no longer took that as a sign that she was safe. Someone had been following her, she now understood. The same man in the red truck who had tailed Inés Avalo in the days before her throat was cut.

27

He drove her home, as promised, pulling into the parking lot, which was empty except for Eric's rented sedan parked near the main gate. Owens slid in beside it, leaving his engine running, twinned headlights shining on the gate's padlock. Caren undid her seat belt, staring ahead. She hadn't thought through this part, the walk in the dark from the gate to the library, until this moment. She could see the deserted security kiosk from here. Gerald wasn't on duty today, and the golf cart was not parked at its station—which meant Eric, who took a set of Caren's keys, probably used it to ferry himself and Morgan across the plantation. Belle Vie, this time of night, absent a wedding or other such catered affair, was black and still, and she could hardly see past the reach of the car's headlights. The gate was locked. But it had been locked the night Inés was murdered, too. And faced now with the prospect of crossing the grounds alone, Caren was almost paralyzed with fear. She hesitated . . . before finally opening the car door. The overhead light popped on, splitting the dark in two, his side of the car and hers.

Owens reached across the distance, touching her arm.

"Hey," he said. "You want me to walk you?"

She zipped up her jacket. "You'd never find your way back, not this late."

"I could stay."

She couldn't imagine what Eric would make of that.

"I'll be okay," she said.

She asked if she could use his cell phone.

"Sure," he said, reaching for the phone, which was sitting in the cup holder between them. Caren dialed over to the library, waiting through four rings. When Eric's voice finally came on the line, she felt Owens watching her. She told Eric to be on the lookout, to do something drastic if she was not on the front steps of the library in the next ten minutes. She let out a low chuckle, awkward and self-conscious, trying to keep her voice light and casual . . . which Eric saw right through. "You okay?" he said.

She told him she was fine.

When she hung up, Owens asked, "That your husband?"

"Uh, no," she said, handing back his cell phone. Maybe it was the way she said it, or the fact that Owens had observed her and Eric long enough to surmise a certain level of complication there, but he smiled in recognition. "Yeah," he said. "I've got one of those, too." He stared through the windshield, at the gates of Belle Vie, biting his thumbnail. "No kids, though," he said. She heard a catch in his voice that she couldn't quite place. It was gratitude, or else deep regret.

"Can I ask you something?"

"Yes, ma'am," he said, his Louisiana drawl curling the words.

"Why does any of this matter to you?" she said. She meant Groveland and Abrams and the death of a woman he didn't even know.

"My granddaddy used to cut cane," he told her.

"Mine, too," she said. Her whole family, in fact, going back before the Civil War, all the way back to Jason. She liked the fact that Owens shared this with her. It made her feel better about leaving Donovan's DVDs with him. In his hands, they would be delivered to his editor in the morning. That was their plan, the pact they'd made. She stepped out of the car, and through the rain-dappled windshield Owens gave her a thoughtful smile. "'Night, Miss Caren," he said. He waited until she was all the way behind the locked gate before pulling out of the parking lot, taking the last bit of light with him.

From the gate to the old schoolhouse was easy. She stayed on the main road as it veered a few yards to the west, before meeting up with the circle drive on the back side of the main house. She followed it to the rose garden, heading toward the library, which was situated at the northeast corner of the plantation. The rain had eased to nothing, but the ground was soaked through from days of this, back and forth, off and on, black clouds one minute, sunshine the next. She made sure to keep to the paved path. It was quiet out here, so much so that she thought she could hear the river in the distance, its push and pull, the swirling current and the chorus of night birds on its shores. Where there was moonlight, it cut through the tree branches overhead, casting sharp, short shadows that darted this way and that, right before her eyes. Still, this wasn't so bad, she thought, shoving her cold hands into her pockets.

It was well past the garden when it first occurred to her that she wasn't alone out there. The sound was faint at first, and she took it for wind in the trees, the whispers of haints on the plantation. Then the weight of the noise deepened into a low *pat-pat-pat*, the rhythm as even as a heartbeat. It sounded, without question, like the slap of feet on wet grass. Twice, she swung around and called Owens's name, thinking, praying, really, that he had somehow followed her behind the gates of Belle Vie. She quickened her steps, breaking into a determined trot, then a sprint. She ran as fast as she could, darting off the main path and cutting across the east lawn. She could see the lamp in her bedroom window. She ran toward the light, dew seeping through the soles of her boots, cold creeping into her toes. She ran, calling Eric's name.

The root of an aged oak tree laid an unseen trap in the dark. She twisted her ankle on it, falling hard, nose-down in the wet grass. When she lifted her head, she was staring at a pair of men's shoes, just inches from her face. She saw the gun next, black in his hand, as the other reached down and grabbed her by the collar of her jacket, yanking her to her knees. Caren started to cry, an ugly sound, wheezing and desperate. She could manage only a few words. "What are you *doing?*"

"Looking for you," he said.

Eric laid the pistol at his feet, kneeling beside her in the grass. When he saw she was okay, he collapsed onto his backside, pulling his knees to his chest. He winced, laboring to catch his breath, leaning against the base of the oak tree. "You said to come get you if you didn't show up. I waited and waited, and then you called again, and I didn't know what was going on. I didn't know what to think."

She stared at him, the line of his profile in the dark.

"What do you mean I called again?"

"You called me," he said, sounding overheated and agitated. "Not ten minutes after the call from the parking lot, you rang the house again. I picked up the line, but I couldn't hear a thing, just someone there and not talking, and I guess I got scared."

"*I* called you?"

"I thought you were in some kind of trouble out here."

Caren felt the same panic she'd felt on the dirt road in the tent city, she and Owens running from someone or something she couldn't see.

"The number," she said. "That second call came from my cell phone?"

"Yes."

"Eric, that wasn't me."

According to the map on her computer screen, the call had bounced off a cell tower not even a half a mile away in the parish countryside, and the closest source location the phone company's website could offer was an address on the river road, a street number that happened to correspond with the Belle Vie Plantation. Whoever made the call might well have been inside the locked gates right now. Eric blanched, backing away from the screen. Caren went for the home phone . . . and then stopped herself. A 911 call about a missing cell phone was almost certain to be ignored. Even to a dispatcher, she couldn't say for sure that the eighteen acres had been breached, that there'd been a break-in at all. And she wasn't going out there in the dead of night to check, not even to open and unlock the gates for Lang. Her only child asleep upstairs, she locked the front door, then double-checked it. She handed Eric the .32, taking the shotgun for herself. They would guard the homestead as best they could.

Eric was sitting on the leather sofa.

It's then she saw his canvas overnight bag, zipped at his feet. There was a printed travel itinerary resting on top. She stared at the duffel bag, and then she looked up at him. "I didn't know if I was supposed to buy two plane tickets or three," he said.

"I still have to tell the staff, Eric. I owe them that much."

He didn't say anything right away, just stared down at his hands.

"And we still have the Whitman wedding next week. It's work I promised them."

"What about Morgan? You heard her today."

"She'll be with her father."

"She wants you, too. She wants her mother, too."

It seemed they were veering toward a larger discussion of what would happen *after* the Whitman wedding, after this place closed for good. "I don't know yet, Eric."

It was the best she could offer right then.

He told her he'd booked a flight for Monday morning, three seats.

"I guess I'm still hoping you'll change your mind."

He was waiting for her, she realized.

He had been for days.

She smiled.

"You hungry?" she asked him.

He shook his head. "No."

"'Night, then, Eric."

She didn't realize he was behind her until she was all the way to the foot of the stairs, didn't realize until that very moment that he'd been following her on her way up to her bedroom. "What are you doing?" she asked, and of course he had no answer, at least none he could put into words. And it frankly didn't matter, anyway. She was perfectly willing to be pulled along by their history, whatever was left of it, still imposing its will on this little moment in time, the two of them on the stairs. She didn't have the energy to fight it. He kissed her right there, her back against the wall, which was papered with linen and pink roses. She took his hand, leading the rest of the way.

They didn't have sex.

She didn't try, and he didn't ask.

Instead, they lay side by side in the dark, staring at the ceiling.

He was so still and silent for so long that Caren started to think he'd drifted off. But when she turned her head, Eric was wide awake. He had one forearm behind him, tucked under his head like a slim pillow. She watched the rise and fall of his chest.

"I lied," he said softly. "When I told you I didn't think I would ever marry you, I was lying." He gazed in her direction, but the look in his eyes was lost to the darkness. "I was just mad."

"I know."

It was her own little lie.

"I had a ring," he said, lifting his eyes to the ceiling again.

This detail hurt more than the rest of it. Fleetingly, she thought to ask where it was. Not to wear it, but just to have it, as a remembrance, something to hold in her hand.

Eric reached across the bed to touch her arm.

"I love her, Caren," he said. "I mean, this is real for me."

"I know that, Eric."

He fell silent for a moment, then whispered the rest.

"Lela's pregnant."

Of course she is.

Eric waited to hear something from her, and when he didn't he let his hand fall from her arm. In the dark, he said, "I want my family together, Caren. I want that."

They lay beside each other for a long time, each growing drowsy in the absence of knowing what more there was to say, the shotgun and the pistol across the foot of the bed. Eric fell asleep first, and then Caren, lulled by his heavy, somnolent breathing, waking only once to tell him, to say it out loud, "I'm sorry, Eric." *More than you know.*

She drifted off thinking about family, the little one that fit beneath this roof, but also the one beyond the library's doors. Lorraine and Pearl and Ennis. Luis and Dell and Donovan, and all the Belle Vie Players. And she thought of the ones who were gone. Her mother and grandparents and great-grands, stretching all the way back to Jason. Which made her think of Inés, too. They were, each of them, connected across time, across the rolling land of a place called Belle Vie, each navigating a life shaped by the raw power of labor, but also love, their relationships built on river silt, thin and shape-shifting, their family lives a work of improvisational art, crafted from whatever was at hand, like the glistening bottles of Akerele's bottle tree.

28

Caren woke up next to an empty space.

Downstairs, Eric was sleeping on the parlor sofa, where he must have returned sometime in the middle of the night. He was lying flat on his back, his glasses open across his sternum. She didn't wake him, nor did he stir at the sound of her movement, her footsteps across the wood floor. She slipped her arms into the sleeves of her quilted jacket, zipping herself in. Then she moved the shotgun and the pistol, well out of Morgan's eyesight. She put them inside the storage room where the plantation's records were kept, and then she left a note for Eric. They couldn't stay here anymore, not after last night. She told him to go. Pack Morgan's things and drive to the airport and don't look back. Don't worry about me, she wrote. She would check into a motel if she had to. There were just a few last things she had to take care of first.

It was a Saturday, always a big day at Belle Vie.

Three shows, tours hourly, and fresh coffee in the gift shop.

She climbed behind the steering wheel of the golf cart to begin her usual inspection of the grounds, marveling at how few more times she had to do this, to observe Belle Vie at daybreak. Dewdrops twinkled in the pinkish light. The sky was streaked with thin, wispy clouds, and Caren thought they might even have sun today. In the distance, the white columns of the main house rose majestically, casting short, pale-gray shadows across the bricks on the main road.

She made three stops initially.

The gift shop: to unlock the door and turn on the lights.

The main house: to unlock the doors on the first floor and turn on her laptop.

The stone kitchen: where she checked to see if Lorraine had arrived yet.

She found the building empty, and so she continued on, inspecting the southwest end of the property, the guest cottages, and the slave cabins.

The rise of land behind the quarters was as dull and depressed as ever.

This morning, however, the sight of it stoked Caren's curiosity.

The land, a patch of yellowed weeds and dirt about twelve feet by fourteen, grown over the foundation of some long-lost building, sat on the exact spot where Jason had once built a small edifice—as was noted on the map she'd found among her mother's things, the bits and pieces of Belle Vie's history Helen had saved, a map her great-great-great-grandfather had filed with the federal land office in New Orleans.

That last little bit hung in the air like a low, cold fog.

Caren leaned against the steering wheel, thinking.

Eventually, she put the cart into gear, pulling in a wide arc and heading back to the main house and her office. Upstairs, she found Jason's map, which she'd photocopied here before she ever showed it to Danny. It was hand-drawn, a thing of beauty, really. The big house and the cottages, the kitchen and the rose garden, and the quarters, of course. It was all here. And with a careful hand, Jason had drawn in the twelve-by-fourteen structure he built behind the slave village . . . shortly before he died. The map, as she remembered it, was dated the fall of 1872, November, and it was stamped by federal seal by the Homestead Land Office in New Orleans. Jason had filed the map with the land grant office . . . yet it was Tynan who ended up with the deed.

Tynan, she remembered.

The last man to see Jason alive.

Caren ran her finger over the lines of the map, connecting one piece to another.

Reaching across her desk, she picked up her office telephone. She used the number Owen had given her, his office at the paper. He wasn't at his desk, but she left a message anyway. There were records of this stuff, right, in the archives at the newspaper? she said. At a time when landowners were the most prominent members of a community, weren't land deals and real estate sales reported openly in the newspaper and its predecessor, the *Picayune*? Could Owens take a look? She hung up the phone, thinking about the sheriff and his suspicions about William P. Tynan. She was close to something, she felt, within spitting distance of the truth. Five generations on, maybe Caren would finally find out what happened to Jason . . . and why.

It was after nine by the time she made it to the old schoolhouse.

The first show was almost always tourists; locals usually brought their kids, parents, and family from out of town only after a late breakfast or soccer practice or other weekend goings-on, usually straggling in late for the eleven-o'clock show. For the first performance this morning, there were fewer than ten people in the audience, including an East Indian couple in matching baseball caps and sneakers, sipping coffee, Lorraine's finest, out of paper cups. The woman had a pocket-sized camera hanging from a string on her wrist. The man, gray at the temples, had a state map folded and tucked beneath the belt of his khaki pants as he sat, taking in the whole of the antebellum spectacle before him. Caren knew the scene onstage. It was the play's climax.

The women of Belle Vie, Madame Duquesne and her un-married daughter, Manette, virtuous gentlewomen reduced to tattered rags and begging food on credit, fall to tears on news of Yankee soldiers commandeering plantations throughout the parish—ordering slaves to leave their work in the fields; stealing jewels and silver hair combs for their mothers and girlfriends up north; and burning pianos for firewood, or just for fun. When the Duquesnes' trusty driver, played with magniloquent obsequi-ousness by Ennis Mabry, delivers the news, Madame Duquesne faints at once, collapsing into her daughter's arms. The slaves are gathered 'round, a last order given by Mademoiselle. That day, Ennis gave what would have been Donovan's big speech. Onstage he laid his hat to his chest. "Dem Yankee whites can't make me leave dis here land. Dis here mah home. Freedom weren't meant nothin' without Belle Vie." It was a grand solilo-quy, meant to paint the slaves as loyal to the mostly good white people of the South. But the soul of the show was always meant to rest with the ladies Duquesne, women who would rather lose everything than watch their way of life turned over for ridicule or sport. Having lost their men to war—husband and son, father and brother—Madame and Manette, played by Val Marchand and Kimberly Reece, respectively, chose to leave the planta-tion for good, seeking shelter with distant relatives in Virginia. "It's over, Paul and Delphine, Anthony and Sera," Manette said, walking down the line of her slaves, like Dorothy bidding good-bye to her improvised, makeshift family in *The Wizard of Oz*. The final word from Mademoiselle: "Belle Vie is no more." Arm-in-arm, the women Duquesne walked off the stage while a boom box on the stairs played a cassette tape of a scratchy Brahms recording. The slaves, left behind on the plantation, did not jump for joy at the end of their incarceration, nor did they hear in the martial drums in the distance—and the coming of

Union soldiers—a life of freedom. They fell against each other, weeping for the end of an era.

Belle Vie is no more.

Later, it fell to Caren to tell the staff the same.

As the audience cleared the schoolhouse, she gathered the cast and crew in the main room in front of the stage: Luis, Pearl and Lorraine, Cornelius and Shep and the rest of the cast, Val and Kimberly, Eddie, Bo, Nikki, Shauna and Dell, as well as Gerald from security.

Caren sat on the edge of the stage, in front of her motley crew. They had about twenty minutes before the start of the next show. "It's done, guys," she said. "Lorraine was right."

And then, because their silence was unsettling, very nearly unbearable, she made sure her words were clear, that each and every one of them understood. "Clancy's shutting us down."

Lorraine sucked her teeth. Pearl sank into one of the white folding chairs, resting her chin in her hands. Luis, the most senior employee, put his head down. The others were all looking at each other, waiting for somebody to speak first.

"When?" Cornelius said.

"A week, tops. The Whitman wedding will be our last."

Nikki Hubbard, of all people, started to cry. She was clinging to Bo Johnston's arm. Together, they made a strange romantic pair, Nikki in her slave rags and Bo dressed as the white overseer. Bo kissed the top of Nikki's head, holding her hand.

"I can put most of you guys on for the Whitman event, if you want to make some overtime. And I'll gladly write a recommendation for anybody who wants one," Caren said. She would do anything for any one of them, she thought, just as she would for Donovan.

"But, either way, it's time to start packing up your things," she said.

"Is it Merryvale?" Val asked. Her nails were painted bright pink today, just like the lipstick bleeding into the corners of her mouth. "Are they building a new subdivision?" She, more than anyone in the room, looked at least vaguely hopeful.

"No. The Groveland Corporation is taking over the land."

"No shit," Shep said.

"Groveland?"

"The farm people?"

Val looked disappointed.

Lorraine, too, though for entirely different reasons. "It's gon' be nothing but cane out here," she sulked. "Nothing but Mexicans and machines for days. You know black folks can't never hold on to nothing good."

Dell, more sullen than usual, said, "It's a *plantation*, Lorraine."

"Yeah, but it was ours."

"Oh, hell, Lorraine, it was never *ours*."

Dell, who played the mammy in the stage play, pulled a loose cigarette from the front pocket of her costume's apron, and Caren didn't bother to stop her when she lit up brazenly, right there inside the schoolhouse. What difference would it make, really, if the whole thing were to burn down now? What exactly was she trying to save? Whatever the plantation had meant to each and every one of them, they would have to take it with them.

"What about Danny?" Ennis said. "He could talk to Clancy, couldn't he?"

"Yeah," Cornelius added. "Danny ought to talk to him."

"I don't think Danny's going to change his mind," Caren said.

"Oh, it's done, y'all, just let it go," Dell said. Shauna, seated beside her, had her head down. Eddie Knoxville, apropos of nothing, announced that he'd like to travel. Lorraine, however, was still steaming. "It's not nothing, Dell, it's history, *our* history."

Dell blew a puff of white cigarette smoke.

Poof.

It would, all of it, be gone.

"Shit, man," Shep mumbled. "Guess it's back to working at Walmart."

"That's if you're lucky," someone else muttered.

"You better hope Walmart will take your country ass back," Cornelius said.

Shauna, her straightened hair held by a knotted kerchief, had said very little this morning. She'd spent most of the meeting fiddling with the hem of her costume. "What about Donovan?" she asked softly.

"It's not good," Caren said.

"Oh, hell," Ennis cussed, twisting his hat in his hands.

"He's got a lawyer, one of the men from Clancy's firm, and they're telling him to take a deal."

"They can't do that."

"Not without his say-so, no."

"Aw, Donovan ain't kill that girl," Lorraine said.

"Then why would he take a deal?" Gerald said.

Cornelius made a face. "Brother-man done lost his head in there, that's all."

Kimberly Reece was looking at all of them like they were fools. "Innocent people don't go around confessing to crimes, y'all," she said, her voice squeaky and righteous and impatient, that of an older sister urging them to grow up. She tucked a lock of blond hair behind her ear and reminded them of Donovan's past troubles with the law. "He was here the night that woman was killed and every one of you knows it, too."

She cut her eyes at Caren, realizing she'd maybe said too much.

"I already know about the movie," Caren said. "I saw the DVDs."

She waved off their surprised looks, their nervous anticipation of a reprimand that she wasn't in the least interested in giving. She no longer cared about breaking the rules. "And the cops know about it, too," she said. "He's liable to pick up a trespassing charge while he's at it. The detectives know he was out here on Wednesday night."

Kimberly Reece nodded, adding, "My cousin works at the courthouse, and I happen to know for a fact they found the murder weapon in Donovan's car."

Caren felt the air in the room cool.

They were trying it on, she knew, the idea of Donovan, their co-worker, as a violent criminal, a killer. Cornelius shook his nappy, uncombed head. He didn't like the picture it painted, but there it was.

Shep mumbled to himself, "Fuck, man."

Lorraine had heard about enough.

"Does Leland know about this?" she said.

"About Donovan?"

"About the sale."

"I'm sure Raymond told his father," Caren said. "He had to sign off, too."

"I don't know," Lorraine said, shaking her head and looking around the room at the others. "Raymond's played dirty in the past. He bought Bobby out years ago for some little bit, knowing that boy can't hold a dollar, drunk as he stay. And now he's gon' make millions selling out to Groveland. I wouldn't put it past him to cheat his own daddy." She had half a mind to drive up to Baker right now and have a bedside talk with Leland, to let him know what his firstborn was up to, to make sure everything was on the up-and-up. "Raymond," Lorraine spat. "With his capped teeth and his dyed hair." She shook her head, turning up her nose at the plastic image.

Caren hopped off the edge of the stage. "What do you mean he cut Bobby out?"

"Years ago," Lorraine said.

"So Bobby's not going to make any money off this Groveland deal?"

"I don't see how."

And all this time Caren had thought that Bobby's sudden reappearance in the parish these past few weeks was about the younger Clancy keeping an eye on his assets, and his brother's handling of the family business. He had said as much, hadn't he?

"That boy don't have a pot to piss in," Lorraine said. "Leland don't like him at the house, and Raymond won't have him. It's something how money changes folks. Raymond, all these years, has gone cold as ice, looking down on his own kin. But Bobby ain't all bad. Some folks just need the love and patience of a real family, need an anchor in this world. He misses that, is what I think. To Bobby, this place is still home."

They were the same words Raymond had spoken just after the murder.

She remembered the night of the Schuyler event, how Bobby had made himself at home in the dining hall, nipping at the food and lamenting at the presence of strangers in his father's house. She wondered if Bobby still had a key. "He hasn't been coming around here, has he?" she asked the room. She remembered, too, the night Morgan swore she heard someone outside her bedroom window, someone Caren was no longer sure was Lee Owens. "Have any of you guys seen him coming around Belle Vie?"

Lorraine raised an eyebrow . . . then shook her head.

"I never met the dude," Cornelius said.

"Me neither," Nikki added.

There were more head-shakes around the room.

Luis cleared his throat, suddenly stepping forward. "He's been here," he said, hands tucked in his pockets and looking sheepish, worried maybe that he should have said something about it earlier.

"You saw him?"

"I caught him in the shed, yes, ma'am. He was taking one of our shovels."

A shovel?

Yes, ma'am, Luis said.

Caren grew quiet then, very still and quiet.

But her mind was already racing, all the way out the front door, flying all the way across the plantation grounds to the cane fields and the open land by the farm road. Into her mind popped the image of the pocked land, the holes in the ground where someone went digging for bone. What in the world did any of this have to do with Bobby? "Do you know where he lives, Lorraine? You know where I can find him?"

Lorraine nodded.

"I know where he stay, baby."

29

All this time and Bobby Clancy had been living just up the river road, not even a mile from Belle Vie's gates, in a run-down fishing lodge that had its back to the water, set back from the river's levee by a hundred yards or so of sand and weeds. There was a propane tank along the west side of the one-story, clapboard house, a few of its graying shingles rotting at the edges, and down in the dirt, an orange extension cord was snaking from the edge of the yard all the way to the front door of the house, where Caren was standing now. She thought she heard some movement inside, and so she went to knock on the door a second time. The shovel, the one Luis said Bobby had stolen from Belle Vie, was resting right there against the railing of the front porch.

A minute or so passed, and still no one came to the door.

Caren thought about a back door, one that faced the river, and wondered if Bobby was coming out that way. She felt the porch's wooden planks creak beneath the weight of her boots, as she started down the steps. The house was a true river hut, with no foundation and all four corners hopped up on blocks of cement. She could see tiny blades of grass blowing beneath the house, as the wind picked up and a huge chunk of blue sky closed over.

She smelled rain coming.

The air had turned gray and dark, and Caren was careful

to watch her step on the unpaved ground, stepping over tools strewn in the dirt, along with empty beer cans and miniature bottles of bourbon, the kind you could still buy at the T&H in town for a dollar or two a pop. She walked all the way around to the back of the house . . . before stopping dead in her tracks. For parked in the yard, at an angle which had made it invisible from the street, was a red pickup truck. It was rusted along the sides and had a familiar dent in the front grill. The headlights were square . . . just like the ones in Donovan's video, shining from the cane fields on the night Inés Avalo was murdered.

Caren slapped a hand over her mouth, afraid she might actually scream out loud. Slowly, she backed away from the sight of the red truck and all that its presence *here* implied. There would be time to sort it out, but right now she felt an almost primal urge to get out of there as fast as she could.

She spun on her heels, turning toward her car.

And that's how she bumped right into Bobby Clancy.

He smelled of pine and beer, and he was sweaty for some reason, the dampness of his cotton T-shirt showing off a ridge of muscles across his torso. He'd grown sloppy over the years, but he was still strong. Capable of God knows what, she thought.

Bobby looked at her and smiled.

"Well," he said, "to what do I owe the pleasure?"

Caren stammered that she was just leaving.

She tried to step around him, but Bobby blocked her, reaching for her hand, and then her shoulder, digging his fingers in, so that she could move neither left nor right.

"Stay," he said. "Let me at least make you a cup of coffee."

She saw a flash of lightning reflected in his blue eyes.

And then a crack of thunder, as loud as a gunshot.

The storm was creeping closer.

Caren looked across the yard at her car, seemingly beyond

her reach, as she nearly withered beneath Bobby's grasp. She looked toward the clapboard house.

A phone, she thought.

Inside, there might be a phone.

And so she let him lead the way.

The place was surprisingly roomy, mostly because Bobby didn't hardly have furniture of any kind. As far as she could tell, he slept on a pallet of blankets in the center of the lodge's main room. Bobby had by now led her into the kitchen, where he'd sat her at a chair against the wall, in such a way that put him between her and the front door. He was standing over a small two-range stove, fiddling with the knobs and a small book of matches. From Rainey's, Caren noticed, the icehouse, where she'd gone the night she went looking for her cell phone. Bobby, getting a fire going on the stove, looked up at her and smiled. "Or I could make us some tea, if you like that better." Caren shook her head. She felt a strange calmness come over her. This was Bobby, after all. She had known him her whole life. Sitting here in his warm kitchen, at a table topped with a sunny tablecloth and toast crumbs, a few loose insides of local newspapers, she felt a surge of hope that she was wrong about him, about all of this. "It was good seeing you last night," he said. "It's always good seeing you, Caren."

She smiled stiffly.

"That's a sweet girl you got, too," he said, standing over running water at the sink, swishing it around an empty coffee mug. "She's, what, in the fifth grade or something?" At the mention of her daughter, Caren felt something acid in her stomach. Bobby had his back to her, and she could see he was wearing blue Wranglers, just like the description of the man the school's secretary said had been looking for Morgan.

"Good guess."

Too good, she thought.

She swallowed hard, then said softly, "Do you think I could use your telephone?"

Bobby, who was setting a percolator on the stove, looked up at Caren and said nothing for a few seconds. But she did notice that his eyes narrowed ever so slightly. Outside, she heard another roll of thunder, this one more like a roar, a scream.

Bobby gave her a queer smile.

"Sure."

From a chipped corner of his kitchen counter he grabbed a dirty cordless phone and handed it to her, meeting her eye for a half second before releasing it to her grasp. He never made his way back to the stovetop, instead hovering over the edge of the table as she dialed the ten digits that made up her cell phone number. Bobby was looking right at her as the line connected and she heard a ringing in her ear. Beyond the kitchen table, the whole of the house was dead silent, and Caren felt a moment of breathtaking relief. Maybe there was some other explanation for all of this. It was a small hope that she clung to . . . up until the moment she heard a faint buzzing in the front pocket of Bobby's Wranglers. Their eyes met over the table. She hung up the line, and a second later, the buzzing in Bobby's pants pocket stopped.

He was still hovering over her.

Caren could see that he had started to sweat again. There were shallow pools of moisture in the deep hollows beneath his tired, bloodshot eyes. She still had the cordless in her hand. She managed to dial a 9, and then the first 1, before Bobby said, "Don't do anything stupid, Caren." He reached down and grabbed the phone out of her hand.

Caren felt a whisper in her throat. "What did you do, Bobby?"

"I'm not going to hurt you, Caren," he said, stepping back, as

375

he tucked the cordless into the back pocket of his jeans. "I don't ever want to hurt you."

"Jesus, what did you do?"

Bobby wouldn't look her in the eye.

"Did you kill that girl?"

"She was on my land, *mine*," he said sharply. "Not Groveland's."

The pools of water beneath his eyes broke free, running in two lines down his face, and Caren realized that Bobby was actually crying. He was nearly shaking with rage. His life had come down to this fishing lodge, this one room by the river, where he lived alone. "That's my family's place," he said. "And it ain't right what Ray's doing."

"What did you *do*?"

He shrugged coldly, as if saying the words out loud didn't matter much. His back was to her, kind of, and she couldn't tell if he was hiding shame or the ugliness of his rage. "My brother told me to keep an eye on her. She had found something in the fields that worried him, something Abrams told him about, and he didn't want it getting out. He told me to watch her." Then, he added bitterly, "That's Ray. Don't want a goddamn thing to do with me till he wants something dirty done."

"So you *killed* her?"

"I was just keeping an eye on her, just making sure she kept her mouth shut, that nobody said nothing else about bones in the fields, not before Ray's big sale. But then she came at me with a knife . . . On my own goddamned property, she's threatening *me*. So I reached out, and I don't know, I grabbed the knife and I just swung. I guess I must have cut her good."

"Oh, Bobby . . ."

The sound caught in the back of her throat, hiding there.

"She ain't have no business out there no way," he said acidly.

"Did Raymond tell you to keep an eye on me, too?"

By now, Caren's voice was shaking.

"I did that for nothing," he said.

He squatted down, so they were eye-to-eye.

She thought he was going to put his hands on her.

She leapt out of the chair, upending the kitchen table as she got to her feet. The whole thing fell against Bobby, knocking him back, and Caren ran for the front door. It was still standing open, and she shot straight through and down the porch steps, running to the driver's-side door of her Volvo. She heard footsteps behind her, but she never looked back. She spun around in the dirt yard and drove onto the river road, heading south toward the highway, toward the sheriff's station. She got about two miles up Highway 1 before she remembered she had left Morgan at Belle Vie with her father. Eric had no idea what Caren now knew, that everything connected to the Clancys was tainted, that he and Morgan were sitting ducks out on the plantation. And without her cell phone she had no way of telling him.

She swung the car around and headed back to Belle Vie.

The library was in the northeast corner of the property, and from the direction she was traveling, it came into view first, even before the main house. Caren dumped her car along the fence and ran to the front gate. As she started up the alley of live oaks, the first drops started to fall. Caren took off running, cutting through the grass.

The front door was unlocked.

The lights were all on, but there was no sign of Morgan or Eric. Caren circled through every room in the building, from the front parlor to the kitchen, where there was a pot of cold coffee sitting on the stove. Upstairs, there was an open, half-filled Samsonite suitcase in the hallway between the two bedrooms, as if they'd started packing and then stopped suddenly, the task interrupted. "Morgan?" Caren called out, over and over. She called Eric's name, too, as she ran back down the stairs. There was only one room left to check: the Hall of Records, holding Belle Vie's history, its heart and soul. Caren ran through the parlor to the narrow storage room. "Eric?" she said, pushing into the room. The door, swollen from the rain, took a moment to pop free. Inside, the lone lightbulb was swinging on a string. Caren squinted against the low light, and it took her a moment to notice what was wrong. The guns were missing. The shotgun and the pistol, the pearl-handled .32. They were both gone.

Caren ran to the phone on the kitchen wall.

She dialed Eric's cell phone. Twice, no one answered.

She turned and ran out the front door.

There was a show still going in the old schoolhouse, but no Eric. He and Morgan were not in the gift shop, either. She tried Gerald, but he was not responding to any of her calls over the two-way. She checked every room on the first floor of the main house, then the old bedrooms upstairs, and lastly her office. Her desk phone was ringing off the hook. Caren reached for it, screaming Eric's name as she answered. There was silence on the line . . . then the voice of Lee Owens.

"Caren, are you okay?"

"Bobby Clancy," she said. She was panting, out of breath. "It was him."

"What?"

Owens seemed momentarily confused, as if he'd walked into a play well past intermission and had missed some crucial turn in the plot line.

"It was Clancy."

"What about Abrams?"

Abrams had never had a real motive, she finally saw.

It was Bobby Clancy who had taken out his rage on Inés Avalo.

Just as it was Bobby who had been digging in the fields where she found human remains—which had worried Raymond terribly when he found out about it, enough that he put his brother to the task of keeping an eye on her, and setting in motion the events that took her life.

"It was him," she said. "It was Clancy."

"Caren, does this have anything to do with that message you left this morning? The stuff you asked me to look up?"

She had almost forgotten.

"What did you find?"

"The Homestead Act," he said excitedly. On the other end of the line, she heard him shuffling papers across his desk. "I didn't actually find anything in the newspaper's archives about the Belle Vie Plantation and land sales. I mean, nothing that caught my eye. Like you said, the government owned it for a time after the war, and then a William P. Tynan took possession after that, in 1872." The same year that Jason went missing, Caren remembered. "But it is true," Owens continued, "that the federal government was using the Homestead Act of 1862, something Lincoln had signed into law, to procure land grants for former slaves. It had originally been written as a law to help settle the West, but during Reconstruction, the feds had other ideas. Any free man could be granted a piece of unclaimed property, including former plantations, as long as he lived on the land and grew crops or built on the place, a structure of at least twelve by fourteen. Long as he could prove he'd made some kind of improvements to the land, any man stood a chance," Owens said over the phone. "That was the idea, at least."

Caren glanced out the window, thinking of the quarters and the patch of land back behind the cabins where Jason had built a small hut, no bigger than a horse's stable but big enough to suit the dimensions required by federal law. She had the map

of the plantation out on her desk, stamped by the federal government in 1872. She now realized that her great-great-great-
grandfather must have made a claim on this very land just before he died . . . and just before William Tynan took possession
for himself. Caren remembered her mother's last words to her:
Leland Clancy knew he hadn't come by this land honestly. And
she guessed that Clancy's two sons knew it, too. They knew what
William Tynan, their ancestor, had done to get his hands on
Belle Vie, that the sheriff's accusations of murder back in 1872
weren't that far-fetched. It made her think twice about the bone
Inés had found, and the possible identity of the body buried in
the fields. "What about state and federal records? Were you able
to check there?" she said.

"I cross-checked what I could from here in the office, but my
understanding is that some of those records have been lost over
time. Before computers, things got moved around, papers disappeared." Then, mulling it over, he said, "Bobby Clancy . . . are
you sure?"

Outside, lightning shot through the sky, brightening the
southern end of the plantation. And in the flash of electric light,
Caren caught a frightening sight. Eric's rental car was in the
parking lot . . . but so was Bobby's red truck. "I have to go," she
said, slamming down the phone. Thunder followed the strike of
lightning, as loud as a cannon shot. Caren ran out of the main
house, searching for her family. On the other side of Lorraine's
kitchen, the vegetable garden came into view. The dirt was
turned over, roots coming up out of the ground.

Caren saw tire tracks in the mud.

She grabbed the two-way from her jacket pocket, calling over
to security again.

Gerald, when she reached him, sounded breathless and
confused. The white golf cart was missing, he said. He'd driven

to the gift shop to use the facilities and when he stepped out again the cart was gone.

"What's going on, Miss C?"

"Call the cops," she said. "Get somebody out here *now*."

She clicked off the line and followed the twin tracks in the mud.

She passed the garden and the stone kitchen and the two guest cottages, searching every corner of the plantation, running all the way. She ran through the slave village, coming up to the white five-foot-high fence, and that's where she saw them. On the other side sat the golf cart, idling near the cane fields. Eric was in the driver's seat, the lenses of his glasses so dotted with rainwater that Caren could hardly see his eyes. Morgan was shivering, crouched in beside him. Eric had an arm around her, not letting go for a second. And behind them both, in the backseat, Bobby was holding the .32 to the back of Eric's head.

When she saw her mother, Morgan tried to stand. "Morgan!" Eric shouted.

Caren told her not to move.

I'm coming, she thought.

Don't move.

She ran for the fence. The bars were slippery and wet, and she had no idea how she made it over in one piece. She did manage to cut her palm in the process. And when she landed in the cane fields, her ankle bent at a sharp angle, a pain that shot up through the base of her skull. She limped toward them, but stopped short when Bobby slid from the backseat. He had the pistol in one hand and the shotgun in the other, the long nose of it carving a trail in the dirt. His gait was loping and unsteady, and he was tilting off to one side. "I told you not to do anything stupid." He's drunk, Caren thought. The .32, still pointed at Eric's head, was wavering slightly in Bobby's hand.

All around them, the tall sweet grass was swaying this way and that in the wind. "I'm not going down for this. Not for nothing," he said. He was shaking his head, back and forth, the motion achingly precise, as if he were gunning some internal engine, revving himself up . . . for what, Caren didn't know. "I'm not going down for this alone."

There was a faint movement behind him.

Eric had climbed from behind the wheel of the golf cart. To Morgan, he held up a single finger, indicating that she was to remain silent and perfectly still, no matter what was about to happen. Then he looked at Caren. He nodded his head toward the shotgun, sending her a silent message with that small gesture. He was going to grab the larger gun, catching Bobby unawares.

But when Eric reached for it, the shotgun didn't easily come out of Bobby's hand. Bobby turned and swatted hard with the smaller gun, landing a sharp blow across Eric's brow. Eric reeled backward, and Morgan screamed. Bleeding from the hit, Eric then charged Bobby at the waist, knocking them both into the dirt and mud. Bobby fell on top of the shotgun, belching out a low moan when the nose of the gun dug into his back. Eric reached for the pistol, and a second later Caren heard a shot ring out. Morgan jumped out of the golf cart. Caren screamed for her to stay where she was. They both watched as Eric rolled over in silence, landing face down in the dirt. Within seconds Bobby was standing over Caren.

"I'm not going down for this one," he said, pointing the pistol at her face, his finger on the trigger, the knuckle scraped raw. "You not gon' breath a word of it, hear?"

Bobby.

She whispered his name.

"It's me, Helen's girl," she said. "It's Caren." Bobby stumbled on unsteady feet, blinking back against the sound of her voice and whatever memories it invoked. In his hand, the gun wavered slightly.

Behind him, Eric sat up.

Bobby turned toward the sound, which is how he never saw where the final shot came from. Even Caren had no idea that Hunt Abrams had followed the sounds of their shouts in the fields. Without saying a word, Abrams aimed his shotgun, the very one he carried in his truck, and unleashed the force of it. Caren watched in disbelief as the blast shredded Bobby's left shoulder. He dropped the pistol and fell backward, as stiff and straight as a stalk of cane. The sound he made, his voice box choked with shock and searing pain, cut through the air.

Abrams jogged across the field, kneeling at Bobby's side. When he got a good look at his handiwork, saw up close what he'd done, he cursed himself. "Aw, goddamnit," he muttered. He sank down into the wet earth and lowered his head, his shotgun still warm at his side.

Eric's right arm was bleeding.

He was shaking everywhere, teeth chattering from the pain.

"Morgan opened the door," he said to Caren, trying to explain, trying to understand himself what had just happened. "She let him in and . . ." His voice trailed to nothing, lost in the rain and wind. He winced and looked down at his arm. "How bad is it?" It was ugly, but manageable, she hoped. It looked like no more than a flesh wound.

A few feet away, Morgan, by a miracle, was unhurt.

"Get her out of here," Caren said.

Eric made his way to their daughter and Morgan threw her arms around her father.

"Go!" Caren said.

Eric hesitated, looking back her.

He didn't want to leave her out here.

"I'm okay," she said, and she was.

She watched and waited as he ushered Morgan into the golf cart, then climbed behind the wheel. He put the cart into gear and spun it in the direction of the river road, kicking up a spray of mud as he sped away. Hunt Abrams was still seated beside Bobby's injured body, his own one-man vigil. Caren limped toward him, her ankle still throbbing. She knelt beside him and rested a hand on Abrams's shoulder. He looked up at her, but had nothing to say. She leaned her weight against him as she bent over Bobby Clancy, patting his damp body, until she found her cell phone in his jeans pocket. In the afternoon rain, she called 911, asking for an ambulance, and then she called the Sheriff's Department.

Lang was already on his way, they told her.

They would need a second team, too, she said, investigators and crime-scene techs with shovels and whatever else was needed for an excavation, to get Jason out of these fields.

30

By Monday morning, Bobby Clancy was out of surgery and resting as well as could be expected at the St. Elizabeth Hospital across the river in Gonzales, no more than a few miles from the sheriff's station at the Ascension Parish courthouse, where he would be housed once he was able to be moved and thereby officially charged with the murder of Inés Avalo—the same courthouse where Donovan Isaacs's hearing to change his plea had been hastily scrapped from Judge Jonetta Pauls's morning docket. All charges, Caren heard, had been dropped.

She was already miles and miles away by then, downriver at the New Orleans International Airport in Kenner, bidding a bittersweet good-bye.

She was not allowed past the checkpoint, and so the setting was awkward. Out on the curb by the skycaps, she kissed her daughter one more time.

Morgan was surprisingly calm, cheerful even. She'd never been on an airplane before, never been to Washington. Eric had mentioned, twice already, a possible trip to the White House. He was trying to put her at ease; they both were. Caren had promised to call every night. It was coming, she knew. She'd made a point to warn Eric, last night and then again this morning as they'd loaded up the cars. It might be a day or two or even a few weeks from now, she told him, but the events of yesterday, the rain and the blood and the guns . . . she will wake up one night screaming.

Or she might say nothing at all, Eric, and you'll have to watch for those moments most of all, when she simply stares out a window or stops eating in the middle of a meal.

Just be there, she told him.

"And what about you?" he'd asked, his left arm still bandaged.

Nothing had been decided, not yet.

There was the Whitman wedding, work she'd promised the staff.

There was a whole house to pack and a history to put away.

Beyond that, she wasn't willing to say for sure, one way or another.

"Mom," Morgan said, turning to run back to her mother just as the sliding glass doors to the terminal opened and Eric stepped inside with their bags. Caren knelt down on one knee and caught Morgan as she threw herself into her mother's arms. *I know, 'Cakes. I feel the same way.* Morgan was the first to pull back, digging her fingers into Caren's shoulders and staring into her eyes as if she felt she needed to buoy her mother up or convince her of her own strength. It reminded Caren of the whispers of encouragement she used to give Morgan when she was first learning to walk on her own. "I won't let them touch my hair," Morgan said. "Or pick out my clothes."

And by *them*, Caren knew she meant *her*.

They were having a discussion about loyalty, without ever mentioning Lela's name. Caren didn't know whether she should feel proud or tremendously sad that her daughter believed that this would make it easier on her, that Morgan felt she had to protect her mother. "No, 'Cakes," she said. "That's your dad, and she's going to be your stepmother, your family." The mother of your brother or sister, she thought.

Caren smiled, touching the curls around Morgan's round face.

"And I'm okay with that, 'Cakes."

Morgan grinned, showing the gap in her front teeth. Bobby was right. She did look just like Helen Gray. "Tell Donovan I love him," she said. And with that, she turned and ran, her backpack thumping against her bottom, as she caught up to her father, who'd been watching and waiting from the glassed-in vestibule of the American Airlines terminal. "Good luck next month," Caren told him, meaning his coming nuptials, his start at something new. Eric gave her a small wave. Morgan, God bless her big, magnificent, forgiving heart, never looked back.

Later, at the sheriff's station, Caren gave Detectives Lang and Bertrand her second of two interviews, the other having taken place last night, on the grounds of Belle Vie, her clothes still wet and muddy from the afternoon storm. Today, she signed an affidavit, detailing the last twenty-four hours and beyond: the early suspicions of someone other than Donovan being responsible for the murder, the discovery of his film script and DVDs and her missing cell phone, the discussions with Lee Owens of the *Times-Picayune* and the information from Father Akerele and Ginny at the church, the stories of Inés being followed by none other than Bobby Clancy, Caren now knew. And this she tied to the bone that Inés had found in the fields. There was an official file for him now, for Jason. Forensic anthropologists at LSU were contacted, and Caren had offered her own blood for a DNA sample, or whatever else this century had to offer in the way of science, to determine who was buried out in the cane fields.

The cops were getting no help from Raymond Clancy on the matter. He'd been stalling about giving his own police interview. Too busy, Caren guessed, dealing with the press, giving multiple television interviews about his unstable brother and the tragedy of the circumstances, a man come unhinged, a man he hardly knew anymore. By the morning's news cycle, he had completely disowned his only brother, and people were already praising him for his frank candor and levelheadedness in the face of a crisis. He was an absolute natural on-screen.

On her way out of the station, Caren spied Owens in the parking lot. He was in the driver's seat of his Saturn, parked next to her Volvo. He climbed out of his car as she approached and leaned his right hip against the front end of his vehicle. He was back in uniform, his khaki pants and a thin T-shirt, even though it was barely fifty degrees outside, and on his head was a faded ball cap, the words BANKS STREET BAR & GRILL stitched in white, yet another blues club in his beloved New Orleans. She wondered what it would have been like to know him when she lived in the city, if she'd stumbled upon him some night at Sweet Lorraine's or the Old Opera House, or if he'd ever had a drink at the Grand Luxe Hotel after work. She liked him, that was easy enough to admit. When he took off his hat in her presence, running his fingers through the snaking curls, she felt an unexpected swell.

He smiled, tapping his cap against his thigh. "So . . . where you laying your head tonight, miss?"

"Belle Vie, for now," she said. "I've got some things I need to wrap up."

"Any chance we'll get you back?"

The *we* being his city, she knew. "I don't know."

"It's not like it was," he said.

"Is that good or bad?"

Owens smiled, kicking his foot against the car's front tire. There was no easy way to answer that. His tone grew serious, wistful even. "The story's dead," he said. "And Clancy's coming out of this deal looking like a star." He shook his head at the exquisite irony of it. "The crime beat will have a go at the killing and Bobby Clancy, but without a murder angle tied to the Groveland deal, and no charges against Hunt Abrams, the paper's a lot less interested in how the company treats its workers. They're going to run a piece about the company's expansion, what it'll do for the state's economy and the future of the sugar business in Louisiana. But most of that research is coming out of the AP's bureau in New Orleans. It won't have a thing to do with me."

"I've got a story for you."

He gave her a curious look, tilting his chin to one side. "Yeah?"

"Just give me some time to get it all straight, Owens."

"Call me Lee."

He slid his cap back on his head and nodded toward the doors of the courthouse. "My turn now," he said, indicating the police interview that awaited him.

He was stalling, though, lingering in her presence.

"Listen," he said finally. "If you do come back to New Orleans, I mean, if you come back for good, would you let me buy you a drink sometime, Miss Gray?"

"I would insist on it."

He was charmed, for sure. And wise enough to go out on a high.

He tipped the bill of his cap, and walked into the parish courthouse.

Two days before the Whitman wedding, Caren led a guided tour for the Groveland brass. The company sent a team of five from the corporate headquarters in Porterville, California, to survey the site, two women and three men, the youngest and tallest of whom—an African-American gentleman with close-cropped hair and smooth, unlined skin—appeared to be the one in charge. They arrived with their own name tags, laminated cards clipped to their matching oxford shirts, the sunny Groveland logo stitched over their right breasts. The black guy was: KEN WIGGAMS, PRESIDENT, SOUTHEAST REGIONAL DEVELOPMENT. The other four were titleless names: Susan, Kathy, Edward, and Jim. Caren greeted them in the plantation's parking lot. There was no rain that day, not a cloud for miles, and so the plan was to tour the grounds on foot. She started at the rose garden, remembering as she went Luis's steady hand, the care he'd shown all these years. The main house was open, the view through the foyer and the dining hall going all the way to the front lawn on the other side, the alley of oaks and the verdant levee in the distance, a roll of grass bright and green in the sun. She showed them the upstairs bedrooms, where the Duquesnes and then the Clancys once slept. And she took them through the kitchen, introduced them to Pearl and Lorraine, who offered a tray of sweet tea infused with orange and honey. Lorraine winked at Caren as the tour group left, stepping around her garden. Down the lane, the windows of the cottages, Manette and Le Roy, were all open, their white, gauzy curtains lifted and then rested in the late morning breeze. She explained that the cottages were once used by guests visiting Belle Vie, but the overseer, a man named Tynan, had made his home in the *garçonnière*, what was now the plantation's library.

In the quarters, she kept an eye on Ken Wiggams.

The ladies, Susan and Kathy, and even the older gentleman, Edward, a white man in his late fifties, were all taken with the scene, reading each placard carefully and going in and out of the cabins, including the last one on the left, Jason's old home. The women asked questions, about the quilts and the field tools and the stove dug into the ground. Edward took a picture of the cabin with his cell phone.

Ken Wiggams, the black guy, was the only one who didn't venture into the slave village, never setting foot on the dirt path. He stood apart from the others, his hands shoved in the pockets of his black slacks, his mouth pinched into a bitter, grudging expression, and it occurred to Caren that she should have found a way to bring this man out here alone, away from his white colleagues, that her last-ditch effort to save the plantation might have gone better if she hadn't put him in the difficult position of necessarily viewing himself as two men at once: a president and a descendant of slaves. He turned at one point and asked her directly, "How much more of this is there?"

The last stop on the tour was a visit to the old schoolhouse.

There was no staged performance today, but the members of the Groveland delegation were invited to watch a different production in progress, the shooting of one of the final scenes of Donovan's screenplay. Caren advised caution as they stepped over a tangled river of wires and cords, connecting lights and sound equipment. The schoolhouse had been made over to look like a court of law, the place where Tynan finally went on trial for the presumed stabbing death of Jason.

The sheriff was on the stand.

It was Donovan, of course, in boots and a badge.

Danny Olmsted, newly added to the cast, played the part of the prosecutor, wearing as his costume the same black trench coat he always did, this time over a frilly white shirt and a poorly knotted ascot. He clasped his hands behind his back, speaking in a manner that was one part Perry Mason, one part George Washington.

The scene of an ancient murder trial played before them.

"What *is* this?" one of the Groveland employees asked.

"Belle Vie," Caren said.

This is what you bought.

391

* * *

Later that day, she said good-bye to her mother, clearing the land and brushing dirt and leaves off the headstones of her family, working in a straight line, all the way back to Eleanor and the empty space beside her that belonged to Jason. It would have been something to know them, she thought, whispering their names. And then, lastly, she told her mother it was long past time for her to go. It was time for her to move on.

That night was one of her last at Belle Vie.

Alone, she ate half a frozen pizza, washed down with warm red wine. She sat in front of her laptop at the kitchen table, looking at law schools in the D.C. area. Just looking, she told herself.

Later, she surveyed what was left of her packing.

As the sun set, she started off with her Maglite and ring of keys, checking and double-checking the front and back gates, riding along in the white golf cart underneath the canopy of magnolia trees. Around the back side of the main house, she stopped cold when she saw a light on inside the building. Caren was supposedly the only one out here. She slammed on the brakes. Looking in through the first-floor windows, she felt in her jacket pocket for the .32 pistol. She was in the habit now of keeping it close by.

She left the engine idling and entered the house through the back door, pausing in the darkened foyer. She held the gun by her side as she walked beneath the winding staircase toward the dining hall, the door to which was cracked open. On the other side, she saw a flicker of light. She crept across the parquet floor, trying to center most of the weight in her hips so her feet fell lightly, making little sound. It was only as she got closer to the door that she heard heavy breathing, like a rattling whisper. Raising the pistol, she pushed open the carved wood door. Inside the dining hall she found Raymond sitting alone, reclining by lamplight. He was stone drunk and sleeping across the wide bottoms of two of Belle Vie's best dining chairs, within arm's reach of a bottle of Cuvée, which was open and stood half-finished on the floor next to him. Caren felt for a light switch on the wall, brightening the crystal chandeliers overhead.

Clancy stirred.

He opened his eyes and looked at Caren, grinning widely. "Gray."

"What are you doing here, Raymond?"

He sat up, chuckling to himself at this situation, him drunk and laid out. When he sat up to his full height, his knees were nearly pressed to his chest in the short dining chair. "Sit down," he said to her, as if she were just dropping by for a visit or an after-dinner spirit. He reached for the bottle of brandy, one she was sure he'd lifted from Lorraine's kitchen. Pouring a small bit into a snifter, he then offered it to her. Caren refused. Raymond took his straight from the bottle.

He rolled his eyes to the ceiling and sighed.

"They're going to tear it down, Gray. I got the call a few hours ago."

"What did you expect?"

Raymond shrugged, and Caren decided she hated him, for, as much as anything else, his smug indifference to all this. Sure, he was sad about losing this place, but sad for all the wrong reasons, a man in midlife coming to terms with the knowledge of what, given the chance, he'd trade for politics. There was nothing but self-pity in this room, and Caren wanted nothing to do with it. There was only one thing she wanted from him before she went.

"I want to see it," she said. "I want to see the deed."

Raymond paused, staring into his brandy.

He tapped a lean finger along the belly of the bottle.

"I don't know what you're talking about, Gray."

"Yes you do."

Clancy took a long sip of brandy, not answering her, behaving for a moment as if she'd never said a word, as if she weren't standing right in front of him. "Listen to me, Gray," he said, finally, his voice as hard and cold as a shard of ice. "Listen good . . . my brother is not a well man, hasn't been for years. I don't know what in God's name got into him, why he went crazy on that girl like that. But I didn't have anything to do with it."

"You knew the story of what happened to Jason, and you lied when you said you'd never heard that your own relative had been the suspected killer. You were the one who took the records out of the archives, trying to erase the true chain of ownership. And when Abrams reported to you—still the stated owner of this land—what Inés had found in the fields, you had a hunch what it was, that the bone belonged to Jason, and you wanted to erase that, too. You had your brother dig up the fields out there, looking for the rest of his remains. And *you* put Bobby on Inés's trail," she said acidly, the words burning on her tongue. "And look what happened."

"He was just supposed to watch that girl, make sure she didn't go blabbing to anyone else," Raymond said. "But I swear, Gray, I think my brother saw an opportunity to tank all I had coming to me, and he was willing to take a life to do it." He lifted the bottle. "I swear he did it to spite me, leaving her in the dirt like that."

"I just need to see it," Caren said. "I just need to see the piece of paper that said this place would have been Jason's if Tynan hadn't killed him. I just need to see it."

Raymond didn't say anything.

He was staring into the dregs of his bottle, the whites of his eyes dull and gray.

"This was never just about Groveland, was it?" she said. "The sale?"

Raymond's voice, when he finally spoke, was hushed and wistful.

"People are funny about this place, Gray," he said. "I've met whites who love it, blacks who can't stand it, and the other way around, and not a damn thing in between. Everybody's got their own idea of what Belle Vie ought to be, who it really belongs to."

"It belonged to Jason," Caren said. "This was all his."

"You'll never prove that, Gray."

"And there was no way in hell you could run for office in a state with a population this *colored*, no way to run on your daddy's good name, and then have the whole world find out your family stole this land from a black man."

Raymond leaped to his feet, knocking over his chair.

He made a move, as if to take hold of her arm, but she still had the revolver in her right hand.

At the sight of it, he backed off, stammering his words. "I didn't steal shit, Gray," he said. "That was Tynan. That don't have a thing to do with me. I didn't steal a goddamned thing. And hell if I'm going to be held responsible for what some crooked white man, family or no family, did two hundred years ago. It ain't fair to me. It ain't fair to anybody. And I don't want it on my back anymore. I wish to God Daddy'd never fooled with any of it, never put it on his kids, passing this shit down, on and on. I don't want it. People been after me for years to sell this land, and I put it off, but I'm finally ready to be done with it." He then turned and fixed a stare out the windows. "Groveland is a good deal, good for the state," he said. "People want history, they can read books."

"Where's the deed, Raymond?"

"It's gone."

The admission wasn't mean-spirited. It was the truth.

She would never see it, not in this lifetime.

"I can still make 2010 work," he said, speaking of his place in the political landscape. "That's a whole year away." He sank into a chair with the bottle of brandy. "People have short memories."

"I remember."

Clancy looked up at her, rolling his shoulders, trying to compose himself. "So I suppose this means you're going to try to block the Groveland deal, lay some claim to the land," he said. "I suppose you're going to pick through dusty records in your family's name, try to find any old thing that says Belle Vie belonged to you all along."

Caren shook her head.

"I don't want it," she said firmly. "Any more than you do."

She repeated the words she'd said over her mother's grave, that it was time for her to leave it behind.

"Where you headed, then?"

"D.C.," she said, finally saying it out loud. "I'm moving to D.C."

"Washington, huh?" he said, making a face, as if he didn't realize they let anybody in the place without an elected seat in government. "You got family there?"

"Something like that."

She left him alone in the big house, driving herself home in the company of the plantation's aged oaks and weeping willows, each branch and leaf dusted with silvery moonlight.

They went all out for the Whitman deal.

Peonies out of season, in shades of plum and rose, with a supporting cast of hothouse orchids, shipped all the way from Memphis; tables set with silver and china trimmed in gold; and a dusky pink carpet sprinkled with white petals, leading from the rose garden to the main house. Lorraine, as instructed, spared nothing for the food: chilled oysters with a mignonette sauce awaited guests on the front porch as soon as the last vows were said; along with a rare Viognier, enough for each guest to have two and three glasses before dinner, served with both Roquefort and Comté cheeses and complemented with a cherry jam dotted with cane crystals. And that was all just to start.

In the dining hall, while Shannon Whitman, resplendent in winter white, beads, and silk, cried through four rounds of drunken wedding toasts, the guests were treated to red cabbage sautéed in cider vinegar; andouille sausage over coarse grits and butter; pork roast in apples and wine; and a whole roasted chicken for each and every table. It was a feast the likes of which Belle Vie hadn't seen in more than a hundred years. Caren watched it all from the back of the hall, overseeing every last detail.

Later, long after the sun went down and the guests had gone, she helped Lorraine and Pearl wheel a cart full of leftovers— buttercream cake and wine and cheese and champagne—down to the quarters, where the staff had gathered. In the end, they'd all begged off the overtime and the prospect of dressing up as slaves and slave masters for a paying audience one last time. They'd spent the evening filming instead, way down by the quarters and out of sight of the goings-on in the big house.

The scene was Jason's funeral.

The stage was still set.

Twinkling lights were strung from the wood gates, and bunches of pansies and daffodils in mismatched glass jars lined the dirt road, where the ex-slaves had gathered to say good-bye. It was kind of pretty actually, out here under the stars on a clear, black night. Sometime after midnight, Cornelius hooked his iPod to a boom box and plugged that into Donovan's generator. It started to feel like a party instead of a funeral—a proper send-off with food and drink and good music, blues and some zydeco, and when it got really late, Earth, Wind & Fire. They danced, some of them; they sat and talked and laughed. Shauna, Nikki, Dell, and Bo Johnston. Luis and Shep and Kimberly, Val and Eddie Knoxville. Cornelius and Pearl and Ennis Mabry and Lorraine and Danny Olmsted . . . and Donovan, of course. Some of these people Caren knew she would never see again, a shame, really. Lorraine was drinking beer from a can, and when she finished, she stood and said it was time to head back, to pick up where the catering crew had left off—bussing dishes and breaking down tables, cleaning the kitchen and any left-behinds in the dining hall. But as Lorraine started to her feet, Caren asked her to please sit down. "Leave it, Lorraine," she said, her tongue light with champagne, her mood brighter than it had been in weeks, years even. *Leave it just as it is.*

Acknowledgments

This book would not exist without the guidance of my agent, Richard Abate; the unwavering trust of my editor, Dawn Davis; the support and candor of my Serpent's Tail family, most especially Rebecca Gray; the love of my husband, Karl Fenske, who is a true feminist and took many a "second shift" so that I could write in the evenings; the sharp eyes of my sister, Tembi Locke, who read multiple drafts and offered great notes (as always); the timely patronage of Gene and Aubrey Locke and Sherra Aguirre; and the deep intelligence of Dr. Cheryl Arutt, who weekly opens my head and heart to the mysteries of human nature, starting with my own.

Additional thanks go to Pete Ayrton, Andrew Franklin, and Ruth Killick, for making a home for me across the pond; to Shanna Milkey, Maya Ziv, Katherine Beitner, Kendra Newton, Jonathan Burnham, Michael Morrison, and the rest of my HarperCollins family, for their professionalism and vision; to Megan Beatie and Lynn Goldberg for helping to introduce me to the world as a new author; and to Bob Myman, Philip Raskind, and Adriana Alberghetti, for being the great constants in my writing life.

And for driving me around in his pickup truck and explaining in great detail the Louisiana sugar industry, I thank Herman Waguespack, Jr., of the American Sugar Cane League. Thanks also to James Wilson at the Center for Louisiana Studies, who made sure I had all the historical research materials I needed, and to my dear neighbor Lowell Bernstein for checking my Spanish.

I could never forget to thank my brother-in-law, Rosario Gullo, for reminding me, so often, that I am right where I'm meant to be; or the many friends and family members who, each in their own way, let me know I had their full and undying support.

Finally, with this book in particular, I want to express my love and deep gratitude to the women who have mothered me in my lifetime: Sherra, my first love; Aubrey, who opened her heart to me from our very first meeting; Mrs. Odell C. Johnson, my literary soul mate; Fanny and Willie Jean, who is a light in my life; Altha Mae, Dolphus, and Douglass; Rhonda, Pam, Cheryl, Lennette, and Michela; Bernadette and Mrs. Willie Sampson; Helen, Opal, Versa, and Elsie; Connie Fenske; my dear sister, Tembi, who has always offered me a hand to hold; and Odelia, who is in my heart still.

And to my daughter, Clara, who made a mother out of me, I say thank you, my love.